The Many Ghosts *of* Donahue Byrnes

Laura McLoughlin lives in Co. Armagh, Northern Ireland with her husband and two beloved dogs. Formerly a web journalist and editor, she currently works as a Digital PR Executive, and holds a BA (Hons) in English with Creative Writing from Queen's University Belfast. *The Many Ghosts of Donahue Byrnes* is her first novel.

The Many Ghosts *of* Donahue Byrnes

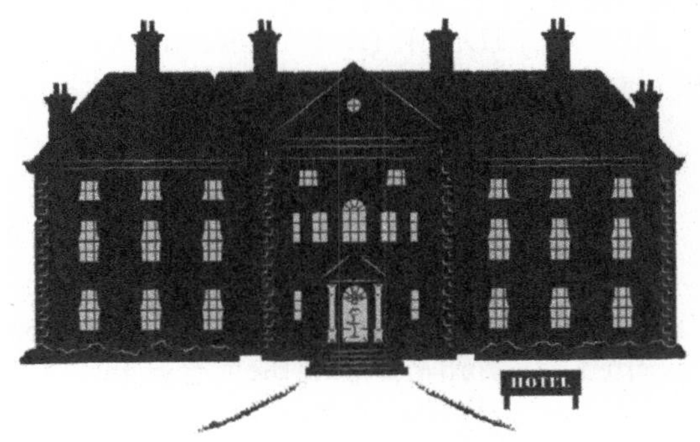

Laura McLoughlin

Black&White

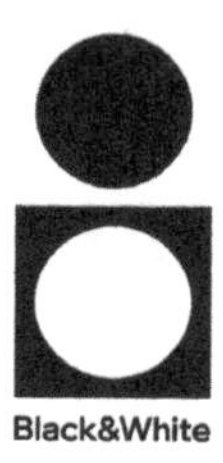

First published in the UK in 2024 by Black & White Publishing
An imprint of Black & White Publishing Group
A Bonnier Books UK company
4th Floor, Victoria House, Bloomsbury Square, London, WC1B 4DA
Owned by Bonnier Books, Sveavägen 56, Stockholm, Sweden

Trade Paperback ISBN: 978-1-7853-0581-8
eBook ISBN: 978-1-7853-0580-1
Audio ISBN: 978-1-7853-0579-5

A CIP catalogue record for this book is available from the British Library.
Typeset by IDSUK (Data Connection) Ltd
Printed and bound in Great Britain by Clays Ltd, Elcograf S.p.A

1 3 5 7 9 10 8 6 4 2

Black & White Publishing is an imprint of Bonnier Books UK
www.bonnierbooks.co.uk

For Blair — we did it

chapter 1
blue for blue

THEY SAID FUNERALS WERE for the living, and that much was certainly true of the funeral of Donahue Eagan Byrnes.

It was late August and unusually warm. As such, clusters of dully dressed people inched their way up the steps of Ballinadrum Presbyterian Church, talking and perspiring in equal measure. The church – dark-grey stone with a half-storey bell tower – offered its condolences by way of blessed shade.

Like everyone else, Mia Anne Moran wore black. It matched her close-cropped hair and made her feel especially pale. She alone, however, wore at her breast a small token of something with which she knew Donahue would have preferred his funeral decorated: a pink hydrangea bloom.

'How did you know, Mia Anne?' she could imagine him asking, bushy moustache bunched over a wide grin. 'I have always loved hydrangeas the best.'

It was a small comfort to her that amongst all of these *funeral things*, she might wear a piece of who Donahue Byrnes actually was. After all, how much had Donahue Byrnes cared for dismal pipe music, limp white lilies, or hushed conversation? Not at all, in Mia's recollection.

As she moved through to the nave, she tried not to engage in conversation. It was all the same sort of thing anyway – how much he would be missed, how well he had done to reach his nineties. A *brave age*, they said, *a good run*. And it wasn't that Mia could disagree – not really – but it didn't matter. Somehow, it still should not have been Donahue.

Even as she found her way to her family pew, Mia felt a sense of unreality, as if he may yet slide in beside her to ask how it was all panning out. 'Who has not cried yet? I would like names, Mia Anne.'

The space beside her was filled only by her grandmother, Brea Moran. The old woman wore a black brocade jacket and a smart suit skirt, but no hydrangea bloom as Mia had suggested. 'It's a sad day, Mia,' she had insisted. 'You wear black on sad days.'

The pews swelled with mourners. The rafters rose with whispers.

Then, the Reverend Rainey – grey, morose, and sporting an unflattering combover – took his place at the pulpit. As he began his address, which was perfectly adequate if over-simplified, Mia's gaze drifted to the altar. The coffin – pale wood, golden handles, weighed down with yet more of those awful white flowers – should have made Donahue's death feel all the more real and terrible, but there was numbness in the sight. The idea merely circled her mind, unable to land just yet.

She thought about him lying there – fine suit, newly trimmed moustache. Eyes closed as though he had simply succumbed to a mid-afternoon nap. He would not rouse, however. His eyes would stay closed.

In life, Donahue Byrnes had commanded entire conversations with those eyes, his gaze as captivating and expressive as a player on a stage.

When Mia was a girl, he had told her that he and her were a matching pair: blue for blue. Such a comparison from such a fascinating adult had made Mia's entire day, perhaps even week, but since she had grown up, she had come to understand that while they did indeed share eye colours, his had always, always been different.

His were electric, dancing. Hers were watchful and demure. His found people across entire rooms and pulled them near with a special kind of gravity, and hers just drank them in.

And now his were closed, and she watched on, still.

Mia's breath hitched. She felt a hand take her own: Granny.

'Are you ready?' she asked. Her head, unlike the smooth black of her granddaughter's, was fluffy and white, and her eyes, by her own description, were the colour of murky dishwater.

Mia smothered the urge to ask, 'Already?' and instead drew a folded sheet of paper from her pocket. She gave her grandmother a nod.

A mere minute later, the Reverend Rainey called upon her. 'Mia Anne Moran, a dear friend and employee of Donahue Byrnes, will now share with us a few memories of his life.'

Mia stood, feeling heavier than she had in her entire life. At twenty-two, she had known loss, but had never felt it so immediate, so close.

When she reached the pulpit, she unfolded the paper and laid it flat against the dark wood: a page of memories crudely translated to ballpoint ink. This was all she had, she realised with a wave of something that felt like fear – this was all there would *ever* be. And yet, for as long as she had known Donahue, there had always been *more*. More secrets, more jokes – some other part of his old hotel he had yet to reveal to her.

Only last month he had told her about *a special role* he had planned.

'A special role?' she had asked, a half-smile on her lips, searching for the punchline. 'What sort of role?'

'It's evolving, I think. Would require a little time-travelling, and an absurd faith. An open mind. Dancing shoes, perhaps.'

'Is that all?' she had said, laughing. 'And what sort of person might you be looking for?'

'A treasure-seeker. A believer. A good friend of mine.'

His stare had been as intense and blue as it had ever been, and Mia's curiosity had risen and stretched like a cat.

'What on earth does that mean?' she had asked, but it had been the wrong thing to say – the wrong password.

'In time, in time,' he'd given as his reply. 'Give it a little more time.'

And yet, now, there was no time. There was nothing at all – nothing but *this*. This page. These memories. This feeling that someone had cut the song in the middle of the bridge and all that followed was aching, echoing quiet.

Mia took a short breath, and began to read.

'Donahue Eagan Byrnes the second was a good man.'

Afterwards, they went to his hotel.

It had not always been Donahue's hotel. It had belonged to his father before him, and his before that. In its lengthy two-hundred-year history, in fact, one-hundred-and-thirty of those years had involved a man named Byrnes.

In a town of two-storey buildings, it was a sprawling, gargantuan structure, grey-bricked and shaped like a lucky horseshoe. Its face was handsomely, albeit deceptively, square, each wing extending to the rear and creating a sweet little cove, used for après dining in the summer and gathering frost come winter. Comprising six floors (not counting its cellar), two wings (only one of which was open), one hundred and twenty guest rooms (those available for bookings obviously half that), and a glittering collection of four hundred and thirty-seven windows (Mia had counted), it was, if you were to ask Mia at the very least, the most beautiful building in the world.

Despite being named for the town in which it was built, the hotel occupied a distant corner of its boundaries, and was so indulgently set back from the road that many visitors missed its iron-gate entrance entirely. When they finally circled around, they would find the seemingly direct driveway was in fact curved in the way of a crooked mirror-maze trick, and crowded with greenery, too, so that their destination was only revealed to them in full as they arrived outside its front door.

Some said it had always felt a little different – built on a ley line, or with ancient magic in its bricks – but most said that no, it was just old, tucked away from the world, and a little cold, too.

Until, of course, Donahue.

What it was exactly about his ownership that made the difference was something without a name. Mia knew it when she felt it though, and similarly, knew it now, when it was gone.

She stood in the lobby of what was no longer his hotel, feeling its absence keenly. He would be glad, though, she thought, to know just how busy it was – more crowded now, perhaps, than in all the time she had worked there.

And it was a hard room to crowd. The lobby was objectively large, with a high concave ceiling and plaster coving. It housed an imposing front desk and wall of guest keys, and on either side of those, twin staircases. Two gold-doored lifts took up east and west positions, though it was only the one on the left that actually transported guests anywhere – to the east wing's guest floors, to be exact. The other lift – and the entire west wing – had been out of action as long as Mia could remember. Even the stairs just went up and up and up, the doors leading off from them bricked closed and papered over.

'Heating bills,' Donahue had complained when Mia, as a small girl, had asked about the hotel's other half. 'Scandalous. Criminal. Priced by a pirate's scales and that's the very truth, Mia Anne.'

On an ordinary day, there might have been a large arrangement of blue or pink or even purple hydrangeas at the room's centre. Today, though, of course, there were only lilies, and people who drifted here and there, picking at the buffet table. Pouring tea. Chatting.

Mia held an egg and onion sandwich she wished she hadn't picked up. Now, she would have to eat it – an unpleasant option – or spend the rest of the afternoon with it in her hand, the buttered egg turning her stomach.

'Did you enjoy the service?'

Startled from her thoughts, she looked at the man beside her. Henry McCullough was a softly spoken, red-haired man in his early forties. He wore round tortoise-shell glasses, and an unremarkable black suit. As the hotel's manager, she often saw him dressed smartly, but today he was missing what she considered his trademark pastels – a powder blue shirt, for instance, or silk floral-print tie.

She wondered if she, too, looked out of character in black.

'It was fine,' she said. 'And you?'

'Not particularly, but I'm not sure if you're supposed to.'

They slipped into an uneasy silence. It was not that they were not friendly with one another, but he was her manager and to call them *friends* was too generous a description.

'Your hydrangea,' he said after a moment. 'He would have liked it.'

Mia smiled for the first time that day. 'Do you think so?'

Henry took hold of his jacket lapel and, after a covert glance left and right, folded it outwards to reveal a blue sprig of hydrangea, winking at Mia from his shirt's breast pocket.

'I thought I was the only one,' she said, smiling in wonder.

'Not quite,' he said, and then his gaze caught on something at Mia's shoulder.

Mia turned and saw her fiancé Rosco Buckley approaching with two cups of tea. He was a young man of twenty-four, with dark, hooded eyes and a tanned complexion. Black suited him, and while he was usually not one for shirts and ties, Mia quite liked the formal look. It made her think of church aisles and bouquets.

'How are you, Henry?' Rosco said. 'You organise all of this?'

'No,' Henry said with a self-deprecating laugh. 'For once, I'm very much a guest of the hotel. I believe Donahue's son was the one to put it together.'

'His son?' Mia asked. 'Is he here? I've never met him.'

Henry stepped back to look about the room. 'I'm not sure, actually. I saw him in the church, but—'

An older woman reached out and grabbed Henry's arm. 'It's a wonderful buffet, Harry, sweetheart. Really good turnout.'

'Oh, I'm not the one—'

'Now, tell me: you're not married, are you, Harry? Because I've this niece, and—'

Henry offered Mia and Rosco an apologetic smile and a quick *excuse me* before allowing the woman to lead him away.

Rosco handed Mia a cup of tea. 'Well, that makes sense.'

'For Henry not to be married?'

'No. Well, yes – maybe. But I'm talking about organising the funeral. I always thought Donahue and Henry were pretty close, so I kept thinking the whole way through the service *why did he order these flowers*?'

'I did the same,' Mia said. 'Though it's stranger still his own son would have chosen them.'

'I heard he hasn't visited since his mother's funeral, so I doubt he knows, much less *cares*, what flowers Donahue liked.'

'You didn't see him at the tea table, did you?'

Rosco shook his head. 'Wouldn't even know who to look for.'

Disappointingly, Mia did not know who to look for either. Donahue had only ever spoken of his son – Cormac – briefly and blithely. *Why didn't he work at the hotel?* Didn't much fancy it. *Why had he left Ballinadrum?* Didn't much fancy that, either. *Will he be back?* It was hard to say, but Donahue would phone him that night to find out.

And yet, today, Cormac Eagan Byrnes had returned to Ballinadrum. Today, the hotel was his.

'You know,' Mia said. 'You could have worn a hydrangea, too.'

'Yeah, well, I wasn't one of Donahue's favourites, so . . . '

'Donahue didn't have favourites.'

Rosco smiled and shook his head. 'Do you like egg and onion?' he asked, blatantly changing the topic before Mia could argue. She had never been able to change his mind, anyway – on this, or anything else. 'I could have sworn you didn't.'

'I don't, really. Actually, not at all. I just . . . '

Without warning, Rosco plucked the sandwich from her hand, and popped it in his mouth.

'Better?' he asked around it.

Mia laughed. 'Thank you.'

'I figure *for better or worse* probably covers egg and onion sandwiches,' he said, brushing his thumb over the ring on her fourth finger. 'Probably not tuna, but egg and onion for sure.'

'Maybe check with the minister before the service, just to clarify.'

'I've got six months. I could probably go over a full roster of sandwich fillings in that time. Make sure I know what I'm getting into.'

A bustle of older women crossed their path, all puffed-up hair and talking over one another, and in their midst was Granny – too engrossed in conversation to immediately notice Mia as her granddaughter had done her. But she did, a half-second later, and her face transformed with delight.

'Mia!' she said. 'The girls and I were just looking for you – and *Rosco*, good. Deirdre was just telling me that her car's axel has been acting up again. Doing that vibrating thing, isn't it, Dee-Dee? And I said to her, you know, my *grand-son-in-law*—'

'He's not *in-law* just yet,' Mia teased.

'Well, I said Rosco Buckley's the one to ask. The last mechanic I was at – you wouldn't believe it – wanted to charge me *two hundred pounds* for a set of new brake pads and—'

They continued to discuss criminal mechanics and the cost of tyres these days, and what a lovely couple Rosco and Mia made – *they had always said so* – and how excited they all were that the two were getting married, and *isn't it so nice to have a man that's handy, Mia?*

Rosco gave Mia a sideways glance, and she smiled back an apology, though she needn't have. Rosco was as used to Granny's girls as she was – each of them somewhere in their seventies, but as giddy and loud as a pack of teenagers.

Granny herself would often say that she only hit her stride at fifty-five. Mia was still waiting for that moment to find her, and even now she could not help but note Granny's way of leaning into the circle of conversation, talking with hands and sweeping gestures, while Mia guarded herself with crossed arms.

'You spoke so well,' one of Granny's friends said – Paula, the one with red spectacles. 'You must have been very close to Mr Byrnes to gather up all those stories.'

'Yes,' Mia said. 'We were friends. I met him when I was . . . Well, I think I was . . .'

'Six,' Granny Brea supplied. 'She was six when she met him – and that old Donahue, he started right into telling her all sorts of nonsensical tales. He was a storyteller, that one, through and through.'

'And do you think there's any truth in them?'

'I certainly hope not,' Granny said. 'And in any case, *I've* never seen any ghosts about here.'

'Neither have I,' Rosco said.

'Have you, Mia?' another asked – Mildred, from choir. 'Seen a ghost, that is?'

'Never,' Mia said.

But she had certainly looked. As a girl, she had spent long afternoons searching for the lonely wolf who apparently lived in the attic, the fairies who were supposed to lurk in the bushes outside, and, of course, the ghosts.

There were those who played music late into the night, and danced, and told jokes, while others staggered about on the upper floors and whimpered in high winds.

They were the most consistent of Donahue's tales, though the stories hadn't begun with him. Instead, they went as far back as the forties when the hotel had offered up its west wing as a wartime hospice for a few months.

As far as Mia knew, it was after that people started to whisper about dead soldiers and tainted ground.

But people liked to whisper in general, Mia thought, and such gossip made good kindling. Donahue Eagan Byrnes had known that better than anyone.

'Maybe you'll see one yet, hm?' Mildred said to her.

Mia was quite sure that whatever magic Donahue had brought to Ballinadrum Hotel was going to seep out of the building like water through a cracked vase, and that any chance of ghostly visitations – or time travel or treasure hunts or *special roles* – would go with him.

Still, she wore her rigid waitressing smile, and answered, 'Maybe.'

chapter 2
rumours like that

A MONTH AFTER DONAHUE BYRNES' funeral, Mia Anne Moran was on the fourth floor of Ballinadrum Hotel, searching for a place to hide.

Her feet were quick, and her pulse just the same, but her mind stalled with indecision. The hallway contained a great many things to hide behind – an armchair in yellow madras, thick indigo curtains lining the half dozen windows; a treasure chest with a cast-iron lock – and not only that, but the corridor itself was uneven in both conception and execution. There was no perfect right angle to be found anywhere, and so there were any number of small alcoves she might sink into and disappear.

A clatter of feet from the stairwell jolted Mia to decision.

She rushed to the nearest set of curtains. The heavy fabric settled against her body, tickling her nose, and she pushed herself flat against the wall.

In the dark, she listened: rain against the window, pipes creaking in the wall. And footsteps – soft and muffled.

They had reached the long runner rug, then. That meant they were getting closer.

Mia held her breath and tried to make herself smaller.

She could hear a soft padding – no more than a few feet away, by her estimations. It slowed. It stopped. Then it retreated back down the hallway and faded to nothing.

Out of nowhere, a laugh rang out: a bell-like tinkle of a laugh.

Mia pushed closer to the wall, anticipating the curtain being ripped away at any moment – but there was no more soft padding across the rug, or laughter, either. By what Mia could tell, she was alone.

That, or the laugh was waiting and listening, too.

Then came a high *ping*: the lift had arrived on the fourth floor – presumably to transport the laughter away.

Mia breathed out once again. It was only when she heard more footsteps still that she realised the lift had signalled someone's *arrival* rather than exit. *These* footsteps could be heard plainly – heavy, rhythmic, self-assured.

'Mia?'

She tried to sink back into the concave wall, but a little too hard. She bumped her head. 'Ow,' she said.

The curtain lifted, and the sudden light from the hallway dazzled her. A tall figure came into focus, his head cocked, and brow furrowed.

'Aren't you too old to be playing hide-and-seek on the job?' Rosco asked.

'*Shh*,' Mia said. 'You're going to give me away.'

'And there's my answer. How on earth does Henry let you get away with carrying on like this?'

She inched further into the recess of the curtain fabric. 'I'm efficient.' When he snorted, she added, 'And well, there's . . . not that much to do.'

'Isn't Saturday supposed to be your busiest day?' he said with a roll of his eyes. He leaned forward, kissing the side of her head. 'What's so funny, anyway?'

Mia frowned. 'Funny?'

'I heard you laughing.'

'I wasn't laughing.'

Rosco shook his head. 'I *heard* you, Mia.'

'No,' she said. 'You didn't.'

'Who was it, then?' He made an act of looking up and down the hallway. 'Doesn't seem to be anyone else here – or have they chosen a more inspired hiding place than you?'

While the hallway did curve this way and that, it did not turn so abruptly to create *corners*, and if someone was to hide along here, they needed to *want* to hide – as Mia had done just minutes prior. It was the same on every floor, in fact: one long, not-quite-straight corridor, and ten gold-numbered doors, with perhaps one extra for linen or cleaning supplies. (Supposedly it was a perfect mirror to the other wing of the hotel, though Mia had never seen it for herself, and had a hard time believing that anything about Ballinadrum Hotel had the ability to behave *perfectly*.)

'I don't know,' Mia said, genuinely perplexed. 'I heard it, too, but I couldn't place it. I thought they were getting into the lift, but if you—'

'There wasn't anyone in it when I got out.'

'Maybe they took the stairs?' she said, feeling doubtful.

'Or maybe,' Rosco said, pressing his forehead to hers, 'you could do a better job of keeping quiet.'

Suddenly, Mia was aware of hard, quick steps coming down the stairs. Before she could attempt to hide herself again though, two figures burst through the stairwell door.

The first and most energetic of the pair was Ruby Gallagher: a plump, buxom woman in her mid-forties who was only seen without her trademark red lipstick on the direst of days, of which this was not one.

She raised a finger and called out, 'A-ha! We found you, Mia!'

Beside her was Sonia McCain; younger by ten years and thinner by several inches, she wore her long, bleached-white hair in a single braid down her back.

Both sported black pencil skirts and white shirts with the lavender crest of Ballinadrum Hotel printed over the left breast – the same as Mia.

'Behind the curtain, Mia?' Sonia said. 'I'd have thought you'd be more creative than that.'

'Rosco gave me away!' she protested.

'You were the one laughing,' he said. 'You'd have been found anyway.'

'I already *told you*, that wasn't me!'

'And we've already confirmed there was *no one* else here. Who would it have been?'

'A guest? Someone's kids? Or—'

'A ghost?'

Mia's gaze latched on to Ruby.

'Well,' Ruby said, twisting a length of frizzy brown hair around a finger. 'You've heard the rumours.'

'Yeah, but . . .'

'They're not true,' Rosco finished.

'Well, I thought that, too,' Ruby went on. 'Until I heard one myself.'

'No, you didn't,' Sonia said, voice heavy with a sigh. 'It could have been anything, Ruby.'

'In the kitchen? With *no one* else around?'

Mia felt the hairs on her arms prick up. 'When did this happen?'

'Last night,' Ruby told her. 'I was just about to clock off. Everyone else was already away home for the night—'

'When a deep and unsettling *cold* flooded the room,' Sonia said, wiggling her fingers. 'And a child's laugh rang out through the hotel.'

'Stop it,' Ruby said, giving Sonia a venomous glance.

'What happened?' Mia asked.

'It got cold,' Ruby said, enthusiasm clearly dented. 'And then I heard a laugh.'

'It could have been anything,' Sonia repeated.

'It was like it was *right in the room*, Sonia. And after what Leslie was saying just the other day . . .'

'What?' Mia asked.

'She actually *saw* one of them – *the ghosts*.'

'She saw a pile of laundry,' Sonia cut in. 'A ghostly, otherworldly *bedsheet*.'

'No, it was a *person*, or something person-shaped, wearing something gauzy and light. Like a veil, you know? And this wooziness came over her, just as it got all cold . . .'

Some feeling flared to life in Mia's gut – thrill, perhaps, or maybe unease. The two were close-knit twins as far as Mia was concerned, and she could seldom tell the difference between them, but this . . .

'That's Leslie, though, Ruby,' Sonia went on. 'I don't know how you can trust a thing she says after she had everyone convinced that Mel in housekeeping was having an affair with the food delivery lady, and there wasn't a pick of truth in it.'

Ruby kept pulling at the hair about her temple. 'She refuses to go down to the laundry room anymore, you know.'

'Just another excuse not to do her job. Come on now, you know the hotel has been jumpy ever since . . .'

Whatever had been flaring to life inside Mia went cold. She looked from Ruby to Sonia to Rosco, all of whom let the end of that sentence float in the air between them.

Mia wasn't going to be the one to say his name. Not tonight. Not again. They had already said it so much in the weeks since they'd lost him – between tears and shifts, in whispers and in passing. Mia had long reasoned that it was nice to use it even when its owner was not there to claim it, as some proof to those still living that he had existed, but saying it did not bring him back. It did not answer the questions he had left in his place, and it did not – not ever – make the loss of him hurt less.

The rain against the windows played on.

'Let's not get carried away,' Rosco said. 'There have always been rumours like that going about.'

Ruby did not look convinced, and Mia felt that uneasy thrill come alive again.

'Exactly,' Sonia said, planting her hands on her hips. 'So, are we going to finish this game or not? I thought you could sniff out Hugh McDermott a mile away, Ruby.'

Ruby gasped. 'I have no idea what you're talking about.'

'Sure, you don't.' Both she and Mia were well aware of Ruby's not-so-secret obsession with the hotel's chef. 'You best hope he's not taken to hiding with Linda. They'll have been coupled up for quite some time now and you never know what can happen in a small, enclosed space . . .'

'Alright, you've made your point. No more dilly-dallying. You coming, Mia?'

Rosco slipped his hand into Mia's and squeezed once. *Stay*.

'I'll catch up,' she told them. 'Won't be long.'

'Oh, to be young and in love and about to start your wee baby lives together,' Ruby cooed. 'Wish it was me. Don't you, Son?'

Sonia, going on five years since her divorce settlement, attempted a polite sort of grimace. 'I'll settle for bridesmaid this time around, thanks. Try not to waste the whole night in a storage cupboard, okay, Mia?'

Ruby cawed a great laugh, and pulled on Sonia's arm. They breezed through the stairwell's door again, transformed purple by its stained glass and already lost in conversation.

Mia looked back to Rosco. He was smirking.

'What?'

'I just think it's funny.'

'What is?'

'That your best friends are twice your age.'

'They're not – well, okay, Ruby is, but Sonia's thirty-three. It's not that weird, is it?'

'I didn't say weird. I said funny.'

Mia wasn't sure if that was better or worse.

'What brings you to our fine establishment, anyway?' she continued in a light tone. 'And be warned: if this is some sneaky way to get me to go drinking downstairs with your mates, I'm afraid I am *on duty*.'

'Yes, I would *hate* to pull you away from all this *hard work* you're doing, but no, it's not that.'

There was something about Rosco's stance that put Mia on edge. He was suddenly too still, too poised.

'Well, what is it then? Did the band cancel or something? I sent the deposit over to them last week. They should have got it by now and—'

'No, it's not that either. It's . . .' He took a step closer, his voice low. 'Mum's got a big story and it's going to break tomorrow, and I know you love this place and—'

Rosco's mother worked on the local paper, so she always had town gossip ahead of time, but it was never anything *big*. Big meant *bad*, in Mia's head, and the way Rosco was talking . . .

Her skin prickled all over. 'What's wrong?'

'The hotel, Mia. They're selling it.'

chapter 3
a mystery he had never solved

MIA LOOKED AT THE HOTEL – the barroom's checkerboard tiles, the golden doors out front. A cocktail, belonging to Ruby, decked with an umbrella and sugar rim. Rosco, on their one-year anniversary, frowning over a cup of coffee.

They were only photographs, of course, but Mia liked to think they were something like preserved memories – fossils in amber, butterflies behind glass.

Today, she was reorganising them – Granny Brea dancing barefoot at a wedding in the top left, swapped for Sonia in a Halloween mask on the other side. Donahue in a luminous green suit on the right, for Donahue with buttercream in his moustache on the left. Donahue leaning on the front desk, gazing out the window here, traded for Donahue waltzing through the lobby there.

Donahue for Donahue for Donahue.

None of the photographs were particularly *good* by technical standards. Mia liked to use a second-hand digital camera that made most shots a little blurred – she had a phone of course, but its lens was too sharp, too sudden – and when she printed them, she used the notoriously unreliable printer at the chain pharmacy in town. Yellow was rendered gold, grey darkest midnight.

She preferred it that way – even if it was somewhat untruthful.

Just as she settled on the new order of her pictures, there was a knock at the door.

'Come in,' Mia said.

At the sound of paws on hardwood floor, she smiled, and two dogs took up their usual spots in her room: Muriel, a West Highland Terrier, small for her breed, took two attempts at leaping onto the blue, floral duvet of the double-sized bed; while long-legged Handsome Boy, a hound-like mongrel, made himself comfortable on the floor's shag rug.

Granny Brea followed them and took up her own seat in the lone, worn armchair. She began to unravel the wool scarf about her neck.

'How was choir practice?' Mia asked.

'Mm, fine. Jennifer keeps doing that thing I said she does – you know the whistling in the high notes? The organist was trying to train it out of her but no luck today. Doubt he'll have any next week either.'

Mia smiled. 'I thought she had that flu thing a few weeks back,' she said. 'Maybe her throat's still not right.'

'Well, if it's not right, she should stay home. It would save us having to listen to her work through verse two umpteen times to get it right – and truth be told, Mia, it's not even *right*. It's *listenable*.'

'I'm sure the Lord doesn't mind listenable.'

It was then Mia realised Granny had that stillness about her. The same Rosco had worn last night.

'What is it?' Mia asked.

Granny answered slowly. 'Heard some news today from Paula,' she said. 'About the hotel.'

'Oh,' Mia said.

'You know?'

'Rosco told me, last night.'

'Oh, of course. That boy's mother knows all.'

'She is the paper's editor. It's her job to know.'

'Well, *I* certainly didn't know. Why didn't *you* tell me?'

'You were asleep when I got in.'

'And we didn't go to church together this morning?'

Mia's smile was weak. 'Would you accept *I didn't want to talk about it* as an answer?'

Granny's grey eyes held on to her granddaughter's gaze. 'I suppose,' she said at last, expression softening.

'I just . . . wasn't expecting it.'

'I don't think any of us were, my love. I had it in my head that Donahue's son would have taken up the reins of such a beautiful old building and yet . . .'

'He's giving it away.'

'Oh, hardly giving it away. He'll make a pretty penny out of it.'

'And you really don't know anything more about him? You must have talked to him, while he was still here.'

'Of course, I did, Mia, but I met him as a boy, no more than twenty – if that. And what would he be now? Fifty-something? Sixty? Decades change a person, you know.'

'Well, what was he like then? Awful?'

Granny tilted her head. 'He was quiet. Shy, though . . . I'm not sure. I do remember catching him in the lobby once that summer before he left, and asking him about his plans for university. I knew he was going to London to study accountancy, you see, because Donahue had told me, but there was no chat out of him. No joke or smile either. I suppose when you're a teenager and you're mobbed by a strange older woman in the lobby of your daddy's hotel, you're not that keen to talk, but still. He seemed so unlike his father that day.'

'And you haven't seen him since? Not once?'

'Oh, he might have come back every now and again, but I never saw him. From what I know, he's very much settled in London. It must have suited him better than this little place – fewer nosy neighbours, maybe.'

'Did you see him at the funeral at all?'

'I wasn't looking for him, truth be told.'

'Henry said he was there. . . But he didn't get up to speak at it. I didn't see him at the hotel afterwards, either.'

'Oh, Cormac and his daddy weren't close, Mia. You know that.'

'Still – you should speak at your father's funeral, shouldn't you? Unless your father is a monster, but Cormac got Donahue as a father. He should have had *something* to say.'

Granny shrugged. 'People don't always see eye to eye, Mia, even when they're blood. From what I could tell, Cormac had his own ideas of who he was going to be, and Donahue . . . well, you know Donahue. He loved the hotel, and I got the impression he wanted Cormac to be more interested in it than he was. But that's kids for you, isn't it? They'll break your heart.'

Mia chewed the side of her cheek. 'I wish he was more interested in it, too.'

Granny gave her a tight smile. 'I'd say a lot of people wish that, my love. But you'll be okay, Mia, no matter what happens. You're young. You've got a lot of potential.'

It was supposed to be comforting, Mia supposed, but so were lilies and organ music, and none of them were – not at all.

A few minutes later, with a chime at the door, Rosco arrived.

He waited on Granny's porch with his hands in his back pockets, and Mia met him with a smile. The fleeting August heat had given way to a brisk September wind, and Granny's narrow street was dappled with yellow leaves from the tall lime tree at the corner. They dotted car bonnets and the rain-soaked pavement – small spots of sunshine on an otherwise grey morning.

Rosco wore a tattered red hoodie. Both it and his light-grey jeans were smudged with oil stains and frayed at the hems.

'I didn't know you were working,' Mia said. 'Or is this a new style I wasn't aware of? If so, it's very bold of you.'

He rolled his eyes and kissed her on the forehead. 'The new guy didn't stick. Dad needed me in the garage to finish off the gearbox on that old Volkswagen. Still haven't got it right – absolute bitch of a thing.'

'You should have said. I could have walked to—'

'Now, don't start. I drive you to work. That's how it is.' He led her down the path to the gleaming red Ford parked on the kerb and held her door while she climbed in.

'Is *that* in the vows, too?' she asked, once he was behind the wheel.

'I'll add that one in. Egg and onion, driving you to work . . . We should probably add in something about no dogs under knee height, too. Have you anything for the list?'

'Hmm . . . no taxiing drunken friends home from the bar at one a.m. maybe?'

'Now that,' he said, one hand on the wheel and the other on her headrest as he reversed onto the road, 'doesn't sound very Christian.'

She marvelled at the ease with which he flicked through gears and pulled onto the main road.

A few years ago, she had tried to learn to drive from him in this very car. He had asserted that the best way to learn was *on* the road, rather than in an empty car park like most people. *It's not realistic*, he had argued – *you'll learn better in the moment.*

Which is how they had found themselves at a busy junction in the middle of Ballinadrum town, Mia panicking and Rosco barking instructions. Once the worst had passed and they had safely pulled over at a layby, he had slipped into the front seat again, and Mia had been a passenger ever since.

To anyone who asked about it, she said she preferred it. She saw more from the passenger seat, she would say. And what was more: wherever Rosco went, Mia liked to go there, too, and wherever Mia went, Rosco drove. It worked.

'Mum was saying we need to get a refund on the venue deposit,' he said now. 'Do you mind checking about that today?'

Heaviness flooded Mia's chest. 'I hadn't even thought about that.'

'Mum thinks about everything. I can go in if you can't—'

'No, I can do it. I wish I didn't have to, though.'

'Don't think we have much of a choice in the matter, babe. But don't worry. We'll find another venue.'

That was as comforting as Granny's *you're young* remark, Mia thought, looking out the window.

'And we've got what . . . five months, now?' Rosco continued. 'That's loads of time. We can look through a few tonight if you want.'

She brightened. 'At yours?'

Rosco laughed. 'We always go to mine.'

'I like yours.'

'Yeah, because you go through baby photos with Mum and have Dad pour you endless cups of tea. I'll wind up doing all the work. We should go to your house. Your Granny's out at church on Sunday nights, right? I know she doesn't like me staying in your room, but if she's not there then—'

Mia would not be swayed. 'I promise I will only look at four to seven pictures, and drink approximately two cups if we can just go to yours.'

'You'd rather hang out in my hectic household than spend a night alone with me?'

'One cup,' she said. 'Two pictures.'

'Fine,' he said, rolling his eyes with a half-smile. 'Have it your way.'

Through the window, Ballinadrum sailed by.

It was a hodgepodge sort of place, where the new grew through the old like pavement weeds. On one side of town was the library and recently disused courthouse, both with grand entrances and long histories, and on the other, there was a petrol station and a supermarket more akin to a warehouse than a greengrocer. Even the oldest buildings, a row of tidy Georgian terraces on a cobbled street, were home to chain-store chemists and big-brand coffee houses – distinguished shells for these hermit crab businesses.

The number of family-run shops were unfortunately few, but those that had survived were all the more special for it – such as The Burning Lamp Bakery, which they passed by now.

It was a constant in Mia's commute, but this morning the sight of it made her sit forward and grab her tiny digital camera from her bag. The cobbled street was empty, so quiet and so still, and dusted with the palest sunlight that smoothed the cracks in the once-glossy red sign, and made the display window, which housed a plastic three-tiered cake and a selection of brass oil lamps, dazzlingly ethereal – an angel's bakeshop.

Mia caught a snapshot before it was gone.

'That'll be blurry,' Rosco told her.

Mia clicked through to the tiny preview screen. He was right.

'That's okay,' she said, secretly admiring the watery scarlet smudge. 'I like it blurry.'

He shook his head like the inside of her mind was a mystery he had never solved.

'You know, I was thinking I could get you a new camera – for Christmas, or maybe a wedding present. I could get one of those good ones, with a big screw-on lens and shutter speeds and everything. I mean, I don't know much about cameras, but they've got to be better than that antique.'

She would have sooner traded in her left arm, she thought, but he was trying to be kind.

'I'll think about it,' she said with a smile.

So, they went back and forth on the price of such cameras, and whether it was cheaper to order online, and whether it made any difference, really, if the printer in town was never replaced, and *why did Mia bother going there anyway?*

Before long, Ballinadrum was before them.

Mia had photographed the building itself many times over – its great, grey face set back from the tree-rich promenade – so turned her lens out the passenger side instead.

It was a tangle of shrubbery and declining hydrangea bushes, unpathed and without signs. And, supposedly, for good reason – or so Donahue Byrnes had had her believe.

When she was little, he had told the most fantastic stories about a fairy family living in the base of one of the trees, and on another occasion, of a small library box, perched upon one timber leg, which had been forgotten over many years and now only held secrets.

As a child, Mia had explored the undergrowth in search of both fairies and libraries, and found only the latter.

'It's locked,' Mia had told Donahue the next time she had seen him. 'I can see the books, but I can't get them.'

'Those fairies,' he had said, shaking his head. 'Such mischief they cause.'

Though she had told no one, Mia had gone in search of the library again in the weeks following Donahue's s death. It had been green and damp and the lock in the front more rusted than she remembered. The books were the same – a total of six, no more, no less – and there was no sign that anyone had visited it in years, never mind Donahue Byrnes himself.

It had been a silly venture, she had thought, traipsing out of the shade and back to the hotel, to think Donahue had left something for her. To think he had meant anything at all by his stories other than charming entertainment.

Now, Mia photographed the darkness skimming by, wondering if it might reveal something she'd previously missed. But no – there was nothing.

Rosco parked as close to the hotel doors as possible, at the very bottom of the steps. It wasn't quite the car park – that was a little further along the driveway, closer to the east side of the hotel than the west – but nobody ever minded. Not even when Rosco let the engine idle, and his parting remarks with Mia stretched longer than whatever song was playing on the radio.

'I'll get you this evening then,' Rosco said. 'And maybe we could get chips on the way home – you know, like a treat.'

She gave him a half-smile. 'I think that's what you said after Donahue's funeral, too.'

'Well, it helped me feel better.' He leaned across the handbrake and pressed his forehead to hers. 'Cheesy chip with beans and a can of Diet Coke?'

'Did I ever tell you I love you?'

'Maybe once or twice.'

She adjusted the hem of her skirt and climbed out of the car, waving as her fiancé drove away. The greenery eclipsed him long before he reached the main road.

'Love's young dream,' a voice said behind her.

Mia, turning to climb the cobbled steps, rolled her eyes. 'You said that yesterday, too, Gerry, and the day before that if I'm not mistaken.'

The doorman wheezed.

Gerry Finerty had worked for the hotel as long as Mia had been alive, and the grey hair on his head and worn fabric of his charcoal suit were testament to this fact.

'Call me jealous,' he said. 'Because that's what I am.'

'There's time for you yet, Gerry,' she said kindly. 'I'm sure you meet plenty of lovely people coming in and out of here.'

'Oh, but lovely's not enough; otherwise I'd be on one knee every other day of the week. No, you need a *bombshell.* Do you still say bombshell, Miss Mia?'

'Not really, but I know what you mean.'

'Then you'll know they're once in a lifetime, bombshells, and you best act snappy, or someone else might take them home first. I'm sure that Rosco of yours didn't spend too long *hm*'ing and *ha*'ing.'

Mia thought back to the first time she had ever spoken to Rosco Buckley.

It was the summer she turned sixteen and she had been outside his father's garage while Granny Brea had negotiated a price for the new alternator in her Clio.

Rosco had been standing at the edge of the driveway, grinding the toe of his black trainers into the gravel, when his dark eyes had flicked up, and caught Mia watching him. He had then proceeded to do the absolute worst thing Mia could have imagined: *smirk*.

That night, after attempts to soothe her mortification with tea and scones and one of Granny's old romance novels, she had logged on to Facebook to discover a friend request from none other than the source of her shame himself.

Hi, Rosco had written, after she had hesitantly accepted.

Hi, she had written back.

'I suppose not,' she told Gerry now. 'But good luck on finding one of those bombshells anyway. I'm sure there will be one visiting the hotel any day now.'

'Thank you very much, Mia. And good luck to you, too. I've heard you'll need it.'

'Me? With what?'

'You haven't heard then? About Cormac Byrnes?'

'What about him?' Mia asked, a sinking feeling coming over her.

'Why,' the old man said, green eyes glinting, 'he's here.'

chapter 4
risotto

MIA HAD LONG CONSIDERED the hotel's lobby its shining first impression – all shimmering terrazzo and florist-fresh hydrangeas – but it also had a side that wasn't quite as attractive. One seen by only those closest to it.

Mia hurried along such an employee-only corridor now, twisting and turning with its seemingly nonsensical design as easily as she might locate her own bathroom in the middle of the night. Its wallpaper, first applied in the eighties, was garish and its carpet had been trodden threadbare, but Mia hardly noticed, well used to it as she was.

She dodged other staff members while she went – some arriving for shifts, others on their way out, all dressed in the hotel's white shirts with lavender crests.

'Afternoon, Mia.'

'Working again, Mia?'

'Did you hear, Mia?'

'About what?' she asked politely.

'The *hotel*,' was the response. 'Rumour was it was selling, and now it's in the *newspaper*.'

Mia smiled and confessed she had heard, but was late and couldn't stop to talk. *Couldn't bear to stop* was more accurate, and she rushed ahead to the locker room, hoping to find a little quiet to collect herself. She found only sinking disappointment and another gaggle of co-workers, wrapped up in the only topic on anyone's lips.

'I can't believe it.'

'Some property mogul has already made an offer.'

'Do you think it's going to close?'

Mia skirted around the edges to reach her locker in the back without conversation. Ruby was preening in the mirror in her own locker beside it.

'Word gets about fast here, huh?' Mia said lightly as she worked at her combination.

'Like wildfire,' Ruby whispered back. 'It went up on the paper's Facebook this morning, I heard.'

'Did you read it?'

'Glanced.'

'And?'

'Nothing we didn't already know.'

Just then, Sonia – hair loose, handbag thrown over a shoulder, neon pink backpack in one hand, and her six-year-old daughter, Lily, pulling on the other – staggered into the locker room.

'You said I could,' Lily said, loud and shrill enough to attract the attention of even the circle of gossips. 'You said yesterday I could go with Granny to the shop and get ice cream.'

'Lily, I already told you that I was sorry. I forgot your dad was picking you up in the afternoon and—'

'But you *said*—'

Sonia dropped her daughter's hand, pulling her fingers through her hair and twisting it into a messy bun. 'Neil's running late,' she hissed to her friends. 'And I'm the worst mother in the world.'

Lily had her mother's eyes, and right now they were blazing with indignation.

Mia took her apron from her locker, shoved her satchel inside, and then shut it – with a *bang*. She gasped dramatically, and Ruby, Sonia and Lily all turned to look at her.

'Did you hear that?' Mia whispered.

'What?' Ruby and Lily asked, near enough in unison. With her daughter distracted, Sonia took a moment to get into her locker and fix her hair.

'You didn't?' Mia continued. 'I just thought . . . Well, maybe it was nothing, but . . .'

'Hear *what*?'

'Crying,' Mia said, deadly serious. 'Like wailing, somewhere in the walls.'

Lily narrowed her eyes. 'I didn't hear anything.'

'I suppose it is an old hotel. It makes funny noises sometimes. But then again, given what happened . . . I wouldn't be so sure.'

'What happened, Mia?' Ruby asked, all feigned fright.

'Well, you see . . . Ballinadrum Hotel wasn't always a hotel,' Mia said. 'A long, long time ago, it was just a family home, and after that, it was a coach house, and then the Byrnes family opened it as a hotel, and for just a little while, it was a hospital. Not the whole hotel, just the west wing, mind.'

Lily stared up, eyes large.

'You see, it was during the Second World War, and lots of soldiers got hurt when they were fighting in Europe, so they had to go to hospital. But the hospitals in the big towns and cities weren't safe, so someone very clever decided to have them in places like Ballinadrum. They took all the poor injured soldiers from the hospitals in the cities and towns, and brought them out here to rest. And you know, lots got better, and they went home and lived fine lives after the war, but three . . .' Mia lowered her voice. 'They weren't so lucky.'

'They *died*?' Lily gasped.

Mia nodded solemnly. 'Their ghosts, however, stayed – right here in the hotel, and that old west wing, in particular. Some say they got lost when they tried to pass over, because they were English souls on Irish ground. Others think they were too tired from all their fighting to go the whole way to the afterlife. But me? I'd say they have unfinished business.'

'Unfinished business? Like what?'

'Well, you didn't hear it from me, but . . .' Mia cast a glance around the locker room. The other staff members were beginning to edge out the door, lost in speculative conversation. 'They say they're still searching for what they lost on the battlefield. It's been said that you can hear one of them, and the *thunk thunk thunk* of the peg leg he was given as he roams the hallways searching for his real one.'

Lily, wide-eyed and slack-jawed, looked up at Ruby, and then to her mother.

'Like . . . a pirate?' she asked Mia.

Mia smiled. 'Sort of.'

'Does he have a parrot, too – on his shoulder?'

'Mm. Not that I've heard, no.'

Sonia, now with mascara on her eyes and her hair smoothed into place, looked considerably calmer. She leaned against her locker with a lopsided smile.

'Is that true?' Lily asked Mia.

'Well, that was the story I was told.'

'And who told you?'

Mia gave her a tight-lipped smile. 'Someone very old and very special, which means you can most certainly believe it.'

Lily fixed Mia with another one of her shrewd looks, and then turned back to Sonia.

'Is Daddy here yet?'

'He's just texted, actually,' Sonia said, tucking a stray hair behind her daughter's ear. 'We'll meet him down in the lobby.'

'Do you think he'll take me for ice cream?'

'You can ask him yourself.'

Sonia mouthed a quick *thank you* in Mia's direction, and then steered her daughter out of the locker room.

Mia thought again of the old story, and for the first time, it struck her that Donahue must have considered unfinished business to be a pretty powerful force, if it was enough to hold three soldiers in place for over seventy years. And yet, if he had known that well enough to spin stories out of it, she could not help but question why he had left so much of it behind.

*

The kitchens were noisier than usual, and Mia didn't have to guess why. Amongst the clatter of pots and cutlery and the flip-flap of the serving door, was the ever-present hum of chatter about the hotel – who would buy it, where they would go, if anyone had seen Cormac. It was as constant and stifling as the steam from the many bubbling pots and pans.

Out in the dining room, Mia tried to let the rhythm of work take over.

It, like the lobby, was an expansive, pleasant space with various markers of past grandeur – polished wainscot panelling, three glittery empire chandeliers – marred by an overriding sense of weariness. Its carpet, for instance, was cream and patterned with luxurious baroque swirls, but tramped thin and faded, and its furniture – dark wood and glossy – was finely made, but use had left small nicks and marks along the otherwise perfect polish.

Normally, for Mia, finding a flow about this familiar room was easy. She had worked here as a waitress for over five years – four full time, the rest in balance with school – and before that, had sat as a guest in possibly every chair in the room.

Today, however, the guests were just as fidgety with gossip as the staff. Any time she stopped to take an order, she was quizzed about what she had heard about the hotel in faux-casual tones, and even when she was clearing plates or adjusting the hydrangea blooms placed at the centre of each table, she could hear them – talking, whispering, questioning.

'Mia Anne Moran.'

Mia, in the process of lifting the dirty plates from a family of six, struggled to right herself.

In front of her stood a tall, skinny woman in a scarlet dress and high-heeled brown, leather boots.

'Miss Fitzgerald,' Mia said with more enthusiasm than she felt. 'I hadn't realised you had already checked in.'

Eleanor Genie Fitzgerald was a regular of the hotel, and the most contrary woman Mia had ever met. She looked close to sixty but liked to tell anyone who would listen she had 'recently' turned forty-five, and was supposedly a native of Belfast city centre – her discernible Ballinadrum accent be damned.

'I've just arrived,' she told Mia with a grand air.

'That's wonderful,' Mia said. 'And will you be with us long?'

'A few days. I just had to get away from the town, you know. So hectic, so bright . . . It's nice to come and slow down somewhere as *quaint* as Ballinadrum.'

Mia's smile remained unchanged as she uncomfortably shifted the plates in her hands.

'I didn't just come to say hello, though,' Miss Fitzgerald went on. 'I wanted to tell you there is just the *strangest* sound in my room. You'd almost imagine someone was knocking on the door. Can you do something about it?'

'Well, if you speak to the lady at the front desk—'

'I have, and she won't listen. Not like you do. You're just so . . . accommodating.'

'Well, I'm just a little tied up right now . . .'

'Oh, of course, I'll let you go put those down first!' The woman gave a shrill laugh, and then strutted off.

Sighing, Mia hurried her tray into the kitchen, before dashing for the lobby.

'A new room?' was Sonia's bewildered response. 'She's already changed twice.'

'Well, she's asked for a third, so if it's not too much bother—'

'It is, it's plenty of bother—'

'And because you love me and you're my best friend, would you please, *please* let her change one more time? You know what she's like.'

Sonia just rolled her eyes, told Mia she was an *easy target* and began to click away at her computer.

Job done, Mia returned to the kitchen, loaded up her tray and tried to get on with her day as best she could, when she heard someone call her name.

Looking up, she saw Hugh McDermott, dark hair slicked back under his white cook's hat, pointing to a lonely plate on the to-go counter behind her.

'You wouldn't take that out for me, would you? Becky's gone walkabouts again and it's going to get cold waiting for her.'

Becky was a petite, blonde seventeen-year-old who had joined the waiting staff over the summer, and had recently developed a bad habit of slipping off to the bathrooms during her shifts. It wasn't the first time Mia had picked up after her, so she just smiled, said, 'Sure, Hugh,' and loaded her tray to return to the dining room, adding Becky's abandoned order to the others.

It was then she noticed something.

'Is this . . . risotto?'

Hugh, who had gone back to chopping vegetables, glanced her way distractedly. 'Oh yeah – special request.'

'Oh, okay. I just . . . The menu's never changed as long as I've been here and . . .' She shook her head, forcing a laugh so as not to appear utterly pedantic, and brightly announced, 'Risotto for table nine, coming up!'

Mia sped into the dining room, dropping off two slices of carrot cake at table three, a hot chocolate for table six, dodged a conversation with a gaggle of Granny's friends at seven, and then, finally, reached table nine.

'Good afternoon,' she chirped. 'Your server is just a little busy at the moment. My name's Mia and I—'

She stopped. She stared.

The person seated in front of her was a lean, angular man in his late fifties. His hair was short and pewter grey, and he wore a fine blue suit over an equally fine shirt and tie.

His eyes, however, were what caught Mia off guard. They were steady and serious, framed with grey, wire-rimmed glasses and etched with age, but the colour . . . She had only ever seen such a lovely, sparkling blue in the smiling face of Mr Donahue Eagan Byrnes.

'Are you bringing the coffee?'

It took Mia a beat to snap on a smile. 'I'm sorry, what did you say?'

'Coffee,' the man said, his accent strikingly foreign – clipped and English, the *coff* rushing into the *ee*. 'I asked for a coffee.'

'*Of course*,' Mia said brightly. 'Now, what was it exactly?'

'What?'

'Your, um, beverage, sir?'

'*Coffee*. I just said that.'

'Oh, I know, but with milk, or espresso or—'

'A *black* coffee,' he said. 'Although, you're probably more used to serving barely brewed tea with milk and six sugars in this town, hm?'

For lack of a better response, Mia nodded, turned on her heel, and disappeared back to the kitchens.

Ruby caught her at the coffee machine. 'Mia, just to check – are you attached to your shift on Thursday, because I was thinking about moving . . . Are you okay? You're all flushed.'

'Oh,' Mia said, keeping her head down. 'It's nothing.'

'Now, Mia, is someone giving you a hard time? You know no one's allowed to bother my waiting staff.'

'No, no, it's just . . .' The coffee machine hissed and groaned, spewing hot black liquid into a clean cup. 'Have you met Cormac yet?'

'*No*. Where?'

'Table nine, I think.'

Ruby dashed to the door, peeping through the porthole into the dining room, while Mia put the cup on a saucer and readied her tray.

'The resemblance is definitely there,' Ruby said, Mia now by her side. 'Donahue was a little heavier, but the hair, the nose . . .'

'The eyes.'

'Well, what I said still goes.' Ruby straightened and opened the door for Mia. '*No one* is allowed to bother my waiting staff. You come and get me if he's being an arse.'

Mia would have hugged her if she hadn't a tray in hand, so gave her a quick peck on the cheek instead, and made her way back to table nine.

She didn't want to keep looking at him, but there was something so transfixing about Donahue's features on an unfamiliar face – an *angry* face. It seemed impossible now that she should not have noticed him at the funeral, but then again, there had been so many people, and she had been so . . .

The coffee cup rattled against its saucer, black liquid lapping over the side. It spilled onto the tablecloth.

'I'm so sorry,' she said, fishing for the dishcloth in her apron.

Cormac held up a hand. 'It's fine. Leave it.'

'Sorry, I—'

'I said *it's fine*.'

Mia looked from the dark-brown stain to Cormac again. His face was creased with irritation and a questioning stare.

'You just remind me—' Mia began, when a sudden awful sound broke through the hotel.

A scream, she realised.

In an instant, every diner had stopped what they were doing – cutlery silent, conversations on pause. Then, the hum of whispers swept in.

What was that?

Mia didn't wait another moment. With a quick *excuse me* to Cormac Byrnes and an expression of practised composure, she slipped out of the dining room and broke into a run only when she was out of his sight.

The scene in the lobby was surreal.

At the bottom of the main staircase, a woman lay at an awkward angle. Several members of staff were crouched beside her, and Henry McCullough was holding her hand, seemingly to encourage her to her feet.

It was when Mia drew closer that she recognised the crumpled heap: Eleanor Genie Fitzgerald.

She was missing the heel from one boot, and her hair fell about her pained face.

'Are you alright? Can you stand?' Henry asked in a low voice. He had a ruddy complexion that coloured desperately when worried, so presently his cheeks were nearly purple.

'I don't need to lie down,' Eleanor barked. It was a relief, Mia supposed, that her voice had not suffered. 'I need to get out of here. Now.'

'We can certainly take you to your room, just let us—'

'My *room*? I need to get out of this *hotel*, Mr McCullough.'

A small crowd began to gather and Mia jumped to work, giving each wavering guest her best waitressing smile, and encouraging them to go about their days. They didn't much want to, though. Miss Fitzgerald's continued diatribe was much too compelling and Mia's small voice like a buzzing fly about a picnic.

Amongst the mumbling and chatter, and Eleanor's shrill complaints, however, came a noticeably distinct accent and it cut through the madness.

'What's happened? What's going on?'

Cormac Byrnes arrived in the lobby like a cold snap. His face did not betray outright anger, but there was a tightness in his jaw and a sense of agitation to his quick step. His eyes flashed when they came upon the fallen woman.

The guests who had been drawn from the dining room and the bar parted for him, entertained now not only by the spectacle of Eleanor Genie Fitzgerald, but this new arrival: Donahue Byrne's prodigal son.

Cormac got down on one in knee in an awkward fashion. He reached for Eleanor and then seemed to reconsider, folding both hands into fists instead.

'Are you a guest here?' he asked.

'Yes,' Henry supplied. 'She's staying on the fourth—'

'I changed rooms, Mr McCullough,' Miss Fitzgerald barked. 'I'm on the fifth floor now. My name is *Eleanor Genie Fitzgerald*, and I—'

'Fell,' Cormac said, loud enough to be heard over the rising whispers. 'A simple accident. We're obviously terribly sorry that this happened to you during your stay here—'

'*No*,' the woman said. 'I didn't fall, and it wasn't an accident. I was *chased*.'

Cormac's jaw jumped with tension. 'Madam, I'm sure you had quite a fright, but I can assure you that no one in the hotel would even consider chasing—'

'I know what I saw. It was a *ghost*.'

All the hairs on the back of Mia's neck stood to attention.

'A ghost?' echoed one guest, and the crowd reverberated with murmurings. 'I thought those were stories.'

'They *are* stories,' Mia tried, but no one took any notice.

'Now, Madam,' Cormac said, trying a firmer tone. 'There is no reason to believe our hotel is haunted. In fact, I imagine what you saw was likely a shadow, or a—'

'No,' Miss Fitzgerald said. 'It was a ghost. It came right along the corridor at an unordinary speed, and then stepped through the stairwell door like it was nothing. And when I ran, it chased me – onto the stairs, and that's where I fell, and—' She huffed into a more upright position. 'And I won't be staying to find where it's disappeared off to. Now, Mr McCullough, help me pack my bags – and call me a cab.'

Cormac's eyes darted from Eleanor to the guests, to Henry once more. He stood, smoothing out his suit jacket, and something like panic or frustration nipped at his composure.

'I need to deal with something,' he said to Henry in a low tone. He took another look about the dire scene. 'Handle this, won't you?'

Henry nodded vehemently, then stooped to aid Miss Fitzgerald once more.

Cormac shouldered his way through guests and staff alike, muttering *excuse me* as he went.

As the throng parted, Mia was pushed backwards. Off balance, she stumbled another two steps, and came, regretfully, into his path.

His eyes met hers. They were blue and cold and nothing like his father's.

'Don't you have any work to do?' he snapped, and brushed past her.

chapter 5
wait and see

MISS FITZGERALD DIDN'T WANT to speak to Mia. In fact, she didn't want to speak to anyone but the porter who carried her bags and Gerry Finerty, who held the door as she escaped the lobby of Ballinadrum Hotel into the light drizzle of the afternoon.

'There's no point in discussing it,' she said, flinging her nylon scarf over her hair. 'I told you what happened already, and now I'm leaving.'

'Yes, but *what* did you see? What exactly?' Mia asked, trying her best not to look like she was tailing the woman – though, really, how else might it be described?

'A *ghost*.'

A red taxi waited at the bottom of the steps, the engine running.

'But was it wearing . . . was it wearing a veil, Miss Fitzgerald?'

Miss Fitzgerald bared her teeth in bad humour. 'I had no idea you would find my distress so amusing, Mia. Others, maybe, but not you.'

The porter closed Miss Fitzgerald's two large suitcases into the taxi's boot, as Miss Fitzgerald herself climbed into the backseat.

Just before she closed the door, though, she tilted her chin in a proud little way, and told Mia, 'It was a man, if you must know – with a moustache. And if I were you, I'd not wait around to meet him on a dark night.'

The door closed, the driver revved the engine, and Miss Fitzgerald was quietly transported away from Ballinadrum Hotel, while Mia stood at the bottom of the steps in the rain, thinking, once again, of unfinished business.

Two hours after Mia's shift ended that evening, she still had not gone home.

Instead, she was sandwiched between Rosco and his friend Ethan in a booth in the hotel's bar, for reasons Mia did not consider more important than a cheesy chip or unwinding in front of the Buckleys' stove – particularly after the day she'd had.

'It just happened,' Rosco had explained when she'd first arrived. 'Ethan was already here, and they wanted one drink. Let me get you a Diet Coke.'

'With chips and cheese and beans?' Mia had replied, hoping to jog his memory of that morning's conversation, but he'd simply guided her into the booth with a short laugh.

And at first, Mia tolerated the change in plans rather well. Yes, she was tired, and no, this wasn't *exactly* what she wanted from her evening, but she liked Rosco's friends. They were a tumble of twenty-somethings she had known since high school, and while she didn't always find their jokes that funny, they had never tried to make her feel unwelcome – not on purpose at least.

However, as the minutes and then hours wound on, her tiredness got the better of her. She grew quiet and her attention drifted over the bar, to its strange assortment of souvenirs: cast-iron kettles and odd road name signs, clay pottery and gold clocks, a small mounted deer head and a tin plate advertisement for the *Titanic*'s maiden voyage. Behind the glossy hardwood bar were rows of Irish gins and whiskies, their Scottish cousins, and the odd American expat – and in the very front, bottles chosen for their surreal and brightly coloured labels.

Above these, there was a collection of framed photographs, mostly in yellowed greyscale, from nights-out gone by – Mia's favourite part of the whole room.

That being said, the bar itself was by far her *least* favourite of the hotel's rooms. It was untouched by the purples and pinks that adorned the rest of the building, instead retaining its distinctly scarlet paint and checkerboard tiles.

'A tragic financial necessity,' Donahue had said, when Mia had asked why he'd not had it redecorated, too. 'And truth be told, the ghosts enjoy playing chess across the floor when everyone is off to bed far too much for me to change it now.'

'You doing alright, Mia?' one of the boys asked.

Roused from her thoughts, she glanced up to see Ethan, yellow-haired and beer-flushed, grinning ear to ear. He was probably Rosco's oldest friend, and was described by all of the boys as the *loose cannon of the group*. To Mia's understanding this meant he was the most likely to act out for the entertainment of his friends, and all the more so if alcohol was involved. The waitress in her didn't much like *loose cannons* – they were *always* the worst customers to serve – but otherwise, she thought of him how one might a particularly rambunctious Labradoodle: a handful, perhaps, but not maliciously so.

'Yeah,' she said. 'Just a long a day, you know?'

'Wanna hear a joke, then? Cheer you up?'

'Oh no, it's okay, I—'

'What's the difference between three hundred and sixty-five condoms, and a tyre?'

Mia gave a weak smile. 'Is this going be gross?'

The boys laughed.

'She's got you pegged, Ethan!'

'Getting a reputation there!'

Mia relented. 'What?' she asked.

'One is a Good Year, and the other is a *great year*!'

The boys howled with laughter – mostly, she thought, because it was such a bad joke – and she forced a laugh, too.

She darted another glance at Rosco. He still didn't look back.

'I have more,' Ethan went on, 'if that wasn't funny enough?'

'No, it's okay, Ethan. Thanks, though.'

'I guess it must be pretty tiring – working in a *haunted* hotel.'

'Well, actually, it's not *haunted*. It's—'

'I heard one of them pushed an old lady down the stairs earlier.'

Mia frowned. 'She's not really an *old* lady, and there's no evidence a ghost was involved at all.'

And, truth be told, Mia had looked. After her conversation with Genie Fitzgerald, she had returned to the hotel, wound her way up the stairs, and found the abandoned room.

It was, as all rooms in the hotel were, eclectically furnished and a little tired, but clean. Warm. And this room in particular had just been cleaned, so it smelled like lavender polish and the carpet was patterned with hoover lines.

The décor of pigeon ceramics and tasselled lampshades notwithstanding, it was perfectly ordinary, and the hallway the same. All that differentiated it from any other floor on any other day was the hastily planted handprint on the glass panel of the door between the corridor and stairwell.

No veil. No moustached man.

No ghost.

'Yeah, I'm pretty sure I saw something, too,' another of them – Kyle – said, and Mia's interest picked up. 'Last week? I was sure that someone was looking at me in the mirror in the men's, but when I turned around, nobody was there.'

'What was it?' Mia asked, just short of enquiring of a moustache.

'He was pissed, Mia,' Ethan explained, and Kyle laughed in agreement.

'You know, maybe that's the problem,' another of the boys said. 'Everybody keeps coming to work hammered. Somebody was telling me that someone heard a little girl laughing in the kitchen – which is basically a copy from every horror movie, ever.'

'It's ridiculous what a few stories will do to people's heads,' Rosco said. 'I mean, I know Donahue told a load of tall tales, but none of them are true.'

Tall tales seemed a rather simple description of Donahue's treasures.

'Talking about being pissed, my dad said Donahue was a bit of a drinker, you know,' Ethan said. 'Probably where he got all his batshit ideas from.'

'Donahue wasn't a drinker,' Mia said at once. It was the loudest, most certain thing she had said all evening, and it caught the boys, Rosco included, by surprise. 'He didn't drink at all, actually, except maybe a sherry at Christmas. He didn't like the taste.'

Ethan exchanged a disbelieving look with the other boys.

'He didn't,' Mia insisted.

'And who told you that?'

'Donahue,' she said. 'Donahue Byrnes.'

Infuriatingly, they laughed. More infuriatingly, Mia suddenly felt tears in her eyes.

'Aw, now look what you've done, Ethan!'

'Great, you asshole – she's crying!'

'She's not crying,' Rosco said, firmly. He moved his hand from her waist to her shoulder, pulling her into him. 'You're just tired, right? It's been a long day, hasn't it?'

'Yeah, of course. I'm fine. Sorry—'

'Yeah, and I should've brought you home, instead of hanging out with these goons. Yeah, you're alright. We're going now.'

'Going?' was the horrified response. 'It's not even eleven, Rossy.'

'Yeah, and Mia's tired, so we're off.'

And to the disgruntled cries of the bar, Rosco and Mia walked out hand in hand.

*

Out on the road, Mia breathed a sigh of relief.

The streets were dark, the rain was light, and Rosco's car smelt like the little pine tree in the window. It would be another ten minutes before they rumbled up the Buckleys' driveway, and while there was unlikely to be much time for venue research, there was certainly enough for a cup of tea and a chat with Rosco's mum. His dad would light the stove and the heat would turn Mia sleepy and stupid, and everyone would insist she stay in their spare room. She would not refuse.

'Sorry,' she said softly.

'For what?'

'Crying.'

'Yeah, well.' Rosco yawned. 'It was getting boring anyway.'

'I wasn't mad, just so you know. I was just—'

'I know you were close to Donahue, Mia, but the guys were just joking around. You didn't have to get so serious. You know he was a bit of a . . .'

'A what?'

'Weird guy.'

They took the next road on the right – when it should have been left. Mia saw the dark road that led to Granny Brea's. Rosco took it.

'Don't you want to . . .' She sat upright, worried. 'I thought we were going back to your house, to look at venues?'

'It's kind of late now. We'll look at them tomorrow.'

'Well, maybe I could just come over and—'

'Mia, I've got work tomorrow.'

'So do I,' she said, and he frowned.

'Look, I know you don't have much on your plate over there at Donahue's old place but I'm pretty busy at the garage. I have to be sharp.'

'Okay,' she said. 'We'll not go.'

'Now, don't give me that.'

'What?'

'The *tone*. The woe-is-me tone.'

'There's no tone. I'm just . . . Well, you said we'd do it tonight.'

'And now it's late, and I'm tired, so I'm saying we'll do it tomorrow. Isn't that good enough?'

Mia slid back into her seat, the street before her dotted with little orange pools of light. 'Yes,' she said. 'Sorry.'

*

Granny Brea's house was a skinny detached house on the very edge of Ballinadrum's main town. Older than Granny Brea herself, it matched the old woman for rattling bones and creaking joints, but it had violas out by the front door and the porch light was always on. Tonight was no exception and the latter buzzed an insistent yellow.

Rosco kissed Mia goodbye, but it was a quick peck at the corner of her lips.

'Are you mad?' she asked, standing on the pavement. The rain was heavier now, and his wipers squealed against the windscreen.

'No,' he answered. 'Should I be?'

'No, I just—'

'You're getting wet, Mia.'

She backed away from the car, its headlights turning the puddles white and glacial, and dashed for the house. As she turned to wave, she realised he had already pulled away.

She closed the door behind her and stripped out of her soggy cardigan, her thoughts already whirring with regret.

Mia had been with Rosco long enough now to know the mechanics of his moods, and particularly how quickly they might snap one way or the other – as they had done this evening. Afterwards, it was simply a matter of snapping them *back*, though that was rarely straightforward.

She was already deliberating whether she would call him in the morning before he came to collect her for work to clear the air, or if a text would suffice despite the possibility that he may not reply for hours, or how it might be better not to make a thing of it at all – he hated it when she *made a* thing – when a light came on upstairs.

'Mia?'

'It's me, Granny,' Mia called back.

She trudged upstairs to the bedroom, the weight of her satchel suddenly infinite, and changed into her oldest, slouchiest pyjamas.

There was a knock at the door. 'Can I come in?'

'Sure.'

'And what about two little people, too?'

'No more people, thank you, but dogs are always allowed.'

The door opened with a whine and in plodded Handsome Boy and Muriel, followed by Granny in a fleecy, blue dressing gown and sheepskin slippers.

'Mia, my love, you look awful,' she said.

Mia flopped onto the bed. 'Thanks, Granny.'

'Have you been crying?'

'No,' she lied, heaving Muriel onto the bed beside her. Handsome Boy lay down at her feet. 'Just a long day.'

'You're home late.'

'We got talking to Rosco's friends.'

'That made you cry?'

'No.'

Granny tilted her head.

'It was more . . . Do you remember all that stupid stuff about ghosts haunting the hotel?'

'Hard not to.'

'Well, it's more of that.'

Mia told her about Miss Fitzgerald and the scene in the lobby, Cormac Byrnes' eyes and his risotto, and the supposed line of would-be buyers sizing up Donahue's beautiful hotel.

'He looks like Donahue, too. I don't know why that makes it feel worse, but it does.'

Granny's face was wrinkled with concern. 'I'm sure his father would be very disappointed in him.'

'Well, I doubt he'll take that into consideration when he's deciding to do . . . whatever he's going to do with the hotel.'

'You'll have to just wait and see, my love. Everything could change tomorrow, after all.'

Her tone was bright, but Mia could hear the doubt in her voice. They lapsed into silence, and Mia's gaze slid across the room to her photographs.

'It's silly,' Mia said. 'But I just hoped . . . there'd be something still there.'

'Something?'

'You know, another . . . piece of him.'

'Like what?'

'I don't know. A riddle, a game? He talked about this *special role* he had for me, and now I'll never know what it was.'

'A special role? A job, you mean?'

'Maybe? I'm not sure.'

'You know you already had a special role in that hotel,' Granny said, and when Mia looked at her, she continued, 'You were Donahue's friend, Mia. You knew every one of his tall tales, all the magic of the hotel. You were always more than a waitress.'

The two women fell quiet again, and Mia listened to the sound of the rain, and Handsome Boy's soft snores, and the car passing along their street, illuminating her bedroom window before passing on.

Granny squeezed Mia's hand. Mia turned to her, and was met with a smile.

'Did I ever tell you,' Granny asked, 'about my first date with your Granda Casey at Ballinadrum Hotel?'

She had, so many times that Mia probably could have told Granny the story instead, but she answered, 'No. How did it go?'

'It was the spring of nineteen sixty-three,' she began, as she always did, warmth in her voice and cheeks. 'And Casey Moran was this no-good, no-money eejit who worked on Billy O'Hagan's beef farm. He was too old for me and drove that motorcycle far too fast, but when he turned up at church one Sunday with his Aunt Bethany, I couldn't help but smile at him across the pews.'

Mia leaned back and closed her eyes, let the present drift away like dust motes.

'And he came back the Sunday after that, and the Sunday after that one. It wasn't until August that he actually talked to me and asked me how I was, what my name was, and what I was doing on Saturday. I told him I was getting an ice cream sundae at Ballinadrum Hotel.'

Even though Mia's eyes were shut, she knew Granny was smiling, and she knew why. This was her favourite part, too.

'He says to me, *'With who?'* And you know what I told him? I told him, *'With you.'* And he laughed and laughed, 'til he shut up long enough to say that's what he thought, too.'

She paused then, and Mia opened her eyes to see her grandmother's flushed face, her eyes slightly damp.

'And you got your sundaes,' Mia continued for her. 'He got chocolate, and you got honeycomb, and then you traded, because you liked each other's better. And then he took you dancing in the bar room.'

Granny's voice was thick, but she laughed despite it. 'You know, I wouldn't be caught dead in a pair of heels now, but in those days, it was worth the pain just to hear the *click clack* of them on that gorgeous floor.'

'You got married there, too, didn't you?'

'We couldn't not have our wedding there, not after all it had done for us.'

'I wish I could have had my wedding there, too,' Mia said.

'But that's okay,' Granny told her softly. 'What's for you won't go by you, my love, and you'll get to find somewhere new – somewhere all your own.'

'I know, but . . . I liked going where you went better.'

'You won't always be able to go where I go, Mia.'

Mia looked into Granny's pale, dishwater eyes.

'I know,' she said.

chapter 6
beetle eyes

WHEN ROSCO CALLED AT GRANNY'S house the next morning, the rain from the night before had turned to weak, watery sunlight. With bluer skies came cooler temperatures, and Mia approached Rosco's car with a shiver of both cold and apprehension.

She was well prepared for the conversation to come, having practised it in her mind over breakfast: she shouldn't have acted like that around Ethan and the others, nor made them leave early, and next time they hung out, she would be perfectly agreeable.

Except when they got into the car, the first thing Rosco said was, 'Olive is coming.'

'Why?' Mia asked without thinking, and then hastened to add, 'Not that it's not lovely to see her, but it's just she – well, she only ever visits—'

'For disasters, I know.'

Great Aunt Olive was a rare sight in the Buckley household, but anytime she visited, it was an all-day affair and a spontaneous one, at that. She was a sharp-eyed old woman, with wiry grey hair and weathered skin, who cared little for birthdays or Christmases or end-of-exam celebrations, but felt it worth her time to visit on days pertaining to misery.

Just four months ago, she had arrived with little more than an hour's warning with the macabre announcement that the reason for the get-together was her late aunt's wedding anniversary.

'They would be eighty years married,' she had said sombrely. 'If they hadn't gone and died.'

Mia asked Rosco, 'It's the hotel, isn't it?'

'Must be, or it's another anniversary we haven't marked on the calendar. It's sure to be . . . interesting, anyway.'

'Yeah,' she said softly. 'Interesting.'

'Think you could leave the hotel a little early? Apparently, she's coming at four and Mum's organising tea for her.'

'I'm sure Ruby wouldn't mind.'

'You wanna stay over, after?'

Mia felt the unease of the night before melt like ice in warm water. 'Yeah, if that's okay.'

'Why wouldn't it be okay?'

The Burning Lamp flashed into view – a short queue of elderly Ballinadrum residents already forming about its door – before they slid along yet another row of big-name coffee shops and chemists, and Rosco took a different turn than the one for Ballinadrum Hotel.

'Are we . . . taking the long way?' Mia asked.

'Sort of,' Rosco said. Stopped at the traffic lights, he squeezed her knee. 'I wanted to drive past the House. Feel like it's been a while. You got time?'

The House, capitalised, was a squat, white semi behind Ballinadrum's main street that Rosco and Mia had put an advance down for earlier this year. It wasn't a dream house or anything – its well-tramped carpet and floral wallpaper desperately needing replaced – but with modest looks came modest prices, and more importantly, it would be *their* house.

'Yeah,' Mia said, smiling. 'I've got time.'

*

After work, Rosco picked Mia up and they drove a little way out of Ballinadrum to the Buckleys' house.

It was a large grey new-build with a square farmhouse profile, surrounded by ten acres of farmland. The driveway still hadn't been completed and had lain in dusty rubble these past five years, which meant Mia didn't even have to look to know she was here. The familiar shudder of her seat did it for her.

Rosco's mother, Heather, greeted them before they had even reached the door.

'Mia!' she called. 'It's been so long!'

'Try four days,' Rosco corrected, giving her an obligatory peck on the cheek before showing himself into the house.

'I'm sure it's been longer,' Heather went on, looping an arm through Mia's. 'I'm glad you were able to come at such short notice.' Her voice dipped to a whisper. 'You know Joseph's aunt – *spontaneous*. I had to leave the office an hour early and everything. I suppose that's the perks of being chief, but let me tell you, I'll get an earful tomorrow about throwing my weight around, just you wait. Say, Mia, did you see the write-up on the hotel?'

Heather drew Mia into the Buckley house as if she was afraid Mia would run off if it was not done quickly enough, and the door was closed behind them. Enveloped in a soft, kitchen-y smell – hot water, steamy air, dinner from another evening – Mia felt some forgotten tension unravel.

'Mum,' Rosco said. 'You're doing it again.'

'What? Oh, I'm talking too much – or was it too fast? Rossy has so many rules, doesn't he, Mia?'

Secretly, Mia liked the way Heather talked. Yes, she did speak as though trying to get as many words in as possible before it was socially unacceptable to *still* be talking, but there was such warmth and enthusiasm to her that Mia believed that she really did mean every word she said – no matter how flighty or brief such a word might be.

She was entirely unlike her son in this way – and the fact she was also a head shorter than him, with frizzy blonde hair, only heightened the contrast between them.

'Anyway, Rossy, your Auntie Olive is in the living room. Go say hello, won't you? I'm just sorting out the tea.'

Compared with the hallway, which was painted mint green and had an air of practicality about it – a row of boots beneath a row of coats, a sturdy sideboard for keys and post and other homeless items – the Buckleys' living room was a distinctly homely space, plush and warm, and scented with woodsmoke.

It was most notable, however, for the expansive number of family photographs it contained. A gap-toothed Rosco grinned in a school uniform, while another dive-bombed into a pool in Spain, and another still showed off a pair of scarlet red hands from an afternoon of finger-painting.

Rosco hated every single one of them.

'I'm never going to embarrass *my* kids like that,' he had told Mia one Sunday afternoon, after Heather had pointed out every picture in which Rosco wore braces.

Mia had wanted to tell him it was sweet to have a parent love you to embarrassing lengths, and to have so many memories you could paper a whole house, not just a wall in a pokey bedroom, but that had felt too pointed and – to quote Rosco himself – too *woe is me.*

It wasn't that Mia never talked about her parents. She and Granny could spend hours going over old photographs and stray belongings about the house, but when it came to other people . . . the mention of *dead parents* had the most painful, awkward effect on them – so much so that Mia had become an expert at steering such conversations back to ease.

She would say things like *I was too young to remember*, and *it happened so long ago* – as though her parents' loss was a disappointment akin to forgetting her favourite teddy-bear at the playpark, or being pushed down by an older child outside school. As though it was not the overarching tragedy of her suddenly, violently two-berth family.

So, when it came to Rosco's childhood photographs, she had just told him his braces were cute. He had rolled his eyes and told her *no, they weren't*, and the conversation had moved on – briskly, comfortably. Back into ease.

'Mia!' Rosco's father, Joseph, stood from his seat at the end of one of the sofas and clasped her hand. 'Sorry to hear about the hotel, sweetheart. Onwards and upwards, hm?'

Unlike Heather, Joseph had made Rosco his biological beneficiary, handing down his brown eyes and short, sharp nose. They once matched with heads of coarse, dark hair, too, but in the last few years, Joseph's had been reduced to a thin layer of grey fuzz instead.

'You remember Rosco's Great Aunt Olive, don't you?'

The old woman sat alone on the only armchair, wearing an oversized knitted cardigan and a pair of worn brown brogues. Her chin was hard and square, and her dark-grey hair had been combed flat against her forehead, though a clump of wisps still sprung out into untamed bushiness by her ears.

Most striking of all were her eyes: they were mean little things, probing their subject for hidden depths. They shone like beetle shells in her worn face.

'Of course, she does, Joseph, it's only been four months, not forty years.' She fixed Mia with her stare. 'We're all in mourning with you today. I, for one, was hoping that the old building would outlast me, and it was a nasty surprise, to say the least, to hear that would not be the case.'

'It was all a little sudden,' Mia said, taking a seat beside Rosco. 'For everyone.'

'That's not what we heard.'

Mia turned to the two sixteen-year-old boys taking up the entirety of the Buckley's other sofa. Matthew and Grant, Rosco's twin brothers and obvious Buckleys by their dark complexions, barely looked up from their phones.

'We heard,' Matthew said, 'the hotel had been going down for years and this was just the final nail in the coffin.'

'And Cormac and his dad never even *liked* each other,' Grant went on. 'So, it wasn't as if he was going to carry on the family business – especially not when it's *haunted*.'

Joseph laughed. 'Haunted, eh? Where did you hear that one?'

'Online.'

'Yeah, some website's sharing it.'

'Website?' Mia echoed.

Both boys tapped away at their phones again. A moment later, Grant turned his phone around so Mia could see his screen: a webpage with simple grey text, and below that, a grainy photograph of an old building, which Mia took several seconds to recognise as Ballinadrum Hotel. It looked so much more like a movie set or silly theme park attraction than it ever did in person.

'Tsk,' Olive muttered. 'What a woeful photograph.'

'What website is that?' Mia asked.

'It's some weird American blog – *GhostHuntHub.com*. Totally tragic,' Matthew said.

'Yeah, but they actually have pretty up-to-date info,' Grant said, taking his phone back. 'Seems like somebody's been spilling the hotel's secrets from the inside, Mia. Was it you?'

'No,' Mia gasped, before realising they were teasing, and the pair burst into laughter.

'What's this *info*, then?' Joseph asked with a grin. 'Hard photographic evidence, backed up by today's best scholars and scientists, I imagine?'

'Well, like somebody said there's this *bride*—'

'Oh yeah, the *bride*—'

'Somebody thinks they saw, like, a veil or whatever.'

'And apparently all the weirdest stuff happens around the west wing.'

'The west wing is closed,' Mia said.

'That's the *point* – it's closed *because* it's, like, cursed ground.'

'Yeah, because of the war. People *died* there.'

'It's closed,' Olive said, 'because Donahue Byrnes couldn't bear to pay heating bills for rooms that were hardly ever occupied.'

'I can hardly bear paying the heating bills for rooms that *are* occupied,' Joseph said.

'Yeah, well, everybody's been sharing it anyway.'

Mia sat up straighter. 'And when you say *everybody* . . .'

'Oh, like four hundred shares on Facebook—'

'Five hundred.'

'Oh,' Mia said. 'That's not *too* many—'

'Yeah, but the page has five thousand views.'

'*Five thousand?*' Great Aunt Olive said with disgust. 'Of *that*? The youth today know nothing of value. Let me show you a *real* photograph.'

Groaning like an old door, she reached for her leather handbag by her feet. She set it atop her knee and drew from it a red square book.

Opening it wide, she turned it to the room: Ballinadrum Hotel in black and white, hazy with overexposure on what appeared to be a radiant summer's day.

'And *this* photograph,' Olive said, 'has only been seen by a dozen or so.'

'Where did you get that?' Mia asked with amazement.

'I took it. July, nineteen-seventy. It was closed then, you know, for—'

'*Spiritual cleansing.* It reopened a year later, right?'

Olive's eyebrows rounded. 'A girl who knows her history.'

'Donahue – uh, *Mr Byrne*s told me about it. He said it was to get rid of the ghosts from the war, but the holy water they used didn't bother them much. He told me they just used it to make tea, actually.'

Olive's grave expression cracked with a laugh. 'Did he, really?'

'And another time he told me the sage they burned to ward them off was used to season steaks when they got hungry at night.'

'I wouldn't have thought ghosts would have got hungry at all.'

'Well,' Mia said, 'those were his stories.'

'Ah, he was an unusual man, indeed – a storyteller, through and through. And yet that boy of his . . . Cormac . . .'

'They seem quite different,' Mia admitted.

'You've met him then? I haven't seen him since . . . Well, Donahue's funeral, but before that it was his mother's funeral, and I'm not sure that even counted, he was there and gone that quick.'

'They look a little alike – around the eyes.'

'But that's as far as it goes.'

'Yes,' Mia said. 'That's as far as it goes.'

'You know, he wasn't always that way,' Olive continued. 'I remember him as a wee tiny thing, just one tooth, and his daddy parading him about the lobby like he was the best thing in the world, and even when he was four or five, doing his spellings for us, because Donahue had said how good he was at them. Bright wee fella, then. Absolutely glued to his father.'

'Really?' Mia said. 'I heard they weren't very close.'

'Well, they were when he was wee, but when he got older . . . it wasn't the same. Might just be teenagers,' she added, with a pointed look at the twins. 'Whatever it was though, I just remember going to the hotel one day and asking Donahue about his boy, and he said Cormac was up in his room – wouldn't come down. Don't think it ever got any easier, either.'

Olive returned her attention to the album on her lap. 'Oh, and this one . . .' she said. 'This is a good one.'

She angled it to Mia to reveal three shirtless boys lounging on a grassy patch. All were clearly Buckleys, with dark hair and dark eyes, even rendered in black and white.

'It's the lawn,' Olive said. 'Out the back of Ballinadrum. Can you spot your daddy there, Joseph?'

Rosco's father edged closer in his seat. 'That's him in the middle, isn't it? My, he looks different without the beard.'

'And do you know your uncles, too? That's Samuel there. . . He went to teach in Dublin, so maybe you didn't get to see him that often, and then there's Dennis on the left. He was the handsome one of the four them, you know.'

'Four?' Mia said. 'Who was the other brother?'

'That would be the man behind the camera,' Olive said. 'Owen Buckley. He worked in the hotel, you know, from nineteen fifty-six, I believe, until sixty-nine.'

'What did he do after that?'

'Nothing,' Olive said. 'He died.'

At that moment, Heather returned to the room with a clattering tray and a cheery, 'Now, remind me, who's tea and who's coffee?'

She began to dismantle the precarious tower of cups and saucers on the coffee table, before ordering her sons to man the milk and sugar.

'Why isn't Rosco doing anything?' Matthew asked, hauling himself from his seat.

'Because he has company.'

'Mia's not company,' Grant said.

'Not anymore,' Matthew added.

Some molten warmth seized Mia then. It spurred her to her knees, where she aided Heather in arranging cups and asking Joseph, once more, whether he had decided between tea and coffee.

Olive's voice cut through the rattle. 'He wasn't well, had never been. We always knew he was shy, but this was different.'

Heather shot the old woman a curious look, then caught Mia's eye with a bewildered expression.

'Things were complicated back then,' the old woman went on. 'I often wonder what I would do differently, if I could go back, or what I might ask him.' She leafed through her book again, murmuring, 'There must be a photograph of him somewhere in here . . .'

'Have a little tea, Olive. We can maybe do photographs later, hm?' Heather said, handing the old woman a cup and forcing Olive to set her book down. 'And, Mia, sweetheart, there's a box of buns from The Burning Lamp in the kitchen there. Would you mind grabbing them for me?'

Olive glowered at Heather – and then those little beetle eyes lit on Mia.

Mia ducked her head as she left the room.

chapter 7
the stories were right

ONE WEEK LATER, AS foretold by Heather Buckley and countless others, the first of the dreaded potential buyers arrived in person.

As much as they might have looked and sounded like ordinary patrons, they had their giveaways: on their own, not staying for longer than a night or a lunch. Some had accents, and many took taxis to the doors of the hotel, arriving in an assortment of mismatched vehicles, armed with overnight bags.

Mostly though, Mia knew them by their unhurried steps and slow, sliding stares. There was money to be mined from these walls, and they were here to count it out.

She detested them immediately and utterly, but managed to greet each with a practised plastic smile. 'Have you dined with us before?' she would ask. 'Will anyone be joining you?'

She received identical answers – *no, never*, and *just for one* – and then she would invite them, these vampires, across the threshold of the dining room and show them to their seats.

Cormac would occasionally appear to wish them a pleasant stay or to remind them they had a meeting at whatever time, and when he did, Mia stayed out of his sight.

Today she was serving a tall skinny man with a north Dublin accent. A buyer, most evidently.

He had a noticeably nervous disposition – changing his order twice, drumming his fingers on the table, and glancing about him with such sparrow-like frequency that Mia wondered briefly if he was expecting someone.

'Do you imagine we really do have a spiritual infestation?' she could imagine Donahue saying, with a comedic glint in his eyes. 'Or is our décor as alarming as I had feared?'

Mia unloaded the man's order from her tray. 'That's one breakfast tea, and a ham and cheese panini, no salad.'

'Thank you,' the man said, immediately dumping four sugars into his tea and swirling them about.

'Is that everything today?'

'Yes, yes. Thank you.'

Mia gave a quick nod and started back for the kitchen when the man spoke again.

'Actually, miss . . . I . . .'

'Yes?'

'Have you worked here long?'

'A few years,' she said with a wary smile.

'Always in the kitchens?'

She nodded.

'Do you . . . often go elsewhere in the hotel?'

'I'm not sure what you mean, sir.'

His fingers played against the white tablecloth. He was a yellowish colour, with a well-groomed moustache, and was wearing a checked suit that was just an inch or two too short.

'I only mean that – if you have ever been walking these halls, have you ever seen anything . . . strange?'

Mia's heart pitched. It wasn't that talk of ghosts and oddities had evaporated entirely from the hotel – rather, it clung to conversation like a peppery cologne – but actual *sightings* had been few in these last days. Those which had resulted in mischief or malady, in particular, had been – so far – contained to just the one.

And Miss Genie Fitzgerald had not returned to the hotel for a second.

'Strange how?' she asked.

'Well, I . . .' he began, frowning. 'It's hard to . . . I only mean . . .'

'Have *you* seen something, sir?'

'No.' He thought, and then again said, 'No. Nothing.'

'Well, if you do, I—'

'Yes. Thank you. That's all.'

Disappointment curled about her. 'Oh, okay. Enjoy your—'

'Where's the bathroom?'

Mia pointed to a narrow hallway at the back of the dining room, adding that the men's room was the fourth door on the left.

He nodded, leaving without another word.

'They're miserable, aren't they?' Ruby whispered once Mia had returned to the kitchen for an order of poached eggs and a lemonade. Behind them, the kitchen bustled with the usual clanging and chopping and chatter. 'I don't think I've met one buyer who might actually be a pleasant person.'

'Has anyone . . .'

'Made an offer? Don't think so. Lots of gossip going around, though.'

'Isn't there always?'

Ruby pulled Mia to the kitchen's porthole, where she pointed out a lonely diner seated nearest to the lobby. 'See *that* one – big beard, grey jumper? His name is Victor Gurning, goes to the Baptist church a couple of towns over.

I've heard he's had a few lunches with Cormac so far. He wants it for *bits*.'

'Bits?'

'Yeah, you know, knock it down, strip out what's valuable. Copper, I suppose, and these tiles are probably worth a few pennies, too.'

'He can do that?'

'If he buys it, he can do whatever he wants with it.'

'But it's not his,' Mia said, before realising how stupid that sounded.

'Not yet,' Ruby replied. 'But we'll see.'

When Mia returned to the dining room, she felt her vision now skewed. Wherever she walked, Mr Gurning was a dark smudge in the corner of her eye – sipping tea from their good china, dabbing his mouth with their good napkins. All while calculating the price of everything he put his eyes to.

It was almost more than Mia could bear, and she was only distracted from this acidic dislike by a flurry of activity a few tables over.

'I just . . . I don't know what I've done with it . . .' a woman was saying, elbows deep in her oversized handbag, while two young children looked on and Becky stood by with a bored expression.

'Hey, Becky,' Mia said, coming close. 'You wouldn't mind grabbing a damp cloth from the kitchen for me? I'll sort this.'

Becky shrugged and took her leave.

The woman looked up from her bag with a sudden smile. 'Little Miss Mia.'

'Hi, Ms McGowan. How are you?'

The Burning Lamp bakery's owner was dressed in snakeskin boots and a purple woollen coat – which would have looked more striking had it not been missing a button or bobbling at the elbows. Even still, she was a zebra amongst ponies in nearly every room she entered, and today was no exception.

'Oh, I was doing alright,' she said, digging in her handbag again, 'until I . . . Well, it looks like I've misplaced some cash. I was so sure I put it in this little pocket and—' Her face suddenly drained of colour. 'Oh, Mia, I've given it to the plumber. He was out this morning, fixing the pipes in the shop, and I didn't even think, I was just trying to get out of the house with these two – they were hanging off my leg and I—'

Mia lifted the empty plates. 'That's alright.'

'Oh, but it's not, Mia – I can't use my card. I'm over the limit and I've left the good card at home—'

With her free hand, Mia took up the bill and stuffed it in her back pocket.

'I'll get it,' she said.

'If I can just run back to get the other card—'

'I don't recall you making me run back to the house when I was thirteen and only had enough money for a top hat but left with a half dozen cream fingers.'

'Now, Mia—'

'Or when Granny needed a lift home from the shop because it was raining—'

'Anyone would have done that!'

Mia kept her eyes low, adjusting the glasses on the tray. 'You've been more than good to us, Lorna, especially with this wedding cake you won't let us pay for, so let me just do one thing for you.'

'Now, Mia, as though our Jim would see anyone else make a cake for you.'

Mia knew this to be true. Before his death, Jim McGowan had run The Burning Lamp alongside his wife Lorna, handing out free top hats to a much smaller Mia when Granny wasn't looking, and sing-songing her name when she came through the tinkling-bell door.

When he had died, nearly twelve years ago now, the bakery had never felt so quiet.

'Please,' Mia said.

Lorna sighed. 'Well, you're going to have to let me do three-tiers on your cake, then. No more of this *keep it simple* nonsense just because you're afraid to run up my ingredient list.'

Mia smiled. 'If you insist.'

'And come in for a tasting, too, won't you? You can sample anything you want.'

'You'll regret that offer.'

'Not as long as I live.'

A sudden flash of movement stole her attention away – along with most of the other diners'.

The Dublin man in the checked suit had reappeared. He was making powerful strides towards the door, his face blotched tomato red.

To Mia's surprise, there was a figure trailing after him. More surprising still was that the figure was none other than Cormac Byrnes. He wore an anxious expression, and one arm was outstretched before him, as though he could simply tap the man on the shoulder and bid him calm.

'Just a moment,' Mia told Lorna with a tight smile, before making a walk-run-dash to the dining room's entryway.

'Sir,' she said. 'Would you like to pay here or if you're staying the night, we can—'

'Oh, no. I won't be staying the night. Just the bill, please. Quickly.'

Cormac caught up to them both, and said, 'Sir, I must insist that we have a quick chat about that offer—'

'It's off the table,' was the curt reply. 'I'm not the man for this hotel, Mr Byrnes. The stories were right.'

His wide brown eyes took one final sweep of the room, and Mia could feel the terrible fear in his expression pool in her own stomach.

'It's haunted.'

chapter 8
a pinch of salt

AFTER DARK, MIA MET RUBY and Sonia in the kitchens and recounted the entire afternoon.

'Cormac started on about how everything was fine, *come back and have lunch for free*, but the man wouldn't hear it. He paid his bill and was out of there in five minutes flat.'

'What do you think he saw?' Ruby asked.

'I don't know,' Mia said. 'I didn't see anything when I went to look.'

The three women were bent over a half-eaten, strawberry-topped pavlova. Arguably, it could have been served to guests the next day, but they had decided it wouldn't be missed *too* terribly.

'You went to look?' Sonia said, her tone surprised. 'In the men's bathroom?'

Suddenly self-conscious, Mia said, 'Well, *something* scared him.'

'Oh, don't tell me you're one of them now, Mia. I thought we agreed about this – everyone's in a tizzy about ghosties, but it'll be forgotten about in a month.'

'Except it's already *been* months,' Ruby said. 'And the rumours haven't stopped, have they? Besides, what do you expect Mia to do? Her customer goes running out of the hotel in fright, and you don't think she should investigate what happened? It may not have been a *ghostie*, but that doesn't mean it was nothing.'

Mia didn't have much else to add. Ruby was a vague believer in the unseen, Sonia was not, and Mia hadn't seen, felt, or heard anything that afternoon that would have given significant sway to either side. The hallway the Dublin man had rushed from had been empty, the bathroom he had visited unremarkable, and there were no veils, or laughs, or moustached men to be accounted for.

But hadn't it been a little cold? Hadn't it seemed just a little *too* quiet? And really, if Cormac Byrnes hadn't interrupted her – his eyes flinty – would something, *anything* have revealed itself? Instead, Mia had apologised for leaving her post and fled his presence as if *he* were the ghost.

'I'm just saying,' Sonia said, taking a generous spoonful of pavlova, 'that if this is the same man in the checked suit that I saw in the lobby, I'm not surprised he was spooked. He'd be scared of his own shadow.'

'He did seem pretty nervous,' Mia admitted.

'Like he'd already *seen something*?' Ruby probed.

'Or heard too many stories?' Sonia said. 'You were telling Lily one just the other day, Mia.'

'But have there ever been *this* many stories?' Ruby asked. 'And all after Donahue dies, too. It could *mean* something.'

'What makes you think it's got anything to do with Donahue dying, and not Cormac *arriving*?' Sonia wiggled her eyebrows. 'How's that for a plot twist?'

'Oh, you never take these things seriously. He *could* be the reason, you know.'

'Except for the fact he's been gone for, like, thirty years or something.'

'He could still have a dark, mysterious secret he's hiding from the rest of us.'

'Ruby, he's an accountant. Accountants don't have dark, mysterious *anythings*.'

Mia snorted.

'All I'm saying,' Ruby went on, 'is he must be a pretty twisted individual to fall out with his own dad – especially Donahue, who was the sweetest man I've ever met.'

'I hear Cormac didn't do the falling out, actually,' Sonia said.

'What?' Mia asked.

'Yeah, Gerry told me. He said *Donahue* fell out with *Cormac* first.'

This brought Mia to a pause. If it had been anyone else at the hotel, perhaps she would have held tight to her resolve, but it being Gerry . . . well, his word came as close to the truth as any piece of gossip could.

'A-ha!' Ruby said. 'So, he *did* do something bad – perhaps even *dark and mysterious*?'

'Doubtful. By Gerry's timeline, Cormac was still a kid when it happened, so it was probably something totally mundane blown out of proportion, but *apparently*, Donahue was pretty angry, and everything changed after that.'

'After what?' Mia said. 'What happened?'

Sonia shrugged. 'Gerry didn't say. Just that it was a *falling out*. Don't think Gerry rightly knew, to be honest, and really, I'd take it with a pinch of salt. I personally fall out with my daughter at least four times a week.'

'Maybe it has something to do with the ghosts,' Ruby suggested.

'Enough with the ghosts, Ruby.'

'I can't help it! *Weird things* have been happening around here lately. It's giving me the creeps.'

'It *attracts* the creeps, more like,' Sonia said. 'You know, I had to check in a lady today who went by the name *Mystical Kate*. She asked if I had ever encountered a *cold spot* in the hotel. I mean, it's *Ireland*. There are cold spots all over the bloody place.'

'Although, I *do* know what she means,' Ruby said. 'It's those little shivers you get, like there might be a draught but you can't feel any breeze, and . . . Oh, don't give me that look, Sonia.'

'Well, at least we can be assured Donahue would be rightly tickled by the chaos he's left behind.'

Ruby sniffed. 'I hardly think so. Hotel to be sold off, people arguing about whether it should be knocked down – I'd say he'd feel pretty sorry about the state of affairs, God rest his soul. And if he knew that Mia wasn't going to be able to get married here because of that Cormac . . . Well, that would break his heart.'

That much, Mia thought, was true. Stories and silliness aside, the hotel was important to Donahue, and so were the people inside it.

'Speaking of which,' Ruby went on, 'did you find a new venue yet?'

'Oh . . . no. We'll get it sorted soon though.'

Ruby scraped her side of the plate. 'You're very calm for a girl getting married in five months without a reception venue.'

'That's because Mia has sense,' Sonia said. 'She knows the wedding day isn't everything.'

Ruby was aghast. 'Of *course* it's everything. Just because the day-to-day stuff is important doesn't mean you *write off* the only wedding day you may ever have! And *Mia* knows that too. She's just too nonchalant for her own good. Tell me, Mia – did you have a look at those bridal magazines I gave you last week?'

They had been a very kind gesture – particularly so when Mia had realised how much they cost – but when Mia and Granny Brea had perused the pages, they'd both came to a similar realisation.

'*Extortionate*,' Mia had said to Granny, sucking her teeth at the price noted in tiny text at the footer. 'And for *one day*.'

'But *the* day,' Granny had argued. 'We could manage.'

Mia disagreed, more convinced than ever that the offerings of online resellers or the high street would do just fine. After all, it was *the* day, but she also had to account for *the* band, *the* food, and *the* venue – which was now another undecided item.

'I had a look,' Mia said.

'*And?*'

'They were nice.'

'*Nice?* Mia, you're killing me here. Did you get a feeling for the style, the shape of the dress—'

'There's no point,' Sonia said. 'Dresses always look great on the models, with all the pins and tucking and Photoshop, and then it's a mystery as to why you look like a lumpy meringue. You have to see them in person.'

'Then, let's go! You free this Saturday, Mia?'

The kitchen door swung open unexpectedly, and the women jumped to hide their forks.

'Henry! We were just—'

'Stop, you don't have to explain.' He had a weary look about him, his floral-print tie pulled loose. 'I just need someone to go to the fourth floor for me, now.'

'Not if it's Mr Murph—'

'Mr Murphy has complained about his sheets being itchy,' he continued.

All three groaned. Mr Murphy was a man in his late seventies, who spent nearly every weekend at Ballinadrum Hotel, waltzing about the hallways, calling room service, and complaining about anything and everything he could think of.

'I'm not doing it,' Ruby said. 'It's not my job and I've had enough of him. I had to bring him a cup of tea to his room last week, only for him to give off that it was too hot. Too hot!'

'Well, it's not my job either,' Sonia said. 'I checked him in. I think that's enough Mr Murphy for anyone.'

'Yes, I know none of you are part of the hospitality team, but it would seem that the late-night staff have gone walkabout, and no one is answering my text messages. It's a good thing I know where to expect you three,' he added wryly.

'I'll do it,' Mia said.

Ruby and Sonia shot her looks of surprise. Henry sighed with relief.

'Thank you, Mia. At least I can depend on *someone*,' he said. 'And I will have you know that we respect each and every one of our guests, and it is a *pleasure* to serve them in whatever way they need or desire. That being said, you won't have to deal with Mr Murphy. He's already been moved. All I need you to do is change the sheets.'

'Oh, lucky break,' Ruby said.

'Yeah, you could have opened with that, Henry,' Sonia said. 'Though, I'd still be careful if I was you, Mia.'

'What?' Mia said. 'In case he comes back?'

'No,' she said, all drama and doom. 'In case you meet a *ghost*.'

Mia, unwilling to admit that was her exact desire, just rolled her eyes and laughed.

Mia didn't go to the fourth floor immediately. Instead, she looped around the lobby, back through the dining room, and quietly entered the hallway Cormac had interrupted her in earlier.

It still seemed ordinary. The overhead lights, dressed in little glass globes, buzzed softly, and the pipes in the walls gave their familiar greetings. There was distant conversation – from the bar, or a bedroom, or maybe the staff locker room above – and while the old hotel was prone to the odd cold draught, this space in particular was comfortably warmed by the clicking, clunking radiator on the far wall.

No cold spots. No ghosts.

Mr Murphy's old room, room forty-eight, was all the more ordinary – infuriatingly so. Mia tore the sheets from the bed, tossed them in a crumpled heap by the door, then tucked, folded, and smoothed the replacement sheet flat.

She stood back, half-breathless, to inspect her work. New sheets did little to change the fact that the mattress was ten years old, nor did they help the way the old, yellowed lamps cast a sallow light on everything.

They were clean, though, and white, and smelt like lavender from the wash.

Mia's gaze softened and she trailed her fingers across the top of the bed.

The first time she had ever slept in these sheets for herself was on her eighth birthday. Granny Brea had tried to dissuade her with offers of bouncy castles and cinema trips, but Mia had been certain: she wanted a sleepover at Donahue Byrnes' hotel.

'He says the ghosts only come out after dark,' she had explained to her grandmother. 'And all the other magical creatures.'

Granny had made it a birthday to remember, of course – a vanilla-scented bubble bath, new pyjamas with silver stars, and ice cream sundaes ordered to the room. Donahue Byrnes had even joined them for dinner, ordering extra desserts and a mocktail with a sparkly curly straw for Mia.

Afterwards, they had searched the hotel for *unusual* goings-on. None had shown up by the time Mia had gone to bed at the mighty hour of eleven, but she dreamed of magic the whole night through.

Now, Mia gently closed the door to room forty-eight behind her. She dumped the sheets down the laundry chute, and then, in the deserted hallway, so quiet it was as though the hotel was holding its breath, she drew her camera from her apron.

Snap.

Mia looked down at the little digital screen, and saw the scene before her. Purple carpets, tall dark windows and a hodgepodge of furniture, collectable plates and candle sconces screwed into the wall. She wished she could have captured the imperfect silence, too, and the vague scent of age and beeswax polish, and the sound of her feet on the carpet – but a picture was all she could take.

She took another, and another after that, her camera singing with each stolen image.

And then, when the photographs began to feel useless and small, and she much the same, she stopped and wondered if

Rosco had been right about getting something new, something better.

She switched to the viewer to look at the images, and was surprised to see a spot – a pale, glowing spot, in the centre of the frame. She wiped the screen and then the lens with her sleeve, glancing between the camera and the hall before her.

There was no lamp, or even anything particularly shiny, and this little dot was so pale and cold that Mia couldn't help but lean closer to get a better look.

And then there was a laugh – a bright tinkling laugh.

Mia recognised it at once, and listened intently for it to continue, to guide her to its source. But nothing came.

Had she imagined it? It certainly felt like it in that moment when all was so quiet and still; when Mia was all alone with nothing, yet again, but the hotel's old walls and floors.

She returned to the world downstairs.

chapter 9
dead man

MIA WAS OFTEN HAPPY because Rosco was happy. This was one of those afternoons.

He had gotten off work and taken her to the House, where they had spent the better part of an hour and a half measuring up walls and windows for furniture they couldn't afford, and curtain rails his uncle was giving away for free. They had danced in the lonely living room, and crept upstairs to their would-be bedroom to kiss like it was their honeymoon, arguing between breaths about whether they needed a king or queen-size bed.

They never came to a conclusion, and Mia didn't care.

Some part of her was still there now – swaying, laughing, scoping out a corner of the living room for their Christmas tree – as Rosco pulled up in front of the hotel.

A light frost had appeared overnight, and in response, Mia had donned her Ballinadrum Hotel sweater – the little purple crest embroidered in the black wool – and upped her forty-denier tights to eighty. The winter would see wool come into play, and an extra coat, too, but right now, in Rosco's heated car, she was luxuriously warm, and he was using her hand as a microphone as he sang along to whatever pop song was on the radio. When she told him that she needed it back, he kissed the flat of her palm.

She leaned forward and allowed herself to sink into another kiss, another moment in which she was utterly, undeniably, unequivocally sure they were going to be happy.

With reluctance, she broke away. 'I have to go to work.'

'Do you, though?' he asked, catching her hands, and pulling her back to him.

She kissed him again. 'Yes, Rosco, I do.'

'You could call in sick.'

'I can't do that to Ruby.'

'She'd understand.'

'I'll see you tonight, Rosco.'

'Or, hey – maybe you could just quit.'

Mia had her satchel in one hand and the door handle in the other. She still wore a smile, but her eyes narrowed in confusion. 'Quit?'

'Yeah, what's your notice? Can't be more than a few days, can it?'

'Wait, you're serious?'

'Well, if the place is selling, maybe you should just get a head start.'

'It doesn't work like that.'

'Sure, it does. You get a new job before you lose the one you're in. I'm pretty sure that's how most people do it.'

'Yeah, but we don't know the hotel is closing.'

Rosco laughed as though she were joking, and when she didn't join in, he rolled his eyes. 'I'm trying to help, you know, Mia.'

'Well, it doesn't much feel like it.'

His hand rested on the steering wheel. They looked at each other a long moment, before he repeated his words. 'I said I was trying to help. Don't you believe me?'

'I do believe you. I'm just saying it doesn't *feel* especially helpful.'

'Would you prefer it if I lied to you?'

'No, but—'

'Then, what's the problem?'

Mia took a quick breath. 'I don't want to quit the hotel.'

'Then don't,' he said, his tone pitched slightly higher. 'It was just a suggestion.'

'Okay, then.'

He looked down between them and then picked up her hand. 'I'm excited about this, you know. About us.'

Mia nodded. 'So am I.'

'Yeah?'

'Yeah,' she said, and then added, 'Even the queen-size bed.'

He broke into a smile, too. 'And what about king-size?'

She leaned forward, and he answered her with a kiss.

Mia had hoped she would never have to repeat her experience of serving Cormac Byrnes coffee, risotto, or anything else while he stayed at the hotel, but that Monday evening, her fears were realised.

He was sitting at a lonely table in a far corner of the dining room, leafing through a stack of papers, and by his countenance, Mia couldn't be sure if he even remembered her from the coffee mishap.

'Black coffee,' he said now, barely glancing up from the menu he pointed at. 'And this . . . steak and chips. Hold the peas.'

'And how would you like that done?'

'Rare. *Actually*, rare too.'

'I'll mention it to our chef,' she said lightly. '*Actually rare.*'

The joke didn't land as well as she had hoped. He looked up at her, frowning this time, and once again, she found herself marvelling at his ability to look so unlike his father in one moment only to surprise her with the similarity in the next.

When she returned with his coffee, she took a quick breath and said, 'You know, you look like him. Your father.'

While the warm evening lighting in the dining room had softened his outward appearance, when Cormac Byrnes looked at her, Mia wished she hadn't mentioned anything at all. His stare was penetrating and tone unimpressed.

'Despite being told, with alarming frequency, since arriving in this town how much I remind people of him, I have personally never seen any great number of similarities. Did you know him well?'

'We were friends,' Mia said.

'Were you? I'm sorry for your loss, then.'

He said it as though the mourning belonged to her alone, and it struck her as something uncomfortable.

'I hope you find a good buyer, Mr Byrnes,' she said, a little too forcefully. 'It's a really special hotel.'

His eyes narrowed. 'Is it? What makes it so special?'

'Oh, everything,' Mia said, smiling. 'Everyone who works here is so nice, and the place just has this—' *Magic.* '—history, you know? There aren't many hotels like this left.'

It was only when he answered her that Mia realised how much she was hoping he would agree. Instead, she felt she had been caught out by the tide, cold, dark water lapping about her.

'I doubt there will be any at all in the next ten years,' he said, not looking at her.

Mia felt her cheeks pink as though they had been slapped, and a hard lump formed in her throat. She smiled around it and returned to the kitchens, to seek out Becky.

'I need you to take my tables,' she said. 'I'm going to get the breakfast slips.'

Becky, who was seemingly waiting on an order from Hugh, gave her a quizzical frown. 'We don't get those until the dining room closes.'

'I'm getting a head start,' Mia told her.

Mia felt immense relief the instant she stepped out of the dining room. The lobby was cool and airy, and there was music playing in the bar – some man with a guitar and a low, sad song.

Upstairs, she snatched up whatever breakfast slips had already been left outside of bedrooms, and then climbed to the second floor, and after that the third, huffing a little that she was out of breath and still just as frustrated.

It was inevitable she would have to make this same trip in a few hours' time, but that was okay. She would do it three times over for this blessed distance between herself and Cormac Byrnes.

He must have thought her such a little girl, she thought now, talking on about Donahue, and the hotel. How stupid she must have looked to him.

On the fifth and final floor, Mia passed through the door from the stairwell to the corridor, and stopped.

She was struck with an odd and immediate sense that someone was already there. Looking along the empty hallway, though, Mia could see without any doubt that she was quite alone. She shook her head, wondering what she had expected – Cormac to have followed her upstairs? A *ghost*? Hadn't she done this before?

Mia stooped to lift just one breakfast slip – *Ulster Fry, coffee, sliced orange* – and, with reluctance, conceded it was time to go back to the dining room. To Cormac.

She turned, meaning to make her way back to the hotel's lift, when she stopped dead.

Just ahead of her, staring out the next window along the hallway, was a large man and a little girl with a head of pale curls.

She wasn't sure when either of them had come onto the floor, or even where they had come from, but she could hear them quite plainly now: muted conversation, and a laugh.

A little, bell-like laugh.

Mia's curiosity was sudden and striking, but she pushed it away. She couldn't carry on like this, taking these ghostly rumours to heart . . .

She passed the two with a soft, 'Good evening.'

The girl swivelled to watch her go, the pleated skirt of her button-up dress swinging about with her, but the man didn't move at all. She saw only his profile – plump cheeks, flat nose – and it snapped at her memory.

She stopped. She turned.

The little girl at his side dashed off suddenly, blonde ringlets bouncing down the corridor.

'Oh, there's nothing up that way, she'll—' Mia said to the man, but as her gaze flicked from the girl to him and back, the little girl was no longer running through the hallway. She had disappeared – into her room, perhaps? But Mia hadn't heard a door, and it all happened so quickly, almost as though . . .

She looked again at the man, and he still did not look back. Taking in his oddly familiar features, Mia had the urge to take him by the shoulders and turn him so she might see the full of his face.

Knowing that was ridiculous, she asked instead, 'You didn't happen to see where that little girl went, did you?'

He kept staring straight ahead, into the night.

'Excuse me – sir? The little girl who was with you? She was just here, and now she's . . . Sir, I don't know where she's gone.'

At long last, the man turned.

Mia gave a sharp gasp. She knew him. She knew him with such paralysing clarity, from his dark-brown eyes to his soft sloping shoulders, that it felt like a crime that she would have ever thought him just another hotel guest.

'Jim,' she breathed. 'Jim McGowan.'

'Little Miss Mia,' he answered with a smile. 'What are you doing out so late? You know you should be in bed.'

For a split second, it felt like flying, and then, it was falling. The shock gave way to horror, and the horror flooded Mia's ears and tripled her pulse.

With swaying wooziness, she stared at Jim McGowan: owner of The Burning Lamp, husband of Lorna McGowan, and dead twelve years. He did not seem to have changed. He had the same curly brown hair and flour-dusted skin, and even wore his baker's clothes, right down to trousers patted with hand-prints.

But it couldn't be real. It wasn't possible. If she were to speak again, she was sure the illusion would disperse, that she may very well wake up on the carpet, having fainted or fallen victim to a collapsed ceiling, or even in her bed, back home in her grandmother's house, so she whispered into the gaping quiet, 'Is it really you, Jim?'

He took one step closer. Mia could see the wrinkles etched into his face, the rosy blush in his cheeks, and still her chest bubbled with a scream that would not come. She held it so tight in her being, so close to herself, that instead of making any sound at all, it shook her from her ribcage outwards.

'You're taller,' he said. 'And your hair – you've cut it, and . . . Mia, are you crying?'

'No,' she said. It burst from her, fraught and wiry.

'Oh, you are. Have you fallen? I've told you not to run in these hallways.'

'No, I haven't – I'm . . .' She shook her head, held her fists tight to her sides, willing herself to see through whatever dream she was having. 'You can't be here.'

'And why is that?' He tilted his head, smiling all the while.

She would have almost thought they were back in the bakery, amongst the clouds of sugar and flour, if the hotel hallway had not been so terribly dim, the shadows so close – if it had not been so unbearably cold.

Cold.

All the rumours of the last month, all the tales Donahue Byrnes had told her, came rushing back, and her hands flew to her temples, as though that alone might hold her mind together, or keep the sudden flurry of black spots from flooding her vision entirely.

'Mia, you don't seem well. Shall we fetch your Granny?'

'You're not here,' she said. 'This isn't happening.'

His big brown eyes wrinkled with confusion. 'Of course I am, Mia. Look at me.'

And then, Jim McGowan held out a hand. She knew what he meant – *touch me, feel that I am real, and I am truly here* – but her fingers were still on her temples, and she could only stare down at it. It was as pink and fleshy as his face, and not see-through, as movies and TV had led her to believe it would be.

She forced her hand out in front of her.

'You're not here,' she said, as her fingers brushed his.

As her fingers brushed his.

It was not air she felt but the rough calluses across his palm, the swollen joints about his fingers, the soft, dry flat of his hand.

He was here. He was really here, and Mia's world cracked wide open.

'Jim,' she said. 'I thought you were dead. How are you here?'

'Dead, Miss Mia? What are you on about?'

She clutched at both his hands now. 'Have you come back to tell me something?'

'What do you mean? I'm right here. I'm quite well.'

'But, Jim . . .' She shook her head. 'I don't understand. I went to your funeral. I've visited the grave.'

Jim frowned, and suddenly, Mia's hands were empty. She looked down and saw that this time, her fingers had passed through Jim's still-outstretched palms, and when she tried to take one of them again, she felt only air.

'Jim, what's happening?'

'Dead?' he said. 'Dead.'

He turned away, face contorted and pained.

'I didn't mean – Jim, I'm sorry. I don't . . .'

But the dead man was leaving her. He rushed along the corridor, faded at the edges now, still muttering, 'Dead? Dead. *Dead.*'

Mia reached forward, trying once again to take hold of him, and said, 'Jim, I'm sorry.'

He whirled to face her. She could see now that he looked like a smudged oil painting, all the colours running surreally, and worse still were his feet – once so firmly planted on the carpeted floor, and now sinking through it.

She wanted to reach for him again, but his face was rendered unfamiliar and frightening, and there was only strength enough in her body to hold herself upright.

Jim McGowan faded into the floor.

His cries, however, did not go with him. Mia could still hear them – his wails like loose floorboards, and the banging of a door in a draft. He was in the hotel, part of the bricks and mortar, and he shook the very walls.

Mia stared at the floor where Jim McGowan had stood. She listened as his cries echoed on.

'What are you doing?'

Mia looked up. Holding the door to the stairwell and wearing an expression of pale horror was Cormac Byrnes.

'I'm . . . I—'

She could hardly get the breath to speak, and he crossed the space to her. She wasn't sure how she would explain it, or if he had seen it, too, and was grappling with how to even begin, when he took her shoulders in two hands and said, 'What did you say to it?'

In his eyes, she did not see shock or disbelief as she had anticipated. She saw fear.

She pushed him away.

'Stop – wait!' he cried, but she was already running for the stairwell. Her feet flew before her, barely touching the ground as she took the stairs two or three at a time.

She did not know if Cormac gave chase. She did not know if Jim returned. She only knew that Granny Brea's house was ten minutes away on foot and she was going there, right now.

She did not stop for anyone.

chapter 10
the extended addition

'Sick day? you haven't taken one of those in years.'

Mia slouched over her cereal, stirring it to mush. 'Must be something going about.'

There was a morning chill about the kitchen despite Granny's little electrical heater, and Mia could see the steam from their tea drifting towards the ceiling. Both dogs snuffled for scraps at the table's edge, and Granny Brea, dressed and ready for her day, only encouraged them.

'I was going to go to the market with Carol this morning,' she said, tearing the crust from her buttered toast and tossing it to whichever dog was fastest – Muriel, on this occasion. 'But if you're not feeling well, maybe I could just stay home with you – watch a few movies, drink a little more tea, hm?'

'It's okay, Granny. I wouldn't want you to miss seeing your friends, and besides, I'll probably just try to sleep it off.'

'Well, do you need me to call work for you?'

'Already sorted. Ruby said it's fine.'

Granny leaned forward to place her palm to Mia's forehead.

'I'm twenty-two,' Mia reminded her.

'I know that, and now I know you don't have a fever,' Granny said decidedly. 'Probably best just to sleep it off.'

'Like I said.'

'And if you're very sure—'

'I am.'

After kissing Granny goodbye and letting the dogs out onto the front lawn, Mia returned to the mess of blankets she had emerged from not so long ago.

With her eyes closed, all the world was dark, but the longer she lay there, the more it felt as though her duvet was smothering her. Suddenly she could bear it no longer and threw off the covers to stand in the centre of her room, breathing heavily.

Her eyes were drawn to the window, to the grey and misty morning. She must have seen every shade of the sky through the night.

Now, she brought her gaze back to her wall – and her photographs.

Donahue grinning, Donahue laughing, Donahue's hotel, Donahue's hallways. His voice drifting about in her head like low-hanging cloud: 'You know the most impossible stories are the most fun to tell, don't you?'

The stillness of the house eventually pushed Mia out onto the front porch.

The air was crisp if not yet cold, and the sky such a reserved pale grey that the street's trees looked all the more yellow. Every now again, one of their leaves would detach to float over the garden, and Muriel and Handsome Boy would rush around under it, snapping and leaping as they went.

These things were enough to occupy Mia's mind. Or at least, they were distracting enough to soften the hard edges of her thoughts. Out here, she might look at the night before with a sideways slant, comforted by the goings-on of ordinary living, and not feel so utterly *buried* in this impossibility.

Jim McGowan, dead but not, in a box but walking the hotel.

And Cormac Byrnes – knowing about it all.

Donahue's stories had always been charming in their whimsy, but now she questioned how he had been able to tell her there were ghosts in his hotel with such bright cheeriness when the reality was so . . . frightening? No, that was too simple a word, too straightforward. She had heard her friend say her name. She had seen him smile. That was miraculous, wasn't it?

She knew she should have told Granny. It was just that the house had been so quiet and calm when she had arrived home, breathless after running all that way from the hotel. The dogs had hardly raised their heads to look at her, and Granny herself had been sleeping soundly.

And really, was there ever a *right* moment to tell somebody about a dead man walking?

Just then, a dark figure appeared on the street.

Mia tensed all over, poised to scurry back into the house, when she realised that she recognised him.

'Hey,' she called out. 'What are you doing here?'

Rosco frowned from over the hedge. 'I should be asking you the same thing. Aren't you sick? You should be inside.'

'Needed some air.'

Rosco slipped through the garden gate, dogs rushing to greet him, all paws and lolling tongues. Mia bid them down, and noticed the prints that now decorated Rosco's jeans. 'Sorry. I keep telling Granny she needs to train them, but I . . .' Her eyes jumped to the brown paper bag in Rosco's hand. 'Were you at The Burning Lamp?'

Rosco smiled. 'Thought you needed a pick-me-up. Now come on – inside. It's not summer anymore, Mia.'

'I'm wrapped up okay,' she said, raising the drooping sleeves of her blue oversized hoodie. It had belonged to Rosco once and had the oil stains to prove it.

He just tugged on her hand, and she followed him into the house.

'I thought you were working today.'

'Yeah, but I get a half-day Friday. Just swapped it around.'

He strode into the kitchen, tossed the paper bag on the table, flicked the switch on the kettle and began to rummage in the cupboards for plates and cups.

When Mia attempted to help with teabags and butter from the fridge, he gave her a gentle nudge.

'You're sick,' he said. 'I'm looking after you.'

'I'm not *that* sick.'

'Sick is sick, so go make yourself comfy on the sofa. I'll bring this in.'

She hovered just a moment longer before giving in.

Granny Brea's living room was thick with cushions and throws and other soft wraparounds, all patchwork patterns and mismatched colours. The TV in the corner was as old as Mia, but Granny knew how to use it and it worked just fine, and there were always a dozen or more magazines and dog-eared romance novels scattered about the coffee table.

Mia thought of turning on the TV and letting the noise drown out the workings of her mind, or flicking through a book to see where Granny had left off, but she was too restless and uncomfortable to do either.

When Rosco appeared in the kitchen doorway, she actually gasped.

'Are you okay?' he asked, handing her a cup of tea.

'Better now,' she said.

'You seem jumpy.'

'I must be tired.'

Rosco set the plate of buttered scones down on the coffee table, before pulling off his jacket. 'So, what's up? Stomach-ache, cold? Your message wasn't very detailed. It mustn't be good if you went home early last night. I really wish you'd have called me to pick you up, you know.'

'The walk helped, I think. And . . . I'm a lot better now.'

'So, what is it? A cold? Flu?'

'No, I don't think—'

'Then what?'

She opened her mouth, but there weren't any words to follow. His brow tensed with concern.

'You know,' he said quietly, 'you can tell me anything because I'm . . . I'm going to be your husband, and I'll see you in every shape by the time we're through, so you don't need to be embarrassed.'

She gave a weak laugh, and he grinned back at her, waiting.

'Well, it's . . . I don't really know how to talk about it. I don't really *want* to talk about it.'

He tilted his head, frowning. 'Okay, but you know it's always better to . . . like, get stuff out. I'd rather you told me.'

'I know, but it's just so—'

'It doesn't matter what it is. You can tell me.'

'It's just . . . Well, it's . . .' Mia took a long breath. 'Ros, I saw something at the hotel last night.'

'What kind of something?'

'Well, I'm not completely sure, but I . . . Well, I *am* sure, but it seems . . .'

'Mia,' he said, his voice threaded with alarm, 'what is it?'

'I think I saw . . . a ghost.'

To Mia, the silence that followed this utterance felt cavernous. In reality, it took just a second for Rosco to ask, 'Where?'

This time she did not hesitate. 'In the hallway, on the fifth floor.'

'Last night?'

'*Yes*. And it seemed *so* real, Rosco, and I was so scared.' She was practically on top of him, leaning half off the sofa. 'Even though I *knew* things like that couldn't exist.'

'Knew?'

'*Know*. And what's really weird is that . . . It kind of looked like Jim McGowan.'

Kind of wasn't accurate. *Exactly* like Jim McGowan was more apt, but it felt hard and aggressive somehow, as if she was coming on too strong in her own testimony.

'The baker? But he's been dead like . . . Ten years?'

'Twelve,' Mia said.

'Well, that's . . . That sounds really scary.'

She spent the next half hour describing her encounter in detail, delving into memories both distinct and immediate, and those more blurred around the edges, and feeling it all afresh in her chest.

Rosco brushed her arm with the back of his fingers.

'And then I knew I couldn't go in today. I didn't want to see anybody.'

'Oh. Sorry.'

'No, not you,' she said. 'I'm glad you showed up.'

He smiled. 'Well, I'm glad I showed up, too. I didn't realise I'd be hearing one of the hotel's ghost stories first hand, but you know – still glad.'

'That's what it was, right? I feel like I'm going crazy.'

'Well, it sounds like the other stories going around, doesn't it? The laugh, the disappearing . . . '

She looked into her teacup. 'And what do you think Cormac meant?'

'Hard to say. Could be anything, right?'

'The way he said it, though . . . It made me think he *knew*.'

'That there are ghosts?'

'Yeah – which is . . . '

'Crazy?'

'It *sounds* crazy, yeah.'

'He must have heard a lot of Donahue's stories, too, I guess. You know, the *three Englishmen*, and whatever else it was.'

'I don't remember the *dead baker* in Donahue's stories.'

'Yeah, well, maybe that's the extended edition. New chapters.'

Rosco was smiling, but Mia wasn't.

'New chapters?' she repeated.

'You know, like – oh, it doesn't matter. I'm just mucking—'

'*No*, that . . . New chapters. After he's gone. That's . . . That makes sense.'

'Does it?'

'Well, no, not entirely, but—'

Rosco laughed. 'I take it back. Maybe you do need another sick day, Mia.'

Now, Mia laughed, and it was a wilder thing than she thought it would be. It burst from her and left behind some trail of sparks – all energy and ideas. 'No, I don't. I'm fine. I'm just . . . I got scared, you know? But it's just like Donahue's stories, isn't it? It's *Donahue*.'

'What's Donahue?'

'*This*. What I saw last night.'

'You've lost me, Mia.'

'When Donahue was alive,' she explained, 'he told me all these *stories*, and then said I had this special role at the hotel, and I've been . . . I've been wracking my head about it, Rosco, ever since everybody started talking about ghosts and weird things. I couldn't shake this feeling there should have been something left behind after he had died, and this . . . This is—'

'This is Donahue?' he repeated, an eyebrow cocked.

'Yeah. Yeah, it's Donahue – another chapter of Donahue; the *next* chapter.' *The one I've been looking for.* 'Like you said.'

'And . . . What does that mean exactly?'

'It means that . . . That it's important, and special, and . . . I don't know. I should . . . I should ask Cormac.'

'You're going to ask *Cormac* about the ghost of a dead baker?'

'Well, if he saw it—'

'And you don't think he'd find that a little . . . strange?'

'Maybe. Maybe not. I think I should try. I mean, what if he's got something to do with Donahue, too?'

'What, his son? I think he has something to do with Donahue, yeah, Mia.'

'No, not like that. I mean, what if it's *connected*? Donahue's death, Cormac coming back, this . . . This—'

'Ghost?'

'Yeah!'

Rosco was looking at her like she was half-mad, but in a good way – or in a way that was amused, at the very least. He didn't understand it, she knew, but that was okay. Few people did. It only mattered that she knew – knew that this was indeed *something*.

'You must have been pretty freaked out, Mia,' Rosco said at last.

'Yeah, I was, but this . . . Now—'

'Yeah, yeah – it's Donahue.' He shook his head. 'Special flower power pals, you and him.'

'You think?' she asked, all earnest.

'Ahuh. Peas in a pod, or hydrangeas in a bush, or whatever. Now, come on – I think it's time you had something to eat before we talk anymore about ghost stories. Cherry scone – butter and jam? Tea?'

She grinned at him. 'Did I mention I love you?'

He leaned forward to kiss her. 'Maybe once or twice.'

chapter 11
absurd faith

AT EIGHT O'CLOCK THE next morning, Mia was in Ballinadrum Hotel's dining room, delivering orders of eggs, bacon, and porridge to tables of sleepy hotel guests – and keeping an eye out for Cormac Byrnes.

For the first time since his arrival in Ballinadrum, she had actually arrived at work *wanting* to see him – she had questions, lots of them – and yet, he remained *un*seen. By ten o'clock, she even asked Ruby and the other kitchen staff about him, to which they responded in relieved tones that *no*, no one had spotted him – lucky for them.

Except Mia didn't feel lucky. She felt uneasy. Was he avoiding her? Had something happened to him when she left the hotel?

Worse still was if it had nothing to do with Jim McGowan or the walking dead, Mia knew there was all the more possibility that Cormac was absent from the hotel in favour of a lunch with a prospective buyer – discussing demolition plans and the cost of copper.

That was, of course, if the hotel had not been sold already.

All in all, Mia was not accustomed to this level of distraction. Her mind boggled with questions about the hotel's ghost – *who had Miss Genie Fitzgerald seen, if not Jim McGowan? But Jim didn't have a moustache, so was there another ghost, or had she been mistaken? And where did the bride's veil come into all of this?* – as well as Cormac's whereabouts, and regrettably, it had begun to show. She had to ask table three for their order twice, brought table seven's coffees to table sixteen, mistook semi-skimmed milk for whole, and managed to drop more food items over the course of two hours than she had in the last two years.

Ruby caught her on her way out with her next order – two soda baps and a bowl of cereal. Her eyes were creased with concern as she looked the dishes over.

'You sure you're okay, Mia?'

'Ahuh, fine – just a little tired.'

'Oh, well, it's just . . . I was wondering if you were maybe still a little . . . sick.'

'Sick? No. I don't even really know if I was all that sick yesterday, to be honest. It might have just been something I'd eaten.'

'Something you'd *eaten*?' Ruby took the tray from her hands. 'If there's any chance you had a bug yesterday, Mia, I'm not sure you should be handling any food today. When was the last time you vomited? Actually, don't answer that. I'm putting you on cleaning duty instead.'

'Ruby, I don't need to—'

'Two sausages, a slice of buttered toast, a coffee, and a trail of tomato sauce from the kitchen door to table three – you're clearly not your full self just yet, so . . . cleaning duty. Now, I need a few plates gathered from room fifty-two if you wouldn't mind heading up there now.'

Mia startled. 'The fifth floor?'

'Yes, is that okay? Unless you're too sick to ride in a lift?'

'No,' she said, gathering herself. 'No, I can ride the lift.'

'Then what's the problem?'

Mia almost told her about Jim McGowan then – about the way Cormac had looked at her, and the little girl who had disappeared without warning – before catching herself. She didn't need this going any further than it already had.

Besides, wasn't this what she wanted – a chance to investigate the scene of the appearance?

'There isn't any,' she said, body singing with nerves. 'I'll go now.'

The ride up to the fifth floor was quiet. Not suspiciously so, as she had anticipated, but normal quiet. The only problem was Mia's head felt anything but, and she knocked on room fifty-two with a rising pulse. A sleepy-looking couple answered the door, and while it felt foolish to be frightened, Mia couldn't help it. Her back was to the hallway, and she felt exposed.

The couple took their time loading up their silver tray and Mia counted the seconds. When the door was finally closed, quick as a flash, she turned around so she could press her back into the wall and be sure no spectral figure was looming at her neck. The tray tinkled its disapproval.

There was nothing there, of course, nothing at all – but hadn't it been that way the same night she'd seen Jim McGowan?

It was Donahue, she tried to remind herself. Donahue's magic and Donahue's stories. All the light he had brought to the hotel was in this apparition – it was what he had told her about all those months ago, even if she hadn't known it then.

And yet, she could not help but long for the warm comforts of the dining room downstairs – Ruby looking over her shoulder, elderly diners sharing conversations over porridge, the soft music on the overhead speakers. When she thought of Jim McGowan, she did not think of the charming tales Donahue had spun, but rather that not-quite-right mouth, the sounds he had made. The way he sank through the floor. The panic in Cormac's eyes.

There would be another time to explore, she decided – *after* she had asked Cormac Byrnes about it. That made more sense, after all, to have the facts before charging into a potentially dangerous situation. Not that Jim had seemed *dangerous*, but he had not quite seemed himself either.

Her mind made up, Mia crossed the hallway to the lift as quickly as the stacked tea tray would allow. The indicator's arrow sailed along the numbers as it rose through the floors, and when it opened, she had all but stepped inside when she realised she was not alone.

Cormac Byrnes stared back at her.

As Mia hesitated, the lift doors began to shut, but Cormac reached out and pressed the button to hold them. He looked at her expectantly.

'Thank you,' she said stiffly, and stepped inside, doors closing behind her.

The lift was as close and small as she had ever known it, and the silence between them was as electrified as its glowing buttons.

Cormac spoke first. 'What is your name?'

From the corner of her eye, Mia took him in: lips pressed thin, blue eyes narrowed.

'Mia Anne Moran,' she said.

He chewed on this a moment, then asked, 'Have you worked here long, Mia Anne Moran?'

'Five years.'

'Never went to university?'

'No.'

'College? Anything?'

'Just a course in hospitality at the high school, but I've been here since I was seventeen.'

'Then you must have heard the stories by now.'

Her heart stuttered. 'Excuse me?'

Just as the lift touched down in the lobby, Cormac reached forward and pushed the button for the third floor. The doors opened, and they closed, and then Mia and Cormac were sailing back up again.

'I'm getting off at the—' Mia tried, but Cormac interrupted her.

'Never mind that. Now, please do be honest with me, Mia Anne. You've heard the stories – ghosts, and that, yes?'

'Yes,' she said.

'So I think we both know you saw one the other night,' he went on.

All the words were choked from her mouth, and Mia could feel her heart pounding harder – in her head, her ears, in the tips of her fingers. The lift pinged at each floor, impossibly slow, endlessly long.

'I don't . . .' she began.

'Why else would you have run? You saw it – same as I.'

The admission drew all the air from the small space, and Mia, who had not moved an inch in what felt like an age, flinched. The surprise was her giveaway, and Cormac's haughty glare his confirmation.

'Yes,' she told him, voice feather soft. 'I saw it. I saw the ghost.'

Cormac straightened, looking ahead once more. 'It was calm, speaking to you.'

Unsure of what else there was to say, Mia filled the silence with, 'He was?'

'Pardon?'

'I just asked . . .'

'You said *he*.'

Mia swallowed, suddenly aware of how dry her mouth was. 'Well, it was a he. His name was Jim McGowan. Or at least, it looked very—'

'You know him?'

'If it was him—'

'Who was he?'

'He used to own The Burning Lamp Bakery, before he . . . he . . .'

'Died.' Cormac's eyes were on her again. 'Mia Anne Moran,' he said, 'I need your assistance.'

The lift pinged as it arrived on the third floor. When the doors opened on the lonely stairwell, Cormac strode out at a decisive speed.

Mia clung to her tea tray as though it alone held her together.

Had that really just happened?

'Keep up, Mia Anne.' Cormac's voice was cold and direct. 'You should know I hate waiting.'

Apparently, it had.

Mia followed him through the stained-glass door and on to the corridor.

'Where are we—'

'What are you holding that for?' he asked of the tea tray, still stacked with cups and half-eaten toast. He took it from her and dumped it on a sideboard. 'Come on. Let's go.'

'Go where?' she asked.

'You'll see.'

They crossed the length of the corridor quickly, and came to the last door: some old linen cupboard. Cormac looked along the path they had come, and then, furtively, reached into his jacket pocket to withdraw a key.

It was a gleaming, golden thing, unlike the other keys Mia had seen hanging behind the lobby desk. After another glance over his shoulder, Cormac pushed it into the lock and turned. The mechanism gave with a satisfying *click*.

Then, the door swung open, and where Mia believed only wooden shelves and copper pipes could be, there was more hallway – and a set of stairs, and a deep, dark world that lay at the bottom of them. Dust motes floated in the opening like snowflakes.

Mia stepped back, feeling the light-headed confusion of walking through a mirror maze, but Cormac pushed on. Unsettling more dust still, he flipped a switch and three light bulbs flickered and buzzed overhead, revealing more stairs and more corridor.

She tried to tell herself that yes, of course, the hotel had different passageways that were no longer used, forgotten rooms that had been closed up over the years – and this was no different. But it felt different.

'After you,' Cormac said.

Mia hovered in the doorway. Surely, it was the stuff of Donahue's stories: a forbidden floor, a secret key, a hidden passageway, and the promise of ghosts. Surely, it was a fantasy, a dream, something Mia would wake up from and laugh about.

But one look at Cormac's face told her that it was anything but.

It would require a little time-travelling, and an absurd faith. An open mind.

Armed with absurd faith, and absurd faith alone, Mia took a step forward.

Cormac Byrnes closed the door behind her, and with the sharp click of the key in the lock once more, she knew without doubt that there was no going back.

chapter 12
all his tales true

MIA KEPT HER HANDS by her sides, but some part of her still felt tempted to run her fingers along the walls and the old, faded wallpaper, scraps of which had peeled away.

'What is this place?' she asked.

'An old passageway, used by servants once upon a time, when the hotel was not a hotel.'

'And where does it go?'

'To the west wing.'

'But the west wing is closed.'

'And for good reason, though probably not the one you heard.'

'I was told it was because the hotel couldn't afford to keep it open, with the heating and electric and . . .' She trailed off, eyes on the ceiling, the floor, the walls – the darkness approaching before her. 'And the water damage . . .'

'Yes, that would have been nice.'

Cormac edged ahead of her, flicking yet another light switch to illuminate the rest of the raggedy hallway, at the end of which waited another door.

'But I'm afraid it isn't the truth,' he went on. 'How much do you remember of the hotel's history, Mia Anne?'

'I know that . . . I know it was built in the eighteen-hundreds, and that it was owned by the Matthews, before it became a carriage house, and then an inn, and then—'

'Yes, and later? The war?'

'I know it was a hospital. People tell stories about . . . Three soldiers—'

'Yes, the Three Dead Englishmen. My father told me that one.'

'He told me it, too.'

'Did he ever tell you it was true?'

'Yes. Well, I'm not sure. He told me . . .'

'Lots of things? Let me guess. He told you about the fairy library in the hydrangeas, and gremlins who ate the leftovers in the fridge, and if anyone ever asked about strange things happening around here, he'd mention his beloved ghosts in the exact some jolly voice. Am I right?'

The tone cut through her. She watched her sensible black shoes take step after step in the gloom.

'He wasn't very good with the truth, my father. You see, he knew what this hotel's problem was, and it wasn't money or style or competition. The real problem, the *true* problem is what you saw last night: *ghosts*.'

They had come to the second door now, and up close, Mia could see it was taller and grander than any of the others she had seen in the hotel. An unnatural cold seemed to permeate from it.

Cormac took the curled brass handle and opened it wide.

Mia's lips parted. Before her, a ball was underway.

A dozen or more people were dancing across the pink terrazzo floor in a wide, languid circle, and a little girl, no older than eight or nine, sat at a large, white piano, pattering out a nonsensical melody – *the* little girl, Mia realised, the one who had been there then disappeared the night she'd seen Jim McGowan. She was wearing the same pale-blue button-up dress and shiny leather bar shoes, and if the people dancing noticed she could not play the piano, they did not seem to mind. They merely trailed about in rhythms of their own choosing.

And then, Mia saw him: Jim McGowan, as round and cheerful as she had seen him in life. He spun across the room with a woman in his arms. Both were laughing.

Most of the dancers were laughing, actually, and if they were not, then they were talking, or kissing cheeks, or singing along to a song Mia did not recognise.

In fact, the only evidence they were not as real as Mia in that present moment, was the way they faded in and out of view. One second, they were here, then suddenly, gone, and then *back*, carrying on with their dance without ever missing a step, stepping between the seen and unseen world without interruption.

Mia's vision swayed before her.

'Ghosts,' Cormac said, returning her to this moment – this surreal and impossible moment. She noticed he had retreated into the harsh light of the corridor. 'More than I ever remember there being.'

Somehow, she found words. 'They're . . . They've always been here?'

'All my life. Though, it does appear we may have lost a few over the years – only to gain others, of course.'

'How?' she whispered.

'A mystery of the hotel, my father would say,' he said, his tone cold. 'He spent much of his life trying to unravel it. There have only been a few deaths to actually occur within the building, too few for the number you see before you, so it's not as simple as geography or proximity.' He sighed, as though reluctant to go on. 'My father favoured the theory that when the first ghosts took up residence here – those three Englishmen, the soldiers from the forties – the hotel became a sort of hub of supernatural activity. They were neither in this life nor the next, so they gave it some sort of . . . charge, and the new ghosts were attracted to it.'

Mia's gaze drank in the scene. 'All the sightings then – they're not just stories.'

'No, I'm afraid not, though maybe no one would have known the difference if my father hadn't died. He entertained them here, you see, kept them quiet and calm, as best he could. He closed off this ballroom and entire west wing for that reason – so they could have a space for themselves without interference or discovery. He'd bring them music sheets, food—'

'*Food*? They can eat?'

'No, for goodness' sake, they're dead. Use your senses. They do like to remember, though, and pick around things – sandwiches and biscuits and that. Doesn't matter if they can taste it if they know how it's *supposed* to taste.'

'So, they just . . . stay here.'

'Exactly – well, mostly. If they become bored, or too interested in what's happening in the rest of the hotel, they go . . . meandering about corridors.' He rubbed his face, pained. 'You've probably noticed there have been more supposed sightings since my father's death.'

Mia nodded.

'Without him . . . Well, they're restless. Searching for entertainment elsewhere.'

There was something that bothered Mia about this. 'But isn't your father . . . Isn't he . . .'

'Isn't he what?'

It was finally time to ask the question she had wanted to ask from the moment she had seen Jim McGowan: *Where is Donahue*?

'Isn't he here?'

Cormac looked at her contemptuously, and Mia's heart sank. 'My father is buried at Ballinadrum Presbyterian Church, if you'd like to visit him.'

'I didn't mean . . . I only thought maybe—'

'That he had stuck around, too? Yes, I am somewhat surprised he could actually let the old place go, even in death, but I haven't seen a single trace of him. And, as you probably know, he could never go this long without being the centre of attention.'

Mia thought about the man with the moustache Genie Fitzgerald had seen in the hallway the day she had fallen down the stairs. She thought of that squirming, too-good-to-be-true feeling she had carried with her since, which was now some ashen version of itself – but didn't push it further.

'So, if he's not here – why not get rid of them?'

'Firstly, even if my father *was* among these creatures, don't mistake for a second that I wouldn't do everything in my power to get rid of them and their hold on the place. Him included.' Cormac's stare was withering. 'And secondly – don't you think I've *tried that*?'

'Oh,' Mia said.

'Holy men, witchdoctors, a woman who goes by the name Mystical Kate . . . I've gone through a dozen self-proclaimed psychics, and my father . . . Well, who truly knows the lengths my father went to? You see, you can't just exorcise them. They're not benevolent spirits or demons. They're just . . . lost.'

'And you can't . . . move them?' She felt silly saying it. 'I mean, what about taking them outside, to the trees, or somewhere people won't come across them?'

'Doesn't work,' Cormac said. 'The soldiers died *in the hotel* and they're tied to *it*. And even though the others haven't died here, that same supernatural . . . charge, or however you want to describe it, holds them here.'

'But they can't *all* be stuck,' Mia said. 'You said you'd lost a few.'

'Yes, well, I *think* that is the case. I . . . I vaguely remember a rather tall, skinny man with a bowler hat, and he hasn't made a single appearance since I've returned, so I can only assume . . .'

'Perhaps Donahue got rid of him?'

Cormac's frown deepened. 'No. My father knew as little as I do about the logic of these creatures. In fact, I don't think there is a pick of reason to them. As fickle as cats and buses, really. They'll go when they want, I imagine, and not a moment before – and so long as there is one of them . . .'

'There will always be others.'

'*And* a ball underway.'

Mia's eyes wandered back to the ballroom – to the ghosts dancing in their individual, timeless styles, and the little girl playing with the piano.

'My father convinced them of that long ago – this endless party,' Cormac went on. 'Told them funny stories, brought bottles of champagne—'

'So they would never want to leave?'

'Exactly. It was safest for the hotel, and its guests.'

'And he . . . he did all it by himself – Donahue?'

Cormac stiffened. 'Mostly. He had help, once.'

'You?'

'No.'

'*Little Miss Mia!*'

Mia looked to the dance floor. The music had stopped, she realised, and the little girl at the piano was staring at her, along with all of the other ghosts. There was an eerie stillness to them, the sort that would have been ruined by a falling chest or beating heart.

Jim McGowan was the only one smiling. He was dressed in the same clothes she had seen him in before – the baker's uniform with floury patches – and holding out his arms, as though to say *what do you think of all this?*

Mia could see Cormac edge further into the corridor as the ghost approached.

'Jim,' she said, her voice brittle. 'Jim, I'm so sorry about the other night. I don't know—'

'There's nothing to apologise for, Miss Mia. What could you have done that would ever upset me?'

'I only thought . . . Oh, Jim, it's really you, isn't it?'

'What, you don't recognise me? Have I lost weight?' He let out a jolly laugh. 'I wouldn't count on it. I've been feasting like a fool. Can't help it when Lorna's cooking's as good as it is, can I?'

Mia cocked her head. 'Haven't you been . . .'

'I so love a dance, though, don't you?' he went on. 'The music, the people . . . Lorna was here just a second ago. She'd love to see you.'

'Lorna?'

He laughed again. 'Have you bumped your head, Little Miss Mia? You look terribly confused.'

'I just . . . I didn't think she was here.'

'Probably in the bathroom. Always touching up her make-up. How about you and I have a dance 'til she comes back, eh? You can stand on my feet.'

Jim McGowan held out a hand, and for a moment, Mia stared at it: dusty and dry, lined with age and work. She placed her own thin, pale one inside his, and found it cold.

Jim's grin widened. Pulling her forward, he grabbed Mia's other hand and then flung her outwards, drawing her in a wide semicircle about him. Mia tripped over her own feet, the squeak of her rubber soles against the terrazzo the only sound in the room.

Jim didn't seem to mind, though. He danced to a swelling melody Mia could not hear.

'You're bigger than I remember. You must be the tallest in your class now, hm?'

'I'm not in school anymore.'

'You're not? What happened?'

Around them, the ghosts began to sway again. They started to whisper, one laughed, and then the little girl took up her piano, tiny fingers playing over the keys, and the dance recommenced as though Mia was as much a part of their group as Jim McGowan.

'Jim, I don't understand. It's been years, it's been . . .'

The Baker cocked his head to the side, eyes creased. 'I'm starting to worry about Lorna. I may go and look for her. She might have . . . gone to the bar or . . .'

Mia took a sudden grip of his hands, ignoring the chilly discomfort. 'No. I'm sure she hasn't. She's probably taking her time, fixing her make-up.' She swallowed. 'You know how she is.'

He chuckled. 'Ah, she does love her make-up. Always buying little bits here and there.'

'She has lovely taste.'

'Doesn't she?' Jim said. 'To tell you the truth, Mia, all her make-up comes from the chemist, not those fancy places, and all the boots and coats . . . second-hand.'

'It looks just as good.'

'She wouldn't say so . . . Ah, Mia, I'd love to just walk in some place and say *Get whatever you want!* like some millionaire type. I've been working on it though, saving up, doing little jobs here and there . . .'

Mia stared into the man's warm smile, his eyes bright and hopeful, while her own stung with tears.

'Going to tell her on her birthday,' he went on. 'I've got everything planned. I'm going to take her shopping and spoil her the way she deserves.'

He leaned forward, right into her ear, but there was no warm breath. She felt nothing but the general chill of his presence when he said, 'I've saved up enough now. Hid it above the rafters in the bakery. Good one, isn't it? She'd never look there.'

Mia drew back. 'What?'

'You know, now that you mention it, you do look older. Perhaps . . . perhaps I've been here longer than I realised. Say . . .' A crease appeared at his brow. 'Did you see where my wife went?'

'Oh, um. Yes. She was . . . fixing her make-up.'

He laughed, expression brightening. 'She doesn't know how lovely she is.'

Mia pulled backwards until her arms were fully extended, and then bowed, as though the song had come to a spectacular finish, when in reality, it went tinkling on in its nonsensical way.

She turned back to Cormac, who had rigidly remained in place.

'They don't know,' she told him in a whisper. 'They don't know they're dead.'

'Yes.'

'But how—'

'They're not people, Mia Anne. Not really. They're more like . . . a collection of memories and traits. They react to what you say, but they'll not remember for long. You could answer them forever and they would still ask the same questions.'

'They're cold.'

'They are.'

'Should they be?'

'They always have been. Though, if I might say so . . . they appear to like you.'

'I'm not so sure,' she said, recalling their uncertain glances.

'Trust me. They like you better than they like me. And you . . .'

'What?'

'You're not frightened.'

Mia looked back to the dancers, to the gorgeous pink and lavender ballroom, all shadow, save for the slip of white light that fell through the poorly drawn curtains. She felt she *should* be afraid, but her heart was calm and rhythmic, and her mind conjured Donahue – dancing here, amongst these people, these spirits, all his tales true and all his magic come to life.

'I need you to come back tomorrow.'

It was the last thing she expected Cormac to say. 'What? Why?'

'You know why. These ghosts . . . they've been unruly since my father died – roaming the corridors, running into people. I can't even have a meeting in the middle of the day without fear that one of the blasted things will . . . *drift through a wall*, or something. They need someone to take care of them, Mia – someone to entertain them enough that they will stay where they ought to. The hotel will never survive if they're left as they are.'

'But I wouldn't even know what to do, what to say—'

'I've just explained it to you!'

'You've explained it very . . . vaguely, Mr Byrnes, if I can be quite honest, and—'

'Look, there is no rulebook I can offer you. I can only tell you what my father did, and what he did was . . . Well, he listened to them, and danced with them. When one of them wanted a cake, he delivered it. If they wanted to hear the piano, he played it. He brought them mops and brushes, mirrors and lipsticks, pitchers of water whenever they asked, and if they grew bored anyway, he found new ways to entertain them. He sang. He told stories. He did . . . what anyone might if they saw a party dying on its feet. It doesn't take a genius.'

'But you—'

'I can't. I need you to do it.'

'And I'm just . . .'

'The only person I've come across who hasn't gone running from a spectre the moment it appeared. The only person I've ever seen *dancing* with one, besides my father.'

The comparison rattled in Mia's chest. As much as it was unsettling, it felt precious, too. Important.

A treasure-seeker. A believer. A good friend of mine.

Standing now, in a ballroom of his ghosts, she felt Donahue all the closer – tapping her on the shoulder, urging her into a world he had only ever alluded to. A world for which he had been preparing her.

All these months later, and it had come to her, at last.

'Don't take that as a compliment,' Cormac continued brusquely, as though reading her mind. 'It just makes you ideal for the job. You know, the way a person without family is suited to working oil rigs, and exceptionally dull people excel in menial work.'

Mia frowned.

'Look, I'm offering you a . . . promotion, so to speak. You would come here, not the kitchens. Report to me, not that woman, that . . .'

'Ruby. Her name is Ruby.'

'And you wouldn't be a waitress, but a . . . a concierge for the dead. No, don't give me that giddy look, it was my father's name for it. Romantic nonsense, of course, but if you prefer the name, it's . . .' He frowned, evidently torn between advertisement, and disparaging his father's thinking. 'I don't have *hours* in mind, but daytime is essential and if something were to happen at night, I could call you and you could come back to . . . fix it. I mean, it's likely it will be more . . . taxing at the beginning, but once they are settled . . . calm . . . well, things can run almost like clockwork, and you can keep more . . . sociable hours. And you wouldn't have to live here or anything – unless you are quite far away, then, but . . . And we can discuss exact numbers for your salary, but I can tell you it'd be better, and—'

Her gaze was drawn towards the pink and the lavender, the figures swaying back and forth, the music that echoed like chimes in a breeze.

'It would be of . . . unparalleled help to this hotel and its future.'

Mia looked up at him, and for a second, she thought she could see through that steely exterior, to something that looked young and fearful, something soft – but just a second.

'I'll do it,' she said.

chapter 13
unlock the universe

THAT EVENING, MIA FLEW from the hotel to Rosco's car.

The rain came down in droves, and had been doing so for hours. Her shoes were soaked through, and her hair much the same, but the world was alight with something different that evening – something rainwater could not wash out.

Because Mia Anne Moran, guided by Donahue Byrnes from beyond the grave, had been placed in this particular position at this particular time in history to save Ballinadrum Hotel from collapse. She knew it as clearly and as closely as she knew there were ghosts dancing in an abandoned ballroom.

When she reached the car, however, that leaping feeling inside her hardened and fell like a stone. Ethan sat in the backseat.

'What about ye, Mia? Bit wet there.'

She slipped into the passenger side, Rosco leaning to kiss her head.

'It's raining,' she said plainly.

'Aye, and you were running like a bat out of hell. Chased, were you?' He laughed. 'Maybe by one of those *ghosties*, eh?'

She pulled her seatbelt on, trying to catch Rosco's eye. 'Oh, they never chase me, don't worry . . .'

'That's not what I heard.' Ethan put his hands on the back of her seat and leaned close. '*I* heard you'd actually seen one.'

Mia's head snapped around. 'Excuse me?'

'Rosco said you saw one. The other night.'

The way he chuckled afterwards did not convey a sense of confusion or awe or question. It just sounded like a joke, like everything Ethan said, and Mia found herself fizzing with irritation – with Ethan, of course, but also, oddly enough, with Rosco.

She shot the latter a questioning look and he kept his eyes on the road.

'Anything today? A bride, or a solider, or what?'

'None,' she answered. 'Sorry to disappoint.'

Ethan bellowed with laughter.

At last, Rosco turned to her. 'And what about Byrnes? Still being a dick?'

'No more than usual,' she answered.

Both boys laughed now, and Mia forced a smile.

As they pulled away from the hotel, Rosco told her about their plans for the evening – *them* meaning Rosco and Ethan, she learned with disappointment.

It was the boys' intention to drive out to the car dealership by the motorway so that Ethan could buy his first car – *and stop relying on* this one *for a lift, y'know?* – and that neither would be back until much later.

Mia's heart sank further.

'Well, will you . . . call me?' she asked, as they pulled up on the kerb outside Granny's house. The rain had not let up an inch during the journey, and it suddenly seemed all the more dismal.

'I'll see when I'm back,' Rosco said.

He planted a kiss on her lips, mouthed *love you*, and then Mia got out, into the rain. Ethan ran around the car, his head ducked, and took her place in the front seat as the car drove off.

Maybe if she called Rosco, and told him it was important, he would come back, and she could tell him everything. But then, wouldn't Ethan ask questions? And wouldn't it feel like the wrong moment entirely to share something so extraordinary?

She turned away from the dark, wet night and went inside – where she was met not with the quiet she had anticipated, but raucous laughter from the living room.

Granny's girls.

'Mia? Is that you?'

With some reluctance, Mia approached the open living-room doorway.

Six elderly women were seated on the sofa, armchair and one spindly wooden chair, borrowed from the kitchen. Granny had taken the latter, and was in the midst of offering around a plate of biscuits, which had undoubtedly already made two rounds of the group.

Handsome Boy slept at her feet, while Muriel was in perfect bliss on another lady's lap, being fed pieces or ham, sandwich crusts, and other things Mia wasn't sure she should be eating at all.

'Mia,' Mildred called. 'Tell your grandmother she's the reason we're as fat as we are!'

'Yes, every time I come here, Mia,' another lady from choir – Simone – said, 'I go home with a box of leftovers fit for a family of six!'

The centre coffee table was stuffed with plates and bowls – more biscuits, crisps, meat, and cheese rolls.

'I've tried to tell her myself,' Mia said with a smile. 'But there's no convincing her.'

'None,' Granny Brea said, and then gestured for Mia to sit beside her, on the corner of the kitchen chair. 'Now, tell us – what's been going on at that hotel tonight? I keep meaning to go up there to look for one of these ghosts myself.'

The group laughed – or at least, most of them did. White-haired Myrtle frowned as she sipped her tea.

'Oh, don't,' Simone said to her.

'I didn't say anything,' Myrtle replied.

'It was the look on your face—'

'*I didn't say anything.*'

Mia didn't take Granny's corner seat, but instead hunkered beside her, briefly waking Handsome Boy before he laid his head back down, while the women around her laughed. Mia, unsure of the joke, looked around for some explanation – which Granny Brea offered in a stage-whisper, 'Myrtle isn't a fan of all these *spooky stories*.'

Myrtle rolled her eyes. 'I'm not trying to be *inflammatory*. I'm just saying it as it is. It was all a good laugh when they were just stories, but now—'

Mia felt unusually exposed. She kept her eyes on Handsome Boy's droopy ears.

'Now what?' the women asked.

'Well, now there've been *sightings*. You heard about that woman Fitzgerald—'

'People see what they want to see,' Granny said. 'Or what they *think* they see. Doesn't mean it's true, Myrtle. They're still just stories – same as they ever were. So long as they're stories, there's no harm, now, is there?'

'Yes, and you liked all those stories when Donahue Byrnes was telling them. Maybe it's just *Cormac* you have a problem with,' said Paula.

'Yes, well, I'm certainly disappointed – I had hoped he would be more handsome,' said Mildred and again the group gave way to giggles – even Myrtle, who accepted a biscuit from Granny with a good-natured shrug.

'I think I'll go,' Mia said quietly to Granny. 'Few things to do.'

'You go ahead. Just shout if we're too loud.'

She kissed her grandmother on the head. 'As though that would stop you.'

Mia left the room to yet more laughter, and closed the door behind her, before heading upstairs to her room. Inside, the air shivered with possibility.

They're still just stories – same as they ever were.

She looked at her photographs, at Donahue, and every other picture she had taken at the hotel – suddenly fixated with the ridiculousness of having walked in the same building as the dead all this time, and never known.

But now she did. She had met them – these ghosts – and spoken to them, too.

So long as they're stories, there's no harm.

With a long breath, she sank onto her bed.

Her life had become a story, even if no one else heard it.

*

The next morning, when Rosco picked her up, it was still raining. The street danced with puddles, and the windscreen drummed with the noise, and Rosco wasted no time launching into a rambling story about the night before.

For some reason, the boys had decided to go to a *different* dealership, fifteen miles away, and then, because they had gone that far, went to another, an additional ten miles away, and then another a while away from that. By the end of the evening, they were sixty miles from home and eating at some hole-in-the-hedge pub, playing pool with a few old regulars.

'And he didn't even get a car,' Rosco went on. 'Can you believe it?'

Mia had been waiting patiently for a chance to tell him her special secret. It wasn't the sort of thing she wanted to just cut in with; she wanted it to have its own entrance, its own time, and for there to be a moment of silence included.

'I can't,' she said, trying for a bright tone.

'And how was your night? What did you get up to?'

'Oh, Granny's friends were over, and didn't leave until . . . I don't remember.'

'They do know they're seventy-odd, right?'

Mia tried a smile. 'I doubt it.'

'You seem quiet. Something wrong?' Rosco pulled up to the hotel and grabbed the handbrake.

She opened her mouth to finally speak – *I saw another ghost, I saw a whole room of them, I've been tasked with keeping them in order and I have no idea how* – and then closed it.

This was the sort of thing you whispered across a campfire, or shared under cover of your duvet. Not a five-minute conversation while the engine was still running.

'Yeah. Just tired.'

'You sure?' he asked.

'Of course,' she replied. 'See you tonight.'

'New assistant? For Cormac?' Ruby looked horrified, tossing a kitchen towel over her shoulder. 'Since when?'

'Just yesterday,' Mia said, not meeting her eyes. 'I know it's kind of weird but . . .'

'Weird? His whole personality is *weird*, but why you? Couldn't he have someone else? Mia, you're my best waitress! What am I going to do?'

Mia shrugged with an apologetic expression. 'Becky could take my tables?'

'Becky might need to take her own tables first.' Ruby sighed noisily and shooed her friend out of the kitchen. 'If you're going, then go. I'll sort it out. You focus on surviving quality time with Mr Cormac Byrnes.'

Henry, too, seemed perplexed by the arrangement when she called by his office.

'But what does he need an assistant for?' he asked. 'He hardly uses *my* time, and I'm—'

'I don't really understand it myself,' Mia said quickly. 'That's just what he told me.'

'Well, it would be *useful* if he could inform *me* of these changes.' He fixed her with an intent look. 'Is the hotel doing alright, Mia? Has he said anything?'

'Oh, I'm not sure. This is my first day and—'

'Because I've been keeping up with the correspondence regarding the sale, and I haven't seen anything of note.'

'There have been no changes as far as I'm aware. In fact, Cormac seems interested in *improving* the hotel.'

'Improving it?'

'Yeah. He wants to . . . you know, get the place tidied up. Put a stop to these ghost rumours. Or that was my impression, at least.'

Henry's frown finally dislodged. 'Why, that sounds – that sounds *fantastic*, Mia. I actually have a few ideas, myself. Some up-to-date photography for the website, a better booking system – maybe even a plan to open the west wing, if we could dream that big.'

Mia blinked. 'Well, the hotel runs quite well without it.'

'Ah, that's exactly what Donahue would have said. The number of conversations I had with the man about it, but if Cormac is open to *improvements* . . . I'll maybe send him a few of my thoughts, or this example of another local hotel that turned itself around, and . . .'

Henry regarded his computer, seemingly lost in thought, and Mia took her opportunity to see herself out.

The third floor awaited.

Mia had anticipated, rather foolishly, that Cormac Byrnes would look different today – a softer expression, a smile perhaps. As she stepped out of the lift onto the third floor, however, he was as grey and cold and un-Donahue-like as the day she had met him.

'This will be your key,' he said, skipping the greeting.

He offered her a small, mottled bronze key. It looked like it had been through a war, and she closed her fist around it as though it could unlock the universe.

'You will open the door and lock it behind you. Do *not* leave it unlocked, for any length of time whatsoever, and if this key leaves your person, there will be legal repercussions.'

'Excuse me?'

'You heard.'

He led her through the same passageway as before, with its peeling paper and buzzing light bulbs, to the ballroom she had been turning over in her mind since the second she had left it.

The cold met her first, and then, all at once, it was there, a scene framed in the doorway – lovely and grey, pearlised and pink, the dancers silent and weightless.

'Now, if they want something to eat, try to bring something that won't go off, so no eclairs or cream tarts or that sort of thing. Remember: they're not *really* eating it, so it needs a good shelf life if it's to sit here all night and day. It's better again if you can just bring something like an old wine bottle, or fancy biscuit tin. And if they stop with the piano, tell them it's still playing. If they insist, play it yourself.'

'But I can't—'

'Neither can they. Just keep them happy, alright? You've done it before.'

Mia cast a worried look about the room.

Cormac, seeming to notice, continued hurriedly. 'It *will* get easier with time. Just . . . ask them questions. See if they want anything. I'm sure you can use your imagination. And well . . . I'll be back in an hour – or sooner if I feel things are going . . . awry, so—'

'Wait – you're leaving?'

Already on his way out, Cormac cast a questioning glance over his shoulder.

'I, uh . . . didn't think you'd be, um—' Mia stuttered.

'I thought you said you could do this.'

'I mean, I *think*—'

'Can you do it, or not?'

She jumped to attention. 'I can.'

'Good.'

Cormac retreated down the long, yellowish hallway, leaving Mia alone – save for the ghosts.

chapter 14
grey in-between

SHE TURNED TO FACE the room of spirits, holding the key so tightly its teeth sunk into her flesh. Today, none of them seemed concerned by her, continuing with their jubilant laughter and ill-timed waltzing instead, so she took a moment to pick them out as individuals.

The most striking amongst them was a young lady in a white bridal gown, her brown hair tied elaborately at the nape of her neck.

She was talking to an older man in black robes. For a moment, Mia wondered if he was a priest, but a second glance confirmed they were academic robes: a scholar, or headmaster, perhaps.

Behind him, a blond man in a cowboy hat sang along to a remembered song in a shuffling, country accent, while three men – clearly the *Three Dead Englishmen* from Donahue's tales, in old-fashioned military uniform, green and well worn – spoke quietly between themselves.

Among the rest, she spotted a man with bright clown-like make-up juggling nothing at all, another man in blue dungarees measuring up one of the ballroom's columns, and a young woman wearing a large, fluffy coat.

She counted them and totalled fifteen but then on a recount, seventeen. Another recount gave twelve and then fourteen. She could see now why Donahue tried to keep them in one room – it was dizzying enough trying to keep track of them in this large, empty space, with their habit of fading in and out of view, never mind in the rest of the hotel.

As though preparing for a fire, Mia charted the key doors around the ballroom: the large double doors that must have opened onto the west wing's second-floor corridor, a smaller, less grand single-panelled door, which could have led anywhere from a cupboard or coat room to something beyond Mia's imagination, and of course, the one behind her, which she would use to slip back to the hotel's east wing and the real world – if she got through today, that is.

She had just decided it would make sense to try each of the other doors to see where they led, when a figure appeared at her side.

'Little Miss Mia,' said the warm voice. 'Haven't you anyone to dance with?'

'Oh,' she said after a small burst of surprise. 'I'm . . . I'm not really into dancing.'

Jim smiled down at her. 'Of course you are – you come dancing into my shop every Saturday. Unless . . . Are you waiting for a suitor to catch your eye, Mia? Don't want to be caught dancing with an old codger when some eligible bachelor comes calling, do you?'

Mia gave a strained laugh. 'Uh, yes. That's it. Trying to meet my, uh . . . Mr Right.'

'Your soulmate?'

'Sure.'

'You believe in soulmates?'

'Um, well, I—'

'I didn't used to believe in soulmates, but then I met Lorna and you know . . .' His eyes glazed over, looking at something beyond the room. 'I just . . .'

'Jim?'

She touched his ice-cold hand, and immediately, his expression brightened. 'Dance with me, Mia?'

This time, she nodded, and Jim McGowan gripped her hand tightly. He beamed as he lifted his arm for her to spin under, and laughed as they made an ungraceful attempt at a dip, and Mia, upon being righted, realised she was laughing too.

'You look just like your father,' Jim said. 'The blue eyes, the dark hair—'

'I know.'

'Malcolm Moran was a good man. Did I ever tell you about the time he came into my shop, looking for currant squares for your mother? Ah, he was in some state – pregnancy cravings this, hormones that . . .'

'No,' she said. 'I haven't heard that one.'

Smiling, Jim asked, 'Heard what?'

'The . . . story? My father and the currant squares and—'

The Baker gave a laugh and then spun Mia out, whipping her across the room, before seeming to forget that they were dancing at all. He let go, and Mia, still in the propulsion of his spin, went stumbling across the floor – and into another figure.

'Oh, I'm so sorry!' she gasped.

The figure turned out to be the man in black robes she had seen earlier.

Up close she could see the purple veins webbing across his thick jowls and short, round nose, as well as the indignation in his dark eyes.

'I'm so sorry, I didn't—'

'Pupils should never run in the corridors,' he said, his voice a trembling baritone. 'When they do, accidents happen, and accidents cost money. Money, I assume, you don't have, hm?' Before Mia could answer, he was shaking his head and wandering away from her. 'No one does, no money anywhere . . . But how do you fix anything without it?'

Feeling a new shadow fall upon her, Mia whirled around and came face to face with a tall, tight-lipped man. He'd not been amongst the ghosts dancing but seemed to have emerged from thin air, and peered down his long nose at her.

'Miss Moran, you haven't been attending Sunday School. I fear your absence is a symptom of a more concerning issue with your Christian walk.'

Mia blinked rapidly. 'Reverend . . . Plunkett?'

What old age and sickness had once taken away from the stern reverend of Ballinadrum Presbyterian, death had clearly returned. He was now the Plunkett of Mia's early childhood – six-foot with a head of black, wiry hair – instead of the frail, yellowed man whose funeral she had attended as a teen. In fact, she might have thought the spirit before her a long-lost son or nephew, if not for the distinctly shrewd stare and sharp tone.

'Have you been reading your Bible, Miss Moran?' he asked.

'I . . . *Yes*, I think—'

'Is that a lie? You know lying is a sin.'

'No, of course, I'm reading it. All the time. Every day.'

He sniffed once, as though her lies carried a scent, and then looked away, regarding the hotel's dancers with as much distaste as he had done in life. 'You must be sure to use the time you have wisely, Miss Moran. One day, you will wish you had spent more time in meditation and less . . . frolicking. You see these people? This is all they will ever have. There is no glory beyond for those who waste their precious years drinking and cavorting.'

Then what are you doing here? thought Mia. The man who preached faithfully on the unavoidable forked road every sinner and saint met at the end of their life was an unexpected sight in this grey in-between. Didn't he have somewhere better to be?

As though reading her mind, the Reverend turned his head and announced, 'I have to go. Time is getting on.'

'Go?' Mia asked, surprised. 'Go where?'

'It's rude to pry, Miss Moran. Adults do not answer to children.'

'Yes, but I was—'

'I haven't time, Mia. I'll be late – the post office is closing soon.'

'The *post office*?'

The Reverend ignored her, and Mia went to grab him. For an instant, he was as real and tangible as Jim McGowan, and cold all the way through, but he would not be held. He tugged his arm back, gave her a withering glare, and when she attempted to take his hand again, she found her fingers passed right through him.

Then, his legs dipped beneath the solid floor, and the sharp angles of his face melted like snow. He was disappearing.

Unable to follow, Mia stood motionless and afraid. If he sank through this floor, he would be on some lower level of the west wing, and she didn't know it nearly well enough to know whereabouts he could go from there, and if Cormac was right about the ghosts searching out activity and people and conversation, there was no telling if he would reach the lobby, the barroom . . .

'I – I haven't been reading my Bible,' she cried out.

Chest-deep into the floor, the Reverend paused. He rotated to face her.

'Excuse me?'

'I haven't been reading it,' Mia said quickly. 'You were right. I started with Genesis a while ago, and that was fine, but it got pretty dull after that and—'

'*Dull*?' The Reverend rose out of the floor like steam off a hot pan in the sink. 'Mia Moran, I sincerely hope that you did not just refer to the immortal Word of God as *dull*.'

Biting her lip, she answered, 'Well, maybe if you . . . explained it, I would see how exciting it really is.'

It was his turn to reach out to her, and he laid a pale, bony hand on her shoulder. Its cold pressure would have been unsettling to Mia, if she hadn't been so glad to feel the tangible weight of it and see his shining brogues planted firmly on the terrazzo once more.

'We'll begin with the Gospels,' he said softly.

Mia did not argue. She simply sat where he told her, by the thick grey curtains shielding the room from sunlight and prying eyes, and listened patiently as the ghost described wise men travelling from distant lands, shepherds thrown into terror by angel song and the undisciplined, unruly, and unholy nature of mankind, from which the Lord Jesus was sent to save us.

To her relief, as long as she nodded where she was supposed to, and asked appropriate questions when his attention wandered, the Reverend did not attempt another disappearing act.

The same could not be said of the other ghosts, though.

In fact, they made the difficulties of settling the Reverend seem almost non-existent, and it was only Cormac's insistence that the ballroom may yet *run like clockwork* that stopped Mia from losing her resolve altogether.

The man in the cowboy hat – the Cowboy, as she had dubbed him – waltzed through a wall and she was torn away from her lecture in a panic, dashing for the nearest door to wherever he had vanished to. Before she put her hand to the dust-laden knob, however, he reappeared with an oily grin and an invitation to dance.

She managed one chilly jive – and then Mia was pulled away again, this time by the Little Girl.

'My teddy,' she said. 'I can't find it. I've left it somewhere and *you* need to find it.'

'I can definitely *try*,' Mia replied, but that wasn't the right answer.

'I need my teddy. It was a very important gift, and the only thing worth anything. Don't you understand? You can't give me money.'

'I wasn't trying to—'

'He gave me money before, but I need *my* teddy.'

Mia was not musical by any stretch, but the tinkle of a few high notes on the piano seemed to settle the Little Girl – but then the Bride began to wail about her train and how it had been caught on an old nail in a floorboard and *look how it is torn, it's ruined.* Mia did her best to assure her it did not need mending, it was perfect, and didn't she have photographs to take?

The Bride pulled the man in the robes – the Headmaster, Mia called him – in for a hug, smiling as Mia obediently took photos of them both. The digital camera, of course, didn't pick anything up bar the shadowy curls of the Bride and the top of the Headmaster's head. Both could have been tricks of light, so faint they may not have been there at all, but when Mia looked back through the digital screen, she could see two white spots.

She tried another photograph, and again, she saw the ghosts as mere pale smudges. They appeared to be the only true sign the ghosts were there at all.

The Bride demanded photos with most of the other ghosts, calling the soldiers her brothers and the lady with soft eyes and big brown curls her mother, and when she grew bored of that, she began to ask why the cake had not yet been served.

'What kind of waiter are you?' she demanded. 'What am I paying for? Or is that the reason that you're . . . you're doing this? Who told you?'

Fortunately, it was at this moment Cormac Byrnes returned to the ballroom.

Mia spied his slender frame from the corner of her eye, standing in that yellow hallway, and dashed towards him without a second thought.

'They can move through the floor like it's nothing!' she gasped. 'And they see things that aren't there!'

Cormac glanced past her to the ballroom. 'You knew that already.'

'Yes but—' *It's entirely different dealing with it for an afternoon.* 'I can't even *count* them. They're here and then they're gone, and I don't know where to, and then all of sudden, they're back again and – and they don't even *look* the way they're meant to. I mean, *Jim* looks like I remember, but the Reverend Plunkett—'

'You know *another* of them?'

'Not especially well – he was the reverend at our church when I was little – but he was so *old* when I last saw him, and he's not anymore. He's *young* – or young*er*! And the Bride – did she die on her wedding day, or . . .'

'They don't always take on their most recent appearance, if that's what you're asking. Just the . . . most important one. Or perhaps it's the one they remember the best.' He looked the room over. 'Have they been disappearing for long periods? As far as I know, it should only be a few seconds at a time. Any more than that, and it's a problem.'

'No, I . . . I don't think so.'

'Any other questions, then?'

Mia was suddenly self-conscious. She gathered herself.

'Yes. You said an hour,' she said. 'It's been—'

'Three, I know. I was busy.'

'What if I'd needed you?'

'Did you?'

She glanced back to the room, to the dead talking and laughing and dancing and preaching and crying. Their all-so-human bodies flickering here and there, like rays of sunshine through cloud. Her afternoon had been crushed into a hurricane of mere seconds, and drawn out into the most chaotic lifetime Mia could have imagined. Her heart was still skipping a beat too fast, and her thoughts tripped over themselves as, even now, she considered which of these otherworldly hotel guests might cause her trouble next.

And yet . . .

Yet, they were still *here*, and better than that: not traversing the hallways of Ballinadrum Hotel. She had kept it safe.

She had done as Donahue would have.

'No,' she said, surprising satisfaction warming her chest. 'I didn't.'

chapter 15
dangerous things

HEATHER BUCKLEY WAS TALKING a mile a minute in the back seat of Rosco's car.

'The pictures were *gorgeous*. I looked through all the reviews last night, and I swear, there wasn't a bad one amongst them. You know the way most places have at least one? Well, this didn't. *Perfect.*'

It was a bright, cloudless day, unusual at any time of the year in Ireland, but more so in autumn, and it spoke of good things to come. Mia hoped the weather was right.

They were speeding along some country road, yellowing fields flashing in her periphery, enroute to some hotel named The Chelsea.

Mia had never been there before, and was only going now because of her original wedding venue's uncertain future, but Rosco seemed positive about it – not that he would let his mother know that. He had spent the majority of the journey attempting to extinguish her upbeat conversation starters and correcting any particularly overblown comments.

This worked for Mia because her thoughts were otherwise occupied – with the ghosts she had left behind. Reason told her they must be able to behave for at least a few hours, seeing as over the past few days, they had been able to avoid getting into much mischief when she had gone home at night, but still . . .

Daytime was different. Cormac had already said as much. There was more movement and noise, too many distractions – and the ghosts would hardly take into consideration Mia's life outside the hotel.

She doubted Cormac had considered it either. In fact, part of the reason she felt as anxious as she did was that she had simply not told him this was her appointed day off – and was currently riding on the thin hope he would simply not notice she was gone.

Of course, she hadn't just abandoned ship without a second thought. That morning, she had made sure to leave the ghosts with enough cake slices and music sheets that they might entertain themselves for at least a few hours. The Reverend had taken issue with this, of course, saying that sugar was simply a culturally acceptable vice, and the Headmaster, too, had complained about the budget and whether it could stretch to *fancy cakes*.

'If you pay for a few books, what do you have left?' he had asked. 'If you're given a sum of four thousand and spend it all, what is there then?'

Mia didn't have an answer for him that morning, and she didn't now, sailing by in Rosco's car.

'Mia, you listening?' Rosco was frowning at the windscreen when she looked up. 'Where's your head at?'

In an abandoned ballroom fifteen miles and counting from here.

'Nowhere,' she said.

She knew she should have told him by now – and had been planning to – but every moment had felt too . . . rushed, too mundane. But then, she had to admit, if only to herself, that there *had* been opportunities: the half hour they had talked in his car outside of Granny's, the night they'd watched a movie at his house after his parents had gone to bed, that winding night-time drive to the chippy.

Part of the problem, of course, was that she hadn't told him immediately, and *whenever* she told him now, he was going to ask when it all happened, and she would have to tell him she had kept a secret this momentous for days on end.

And so, she kept quiet, allowing her string of mistruths to tangle into knots.

'I was just thinking,' Heather said, 'maybe we should go to lunch afterwards, hm? Have a chat about the place over some tea and a scone.'

'Well, I was going to . . . I was going to head back to the hotel.'

'Oh, that's too bad. Maybe another day, then?'

Rosco wasn't as easily satisfied. 'I thought you had the day off?'

'I *did*,' Mia said. 'But my role's changed a bit since Cormac's arrived. I just have a few bits and pieces to pick up – nothing major.'

'So, do them tomorrow.'

'It's not that simple.'

'How?'

'No need for arguments!' came Heather's cheery voice. 'Today is meant to be *romantic*.'

'Then what are *you* doing here?' Rosco asked, eyeing his mother in the rear-view mirror.

'I'm providing an objective outsider's perspective – you know, to stop you two getting carried away and booking the first venue you visit.'

Mia did not believe Heather's opinions would offer any clarity on the current situation, but she kept that to herself, and soon, they were pulling into a leafy driveway.

It was different from Ballinadrum, of course. The leaves were those of slender silver birch trees, pretty and petite, and the lawn beneath was a tidy green carpet. Neither distracted from the view of the grand, sprawling building of sand-coloured bricks ahead, but framed it green and whimsical.

'Oh, it's *lovely*,' Heather breathed.

'Yeah,' Mia said, because it was – in every way.

The lobby was lovely, with its springy grey carpet and vase of fresh carnations, and the dining room was lovely, too, with well-organised tables and every surface gleaming like new. The lady showing them around had a lovely white smile and a list of lovely reviews to share with them, and assured them their wedding would be perfectly *lovely* too.

Rosco took Mia's hand and led her out to the gardens, where they could be alone for a moment.

The sunshine glittered against the pearly gravel, and if she tried, Mia could imagine a swathe of guests in formal attire sipping from champagne glasses and saying, 'Congratulations, Mia Buckley, welcome to the family.'

She pulled her camera from the satchel she wore across her chest, and snapped a couple of photos – the sun high in the sky, and the grass trying to grow through the brick lawn verge.

'So, what do you think?' she asked.

'Looks expensive.'

Mia let out a loud, barking laugh.

'You know I'm right,' Rosco said, laughing too.

'Your mum said it was in budget, though.'

'Mm, I'd be interested in seeing those figures now I've had a look around. She's been known to smudge details if it means she gets what she wants.'

'Well, I can see why she wants it.'

'Do *you* want it, though?'

She looked around: the shining windows, the pretty pot plants, the archway hung with ivy that they would no doubt pose underneath for photographs.

It wasn't Ballinadrum, but nowhere else in the world was.

'It's lovely.'

'Ahuh. And what else?'

'It's . . . It's big and fancy and I'll feel like I'm playing dress-up in a silly white dress, but I don't want to hurt your mum's feelings, because it really is nice.'

Rosco laughed and pulled her to him. 'Mia, she already likes you. You don't have to worry about what you say to her.'

A door opened. Heather stepped into the courtyard, waving wildly as though they may not have spotted her.

'Can't take her anywhere,' Rosco muttered.

'*So?*' Heather asked, beaming.

Mia glanced at Rosco. 'Well, it's great, but . . .'

'It's a no, Mum. Sorry.'

Heather's smile dropped. '*Why*?'

'Didn't you say you'd be objective?'

'Well, that was before I *saw* the place! Did you even look at the bridal suite? It's so *lavish*. I'd ask to be buried in it, if I could afford the nightly stay. Don't you even want to take a brochure home – see what your granny thinks, Mia? And remember, it's only a tenner more per head than the other—'

'It's too far from what we had going at Ballinadrum, Mum. Mia wanted something low-key, and this is the palace gardens.'

'Oh,' Heather said, unashamedly crestfallen. 'Well, I suppose it's up to you, Mia – it's the bride's day, isn't it? And of course, we'll find somewhere better than this . . . old place. So, where's next then? I think it was called Hamilton something, wasn't it . . . ?'

'Hamilton View,' Rosco corrected, and then squeezed Mia's hand. 'Might be more your style.'

They left with *thank yous* and *see you soons*, even though Mia knew neither she nor Rosco would step foot in The Chelsea again.

Heather kept up her disappointed routine until they reached the car park, and then spiralled into an adoring monologue about the next venue.

'Hamilton View *is* a little more casual – more family-like, you know? Warmer, I'd say. And the drinks wouldn't be as dear. That's the problem with swanky hotels at the end of the day: all the extras cost a bomb, and your guests never appreciate it at midnight when they just want a decently priced pint, do they?'

Rosco glanced Mia's way, a barely concealed smirk on his lips, and she ducked her head to hide her giggle.

Her phone suddenly vibrated in her bag. Mia fished it out to see an unrecognised number.

'Hello?'

'*Where are you*?'

Her stomach dropped. '*Mr Byrnes*, I . . . I'm just out.'

'What do you mean you're out? Why aren't you here? I thought we had a deal.'

'We did – *we do*. I'm just . . . Is everything okay?'

'No – why else would I have called you? Your *friend* has been *seen*, and now I learn you're not even *in the hotel*.'

'I'm sorry, I—'

'I thought you said you could do this.'

'I *can*—'

'Then *where* are you?'

She drew a quick breath. 'I'll be there as soon as I can.'

'You need to be here *now*.'

'But I—'

Cormac Byrnes had already hung up. The dial tone droned like an alarm.

'Everything okay?' Rosco asked, unlocking the car.

'Mr Byrnes called,' she said. 'I have to get back to the hotel.'

'What?' Heather gasped. 'But we've only seen one venue!'

'I know,' Mia said, scratching at the rubber of her phone cover. 'I'm sorry, I . . . He's just . . . He sounds really mad, you know? So, I should probably head back, and maybe we could . . . Can we do this a different day?'

Heather reached an arm around her. 'Of course we can. Don't be getting upset. There's still plenty of time before February, isn't there?'

Rosco frowned. 'Can't you say you're sick?'

'I . . .' Mia took a breath. 'I already said I'd go.'

He shrugged and climbed into the car, and Mia rushed to get in beside him.

'Please don't be mad,' she whispered.

'I'm not,' he said, but when she reached for his hand, he changed gears jerkily.

Mia laid her hands in her lap, and let the countryside whip by.

Mia Anne Moran climbed Ballinadrum Hotel's steps, already breathless. She had hoped with blistering fervour on the drive back to town that Cormac would not be waiting for her in the lobby, but of course, that was exactly where she found him.

He was a jagged figure by the bowl of hydrangeas at the centre of the room, and guests moved about him as though he was an unattractive décor choice. When his eyes fell upon Mia, however, he came to life and, with a commanding jerk of the head, bid her towards the lift.

'What took you so long?' he hissed as they waited for it to arrive.

'I was a little while away. I came as soon as—'

'And where is your uniform?'

Mia had never been more mortified by her baby-blue knit sweater. 'I'll change.'

'No. It's already too late.'

The lift answered and they stepped inside, doors closing behind them. Here, Cormac's restraint untethered. His hand came up to pinch the bridge of his nose, while the other leaned on one of the railings.

'I believe I made myself clear when I said I *needed you here*.'

'Mr Byrnes, I'm—'

'Look, you need to understand that it's not just as simple as people *seeing* something out of the ordinary. *That* can be explained away – other guests, shadows, one too many drinks. The *other* things? The *dangerous* things? No – they can't be changed. That's why I needed – need – you *here*.'

'Dangerous?' she repeated. 'But Jim—'

'Yes, of course, *this* ghost is quite nice. He drifts here, walks through a wall there, but that's not always the case, Mia. When they are left unmanaged, unchecked, they can be . . .'

Mia thought back to Jim's eyes that night on the fifth floor, the way he sank through the floor and felt like a perfect stranger – so different to the spirit she had danced with since.

'Dark,' she said.

He shook his head brusquely. 'Look. It doesn't matter now. Just – just fix it, okay? I've had word via that busybody Henry that room forty-two is *incredibly cold*, and another room on the same floor made a noise complaint. A man *shouting*, apparently.'

'I'm sorry,' Mia said. 'I didn't realise . . .'

The doors opened.

'Fourth floor,' Cormac said. 'Start here – and fix this. *Quickly*.'

Mia, obediently, stepped out of the lift. The golden doors slid closed with an air of finality, and she was all alone – or at least, she hoped she was. The air around her felt thick and sluggish, hard to trust and impossible to know.

She approached room forty-two with trepidation.

The occupant answered after a moment's muffled shuffling. 'Are you with . . . housekeeping?' she asked, eyeing Mia's lack of uniform.

'The office, actually,' Mia said hurriedly. 'I received word about a temperature issue. Is your room still cold?'

The woman shook her head. 'No . . . it's . . . It's better.'

Mia waited.

'It's only that . . . Well, the radiator was *on*.'

'Oh?'

'I thought maybe it was broken and that was the problem, but it was still . . . I don't know if you have a lot of draughts around here, but it just felt so strange for the radiator to be hot, and everything else just . . . not right. The bathroom was warmer. You see what I'm saying.'

Mia did – all too well. 'I'm so sorry to hear that. I'll pass along your comments, and we can see what we can—'

'Oh, well, if you're passing along comments—'

'Yes?'

The woman held the door a little tighter. She cast a quick glance back into her room. 'It's probably nothing, but it's just that . . . I thought I could hear someone . . . talking. Like, they were *right in the room*. Maybe someone left the TV on in their room, or the walls are just really thin in some places, but it just felt like . . .' She thought a moment, her brow tight. 'I probably heard it wrong, but on the off chance I didn't – it wasn't like a general mumbling. It was a man, talking about . . . blond hair. And make-up. A woman doing her make-up.'

Mia struggled to keep the concern from her face. 'I can pass that along. Of course.'

'I may have misheard it. Right?'

'All feedback is valuable.'

The woman just nodded and closed the door with the same wary expression, and Mia stood in the middle of the hallway, worry flaring all over her body.

Where was he?

Had he really been in the room, or just nearby, in some unseen in-between, or had he simply been passing through, before heading onto the next room, the next floor? She didn't know these ghosts well enough to guess their next moves – not even Jim McGowan – and her thoughts ping-ponged with possibilities.

'Can you believe it?'

'*Never.* As if they would let people like that in here.'

A middle-aged couple marched up the hallway with such ferocious purpose that Mia's first instinct was to step back to allow them past, but she forced herself to stay put.

'Sorry to interrupt, but . . . Is there a problem I can help you with?'

The sandy-haired man gave a dramatic sigh. 'No. It's already being handled.'

'Yes,' said his partner, a heavily made-up lady. 'We told the lobby downstairs and they said they'd deal with it *immediately.*'

'With what?'

They swapped a haughty look. 'There was a man,' said the woman. 'In the *ladies'* bathroom – and he didn't apologise – didn't even *look* sorry.'

Mia's coiling anxiety was burning inside her now. It made her want to run, though in which direction, it was yet to say.

'Did you . . . You don't happen to remember what he looked like?' she asked.

The couple seemed bothered by the query, but answered, 'A big man, with curly hair. White clothes, too. Seemed like he worked in the kitchens. It's a disgrace, you know.'

'Yes,' Mia said. 'I know.'

She rushed for the lift, and when it didn't arrive fast enough, her nerves drove her to the stairs.

The one thing she could be grateful for this afternoon, she thought, was Jim McGowan's timing. On a Friday night, there might be a queue of bar patrons waiting for the bathroom, and on Sunday afternoons, too, guests on their way to check out might decide on a last stop before hitting the road. Now though, Mia arrived in a lobby that was conveniently quiet – only three or four people in the whole room, and two of those were manning the desk.

She slipped down the side corridor to inspect the bathroom where Jim had been spotted – and came face to face with a tangle of blonde hair.

The woman had her hands pressed against her cheeks, her mouth forming an exaggerated *o* of surprise.

'Sorry to bother you but—'

'Did you . . . I could have *sworn* I saw somebody in the mirror . . .' The woman brought her hands to her chest, and then gave a laugh that echoed around the tiled room. 'Maybe . . . too much coffee, hm?'

The woman made her way out, and Mia checked every stall in the bathroom – even whispering Jim's name into the walls, like it might call him back to her. When that didn't work, however, she returned to the lobby.

Panic gripped her in a slow, unravelling sort of way. If she couldn't find Jim, or return him to the ballroom, what would happen? Surely, he couldn't be violent – he was not a physical thing, after all – and in life, that had never been his character.

Had it?

Mia had known Jim throughout her entire childhood, but there was nothing to say, for absolute certain, that he had not been capable of unkindness or even cruelty. And then there was Cormac's intimation of *dangerous things*, and she doubted all the more than ever in this form he – and the ghosts in general – did not have the capacity for harm.

As she whispered to the walls and the shadows, the desire to return to Cormac simmered inside her. But then, what would he do – relieve her of the duties for which she was so poorly suited? Her entire contribution to the salvation of her beloved hotel and the legacy of her friend Donahue Byrnes would have totalled a measly couple of days and one runaway spirit.

Then: the thunder of footsteps. Three little boys raced up the corridor.

'She'll never believe you!'

'I'm telling her first!'

'He really *did* walk through the wall!'

'*Hey.*'

The boys, all motion one moment and stock still the next, looked at her, blushing as though they were already in trouble. By the looks of their dark, wily eyes, Mia had a feeling it was a state in which they often found themselves.

'Did you see someone walk through a wall?' she asked, her voice a little thick. Swallowing, she added, 'Just now?'

'Yeah,' said the smallest, just as the tallest amongst them said, 'No.'

'Where?'

'Just back there,' the small one said. 'Beside the bathrooms!'

'And then where?'

'I dunno. I ran away.'

The others pulled his elbow, and once again, they were off, tripping over themselves to be first, and Mia took a deep breath.

She crossed the bright lobby, slipped down the side corridor, listening to every creak and whisper the old building made – searching for something, *anything* out of the ordinary.

It was then she realised just how cold she was.

There was a flicker of movement by her ear, and Mia jerked to the side. Shock barrelled through her, and her heart raced on, but looking at the figure emerging from the tired wallpaper, Mia couldn't help but let out a giddy cry of relief.

'*Jim!*' she whisper-cried, reaching out a hand.

The Baker did not pause to take it, however, but drifted further up the corridor, towards the women's bathroom. A woman's laugh rose on the air, and Jim, seemingly transfixed by it, wandered ever closer.

'Jim,' Mia repeated, more urgently.

Ignoring her, he reached out a hand to touch the bathroom door, and Mia dashed forward to take his arm. Her fingers passed right through his skin, but the sensation still seemed to register with him. He turned to look at her.

Mia paled.

The jolly, endearing face of the man she had known in her youth, and become reacquainted with these recent days, was dark and bleary-eyed. He answered her in a moan, a sound like a rusty-hinged door.

It was the same as that night she had told him he was dead, and yet Mia was still surprised. How could this be the man who had danced with her across the abandoned ballroom and called her Little Miss Mia? How could the figure before her complain about the cost of lipsticks, or plan birthday surprises, when his eyes looked so lost and his expression so unfamiliar?

'Jim, I was . . . looking for you. I thought you would be at the dance.'

The ghost turned away, and Mia's chest tightened.

'*Jim*, we need to go back.'

The woman inside the bathroom continued her conversation. Mia stepped forward to try to take Jim's hand once more, but her fingers slipped through his and his hand disappeared through the solid wood door.

'Jim! That's – that's the *ladies' bathroom*.'

The Baker paused. His gaze drifted towards her.

Mia, hardly thinking a word ahead of herself, continued. 'What would . . . what would Lorna say? I was just speaking with her, actually. She was . . . she was asking if you had that lipstick of hers.'

A flicker of recognition passed over Jim's face. There was something more . . . *himself* there now – something Mia could tug on and draw out.

'Do you have her lipstick, Jim?'

'No.' He patted his pocket, eyes downcast. 'I . . . forgot it.'

'That's okay, I'm sure it doesn't matter—'

'I was going to buy a new one, you know, one of those fancy ones, in the shiny tubes and . . .'

'I know, Jim.'

Still fumbling through his pockets, he said, 'I just didn't get the time.'

'That's okay. It's all okay.'

'And I've . . . I've been saving, Mia.'

'That's great. But I'm sure she'd much rather see you in the—'

Jim smiled, closing his eyes. 'It's in the rafters, Mia, right at the back. I was going to give it to her for her birthday. And I'd go get it, but I just . . . I'm forgetting it all, Mia.'

Mia dared to hold his hand again. 'No, you're not. You'll remember. I'll help you.'

'I need to tell her before I forget. I need to see her.'

'And you will – after the dance, right? That would be a nice time to announce it, huh?'

The concern melted away. 'Yes. Yes, of course – she'll be so pleased . . .'

'I bet,' Mia told him. 'But you know what she said to me earlier when I met her?'

He tilted his head, eyes soft and brown and curious.

'That all she's wanted to do tonight is dance with you – in the ballroom.'

The bathroom door opened suddenly, and the woman's laughter went from muffled, to bright, sharp, and *there*.

Mia gasped and drew back.

'Oops,' the woman said, pulling a phone away from her ear. 'Hope I didn't scare you.'

'No, not at all. Just . . . wasn't expecting you.'

She just laughed. 'This hotel is so jumpy. Must be all the *ghosts*, hm?'

The woman sauntered off then, continuing her conversation, not even noticing the last of Jim McGowan's ghost as it passed through the wall, and disappeared.

chapter 16
blackberries

THE NEXT DAY, MIA approached the ballroom differently.

Firstly, she woke early and threaded Cormac's bronze key onto an old chain, pressing it flat to her chest.

Then, she skipped her usual chat with Sonia in the lobby, instead making a beeline to the hotel's lift. She rode it to the third floor, where she multiplied her two over-the-shoulder glances by three before unlocking the door and slipping through the passageway to the west wing.

There, most importantly, she stopped in the corridor to assess the ghosts.

She watched for Jim McGowan, in particular, and spotted him drifting idly through the middle of the room, discussing something seemingly serious with absolutely no one at all. Fortunately, while he did not appear especially jubilant, he was still *himself* – no dark eyes, no blurred expression.

It should have warmed Mia, but she wondered how long it would be until he changed, and what would trigger it today.

He was ultimately – as they all were – unknowable.

'Have you seen the caterer?'

Mia flinched at the sound of the voice by her ear. The Bride stared at her with wide long-lashed eyes.

'He was supposed to be here,' she continued as though Mia had already answered. 'He said he would be here early, but *look*. Can't depend on anyone, even *today* of all days.'

She turned with distress, her gown spinning out behind her. It passed through the toe of Mia's shoe and Mia shivered at the cold.

Moving her foot, she tried, 'The caterer is on their way. Everything will be on time.'

'Oh, you say that,' the Bride lamented. 'But that's what *they* said, and what they said wasn't what they meant, and what they meant wasn't what they said, and . . .'

'*Actually*,' Mia said, pointing out across the ballroom, 'I think I see them now. Over there.'

The Bride twirled again, and Mia was careful to retract her foot this time. The train flowed like a frosted river, and then melted to nothing.

Then, Mia decided to photograph the ballroom. Yesterday, she had learned a valuable lesson – ghosts could not be trusted. Not to stay in the ballroom, not to listen to her, and not to be particularly consistent, either, but on camera . . . There, they could not flicker in and out of sight. They could be lined up and counted – and kept in some sort of order.

As she did so, the ghosts took notice, and, just as curious, silvery fish, they drew nearer to this oddity in their waters. Blue Dungarees confessed that he had lost the love of his life and did not know how to get her back, and an older woman with ash-coloured hair – who the Little Girl kept calling *Beverly* – insisted she had done the exact same thing. The Clown twisted non-existent balloon animals to the applause of a non-existent crowd, and the Lady, in her hefty fur coat, barely glancing in Mia's direction, asked for an old fashioned – *hold the ice.*

When Mia finally had a moment to count the little white dots captured in her camera lens, she had expected around fifteen or sixteen. To her dismay, however, there were more – nineteen, in fact.

So, she counted again, and then recounted. She took more photographs and counted those too, and each time, she found the same thing.

Nineteen.

Nineteen ghosts.

'Boring, isn't it?'

Mia tore her gaze from her camera and its concerning details to look at a shaggy-haired spirit leaning casually against the wall.

Taking a step sideways, Mia answered, 'What is?'

'The music. It's all so . . .' The ghost made some vague, unintelligible movement with her hands. 'This place should hire some *real* artists. It takes *zero* talent to get a crowd singing a cover of "Sweet Caroline".'

'Oh, well, we could change the music, if—'

'I could do it, you know. I play all my own instruments. Write my own songs.'

'That's—'

'Even played Ballinadrum a few times. Small, but . . . it's got something special, you know?'

Mia smiled at her. 'Yes.'

'Even after I'd given up the gigging stuff, the old place would still let me play the odd Friday night. That Donahue guy . . .'

'Donahue Byrnes?' Mia asked, beaming now. 'You knew him?'

The ghost's expression changed entirely. 'Knew him? Hardly. I played and got out. They hardly even paid me. People always said I got favours but listen here: I didn't get anything.'

'Oh, I'm sure if he didn't pay you, it must have been some misunderstanding and—'

'*You don't know what happened.*'

Some darkness tugged at the edge of the ghost's eyes, as though her smoky make-up had taken on a life of its own. She held Mia's gaze with ferocious intensity.

Then, she corrected the angle of her jagged fringe, stalked off towards the piano.

Mia almost followed, an apology on her lips, but halfway across the room, the Singer lost herself in a dance. When she swung around in the Cowboy's arms, Mia could see she was now laughing – all hurt forgotten.

*

On the way home, Mia wasn't feeling especially chatty.

Fortunately, Rosco was.

He told her about the new fried chicken place he and Ethan had gone to for lunch, and how he had seen Granny at the chemist, and then asked whether she thought Ethan should buy the blue Toyota with a hundred thousand miles, or the silver Ford with sixty thousand – they were going to see both again at the weekend.

Mia didn't know, and told him as much.

'Tired again?' he asked.

'A little. Just a lot of customers to talk to today.'

'Well, I hope you're not *too* talked out.'

The car slowed, and Rosco pulled in off the road, manoeuvring into a space outside The Burning Lamp. Mia could see through the large display window that there was just one customer in the shop, thanking Lorna, it seemed, for the crisp, white box in their hands.

Mia sat up taller. 'Ooh, a few treats for dinner?'

'No,' Rosco said slowly. 'We're doing our cake tasting.'

'That's *today*?'

'Time flies when you're assistant to the Devil, huh? Come on, did you really forget? I thought this would have been the highlight of your whole year: you get to sample *everything* in The Burning Lamp and Lorna can't tell you to stop.'

Mia tried a light chuckle but the truth of it all – that she *had* forgotten, completely and utterly – hit her like catching her hip on the corner of a table.

They stepped onto the street, and Mia grabbed Rosco's hand tightly. He answered her with a smile.

Lorna welcomed the two of them into the bakery with her usual cheer, asking about Granny, and the dogs, and whether they ever got that pipe in the shower fixed. She sparkled in a fuchsia pink cardigan thrown over a glittering graphic T-shirt, and was a supernova in an otherwise dull galaxy.

'Forgive the mess,' she told them, leading them to the kitchen, which was warm from the day's baking. There was a pile of burnt or misshapen scones piled in a box by the back door, and the floor in here had not yet been swept. Mia wondered if the air, too, might be brushed down, to rid it of the thin, floury haze.

'There's only so many hands,' Lorna said, gesturing for them to take a seat at the two little stools she had arranged by a cluttered desk. 'And so much dough.'

Mia smiled. That had been one of Jim's favourite jokes.

She suppressed the desire to hold a hand to her chest, where the ballroom key lay against her skin, and instead let her gaze drift from Lorna and her neon nails to the fresh paint on the architraves, and the splash of pink sugar by one of the benches – a staple of Lorna's raspberry and rhubarb tarts.

It was easy to imagine Jim here, and easier still to see why he kept trying to come back. The ballroom was only so entertaining, and a home all the more . . .

'Don't you think, Mia?'

Mia's eyes snapped back to Rosco. If she had hoped to get away with being absentminded, one look at his face told her she hadn't.

'Fruit cake,' he said. 'It's out, right?'

'For sure,' she said with feeling. 'The real battle is between chocolate, and jam and cream.'

Lorna laughed. 'I had a feeling that would be the case. How about this – we call it a tie, and I do one layer chocolate and one layer jam? That's how my Jim always liked it.'

'He did?'

'Oh yes, every birthday, that was what I made him. And I'd recommend blackberry jam, but that's a little controversial.'

'I probably prefer—' Rosco began, just as Mia said, 'Which did Jim like better?'

He looked at her quizzically.

'Sorry,' Mia said. 'I didn't mean to interrupt.'

'It's fine. Weddings are *exciting*,' Lorna said. 'Jim preferred the blackberry, but what was your preference, Rosco?'

'Oh, well, I'd say strawberry. You want strawberry, right, Mia?'

Mia's eyes darted between Lorna and her fiancé. 'Well, I . . . The blackberry sounds interesting, right?'

'Yeah, but more people would like strawberry.'

'I guess that's true. It's just . . .'

'What?'

'Blackberry might be special.'

Rosco frowned. 'Since when?'

'Well, since . . . now. I hadn't thought about it, really.'

'Yeah, I *know* you hadn't thought about it—'

'No, I don't mean the tasting. I—'

'There's no need to decide today, of course,' Lorna interjected. 'We have plenty of time for the specifics. We just need to get some *ideas* down today.'

Rosco's face was drawn, his eyes darker. Suddenly, blackberry seemed an absurd option.

'Sorry,' Mia said. 'You're right: strawberry is more popular.'

'Decide later, sure,' Lorna said gently. 'It's early days yet.'

Mia nodded along, and tried to pay attention as Lorna went over the different kinds of icing – fondant, buttercream, a special blend of both – but still her mind wandered, circling Jim and his ghost, and the rafters he had spoken of so desperately.

If she could just have a look around, she thought, she might be able to settle herself long enough to actually pick a cake without all of this nonsense floating about in her mind, and she would only be gone for a moment . . .

'Do you mind if I go to the bathroom?' Mia asked, rising from her chair.

She climbed the corkscrew staircase, savouring each familiar creak, and came to a pokey, untidy room – made smaller by the slanting rafters and lack of windows. The worktops here were bumped and scratched, and the large fridge-freezer somewhat yellow, but in Jim's day, Mia knew, all of it would have been shining and new.

His ghost likely thought it still was.

She stopped short of the bathroom, and looked to the rafters. Suddenly, it seemed so silly to take any of the ghosts' words seriously, and even sillier to act on them.

Then again, where was the harm in looking? Granny had said it already – there wasn't any harm in a story – and if she didn't find anything up here, that would be fine. She could go downstairs, argue a little more about strawberries and blackberries, and things would be normal.

But if she *did* find something . . .

Rosco and Lorna's conversation was softened by the floorboards, and Mia shifted the step stool by the bathroom door as quietly as she could to an advantageous position beneath the beams. She probed the edge of the timber. The wood was rough, but there was space to stash a small sum of notes behind it, she thought, though her fingers found nothing.

She stepped down from the stool and moved it along again, repeating her search. She felt every grain along the wood, so intent on her mission that when she noticed that the murmurs from downstairs had all but evaporated, she couldn't be sure how long the quiet had been there.

She moved to the last rafter and ran her fingers along the length of the beam. Her hand brushed against something *not wood*, tucked just out of sight against the plaster, and she gasped with the shock of it.

'Mia?'

Rosco's voice sent a greater shockwave through her than her discovery.

'I'll just be a minute!' she called back.

'You've been . . . a while.'

This time, his voice was accompanied by the unmistakable groan of the staircase. Her hurry turned to panic, and she jammed her fingers into the crack, and pulled.

She half-fell from the step stool, not at all lightly, holding in her hand Jim McGowan's secret: a thick, yellow envelope with *Lorna* scrawled across it in scratchy blue ballpoint.

'What are you doing?'

Mia whirled around, tucking the envelope into her waistband. 'Nothing.'

Rosco frowned at her. 'You said you were going to the bathroom.'

'I got a little distracted.'

'That's been you all over today.'

She tried a laugh, but he didn't return it.

'I . . . I haven't been myself recently,' she tried instead.

'No,' he said. 'You haven't. Now, what are you doing? Come here.'

She drifted across the floor. 'Sorry.'

'For what?'

'For . . . being distracted.'

'Why are you distracted?'

His voice was low and quiet. Mia's, by contrast, was a flimsy old cardigan, stretched out and uneven.

'I was looking for something,' she said.

'What?'

'I didn't plan on it, but I just . . . I got here, and I had to see if it was really there—'

'You're not making any sense, Mia. What could you possibly be looking for up here?'

She closed the remaining space between them, fitting inside his hard-angled shadow and looking up into his suspicious, narrowed eyes. There would be no *right* moment anymore. She had allowed herself to run out of road and here she was on the edge of it all, wishing she had just said something a week ago.

'Do you remember when I told you about the hotel – about the ghosts? It's that again. It's . . . It's Jim McGowan, Rosco.'

'What?'

'I saw him again. I *keep* seeing him.'

Rosco took a long breath, and Mia waited for the blow to hit: *why didn't you tell me, how long has this gone on, when did you start keeping secrets?*

'Mia, you're letting these stories get the better of you.'

The words were ice water, but his eyes were softer than before – warm, even – so she stood there, disarmed, and unsure.

'What?' she said.

'One time, I can understand, but to be entertaining this delusion . . .'

'Delusion? I was *serious* when I told you that.'

'Well, I know you were *serious*, but you were scared. Being scared makes you see all sorts of things. And you said it yourself: it was Donahue's stories getting to you.'

'I meant it was . . . It was Donahue's stories . . .' *Coming to life, being made real.* 'I meant that what I *saw* was what he had seen before. That the stories weren't *just* stories.'

His brows cocked at crazy angles. 'You do hear yourself, right? Donahue Byrnes' silly stories about fairies and ghosts and the rest . . . are now *real*?'

She *had* heard herself, but Rosco's tone, his expression, made her tongue shrink to the back of her mouth and her toes curl in her shoes.

When she said nothing, he threw a hand up, gesturing to the room, as if she had been caught smearing paint across the walls.

'And now you're on about blackberries because Jim liked them, and rummaging about in Lorna's store. You do know that Jim is Lorna's *dead husband*, right? It's not fair to be talking about him like that.'

Mia's eyes found the floor.

'Imagine if I started talking about seeing your mum or your dad, drifting about the hotel's halls. You wouldn't like it. You'd want me to leave them be and stop telling silly stories.'

'But it's not like that.'

'How?'

Because my story is true.

'Look,' he said. 'This is our cake tasting. It's meant to be fun, okay? Let's just go downstairs and put this behind us. I know you've been *seeing* things, but . . . It's important you remember they're not really there, Mia. You *know* that, don't you?'

She nodded soundlessly.

'What, you won't even speak to me?'

She swallowed. 'No.'

'Come here,' he said. His large palm encased hers and he squeezed once, offering her a sideways smile. 'You can be so strange, Mia Moran.'

Mia smiled back, and followed the tug of his hand down the stairs to the kitchens, stealing only the briefest of glances over her shoulder.

Jim McGowan's envelope rested on the hardwood floor where she had dropped it.

chapter 17
all or nothing

THE NEXT MORNING, MIA arrived at Ballinadrum Hotel, bringing a scattering of autumn leaves with her. The doorman Gerry shooed them out like a gang of stray cats, and across the way, Sonia, with her hotel sweater sleeves pulled over her knuckles, waved a sleepy good morning.

But Mia was already stepping into the lift, her thoughts on the third floor alone.

She wanted to see Jim. She wanted to tell him *everything*.

She bounced into the ballroom, camera already in hand. It was a little much for the ghosts, however, because two or three who were closest to the door startled and disappeared at once.

Mia stilled herself, watching as the Bride reappeared across the way, her lips pursed with displeasure, and following behind her, a woman with a long, pointed nose, who muttered, 'Well, I never . . .'

They settled slowly, and the Little Girl pattered away on the piano. A man in a fine suit with a thin moustache clapped along, though did *not* keep time, and the rest flitted in and out of view with delicate grace – their feet soundlessly skating across the ballroom's floor.

The rest, Mia noticed, with a sudden twinge of unease, except Jim.

No matter, she thought. He would materialise any moment now – and she had the perfect lure with her, too.

From her satchel, Mia produced a half-loaf of seeded bread wrapped in brown paper, a trio of silvery teaspoons, a dull butter knife, and, at last, an empty jar, topped with a gingham-printed lid. She set up her collection of treats on the side of the piano, and the ghosts, like insects about a buzzing porch light, drew close.

'I didn't know we had arranged an arrival tea,' the Bride cooed. 'How very luxurious.'

Mia cut thin slices of the bread, topped it with the imaginary contents of the jar, and handed them out to the ballroom's occupants.

The Little Girl announced that it was the best birthday cake she had ever received, and one of the soldiers complained that his toast was *stone cold.*

'Oh, I like onion chutney, so I do,' the Cowboy said as Mia handed him a slice. 'Good with cheese, isn't it?'

Mia liked to see them like this. Happy. Contented.

And yet . . . there was still one missing.

'It's blackberry, Jim,' Mia called gently. 'Blackberry jam.'

She fished into her apron for her camera, keen to be sure that nineteen little dots were still present.

'Are you looking for someone in particular?' the Cowboy asked. 'I could give you a hand making them *jealous*, if you are?'

'No, thank you,' she replied. 'But you're right – I am looking for someone.'

She snapped a photograph.

'Someone *special*?'

'Yes. Definitely.' Mia looked into her tiny screen, counting the dots.

'Say, I haven't got your name yet, have I?' the Cowboy went on.

'You tell me yours first,' Mia said, eyes still on the screen. *Seventeen, eighteen . . .*

'You want my name? My lady, only ask, and I should give you my hand as well.'

'A name would do just fine.'

'If you insist . . . it's Wayne.'

Distracted from her count, she looked up at the ghost. 'Wayne?'

'Yeah. *John* Wayne.'

He erupted into riotous laughter, and Mia shook her head: *impossible man.* She looked back into the camera screen, squinting as though that might provide better fortitude against the Cowboy's disturbances.

Fourteen, fifteen . . .

'Oh, I'm only kidding around. It's really Clint – Scout's honour this time.'

Sixteen, seventeen, eighteen . . .

Where was number nineteen?

Where was Jim?

Mia tried a different angle, but this photo also showed only eighteen smudges, and the one she took from the far side of the room did the same.

Eighteen ghosts.

'Oh no,' she whispered, and raced out of the ballroom.

To Mia's relief, the women's bathroom downstairs was decidedly un-haunted, but her gut still squirmed with worry as to where her Baker had got to – and whether Cormac knew about his disappearance yet.

Her next stop was the lobby, where Sonia was busy on the phone. Mia danced with impatience until the irritated receptionist placed a hand over the phone receiver, and hissed, 'Give me a minute, will you?'

'It's important,' Mia whispered.

'Ahuh,' Sonia said, returning to the call. 'Are you very sure? We'd love to have you and there really is no reason to cancel as far as we . . . Well, of course. Yes, I can do that for you now. Thank you, sir.' She set the phone down. 'That's the third one today, so I don't need you hopping up and down like that when I'm trying to do my job, Mia.'

Mia, caught off guard by the sharp tone, stilled. 'Third what?'

'Cancellation.'

'What? Why?'

'Well . . .' Sonia drew a newspaper out from under the desk, and tapped a column on the first page:

Haunted AGAIN? Ballinadrum Hotel guests speak out about alleged ghostly happenings – nearly 70 years on from first rumours

'You might want to ask your mother-in-law-to-be to ease up on the gossip.'

Mia snatched up the paper, eyes scanning it so quickly the words blurred together, and all she could say was, 'Is this today's?'

'Mhmm,' Sonia said, already back at her computer and typing. 'It was bound to make the news one of these days. Every day is a slow news day around here.'

'But it's not true.'

'It doesn't claim to be. See – *alleged.*'

'But people are still cancelling?'

'Haunted hotels don't make for family-friendly destinations, Mia, or romantic getaways. But don't look so worried. It's a county paper – it won't get too far. Now what can I do for you?'

Mia's thoughts swung like a pendulum from this fresh disaster to the one she was already dealing with. 'Complaints,' she said. 'Have there been any?'

'Aside from the rekindled haunted status? No. Why?'

'No weird calls? Or . . . men in bathrooms, or . . .'

'*Should* I have got a call about a man in a bathroom?'

'No. Definitely not. I just . . . *Cormac* wanted to know. He sent me – to, you know, ask.'

'Well,' Sonia said incredulously, 'you can tell him that we've had no complaints, about men in bathrooms or otherwise.'

'Great,' Mia said, cheeks pinned by a rigid smile. 'Perfect.'

With few other options besides searching every room in the hotel, Mia decided to return to the ballroom on the off chance Jim might have reappeared.

Only when she was standing in the lift, waiting for the numbers to flash *3* did Mia Moran stop to think about The Burning Lamp, and the envelope she had found.

About Jim McGowan and his constant wandering, and his forgetting, and always, always talking about Lorna, and how much the money would mean to her.

I'd say they have unfinished business, she had told Lily once before, and it suddenly struck her she had never taken those words seriously enough.

When the lift finally arrived on the third floor, Mia made the short journey from the hallway to the ballroom, and snapped another photograph of the dancers.

Eighteen.

Eighteen, again.

At seven o'clock, Mia knocked on Cormac's office door.

It had once belonged to Donahue, and Mia remembered it as a plush, purple place of old photographs and unique ornaments. Now, it was more like a hollowed-out pomegranate, scraped clean to rind, with all the pictures taken down, and soft furnishings moved out. Everything that made it Donahue, bar the lavender wallpaper, was gone.

The room's new owner sat at the hardwood desk with a singular folder propped up in his hands so that he might read it more closely.

'Finished for the day?' he asked, barely glancing up.

'Yes,' Mia said. 'But I have good news, too.'

'Oh, really?'

'Jim, the Baker – the ghost is gone.'

Cormac dropped the folder. '*Gone?* What is this, a joke? If you aren't going to take this work seriously, and it very much looks like that is the case—'

'No,' Mia said, interrupting him. 'He's *gone* gone. Like, isn't in the hotel.'

Cormac's eyes narrowed. 'Excuse me?'

'I looked *everywhere*. Every bathroom, every floor. I even looked around the old corridors in the west wing, and I can see why the ghosts aren't as interested in hanging out there, because it really is just dusty and dark and—'

'Mia Anne, get to the point.'

'Jim McGowan left money for his wife before he died,' Mia explained. 'But he didn't get the chance to give it to her. That's where he was always wandering to, why he kept turning up in women's bathrooms – he wanted to find her and tell her about the money. But he told *me* where it was. I found it, and left it for his wife to find. And now he's . . . gone.'

Cormac was on his feet now. 'Gone,' he said. 'When did you . . .'

'Yesterday. And today . . .'

'Gone,' Cormac finished. 'And you're . . . you're absolutely sure he's not still here?'

'I looked everywhere, all day,' she said. 'No one has reported seeing him either.'

'Gone,' he said again. 'One of them is gone.'

'As far as I can tell anyway, and I really have looked. I think it's to do with *unfinished business*, you see, and before Donahue – I mean, *your father* – died, he had told me about this special—'

'I need you to do it again.'

'Excuse me?'

'Mia, if you can . . . If you are capable of actually getting rid of ghosts and not just keeping them entertained with stale biscuits . . . I need you to do this with *every* ghost.'

'Every ghost?' Her confidence wavered. 'I mean, I could – I could *try*, but, Mr Byrnes, I *knew* Jim.'

'It doesn't matter. You can get to know the others. You can . . . work it out, make an investigation of it, *I don't know*. Just – Mia Anne, if you can do this, the hotel could actually be *free* of ghosts for the first time this millennium.'

Something like a smile passed over Cormac's face. He looked younger – like he really could be Donahue's son.

'You mean, we could save it?' Mia said. 'You wouldn't have to sell?'

As quickly as it had come, Cormac's smile withered. 'What?'

His expression caught her off guard, and Mia straightened her shoulders. 'Isn't that what this is about? I thought that if I took care of the ghosts . . . then, you'd want to keep the hotel? And now if I could actually get rid of them for good—'

'I was always selling the hotel, Mia Anne. The ghosts just make it damn near impossible. I mean, you saw that old fool run out of the dining room, didn't you? That wasn't the first time, you know, and then there are all the rumours, and . . . Well, you understand the issue, but since you've been working with them, it's been *much* easier.'

Mia's stomach dropped. 'You wanted my help . . . in *selling* the hotel?'

'You really thought I would *keep* this old heap? Mia Anne, I'm here to sell it and then get going. I have a life in England, you know, and I'm planning on heading back to it as quickly as possible, but until then . . . this is your job.'

She stared at him – sitting in his father's chair, with his father's eyes.

'I'm an assistant,' she said finally. 'That's my job.'

'Well, yes, on paper, but you and I both know what you do here.'

She shook her head slowly. 'I'm not helping you to sell this place off to be bulldozed.'

'Now, no one said anything about *bulldozing*—'

'Mr Gurning,' she said. 'That's what he wants to do.'

Cormac threw his hands up. 'And it's in his rights to do so *if* he buys the hotel, but as it currently stands, he hasn't made an offer yet. Does that make you feel better?'

'No. It doesn't – but there is something that would.'

'And what would that be?'

'You may hate this hotel, but you're the only one,' she said in a quiet voice. 'If you sell, I want you to sell the whole thing. The building, staff, the grounds – everything. Not parts, not land. All or nothing.'

Cormac's eyes narrowed. 'You're asking for the impossible.'

'Then so are you.'

He turned away. It felt like an age lived in that silence, until at last: 'Fine,' he said. 'All or nothing – but the same goes for you.'

The elation in Mia's chest was punctured with confusion. 'Me?'

'You want the hotel to be sold in its entirety? Fine, but I expect the hotel to be rid of ghosts – *entirely*. If even one is left . . . I'll do with it what I want.'

Mia pursed her lips together, fingers knotted together before her. 'That'll take time.'

'You have two weeks.'

'Two weeks? There are too many. Giving it until Christmas would be—'

'As though I will still be here at *Christmas*.'

Mia's phone began to ring. It was shrill and loud and maddening. She ripped it from her pocket and hit *end*, Rosco's face fading into the black of the screen.

'Two months,' she told Cormac. 'That's sensible.'

'It's an age. A month – no more.'

'At *least* the end of the month—'

'Halloween? Really?'

The phone buzzed again, insistent. She ended the call without looking.

'If you give me a little more time, then you can be sure I'll actually do it.'

'Mia Anne, do you want the deal or not?'

'I'm the one doing *you* the favour, you know.'

'Your point being?'

Her phone began again, a nest of angry hornets.

'Fine,' she told him. 'No ghosts by the end of October. I hope you get a good buyer.'

He smiled, but this time, it cast shadows in nasty places. 'As do I.'

chapter 18
a secret in ballpoint

IN THE WEEK THAT FOLLOWED, the sun began to elude Mia. She arrived at the hotel before it had risen, and left only when it had retreated behind the hills of Ballinadrum.

Such workdays, she felt, were longer than Cormac had originally described, but he had also warned her that these things took time, and effort. The ballroom may well come to *run like clockwork*, but not in a mere matter of days. She could not expect ripples upon a pond to still in an instant, after all – though that would have been exceedingly preferable.

Fortunately, Rosco did not probe too deeply about the change in her hours.

'How was today?' he would ask when he picked her up.

'Fine,' she would answer.

And then, suddenly, she was back in his car, rubbing sleep from her eyes, and he was asking, 'How did you sleep?' and she was answering, 'Fine.'

But even those long hours, Mia was starting to worry, weren't enough – not with Cormac's impossible deadline on the horizon – so the following Wednesday, she interrupted their typical schedule.

Granny Brea watched her whirlwind about the hallway, holding a generously buttered slice of toast in one hand and a steaming cup of tea in the other.

'Is Rosco here already? I didn't hear the doorbell.'

'Rosco's not taking me today.'

'Oh, why's that?'

'I told him not to.'

Mia tried not to notice the tilt of Granny's head as she buckled her patent shoes and flipped through her satchel once more.

It was, of course, quite unlike Rosco to accept Mia walking to work instead of riding in his passenger seat. However, it was also unlike Rosco to be awake at this time in the morning, and therefore he probably hadn't even seen her text message.

'I'm going to work earlier now, you see.'

'I'm sure he wouldn't mind taking you anyway. Did you ask?'

'No—'

'And it's raining.'

Mia shook her head, laughing. 'I won't melt, you know.'

'Just a grim morning to stake your independence, is all.'

Mia changed the topic. 'Hey, you wouldn't remember that old notebook I had from school, would you? It was *almost* done, but not quite, and it had that shiny cover . . .'

'Can't say I have. What do you need it for?'

'Oh, I just wanted to take some notes. At work.'

Granny observed her. 'Taking this pretty seriously, huh?'

Mia fixed the key beneath her shirt so it lay flat. 'There's a calling for everyone, I suppose.'

'Well, I'm afraid I don't know where *that* notebook is, but you could take an old one of mine.' Granny popped the last of her toast in her mouth, patting the crumbs onto her nightdress, and then rummaged in the drawers by the front door. 'Now, I've a few old plain ones, and then this one Paula gave me last Christmas . . . *This* one Donahue left here one afternoon he stayed for tea and wouldn't allow me to return—'

'That one,' Mia said, already reaching out.

Donahue's book was a rugged, stoic thing in brown leather. It looked as though it might have held spells or ancient chants or the last account of a lost explorer – or perhaps, when Mia was done of it, tales of dead men and women.

Granny released it into her granddaughter's care.

'It might be a little difficult to write in, with that stiff spine.'

'That's okay. I'll wear it in.'

'If you're sure.'

'Completely,' Mia said, slipping the book into her satchel. 'And, uh . . .'

'Yes?'

'If Rosco comes by—'

'I thought you told him—'

'Yes, but he doesn't listen all that well sometimes.' Mia took a breath. 'Just tell him to check his phone, alright? And maybe that I'm not mad.'

'Should you be?'

'No. And I'm not.'

'Alright then. Don't forget your umbrella.'

By the time Mia reached the hotel that morning, the clouds had begun to peel away from the sky, revealing a clean sheet of pale blue – but not before Mia had been soaked right through.

The hotel met her with the warm, open arms of its golden doors. The ghosts, however, were less than sympathetic.

'You're causing *puddles*,' the Reverend told her. 'And little *rivers*.'

The Bride complained of the weather on her special day, and Blue Dungarees insisted that there was *no work to be done* on a day like that. The Florist was staring out the window as though the world was ending, and the Clown had stopped juggling, opting for listless spinning instead.

Despite their displeasure about the weather, Mia was pleased to find she was making progress with the ghosts in other ways. The Little Girl had started to play a jaunty, chaotic tune on the piano when Mia arrived, instead of hammering out some low droning notes, and the Soldiers had begun to utter one or two actual words instead of general grunts when Mia attempted conversation. The Reverend had even *laughed* the other day when she'd told him a joke about an organist running away with the minister.

'Fiendish!' he had declared through chortles. 'And so very true.'

Better yet was that, as of this week, Mia was finally acquainted with every one of the eighteen ghosts she had spied through the camera lens – and had given them names, too.

The slim blonde lady with a pointed nose was The Gossip because she liked to talk the ears off the other ghosts, and the well-dressed man with the thin moustache, who followed the Lady in the fur coat about, was the Butler.

Mia had called the last one the Florist, though, as with all of the ghosts, she could only guess at what and who they had been in life. He was a tanned, thick-armed young man who'd gained his title when he had made a fuss of fixing a bouquet of flowers Mia had rescued from Granny's bin and brought to the ballroom in an attempt to dress it up.

Today, Mia's offering to the ghosts took the form of an empty wine bottle, swiped from the kitchen's recycling bin.

They clamoured about her, enthralled and elated – all upset from the rain forgotten. Mia passed around glasses, and they tipped back their imaginary drinks. The Singer tasted a full-bodied red, Beverly, or *the Nanny*, the tingle of bubbles, and the Headmaster a sensible port. Blue Dungarees enjoyed his apple cider, and the Little Girl was warned against having any at all, huffing only until she was distracted by the Florist, plinking away at the piano.

With the spirits entertained by their drinks, Mia reached into her satchel for her notebook. She opened it up, cracking the unyielding spine, and wrote *Jim McGowan* in careful script. Then, after a long look, she crossed it out.

She turned to a new page. *Ghost #2,* she wrote, *The English Soldier*.

There were, of course, *three* English soldiers, so Mia scribbled underneath *with a blond moustache and bandaged arm* and then made a face at her work. Her holy text was taking a more juvenile tone than she would have liked.

Did the Bible have first drafts?

She pushed on, describing the soldier as best she could.

Firstly, he was – as far as Mia could tell – the ghost Miss Genie Fitzgerald had come across that afternoon back in September. Moustachioed and male, he was the only one who fit her vague description, and seeing as Cormac was quite convinced there was no possibility it was his father, returned from the ether, this seemed a safe and reasonable (if somewhat disappointing) conclusion.

Secondly, this spectre was perhaps the least friendly of all of the ballroom's residents – followed closely by his two companions. He was yet to reveal any sinister side, but all three of them were often seen trudging about the dance floor, spitting at the feet of their fellow dancers or grumbling bitterly about one thing or another.

Some party, eh? Shame the birds are so damn ugly, Mia might hear them say, or *the beer's shit and the gin's shit and the only way it tastes better is to drink more of it*. It was rarely anything more positive than that.

They were funny, though, she thought, and Blond Moustache had the driest wit of them all. If he cracked a joke, it was with such a deadpan expression it took Mia a moment or two to realise he was actually being funny.

Angry, she wrote. *Always angry*.

Of course, there was only so much one could learn from observation, so, with notebook in hand, Mia approached Blond Moustache.

'Good morning!' she chirped.

He didn't answer, but raked her up and down with unimpressed eyes.

'I'm making a few notes here,' Mia said, lifting her book a little. 'And I wanted to ask you a few questions about . . . Well, your life.'

'Started slow, and ended before it really got going. How's that?'

'Oh,' Mia said, surprised. 'That's . . . uh, great, but . . . Let's start with a name.'

'A name?'

'Yes. Yours, preferably.'

Blond Moustache narrowed his already squinted eyes. 'You don't know my name? Went to battle and shot men so they wouldn't shoot me, lost a brother and a sister, and my mother's at home worried sick every day of her life, and you don't even know my *name*?'

His mouth twitched, his eyes darkening. Mia held her book tight and took a precautionary step backwards.

Blond Moustache did not lose himself to whatever darkness pulled on him, though. He only allowed it to tug on his edges and, with those disconcerting, blurry eyes, leaned close – close enough that Mia should have felt his breath, but there was only cold, cold, cold.

'It's fifteen, forty-two, sixty-eight, five to you.'

Then, he was gone.

Mia scrawled down the numbers. She couldn't let any sliver of information loose to the wind.

She glanced up quickly to make sure that Blond Moustache would resurface – and he did, though a little later than Mia would have liked, and looking as malcontent as ever.

'What have you there?'

Mia jumped, and the pretty ghost at her side giggled.

She was one of the lesser seen spirits – a lady with long brown curls, and childishly wide eyes, who Mia had dubbed *The Writer*. She wore a simple sundress with a cardigan, and could have walked any street in Ballinadrum unnoticed, if she hadn't been dead.

'Well?' the ghost said, and this time, she pointed to the book in Mia's hand. 'Can I see it?'

'Sorry, it's . . . private,' Mia said.

'Oh, a diary. You really ought to be careful about what you write in it, then. Words you say are dangerous enough, you know, and they only live so long as there is anyone to hear them. *Those* words though – they belong to whoever has eyes. Such disloyal things.'

'Well, actually . . . it's not a diary.'

'No? Then why are you holding it like that? Oh . . .' She nodded. 'I understand: it's a *story*. I love to tell stories, too, and I'm just as frightfully shy about them. I wrote maybe a hundred of them, but they never left my bedside table. I didn't even show my mother. You should know, though, you'll regret it someday – keeping it to yourself.'

The ghost reached for the notebook again, and Mia, more curious now, put it in her hand.

The Writer leafed through it faster than any human eye could master a sentence, and laughed raucously from start to end.

Mia reddened. 'What?'

'It's so funny. I love it. You're a wonderful storyteller . . . What was your name, again?'

'Mia. Mia Anne Moran.'

'What a great name for an author. You know, the best authors always have a middle name in print – gives it a bit of self-importance, doesn't it? Although, if I might be so rude, could I . . . ?' She gestured for the pen, and Mia gave her that, too.

The ghost scribbled hastily across the page, although oddly, her eyes did not leave Mia. 'You should do the things you want to do while you still have time to do them – understand? You can't plan for next year because you only have this minute, this hour, this day to get it done, and if you don't – well, what if you don't get a second chance?'

She was writing faster now, more frenzied, and Mia worried about the structural integrity of the plastic ballpoint, pushing harder and harder into the page.

'I'll remember that,' Mia told her gently, and then, all at once, her expression brightened and the ghost handed the notebook back, along with the pen.

'Good,' she said. 'And I wish you luck with your little story.'

She turned away with a wave of curls, and Mia reached out to stop her. 'Could I just get your name?'

The ghost, however, slipped from sight – only to reappear halfway across the room, congratulating the Butcher on his birthday.

Mia opened the notebook. In a crazy scrawl, with looping letters, harsh capitalisations, and no sense of uniformity whatsoever, the words *Rebecca Davies* had been written over, and over, and over again.

Mia turned the page. *Rebecca Davies*, she wrote in her own hand underneath the title of *The Writer*.

Before she closed Donahue's notebook, however, she flicked back to the Writer's page and put a finger to the indents and lines the ghost had carved in the paper. Here was Rebecca Davies, dead but not gone, leaving a trail of who she was only in places where no one might find her.

Then, Mia's fingertip strayed across words that were not *Rebecca Davies*.

He's still here.

The letters were so light, they were almost invisible when compared with the heavy scores of the ghost's name – like a whisper across the page. A secret in ballpoint.

Mia thought of Donahue. She thought of Jim. She thought about all the other ways this ghost could have been trying to communicate with her, and eventually thought, maybe – just maybe – the words didn't mean anything.

Still, she thought, they *seemed* important.

Mia turned the page in her journal. *He's still here*, she wrote, and folded down the corner.

When Mia finally emerged from the ballroom, the hotel had taken on the glinting, golden tones of candlelight and old halogen bulbs.

'Hey, Mia – wanna give us a hand?'

Mia turned to see Sonia, her body tilted to accommodate the large cardboard box balanced on her hip, crossing the lobby towards the lounge.

'With what?' Mia asked.

With a little difficulty, Sonia angled the box so that Mia could lift a flap and see the jewels within: glazed ceramic pumpkins, a clattering of plastic bones, a tangle of purple and black bunting, printed with bats, cats, and stars.

'It's Halloween! Or at least, it will be, when I get this stuff up. Alex is already working on the bar and, let me tell you, that kid has *enthusiasm*. It might upset a few of the regulars, but if it's our last Halloween, I say to hell with anybody who gives us crap for over-decorating – including Cormac.'

'I doubt he'd even notice,' Mia said, though she knew he would.

'So, what do you say – want to string up a few spiderwebs for me?'

'I would, Son, but—'

'Mia!' Gerry called from the doors. 'The fiancé is waiting outside!'

'But that,' Mia said, rolling her eyes with a laugh. 'Maybe tomorrow.'

'Can't tell whether this is a perk of being single or a horrifying reality,' Sonia said. 'Say hi to Rossy for me.'

She wiggled her hips to readjust the box of decorations, before heading to the lounge.

Rosco leaned on the driver's side door, wearing an old denim jacket and pair of beat-up trainers. He looked, she thought, so much cooler than she did.

'Do I win?' he asked. 'Now that I've found you?'

She shouldered her satchel. 'What do you mean?'

'Hide-and-seek?' he said, giving her an unexpected smile. The light from the hotel cast dramatic shadows across his face, and darkened his already dark eyes. 'You're hiding; I'm seeking?'

'I . . . wasn't hiding.'

'Could have fooled me. I mean, when's the last time you took yourself to work, huh? At risk of sounding exceptionally clingy . . .' He leaned in and whispered, 'I missed you.'

A flutter went through Mia, loosening the tight coil of unease she had carried with her all day, in anticipation of the moment she would see him again.

'I missed you, too,' she said.

'So, what's going on? You trying to get a little more exercise in or what? Because I'm telling you, you *look* . . .' He scooped her hips with the hollow of his hands, and she laughed.

'*Quit that.* I just wanted to get in early, and you don't work until eight, so—'

'You know I'll take you whatever time you need, Mia.'

She raised her eyebrows dramatically. 'At the cost of your precious ten hours in bed? I could never.'

'Well, I could,' he said. 'Unless it's not about that.'

'What else would it be about?'

He opened her door, and she got in.

'I *think*,' he said, taking his own seat behind the wheel, 'it's about the other day. At The Burning Lamp. I didn't mean to hurt your feelings, you know.'

'Oh,' Mia said, a little taken aback. 'Well, I . . . I'm okay. I guess I don't like you thinking I'm crazy.'

'Yeah, I was probably too . . . direct – I'm sorry. I know how sensitive you can be about the hotel, and . . . Look, I could have been nicer. That's what I'm trying to say.'

Mia nodded slowly. 'And the ghosts . . .'

'I think we've had enough of ghosts,' he said, and laughed.

She felt her shoulders sink back into the seat.

'So, how about we swing by my house, huh? I know it's a little late, but Mum's been wanting to see you – something about a new venue she was looking at – and maybe we could watch another episode of something? That dumb alien thing seemed okay.'

Mia considered her words carefully, and decided on a light tone. 'How many baby photos am I allowed to comment on?'

'As many as you like,' he said, taking his eyes off the road just long enough to shoot her a wink. 'I'm feeling generous.'

chapter 19
an unfamiliar problem

OVERNIGHT, THE HOTEL WAS DRESSED in its seasonal colours. The front desk now sported garlands of autumn leaves and a wearied, plastic skeleton head, filled with glittering chocolate coins, and the bowl of hydrangeas at the lobby's heart had been removed in favour of a collection of orange, white, and yellow pumpkins.

Even the lift had been victim to Sonia's zealous decorating, and when the doors closed in front of Mia, she looked like an oversized fly caught in the web strung up behind her.

The ballroom went untouched.

'You look terrible,' the Reverend announced as Mia joined the dancers. 'In fact, it looks as though you may have been out *partying*. And *drinking*.'

She thought it peculiar he could fathom a difference in her appearance at all, but there was nothing *un*-peculiar about the ghosts on any given day, so she just rolled her eyes and said, 'Trust me, I was doing nothing of the sort.'

'Do tell.'

'I was reading late. How's that?'

'A lie,' he said.

'No, it's not,' she retorted – and it really wasn't. Not entirely, anyway.

She *had* been out late with Rosco – her dream of cheesy chip and an evening at the Buckley house finally realised – but after he had left her home, she had not slipped straight off to bed as she may have ordinarily done. Instead, she had stayed up for a few extra hours – combing through the scribbles inside her leather notebook, reassessing the ghosts' nonsensical ramblings by soft lamplight.

She put Blond Moustache's numbers through a search engine. She ran *Rebecca Davies* through a dozen genealogy websites. She made note of the Lady's complaints, and underlined the most plausible stories the Gossip had divulged in the last few days.

Any one of them could have been significant, she reasoned, though equally, any and all of it could have been utter rubbish. It was impossible to say – just yet anyway.

'Well, if you were *not* out drinking *or* dancing *or* anything *worse*, I must advise you to rest more often. As a young woman of God, you ought not even give your neighbours the *inkling* that you are capable of such things – such is your duty as a reflection of Christ. What would the children think, and *your grandmother*, and – Miss Moran, *are you listening*?'

When Mia had asked Granny what she could recall of the late Reverend Plunkett, she recounted a similar picture to the one Mia already had: a prickly man who had only gotten pricklier with age. Amongst the numerous instances of his cantankerousness, Granny could distinctly recall him falling out with the church's insurance provider, favoured florist, grass cutter, a door-to-door salesman and, on one particularly ridiculous occasion, a parishioner who had used a novelty stamp when writing to their local politician.

Therefore, Mia knew if there was one ghost she should probably not wind up, it was the Reverend – but her headache was bright and her patience thin.

'Doesn't the post office close soon?' she asked.

The Reverend Plunkett's face dropped at once. He made a beeline past her, wringing his hands and muttering, 'It can't be, can it? I'll miss it again. *Again*.'

As he walked, his feet began to slip through the floor. His edges became blurred and insubstantial, and Mia – with a whispered *oh no* – dashed after him.

'Reverend,' she said. 'The children were reorganising the Sunday School cupboard. If you'd like to come this way, I can show you their—'

At once, the ghost stopped. He turned with a thunderous expression, and then marched straight past her. 'They don't understand the order,' he was saying. 'And everything will be sticky, and—'

She watched him long enough to see him become distracted by the Bride's fluttering edges, and slow to his usual measured pace.

Crisis averted, she took her camera and raised it to the scene – a task she now did so often throughout the day, the lens was sometimes already in front of her eye before she even realised.

The Singer lingered at her ear. 'What have you there?'

'A camera,' Mia answered.

'No, not that. *That*.'

Mia glanced down at the notebook tucked under her arm. 'Oh, a list,' she said. 'Of people the hotel still needs to pay. Could I check your name?'

'Syvita,' the ghost said warily. 'Syvita Green.'

Mia cracked her notebook open and wrote the name down under *Ghost #8 The Singer*. 'Well, there you are. You're on the list.'

The ghost's expression clouded. 'Oh. I could have sworn I'd been paid already.'

'Well, you mustn't have because it's in this little book, so don't worry about it. Actually, if you want to tell me about—'

'You have that on paper?' The ghost's face grew a little darker, her eyes a little murkier. 'It wasn't my idea, you know. I live nearby but it doesn't mean I know what goes on in the hotel, okay?'

'Of course not, I never said—'

'I've played this bar a hundred and one times. It was so kind of him to let me. It was so kind and I—'

'Syvita,' Mia said firmly. 'Syvita Green.'

At once, the bleariness in her eyes evaporated and with piercing clarity, she looked at Mia and said, 'He's still here.'

Then, she was gone.

He's still here.

Mia watched for the Singer to resurface on the ballroom's floor, and, as Syvita Green took a seat at the piano, she withdrew her notebook, and flicked back through her work.

She turned to the Writer's section, and the folded down page.

He's still here.

But what did it mean? That the ghosts were capable of repeating themselves, or each other, or – and Mia was careful not to hope too dangerously – that these seemingly silly, nonsensical beings were actually trying to tell her something?

Looking out at the ballroom again and its flickering dancers, she could not help but repeat the Singer's words in her head, and think of Donahue Eagan Byrnes.

He's still here.

She took out her camera – snapped another photo, did another count.

The Cowboy swayed at her shoulder, daring her to guess his name, and Nanny Beverly began to shout about the price of drinks, and that quiet little Writer sighed by the window. The rest of the silent smudges of light were steady in the digital screen of her camera.

Nineteen, she counted.

Nineteen, she recounted.

Mia looked between the dance floor and the camera, to the big double doors and that little door in the rear, and then back into the camera, where she counted the ghosts once again. It was then that she knew she had to acknowledge – with dizzying concern – she had an unfamiliar problem.

There was one ghost too many.

He's still here.

Her first thought was that Jim had not disappeared from the hotel as she had believed, but then, she reasoned, where had he been all this time? And she hadn't seen him in *so* long, either, which was entirely out of character for him – even though a ghost's character was fickle at best.

No, it was more likely to be someone new – someone she hadn't met yet. Or perhaps even someone she *had* met, and was yet to be reacquainted with.

Her mind circled moustaches, and old hoteliers.

She waited and watched, but no new face appeared before her. Mia snapped another photograph, counting once again, *nineteen* ghosts, and watched while the Bride spun in circles, and the Florist made conversation with the Butler, and Blue Dungarees sized up the room like it was still a work in progress.

Where are you?

And more concerningly still: *who* are you?

*

'What are you writing?'

Mia jumped at the voice, hands flying over the notebook in front of her.

The barman's grin was tilted like it was snagged on a hook. He did not withdraw.

Alex was eighteen with a head of rumpled blond hair and a charming air of cluelessness. It was no secret that he had only applied for the job of barman in a bid to meet pretty girls, and it was also public knowledge that the ratio of pretty girls to old, gruff patrons of the male persuasion had deeply disappointed hm.

Mia had rather hoped taking a seat in one of the bar's booths would have been enough to win some privacy, but perhaps that was too much to ask in a largely unoccupied room. It was still too early for the majority of the regulars to find their seats, and so it was mostly filled – that is, perhaps only a quarter – by hotel guests exploring the limited offerings of their accommodation.

'I didn't know you wrote stories, Mia.'

'I don't, I'm not—' She took a breath. 'I'm copying out *someone else's* story if you must know. I was asked to.'

Specifically, it was a dead woman's story, but Alex didn't need to know that. The Writer had been relaying all sorts of imaginings that day, and Mia, ever the hoarder of ghostly conversations, was trying to piece together her meandering plot – if there was one at all.

'I'd work on a better excuse if you don't want people asking about your stories.'

'It's not *my*—'

'Anyway, you seem a little tense. Would it help if I gave you a little discount on our new Halloween range . . . ?'

He pointed to the chalkboard next to him, which had been cleared of the regular drink specials in favour of Halloween-ified versions.

'Come on, Mia, you know I hate pulling draughts and that's all anybody in here ever drinks. Get a piña ghoul-ada, please? I never get to use the fun syrups.'

'Stop preying on the weak, Alex. You know there's only so many times Mia will say no to you.'

A familiar face took the seat next to her.

'*Ruby*.' Alex's face brightened. 'Fancy trying a strawberry *drac*-iri, or maybe a *poison* appletini?'

'Can't: still on the job. Got fifteen minutes, and I doubt your measures would have me heading back to the kitchens in any fit state.' Ruby turned her attention to Mia. '*You*, my friend, are a hard girl to track down these days. Where has Cormac got you squirrelled away?'

'In the walls, mostly, if I'm very good. Bad girls get the laundry chute.'

'I'd lock them in Mr Murphy's room myself, but each dictator to their own. Now, tell me this . . . How *close* would you say you and Mr Cormac Byrnes are these days?'

Mia stared at her friend.

'See, I've elected myself the head of the committee to get this year's Halloween party on the calendar, and thought

I would come to *you* as the next best thing to talking to Cormac himself.'

'No,' Mia said. 'I'm not the next best thing. Dialling *Hell* might put you in contact with someone a little closer.'

'Hey, that would be a cool cocktail name – *Dialling Hell*,' Alex told them. 'Something like a Bloody Mary with some spice, you know? A few chilli flakes, a shot of sriracha . . .'

Ruby ignored him. 'Look, I know it's not a compliment, but you're pretty much Cormac's right-hand lady. Henry doesn't even know what he's up to half the time – and *hates* it, I might add – so I'm *requesting* you, as the person who at least *sees* him on a regular basis, mention this party to him.'

'No,' Mia said again.

Ruby sidled closer. 'Look: you know how things are going well with Hugh at the moment?'

'Go on.'

'*Well*, I was talking to him earlier, about the decorations and the little pumpkins and *blablabla*. And then we talked costumes, Mia. Couple costumes. I don't know how it came about but he said, and I *swear to you*, he said that we should pair up for a costume this year – *if* it's happening.'

'That's what he said, huh?'

'*Gospel*.'

'Let me get this straight then: you want me to ask *Cormac*, who hates the hotel and everything in it, whether he will hang on to it long enough for us to have a *party* so that my best friend can maybe, possibly, do a couple's costume with the man she's been stalking for the better part of a year?'

'More like a year and a half. But yes.' And then added, before Mia could argue further, 'And if not for me, then for the overall *morale* of the hotel. People are dropping like flies around here.'

'Excuse me?'

'Well, not *flies*, but Becky's gone. And Tim left this morning.'

'What?' Mia breathed. '*Why?*'

Ruby shrugged. 'Job security, I guess. Can't blame them, really.'

Mia let out a long breath. It seemed unfair that the hotel should begin to fall apart from within while the building itself still stood.

First the owner, now the staff.

'Fine,' she said. 'I'll ask him.'

Ruby beamed. 'Oh, you won't regret it, Mia, honestly. It'll be a night to remember if we manage to pull it off! Imagine it – me and you and our girl Sonia, up there on the wall of riotous evenings held in this fine establishment, however long it may stand!'

Ruby pointed up to the collage of frames behind the bar. Old men shared pints around the familiar booths, and couples danced about the tiled floor, and in one particular shot, the barkeeper looked on in horror as a pair of ladies kicked up their feet on his bar. Elsewhere, Donahue, sober as a judge, learned a cancan dance from a trio of revellers.

'It's nice he's still here,' Ruby said, mostly to Mia. 'In a way.'

Mia looked up at the photographs and felt the hairs on her arms lift. 'Yes,' she replied. 'Very nice.'

It was then, staring up at Donahue, that her gaze snagged on another photograph.

'Alex,' she called suddenly. 'Can I see that picture?'

He looked over his shoulder. 'Which one?'

'That . . . See the one with the three old guys, and the silly hat in the middle? Yeah, that one. Give it here, will you?'

Alex, ever obedient, lifted it down and handed it to her.

'You alright?' Ruby asked, as Mia turned the picture over to fight with the pins that held it all together.

Mia didn't answer, but instead pulled the picture free of its frame, turned it over and read the scratchy handwritten names.

Johnson Cottony. Eric McGiver. Trevor Shields. July 1972.

'How'd you know that would be there?' Ruby asked.

Mia stared down at the names, committed them to memory, and then turned the photograph over again. Across the years, held in aged ink, her yellow-haired Cowboy grinned up at her.

'Donahue always wrote on the back.'

'You know one of them, then?'

'No. Not really.'

'So, what's the fascination?'

'Oh, I just thought . . .' Mia replaced the photograph's frame. 'I thought I did.'

Ruby shook her head. 'All that work with Cormac's got you a bit loony, Mia, my love.'

'And all that chasing Hugh McDermott's done the same for you, Ruby, my dear.'

'That's love for you,' Ruby said and she pressed a luminous lipstick stain to Mia's cheek. 'Though I'd have thought you knew that already.'

chapter 20
predator

BALLINADRUM HOTEL WAS WELL-USED to regulars. It knew the one-night-stay stopovers and the gentle to-the-country escapees.

The couple which entered its golden doors, today, however, were difficult to place – at least, as far as Mia was concerned.

They looked ordinary enough, save for their large back-packs, stamped with brightly coloured patches. In all likelihood, Ballinadrum was just a stopover town for them. They would probably be gone by the morning, Mia thought as she glided through the lobby, off in the direction of some bigger, brighter town.

But then the woman said to Sonia at the front desk, 'For the week.'

Mia took a second glance. No one spent more than a few days in Ballinadrum Hotel, especially not those as young or adventurous-looking as this pair.

'Never,' Mia could hear Sonia tell them. 'But I'll let you know if that changes.'

Whatever the topic of conversation was, the two laughed good-naturedly, before taking their keys and cutting ahead of Mia to the lift.

Mia hopped in before the doors closed.

It was the woman who spoke first.

'Say,' she said as though already in the middle of a conversation, 'you work here, right?'

Mia folded her hands in front of her. 'Yes.'

There was a charged look between the couple, before the man asked her, 'And have you ever . . . seen any ghosts?'

'Ghosts?'

'Yes, spirits. We read that this place was *especially* haunted, and, well, we've been to *lots* of haunted hotels, but we've never actually seen anything. We're hoping this will be our first real encounter.'

Mia picked out the woman's accent then: a little lower than her own, a little rounder. Scotland, she believed, though no notion as to whereabouts.

'Where did you read that?' she asked.

'Oh, this website,' the woman went on, reaching into her back pocket for her phone. 'I don't know if you're into the supernatural, but it's the best if you want up-to-date information on hot spots.'

'Hot spots,' Mia repeated softly.

The woman swiped at her phone and then passed it to Mia. On her screen was the familiar grey text of *GhostHuntHub.com* – and in the corner, a white counter that told Mia that she was the nine thousand and sixty-seventh person to see it.

That was four thousand more than when she last checked.

'You came here,' she said, 'for this?'

'For the ghosts,' the man said cheerfully.

The lift pinged as it reached the third floor, and Mia gratefully disembarked.

If only they knew, she thought to herself, where she was headed now.

She took extra care to check over both shoulders before she slipped through the passageway.

In the ballroom, she made the ghosts her offering.

They declined.

'But—' Mia began to reason, before recalling what a fruitless exercise it would be.

Instead, she returned the packet to her satchel with a sheepish apology and more disappointment than she cared to say – because, in her opinion at the very least, they were *good* biscuits. They had scalloped edges, a chocolate cream centre, and, best of all, *real* sugar and calories and crunch – unlike the empty jars, tins and cake stands she normally collected for the ghosts.

That, and she remembered that Donahue Byrnes, in life, had very much enjoyed this particular brand.

'My singular vice,' he had named them. 'Sweet, chocolatey temptations.'

And yet . . .

'Watching my waist,' the Gossip said.

'Don't like chocolate,' the Little Girl announced.

'Not time for breaks today,' was Blue Dungarees' excuse.

It wasn't about the biscuits, of course – not really. Not entirely. It was – as most things were these days – about Donahue.

But then, what had she really anticipated? That Donahue Byrnes would materialise from the ether, dead but not gone, to grab a handful of biscuits, saying *I haven't had one of these in months*?

The answer, of course, was *yes*.

But that was a silliness she couldn't indulge this morning. Instead, Mia withdrew a few sheets of music from her satchel and handed them out to the ghosts with varying degrees of success. The Bride admired her invitations, and the Headmaster reviewed the latest test scores. The Butler considered an important piece of correspondence, and the Florist twisted it into an origami rose.

Entertained by paper *and not biscuits*, Mia thought with bafflement. These ghosts really were *not* to be understood.

So, rather than try, she just counted them – first, by faces, and then, by photographs – and as she tallied up the small white dots, she realised something rather odd.

There were only eighteen ghosts to be counted.

There was no additional, mysterious nineteenth spirit.

Mia didn't know how to feel – had the mystery of her nineteenth ghost reconciled itself before she even had a chance to unravel it? Surely, that was a good thing, and fewer questions were better than more, but then there was that ever-hovering possibility of Donahue and all the hope she had gathered into a few chocolate biscuits and . . .

Then, she realised it.

The Cowboy. He wasn't here – and he really should have been. He never passed up an opportunity to ask Mia to dance, or offer up some eyeroll-inducing remark, particularly when she had some sort of gift for all of them.

But from what Mia could see – and from what her camera told her – he was simply . . .

Gone.

Was that it? she thought, hardly daring to believe it could be so simple. Had it been the picture, which he had wanted taken down from the bar, or perhaps for someone to take notice of – or had it been his name, finally learned and no longer a game?

She didn't even know which of the three names was his. She had been planning on asking him today.

But then, didn't that mean . . .

Mia pulled her camera from her pocket and looked at the picture she had taken earlier, the dots strung up beside one another: eighteen, in total.

Yet no Cowboy.

Looking at the photograph now, Mia thought perhaps this strange white spot, which had distanced itself from the others as though trying to keep out of frame, might be a better fit for that mystery nineteenth ghost – or rather, *eighteenth* now.

He's still here, the ghosts had told her. *He's still here*, Mia still hoped silently.

She opened her notebook and flicked to the Cowboy's page so she might update it, but the music sheets had, seemingly, lost their lustre, and the Writer was now at her elbow, launching into a daring tale of pirates off the coast of South Africa, and the Gossip, too, had begun her usual, 'Did you know . . . ?'

Both, however, were chased from her side when the Reverend appeared.

'It's late,' he announced with doomsday gravity. 'It's very, very late.'

Mia recovered herself. 'I'm sure it's not,' she said. 'The post office stays open late on Tuesdays.'

'Too late,' the Reverend said. 'Too late for the post office entirely.'

'Well, if you say so. You could . . . always go tomorrow? If it's a letter, of course, you could always just drop it into a post box. I have stamps if you need them.'

Mia did not have stamps, but she had little squares of paper, torn from her notebook. They were much the same – to her ghosts anyway.

'No,' he said. 'Don't go near it.'

'Okay. I won't.'

'I said leave it. Leave it be now.'

His voice rose and Mia drew back, checking his eyes for shadows. He seemed rather present, but all at once, took off across the ballroom, faster than she had ever seen him do so in life.

The other ghosts paid him no mind, but Mia's heart leapt as she saw him reach the other side of the ballroom and then cross straight through the wall.

She was off like a shot.

It's fine, she told herself, *it's just some storage space, some old lockers*. But there was no knowing where he might go next.

'Reverend!' she called. 'I'm sorry!'

She opened the door with a tug. It was stiff and swollen and, from within, a great breath of cold, dank air poured out.

'Reverend?' she called again. 'I . . . I need to ask you an important question. It's about my . . . um, salvation?'

She took out her phone and shone a light into the darkness to reveal peeling wallpaper and a once-handsome sofa left to mildew, mould, and the teeth of vermin. It was a sad sight compared to the ballroom, which had retained at least some of its grandeur with its tall columns and pearly floor.

'I'm doubting,' Mia told the darkness. 'And thinking maybe Catholicism is a better choice for me.'

She was met with silence, endless and thick.

'I didn't tithe last Sunday, and I'm not sure I will next week.'

No answer again.

'I'm having sex,' she said, and then, there was a terrific rustling from further down the hall.

'Paul clearly writes in Corinthians chapter six,' came a sharp voice, 'that you must flee sexual temptation *for thine body is a temple . . .*'

The Reverend may not have revealed himself, but the ongoing lecture was enough to relieve Mia of her fears that he had run off to torment the hotel's guests and staff. She didn't even have to keep him talking – the ghost managed that all by himself – and she stepped lightly into the forgotten space.

A figure passed the corner of Mia's eye. Or at least, she thought it did.

She spun to find it, but the white light of her phone found nothing but walls.

And then footsteps – footsteps running by her.

A door slammed up ahead. Mia's heart jumped, and she pressed a hand to her chest with a tiny shriek caught there. Following the sound – deeper into the dark, unfortunately – she came to the door. It was faded and worn but otherwise in good shape.

She took the handle and was shocked by just how cold it felt in her grip. A shiver ran right through her.

'Reverend?' she said, opening the door.

Her phone lit not another room as she had anticipated but a single staircase, tall and narrow and leading to a second door, just a little further up. It was a tight space, all muggy air and endless shadow. It was cold too, so much colder than the ballroom ever was, and something deep within her told Mia this was as far as she should go.

But, if the Reverend was up there . . .

She put a foot forward, and then he appeared.

It was not the Reverend as she had expected. It wasn't even the Cowboy.

Instead, three or four steps up the staircase, stood a tall, thin man dressed in a suit not unlike Cormac's. His dark hair was slicked back, almost wet-looking in the harsh torchlight, and he did not look down at her, but kept his head tilted upwards so she could only see the razor-sharp angle of his jaw and the pale expanse of his throat.

It was *not* Donahue.

Mia couldn't help it. Disappointment caught her in the gut.

He really wasn't coming back.

She took a sharp breath – there was no time for self-pity – put on a smile, and said, 'Excuse me. I don't believe we've met. My name is Mia and I work here at the hotel.'

At her voice, the man before her seemed to thaw to life – if you could call it that, of course. One hand flexed long, thin fingers, while the other held something, she thought.

'Have you been at the hotel long? I could . . . take your name, if you'd like?'

Mia took another step, and the man's head snapped down, revealing his face. She stumbled backwards.

The ghost did not wear a human expression. Rather, like Jim before him, his hooded eyes were impossibly dark, all jet-black ink, and his mouth, too, made her wince. It was pulled into some too-wide, too-thin shape – a grin perhaps, if it didn't look so terrible.

But ghosts like this could still be talked to, Mia told herself. They could be talked down from whatever height they were scaling.

'Is there anything I can help you with?' she asked, though the sound of her voice made her feel she was breaking twigs underfoot in a forest in which she was prey, and the predator . . . The predator was a nameless thing she couldn't quite trust.

'I don't know much about you, but I'm sure I could do something for you, or you could tell me a little bit about why you're here, and—'

The ghost roared. With jaw unhinged and teeth bared, a terrible sound escaped its animal mouth, and at the very same time, the wallpaper on either side of the staircase was ripped away.

Mia staggered backwards as it fell in ribbons about her, and tripped. She dropped her phone, too, and it skidded across the carpet, the light flashing across the room.

She didn't know if she was hurt just yet, but her heart was pounding, and her head was screaming, and there was nothing more she wanted or needed to do in that second but get out of that hallway and *fast*.

She did not stop for her phone. She scrambled to her feet and took off running.

Crashing through the door to the ballroom, she was met with the unperturbed faces of the other ghosts and a rush of warmth she knew couldn't truly be *heat* but just a lesser cold. Only there did she slow.

She turned back – and realised, suddenly, that the hotel was shaking. It was shaking with the noise of this creature, and it sounded like a storm battering the roof, a wind trying to dismantle the brickwork.

The spirit appeared in the doorway.

It did not step inside, though, but stood on the threshold, wearing that same not-grin, and watching her with those bruised-black eyes.

Mia turned as quickly as she could, almost too hastily for her clumsy feet. She fled through the hidden passageway and onto the third floor, knowing she had to find Cormac, to tell him what was happening – to ask him *what to do.*

She did not make it to his office, however. She found him in the lift.

'What the hell,' he breathed, eyes wide with alarm, 'is going on up here?'

chapter 21
all of his life

CORMAC MADE TEA. IT should have been most surprising that he would volunteer to do so, but Mia was more transfixed by the secret mini fridge stashed under his office desk.

'Milk?' he asked. 'Sugar?'

He pulled both from inside the fridge, and then went to a cabinet, where he lifted out two white cups, and a teaspoon – obviously borrowed from the kitchens and never returned.

Mia, sitting – or rather perched – on the sole chair in the room, Cormac's high-backed office chair, nodded. 'I didn't think you took them.'

'Took what?'

She gestured to the desk upon which he doled out the milk and sugar to not one, but both cups, and he looked at his hands as if they had acted of their own volition.

'Yes, well, not usually, but in times of stress, I have heard it can be . . . relaxing, and . . . Alright, okay, you caught me. I like it, alright? How's that?'

He took a noisy, defiant slurp of his tea, before leaning back onto his desk and staring at Mia.

'It's going to take some talking to convince the guests it was a freak wind, you know. It's too good a day for nonsense like that to be going on.'

'Do they . . . always do that?'

'What?'

'Shake the place,' she said hesitantly.

He frowned at her. 'They make their feelings known, and sometimes, the only way to communicate, in a rogue ghost's opinion, is to . . . shake things, yes, but also strip wallpaper, shred carpets, break things. They can cut the electric if they really feel like it.'

He had named it *the Rogue ghost* almost immediately after Mia had described it to him, as though it was part of some hidden ghost manual. More likely, she thought, was that Donahue had coined the term.

'Did you ever . . . see that happen?' she asked.

Cormac was quiet for a moment. 'I saw a lot of things when I was small. Often, I recall, lights going out on perfectly still nights, and I would go to my father's room, only to find he was not there. He would be with them. I would know then they were upset in some manner – in need of his care. As they require yours, now.'

'But they don't *all* do that. I've never . . .'

The memory of Jim McGowan, eyes dark and lost and unfamiliar, resurfaced in her head, and she remembered how the floorboards creaked with his cries.

'When they're rogue, they'll do anything. They're unpredictable, destructive. They'd bring the whole place down if they really wanted to.'

'You said that they could be dangerous. I thought you meant more dangerous . . . to the hotel – its reputation. I didn't think . . .'

'In truth, I didn't want you to think it. I didn't want you to . . .'

'Run screaming out the front door?'

'Something like that.'

'But they don't . . . hurt people, do they?'

Cormac paused. 'They can do. I've seen it. Not that they necessarily *mean* to . . . but you know what they're like. Confused. Unruly—'

Mia thought on this. 'Your father?' she asked.

'What about him?'

'Did they hurt him?'

'No, not him. It was never him,' Cormac said in a brusque tone. 'Only other people. People who didn't deserve it.'

'How do you . . . fix them?' Mia asked.

'I don't know. I mean . . . Look, Mia Anne, I helped my father with his work for quite a short time of my life. Now, after being raised around ghosts and all the other things my father subjected us to, I know *some* things.

'But by the time I was ten years old, my father didn't want me to be part of the ballroom anymore. I won't get into it, but there was . . . an incident. He thought it was too dangerous for me, and for the hotel, and everything around that time was . . .' Cormac winced. 'It was unpleasant. I was not asked back to the ballroom for many years, by which time, I had no desire to be part of it. What you need to understand is I have not stepped foot in that ballroom since I was . . . My, since I was fourteen years old, Mia Anne, which means if you are looking for help with your *task*, then I'm afraid you will find my advice of very little value.'

Mia looked across the room to him. She wondered, then, whether this had anything to do with those stories Gerry had been telling – of Donahue falling out with Cormac. She decided not to ask.

'I didn't know that,' she said instead.

'Well, don't go spreading it around.'

'I'm quite good with secrets.'

'I've noticed,' he said with the faintest of smiles. 'But we've got away from the point of this. Your rogue. Can you describe him for me, again? He was dressed in a suit, correct?'

'With a crest,' Mia said. 'On the right-hand side. I couldn't see the detail, but it was definitely purple.'

'In the sixties they had a slightly different uniform here. I mean, they got rid of it reasonably quickly, as it was too formal, but . . . Well, you know what I'm saying.'

Cormac's fraying edges were beginning to unsettle Mia. She had run to him hoping to find that ice-cold figure, the one who would *nonsense* this and *idiotic* that, rather than take it as seriously as she feared it was.

Instead, he had wanted to go back – immediately. Mia was less enthusiastic, so Cormac had suggested she go downstairs and wait for him, but that hadn't felt like an option either. Not when the hotel needed her.

The ghosts had been unhappy. The Reverend had reappeared and had never wanted to visit the post office more; the Headmaster had demanded to see the accounts for the school; the Bride was spinning in circles and wailing it wasn't her fault; and none of them would stay visible for long. They flitted in and out of sight, mere flickers of light across the dull room.

Mia and Cormac had crossed into the rear hallway, up the stairs and into the room the Rogue had blocked before.

It had not reappeared.

Instead, they found a small room with a low ceiling and lines of lockers against the walls, which Mia assumed had once been a coat or staff room before the west wing had closed. In the centre, there was a stack of boxes, and when Cormac lifted a flap of one, they had discovered forgotten fur coats and old, musty-smelling curtains and sheets.

No ghost. Nothing out of the ordinary, in fact.

Mia had reclaimed her phone, settled the ghosts as best she could, and then she and Cormac had gone to his office.

'He was holding something,' she said to Cormac now. 'I never saw what it was.'

'Well, do any of your ghosts carry . . . a wallet? A pen?'

'I . . . I'm not sure. I've . . . never seen *that* one.'

'Never seen it? But you have all your nicknames picked out. The Bride, the Baker, the . . . what was it a – Blue Jeans?'

'Dungarees. But that one, the Rogue . . . it only appeared on the photographs recently. It's new, or . . . was hiding.'

Cormac stilled. 'How recently?'

'A few days ago. I was going to tell you, but I didn't think it made a difference. The deal was the deal and—'

'Show me,' Cormac said, and Mia obediently clicked her camera on to reveal the image.

'What the hell is this?' he asked.

'Those are the ghosts and—'

'No, the metallic relic. *This* is what you've been using?'

Mia flushed. 'I . . . It's all—'

'Forget it. Explain what's happening here.' His finger hovered over the screen, too disgusted to actually touch it. 'Why is it so far from the others?'

The glowing spot he pointed to hovered in the corner of the image, while the others, crushed together to be on the other side.

'I don't know,' Mia said.

'And you didn't get a name? Any other identifiers?'

'Dark hair, dark eyes – but then, they all have dark eyes when they're upset. That, and I know now . . .'

'You know what?'

'That it's not him,' she said.

'Excuse me?'

'I half-thought it might have been . . . Donahue.'

Cormac pulled away.

'But I figured it couldn't be,' Mia went on, 'not now, after so much time and . . . After today, I know it isn't. He would never try to hurt me. He would never hurt anyone.'

There was a crispness to Cormac's movements as he strode across the room. He turned back to face her. 'How much do you know about my father, exactly?'

Mia, unsure of his tone, answered, 'Lots of things. I know his birthday, and that he was born in Ballinadrum, and went to our church. And . . . his stories.'

'Is that all?'

'Well, there was . . . He liked two sugars in his coffee. And silly ties, but only if they were gifts. His favourite kind of music was country, but he pretended it was something classier instead. And he polished his shoes before bed, but never on a Sunday, and he liked summer better than winter, but Christmas better than any other time of the year.'

There were myriad other things she could have added, but her throat was tight, and her headache had resurfaced.

'He loved hydrangeas,' she said softly. 'And when I was small, I thought he was a wizard. I think I needed a wizard when I was small.'

Cormac looked at her steadily. 'Quite the list.'

'I've known him all of my life.'

'Ah, but not all of *his* life.' Cormac Byrnes fixed her with a cold look. 'Do you know what *I* remember?'

Mia looked at him, waiting.

'Donahue Eagan Byrnes the second,' he said, 'had nightmares which woke him at least two to three nights a week. When he woke, he drank a glass of milk, followed by a glass of water. He was not quiet about it. He was not quiet about anything. If he wanted to do something, he told you, but never to ask permission. It was a warning.

'Before I could read, he wanted me to mind dead people. He wanted me to make conversation with soldiers who should have been quiet in their graves, but instead traversed this damned hotel like it was the only place to be.'

Mia struggled to keep her expression plain and smooth.

'He spent nights chasing them through these hallways, trying to gather them together so they wouldn't frighten hotel guests. His son, though, was to be subjected to their everyday horrors, as was his wife. Neither were to complain.

'He had two real friends, as far as I knew. Neither of them was family, nor did they hang around too long. Mystery as to why, you might say, but . . . you're right about the coffee, Mia. I remember that, too.'

His eyes searched her face, as though he were curious about his talent for turning her skin splotched and red, for wringing emotion out of her with just a few sharp flicks of his tongue. There was no penitence, though, or if there was, Mia didn't see it. There were just two cold blue eyes and a scratch of a mouth.

'Don't sit there and tell me that that man didn't have it in him to hurt people. He hurt *plenty* of people, Mia Anne. You just weren't around to see it.'

Mia rose from her seat in a hurry, sloshing the tea as she set it down on his desk. She turned away from him before he could see her tears, and when she slipped through the door, he did not call her back.

chapter 22
speculation

WHEN MIA FINALLY ARRIVED HOME, hours after she had anticipated, she went to bed, visions of ghosts dancing behind her eyes. She didn't know for sure how well they would behave overnight, but she had done what she could for now – whispering to them until they were still enough to photograph, playing a few tinkling tunes on the piano to encourage at least one or two of them to dance.

They had seemed as wary as children listening to a thunderstorm.

Besides, if any of them needed her help, she reasoned while changing into her pyjamas, Cormac would phone her. And for now, *she* needed sleep.

Except sleep wouldn't come.

Cormac's words were crows come to roost in Mia's head. They pecked her with delight in the dim of her bedroom, and she let them, turning the moment in her mind over and over again just as she turned on her pillow.

He hurt plenty of people, Mia Anne.

Which people? She found herself wondering. Who? Other than Cormac, she had never known anyone who actually *knew* Donahue Byrnes to have less than a shining opinion of him.

Yet to believe Cormac was to accept there was more to Donahue than even Mia may have realised. There was the Donahue of her day, of course, the one who had told her a thousand and one tales of impossible heroes and dastardly beasts, but there was a Donahue before that – perhaps multiple Donahues.

Much like those unread books, untouched in the little library amongst the hydrangeas, there were volumes to him she had never been allowed to read.

Mia left in the pre-dawn light, nibbling a flapjack on her way, unwrapping it with cold, reluctant fingers, and thinking of hot tea in the hotel's kitchens – the staff cooking up spiced scones and nutmeg-scented cakes for the day ahead, and laying out honeyed porridge for guests with early-morning plans.

And Cormac, somewhere in the building. Drinking coffee. Talking on the phone.

She knew she wouldn't stop by his office that morning, nor that afternoon. In fact, she made her way to the hotel with the intention of not seeing Cormac Byrnes even once that day if she could help it.

But she couldn't.

He was already on the third floor when she arrived. She caught him arms crossed, brow furrowed, mid-pace, as though he were waiting for her. Except, when their eyes met, he did not look relieved.

'I heard noises.'

She looked at him, her hurt from the evening before still there, but side-lined by the immediacy of this problem. Unease swallowed her.

'Just now?' she asked. 'You didn't call.'

'It was only an hour ago, and then it stopped. It was . . . laughing.'

'Oh,' Mia said, her anxiety uncoiling ever so slightly. It wasn't that laughing was *good* – any ghostly sounds heard around the main hotel were obviously unwanted, but laughter was better than crying, or shouting, or *appearing*. 'I'll . . . handle it.'

'Yes. Good.'

He was, all at once, speeding past her, and before she could decide exactly what she was going to say, she said, 'Mr Byrnes, about yesterday—'

Whether he had heard her or not, Mia did not know for sure. What she *was* sure about, however, was she had not whispered, and that Cormac Byrnes did not slow. He pushed through the purple stained glass without hesitation, and did not wait for the lift, either.

*

Mia didn't work out which of the ghosts had been laughing. Perhaps it was the Little Girl again, running amuck in the early light before heading back to her piano, or maybe the Gossip, overhearing some particularly interesting scandal in the employee locker room, and then drifting homeward to the ballroom, where she might spread it around.

Maybe it was the Rogue.

Or maybe, Mia considered, there hadn't been any laughter at all, but a paranoid Cormac Byrnes waking in the night with a racing heart.

But this was all speculation, and while speculating was a large part of Mia's process, she knew unwavering *fact* had to come into play at some point, if she was to do anything of value. So, she counted her ghosts, and found eighteen glowing safely in the confines of the digital camera's screen, and she spoke to them – in low, calming tones, and jovial singsong, and sometimes, where necessary, strict instructions.

The Reverend asked about the post office, and Mia offered him a strip of real stamps. With measured slowness, he peeled them from their adhesive paper, and then, just carefully, replaced them, only to repeat the process again.

The Bride was still insisting that *none of it* was her fault, and Mia agreed wholeheartedly, before playing what she could remember of the bridal chorus – the chords of which she had looked up. This brought the Bride in line, and then, to Mia's surprise, the Soldiers joined her, lifting knees high and swinging arms.

Mia offered them ginger nuts and custard creams and scones. She brought candles, and the Florist leapt through the flames with gleeful abandon, while the Butler advised Mia on the correct way to extinguish a candle without upsetting the melted wax.

And all was fine – if it wasn't for that back door, and the threat of a nineteenth figure entering this soft-lit space at any moment. If it wasn't for Mia's pained heart, and the questions that still tumbled about there.

That night, she left on time. She did not call by Cormac's office, and when she arrived at the hotel at a brighter hour the next morning, he was not waiting outside the ballroom.

She told herself it was how she wanted it, but could offer no explanation for the sinking in her chest except that it felt like a bad thing.

And four days later, though she had hoped otherwise, she realised her feeling was right.

*

It was a blustery start when Mia arrived at the hotel. The avenue's trees had turned yellow and brown, and their lost leaves blew right through, chittering when they caught along the walls and steps and hard places around the hotel.

The lobby, too, seemed whipped up by the seasonal wind. It was jumbled and uncomfortable, with too many bodies – a far cry from the usual sleepy greeting Mia received from the old building – and her first thoughts were of her ghosts.

'What's going on?' she asked Sonia, just as someone from housekeeping dodged past her.

'The electric went out,' Sonia said, hardly looking up from her computer screen. She appeared to be firing off frantic emails. 'Or at least, the electric for the refrigerators. Not sure for how long, and all the food . . .'

'Oh no.'

'Henry's beside himself, of course, and everyone's in a flurry – but don't you worry, Mia. I've already texted Ruby.' She finally looked up, and surprisingly, grinned. 'I've asked her to keep the best stuff for us. I mean, how bad can a chocolate gateau get overnight?'

Mia didn't know what to say so she laughed.

Really, she wanted to apologise, but didn't know how. It's not that she had left the ballroom in terrible disorder – the ghosts had been in fine form, actually, compared to a few days prior – but an unexpected power cut seemed rather . . . ghostly.

She turned to find Henry, looking more flustered than usual. His top button was undone, and his ginger hair looked as if he had raked his fingers through it too many times.

'Mia!' he said. 'I wasn't expecting you until later.'

'I like getting a head start. Can I . . . help at all?'

'How are your plumbing skills?'

Both Mia and Sonia looked at him quizzically.

'Oh,' he said with morose sarcasm. 'You didn't hear? There's a leak in the dining room now, too. It's been the morning from Hell, ladies – *Hell*. And the plumber I called was meant to be here by now but apparently, he's gotten lost somewhere enroute and – *Gerry*, I said a *bucket*, that's a coal bin.'

Henry supressed a sigh and turned back to her.

'As you can see, Mia, I'm frightfully busy at the moment, but give me ten – no, *twenty* minutes and I'll show you to the records room.'

He began to march off, and Mia gave chase.

'The records room?' she questioned, in step with him.

'Yes, Mr Byrnes instructed me to give you access – said you had some research to do or something? Bit of a fact-finding mission, I believe – *Leslie*, no dilly-dallying, please. Is that correct?'

It took her a moment to realise he was speaking to her again. 'Oh,' she said. 'Yes, that's right. That would be . . . Well, that would be great, actually.'

'Okay, great, and remember – while Mr Byrnes is gone, I'll be your acting manager so if you need *anything*—'

'Gone?'

'Yes, last night.' He slowed. 'You look surprised.'

Surprised felt like a milder word for the bruise-like feeling this news inspired.

'I am,' Mia said. 'Did he . . . say where he was going?'

'England, I believe, for a few days or so, although he wasn't too forthcoming with his return date. He didn't mention it to you?'

'No. He didn't.'

At last, Henry came to a stop, frowning. He took a quick glance at the lobby about him, and then said in a lower tone, 'Don't take it personally. He tells me nothing, and I'm the manager.'

'I guess so,' Mia said.

'And to be truthful with you, Mia . . . what he does with the hotel isn't down to us, as much as we try. I know you're doing your best for this old place, and Donahue would be proud of you.'

But which Donahue? Mia wanted to ask. The Donahue of fairy dens and ghostly ballrooms, or the Donahue who seemed to have raised a son who hated him?

*

Mia had never seen the records office before.

Unfortunately, it was a dull room – decidedly porridge-coloured – and in the places where it failed to be dull, it was dank, with speckles of mould gathered in corners, or displayed quite unashamedly across the patchy ceiling. The fire escape sign threw a ghastly green about the place, and the low bulb overhead did little to counteract it.

There was no need to dress it up, Mia figured, if no one got to see it, and yet, there was some part of her that felt immense disappointment at the sight. Surely, it should have been a dragon's nest, or a glittering aquamarine cove.

'Did Mr Byrnes say what you should look for?' Henry asked. 'Perhaps I might be able to point you in the right direction, because as you can see, there is *quite* a large collection of information here . . .'

'No,' Mia said. 'I'll just make a start . . . somewhere.'

'Oh, well . . . That's very brave of you. Now, he said you had your own key – is that correct?'

Without thinking, she put a hand to her chest. 'I didn't know it opened this room.'

'Apparently, it opens most rooms. Now, if there's nothing else you need . . . I suppose I'll leave you to it? Are you sure you don't need any help with this?'

Mia was *not* sure, but assured Henry she didn't – yet when the door was closed and there was no pale daylight to lend a hand to the dim light bulb in forcing back that sickly green, she dashed out after him.

'Did you need something?' Henry asked.

'No,' she said. 'Well, yes, I'm going back but—'

She crossed the lobby to the new bouquet of hydrangeas at its centre, plucked a few and then turned back to Henry, 'I thought it needed a little more Donahue first.'

There was a soft knock at Mia's door, followed by insistent scratching.

'Yeah?'

Handsome Boy's nose pressed through the crack, and Granny Brea entered with a beam of light. She was dressed in a pastel pink cardigan and her throat shimmered with a string of pearls. 'You're up late,' she said.

'No later than you,' Mia teased. 'How was Margaret's?'

'Marigold's,' Granny corrected. 'You ought to know their names by now, Mia Anne.'

'I do. Mostly. There's just so many of them, and they all talk at once.'

Granny gave a soft laugh. 'Well, just because I'm up, doesn't mean you ought to be. *I* get to sleep the day away if I should please – and I just might tomorrow. *You*, on the other hand, don't have that luxury. Now, what's keeping you awake tonight anyway?'

Mia looked down at the files scattered across her bed. 'Cormac let me into the records room.'

'Did he? What for?'

'Oh, just to have a look through the history of the place. You know, marketing stuff.'

'Is that what you are now – a marketer?'

'I'm an assistant.'

'And assistants do these things, do they?'

Mia pressed her lips together. 'Yes.'

'This late at night? At home?'

'*I* do. I'm . . . interested in it.'

Without invitation, Granny Brea came to sit amongst the files. Handsome Boy followed and rested his head heavily on her knee.

'The forties,' she said, fingers and eyes passing over the papers. 'A long time ago. Are you looking for something in particular?'

'Just . . . exciting things, I guess. Don't suppose you recall anything?'

'I was just about born, if that helps.'

'Mm,' Mia said. 'Might need a little more than that.'

'Well, what do you want to know? It was wartime, you know. The hotel wasn't even a hotel.'

'I know. I'd like to learn more about the soldiers who died there – stayed there, I mean. It seems sad that we know so little about them. And I have these numbers . . . They're not phone numbers, or postcodes, or alphabetical codes – they're something else . . .'

'How many numbers?'

'Eight.'

'Might be a service number.'

'Is that a thing?'

Granny laughed softly. 'Yes, it's a *thing*. During the war, all soldiers were given a unique number – made keeping track of them easier apparently. Suppose you might have a dozen or more John Smiths or something like that.'

'Seems a bit . . . cold, though.'

'Does it?'

'I mean, not to be given your actual name.'

Granny gave Mia a quizzical look, so Mia pushed on.

'Are these all recorded still? Like, online?'

'You can search them, I think,' Granny replied. 'Myrtle's daughter is awfully interested in family trees – she searches things like that, I think.'

Mia nodded thoughtfully, and Granny tilted her head.

'You've never been interested in history before.'

'Well, Cormac asked me to do it. He mentioned there might be something on Donahue and the old hotel, you know?'

'Oh.' Granny's face softened, and she reached out to tap Mia's chin. 'I see what this is about.'

'What?'

'Donahue.'

'No,' Mia told her firmly. 'It's work stuff. Cormac asked me—'

'To have a look through decades-old files and ask your grandmother about decades-old people?' She raised an eyebrow sympathetically. 'We all have our own ways, you know. When your daddy . . . Well, I didn't think I'd ever recover, and I spent an age looking at old photos and things he'd left lying around like they were the most important things in the world.'

Mia could not remember those days well, but she did recall the box of expired cereal stashed at the back of the cupboard that Granny had forbidden her to eat, and the bag of clothes that had been on its way to the charity shop for eight years now. There were a dozen or more crime thriller books in the bookcase, which she nor Granny had ever read, but still retained folded down pages and the odd splash of coffee.

'But I think you should be careful, Mia. I know you loved Donahue. He loved you too and I'm not sure he would want you to . . . ignore your own life. He was so excited to hear you were getting married, wasn't he?'

Mia thought back to that day – an ordinary Tuesday, wet and cloudy. Donahue had filled the entire lobby with his laughter, with his being.

'Mia Anne, you couldn't possibly be getting married. You have to be at least eighteen and I am under no illusion that you are any more than thirteen. I myself am only sixty-one, you see, so there is no deceiving me.'

'And,' Granny continued, 'I would imagine a bride-to-be sitting up late to look at veils, or bands, or the weather predictions for her special day, not . . .' she gestured to the scattered files ' . . .doing whatever it is assistants do late at night.'

'I suppose you're right,' Mia said quietly.

But when Granny had gone, and the dog had followed her out, and Mia was alone again, she didn't push the files off her bed in favour of sleep. She drew them close, instead, and read them even more fervently – pulling out new pages, jotting down inky notes.

Trying to tie strings to passing clouds.

chapter 23
faithful murmurs

A FEW DAYS LATER, Mia warmed her hands on a to-go coffee and looked out the passenger side's window.

'It's nice, isn't it?' she said.

'Yeah,' Rosco replied, leaning forward so that he might rest his hand on her thigh and get a better look at the House. 'For now.'

Mia laughed. 'Don't tell me you're already thinking of moving.'

'I'm only thinking of practicalities. Where would you put the nursery?'

'Oh, now you *really* are thinking ahead.'

There was no reason to visit the House, really, other than to look at it and confirm it was just as tall, narrow, and vaguely unattractive as the last time they had been, but that was fine. It was enough, Mia thought, to know it was there – that their future still stood.

Today, specifically, it stood behind a thin veil of fog, which had snaked through the town the night before. It gave the House a faded effect – like one of Mia's poorly printed photographs, a memory before it had even begun.

Rosco tugged on Mia's arm and pressed a kiss to her head. 'Aren't you thinking it, too?'

'I guess so,' she lied.

In truth, Mia was thinking about ghosts – about whether she had been right to leave them so she might come here with Rosco . . . and if any of them had begun wandering in her absence.

It would be her own fault if they did, of course. This trip to the House had been her suggestion – a peace offering, something to say when she'd climbed into his car that morning to smooth over the argument they'd had the night before.

'It's bound to be lonely without us,' she had told him, coaxing him into a smile. 'And I can hardly remember what colour the front door is.'

The argument had been petty enough that this small suggestion had worked. It had been the same old thing, in Mia's opinion: Rosco had phoned, and Mia had been less than attentive. She had ignored his texts. She didn't have time for him.

She was always somewhere else.

That latter part was, at least, somewhat true. Last night she had been in Ballinadrum Hotel circa nineteen sixty-five – thanks to the bundle of files she had yet again brought home with her.

The evening had slipped into night while she read through staff lists and the like, so she might have a comprehensive list of everybody who had worn the Rogue's nineteen sixties uniform.

Through her search, she had stumbled upon the name *Kelsey Cunningham*, recorded among the otherwise uninteresting details of yet another wedding hosted by the hotel. She had known the Bride at once by the date – April seventh – because the Bride herself had referred to it on more than a few occasions.

Mia had copied the hard-won name into her leather journal with relish.

She had read on at speed and it was then that the second revelation had – literally – fallen into her lap: a slight, fluttery thing, not unlike a dream.

It was an incident report, detailing the theft of a painting from the hotel. Specifically, it was a rather expensive piece of artwork entitled *The Field by Our House*, valued between six and ten thousand pounds.

The figure alone had been enough to surprise Mia, but what truly arrested her was the name of the supposed thief: Owen Buckley.

Olive's Owen Buckley.

She had copied the rest of the details down with haste, including the name *Francis Croft* – the person who had reported the apparent crime. Mia had whispered it under her breath, quite liking how it hushed in her mouth, before searching out other incidents from that same year.

She had duly found a report dated August nineteen sixty-nine in which a Maria Buckley, aged eight, had experienced an asthma attack, and needed an ambulance to collect her.

Mia wrote this down too, puzzling at the relationship between Owen and Maria – father and daughter, perhaps? Then she began to scour the rest of the documents for other mentions of Buckleys she might added to her extending puzzle picture.

There, she had found Owen's staff number and the dates he had worked at the hotel. He very well could have worn that nineteen sixties uniform.

And then, Rosco had called.

She had tried to tell him about the painting, because at the very least, that was something interesting and truthful, wasn't it? And maybe he would know more about Owen and this *Field By Our House*, seeing as it was his own family embroiled in the situation, but he had been flat with her. He said he didn't want to talk about *hotel stuff* anymore. She said it wasn't just *hotel stuff* – it was history, and family, and Ballinadrum itself. But it hadn't mattered. They had argued anyway.

Now, though, Rosco smiled. They talked about paint colours and plumbers, duvet togs and lampshades. He kissed her head and her fingers, and told her he hoped that their children would have her blue eyes and his tanned skin.

This was how it should be, she thought. This was who they were, who they were supposed to be. All she had to do was find balance: Rosco and the hotel.

Rosco and everything else.

'We better get going,' Mia told him, glancing at the car clock. 'Or I'll be late.'

'You could always skip it,' he said, a hand gliding behind her ear. 'I don't even know why you want to go. You've never gone to the prayer meeting before.'

'It's for Granny,' she lied. 'She'd like me there.'

'And I'd like you here. Or at home. If she's away, we can—'

'I told Granny I'd be there. I can't lie to her.'

Rosco rolled his eyes and plugged the keys into the ignition, starting the car. 'You always have to be so *good*, Mia.'

As they took to the road, Mia pulled out her phone to check her emails for any updates on ghostly enquiries, and then *GhostHuntHub.com*'s page on Ballinadrum Hotel.

It was strangely addictive to refresh the page and check if any new comments had appeared:

Anonymous: NEXT VACATION DESTINATION FOR SUUUURE.

MarjBarj: Does anyone know if this place is REALLY haunted? Not wasting my money again.

DerekJ: @LindaJ – Halloween next year? Spooky!

Anonymous: What a place. Would love to visit.

Apparently, the trend of ghost-hunter check-ins was still a thing, and Mia was conflicted. On one hand, these visitors seemed a little too curious – exploratory and nosey. That didn't pair well with a secret ballroom full of ghosts.

On the other, though, it was hard to be too resentful of them – not when they were so positive about the hotel. And any bookings at all were better than none when faced with this recent wave of fearful cancellations.

'Do you have to do that?'

Mia looked up from her phone. 'Oh, sorry. It's only quick.'

'What is it?'

His tone caught her. 'Sorry, it's nothing—'

'No, really, what is it? I want to know.'

She stumbled over her explanation. 'Henry sent me a meal plan from a wedding in the twenties. He wanted to know whether Cormac would want to see it for . . . marketing things.'

'Then he should ask him himself.'

'But I'm his assistant.'

'Right,' Rosco said. 'Fine.'

'Did I . . . do something?'

She looked into his face, and its hard lines where there had been a soft smile just minutes ago, and cursed her phone, her hands, *GhostHuntHub.com* and how fascinating she found it.

'No,' he told her, but she knew she had.

They rode the rest of the way across town in silence.

The car rolled up onto the kerb outside Ballinadrum Presbyterian Church. It had a high pointed fence and even taller gates, which were propped open for the weekly prayer meeting, the light from inside the church giving it an other-worldly air through the fog.

It was mostly elderly ladies who climbed out of their cars now, greeting each other with jovial smiles, and the minister, Reverend Rainey, who welcomed them at the doors.

'Are you really sure you want to go to this?' Rosco asked.

It wasn't the first time he had asked this today, and if Mia revealed even a hint of reluctance, she had a feeling it wouldn't be the last.

'Already promised Granny,' she said, and kissed him goodbye.

Inside the square grey house of God, the heating was on full blast, and Mia promptly shrugged out of her chunky dogtooth cardigan. In the back hall, a small circle of seven worshippers gathered upon plastic school chairs.

Granny Brea stood to welcome her. 'I didn't know you were coming!'

'Took a notion,' Mia said, sitting opposite her. 'How was choir practice?'

'Angelic, if I should say so myself.'

The ladies on either side of Granny tittered and then began to gossip about the funeral they had attended at the weekend, until the Reverend Rainey closed the doors and called the meeting to a start in his deep, booming voice. 'Let us pray.'

With all eyes closed, Mia counted down thirty seconds, and then got up.

Out in the hall, she made her way to the connecting doors between the extension and the main church building, and thanked the Lord above when she found them unlocked.

The church was exceptionally quiet, as though the stone walls leeched the sound right out of the air, and Mia hoped that she was right. It was a chance, really, as all things were with the ghosts, but given how agitated the Reverend had been today, she considered it a rather likely chance.

'I'm going to be late,' he had said. 'The post office will close soon if I don't get there in time and . . .'

'It's okay,' Mia had said. 'It'll be open long enough. There's no need to rush.'

'Rush where?'

'Well . . . the post office. You needed to go to the post office, didn't you?'

'No,' he had snapped. 'I don't. I never did.'

'I'm sorry—'

'And don't you go looking. I'll do it myself. I just . . . I just don't have the time.'

'Well, I've actually taken care of it. You don't even need to go.'

She had hoped this would reassure him, but instead, the Reverend had turned on her with ferocity and pain in his shadowed eyes. '*How dare you read it?*'

'I didn't,' she had insisted. 'I didn't even open it.'

And then, he had calmed down. 'It's only that . . . Was it not hidden? Did you look in the pews? Is that where you found it? I could have sworn . . . ?'

He had begun to fade then, his thoughtful look sending him further into the nothingness of the air, and while Mia had tried to take hold of his elbow and keep him with her, keep him talking, he had already gone.

It had taken fifty seconds exactly for him to reappear across the room, and when he did, he looked as stern and sensible as ever, asking the passing Florist, 'Where do you think you go when you die?'

Mia might have laughed at his obstinance to have an honest conversation about his own afterlife if it was not so frustrating. He had told her enough, though – enough for her to make an excuse to get to church that evening; and enough to go creeping through the silent, unused pews in search of a mysterious letter.

She found a lot of gum. She found discarded song sheets, a tiny toy car, and a couple of pens, but just between the pulpit, raised up on high, and the very first pew, she also found the smallest of gaps. It was just a sliver of space, big enough for something like a letter – if you knew it was there at all.

And Mia did know, or at least, had good reason to believe.

She used the pen she had found to dig where her fingers could not go, and when it came up against something, she angled the pen in such a way that she might inch it out, little by little.

It took a frustrating length of time – time Mia wasn't sure she had. The Reverend Rainey was an enthusiastic prayer, and the ladies from choir were not shy about taking their time with thanksgiving and requests either, but Granny was never home any later than a half hour after it began.

She wiggled the pen more hastily, and then, with a heart-stopping feeling, she felt whatever was stuck come free, revealing itself as a white envelope.

She gasped audibly, and held it up in front of her.

Elliot Curran, it read, followed by an address not too far from Ballinadrum. Mia did not know any Currans and she flipped the letter over, inspecting the unbroken seal.

The smallest *x* was placed in the topmost corner.

Mia put the letter into her pocket. It would be posted the next morning by first class stamp and whoever needed to read it, would, and those it *wasn't* intended for would never see its contents – including, tempting though it was, Mia.

She left the church and the pews and the silence and returned to the heat and faithful murmurs of the back hall.

Sidestepping into the circle of chairs, Mia closed her eyes and nodded along to one woman's petition for good weather, good health and for Mr Bell to return to church after ten years away.

The Reverend Rainey finished the prayer in less than a minute, and Mia shivered with relief that she had made it back without anyone being any the wiser.

chapter 24
lost property

MIA WAS ONLY VAGUELY AWARE of the sounds around her: a fridge door opening and closing, cutlery clattering together, laughter louder for the otherwise quiet.

'Did you see Lorna earlier? New coat, new shoes – and the *heel* on them, Sonia.'

'I *did* see her. How could I not? That coat was *luminous*.'

'She looked happy, though. Happiest in years.'

'The bakery must be doing better than I thought.'

'How about you, Mia? Did you get a look at the new and improved Lorna McGowan?'

Mia had not. She had been, as always, hidden away in the secret ballroom of Ballinadrum Hotel.

Her day had been difficult.

The Little Girl had screamed about how dark it was until the bricks began to shudder, and Mia had to light six additional candelabras to even distract her from her crying. The Headmaster had been rubbing his hands like Macbeth's wife and would stop for nothing – not even a question about the school he had cared for so long.

In fact, all of the ghosts had seemed that bit more agitated than usual – though what was *usual* for ghosts was probably not that usual at all. But Mia felt she knew them well enough to know there was something . . . strange going on.

She had wondered whether the Rogue was back, but when she consulted her photographs, he could not be found.

So what *was* it?

'Must have missed her,' Mia told her friends now.

'You miss everything these days,' Ruby said.

Sonia hit her with a spoon. 'Don't be rude. She's working hard. Now, Mia, seeing as you haven't made the last couple of late-night luncheons, you get to pick. Pumpkin spice or strawberry?'

Mia glanced to the large open fridge, now humming and cold once more after their unexpected outage. As Sonia had hoped, the cakes inside were too far gone by serving standards, but perfectly fine for hungry, night-time staff.

Mia wondered if ghosts liked cheesecake.

'Pumpkin,' she said.

Ruby pulled the cinnamon-dusted cheesecake out of the fridge. The mock-cream swirls had sunken like snowmen in March, but it was otherwise fine, and Ruby handed spoons to her friends.

'A toast,' she said, 'To a Cormac-less Ballinadrum Hotel, for however long it lasts.'

'Ballinadrum Hotel or the Cormac-less-ness?' Sonia asked.

'Both,' Ruby told her, and they clinked spoons.

'What do you think he's gone back to do?' Sonia asked. 'I would have thought he'd have the place sold by now, with that man, Gurning, in and out the last few weeks.'

'Gurning?' Mia said. 'The bits guy?'

'Oh yeah. Comes in for tea and a biscuit, has a look around – never checks in. Maybe Cormac's doing all his business over the phone these days.'

'Henry says nothing's gone through officially,' Ruby said. 'And he'd be the first to know. But whatever business Cormac's doing, I'm just glad he's eased up on our poor Mia. When was the last time you got a break, my love?'

'Oh, I . . . I don't mind,' Mia said.

'Well, you should. You're supposed to be planning a wedding and you're spending more time here than ever,' Ruby said. 'Come to think of it, have you even got your venue sorted?'

'Going this weekend,' Mia said. 'Think it's going to be Hillwood Hall.'

'Oh, that's *lovely*,' Sonia said. 'Lily and I were there for Pappy's sixtieth not that long ago. Try the goat's cheese balls if you can. *So good*.'

'And what about the dress?' Ruby asked.

'Ehh . . .'

She gasped. '*Mia Moran*, you haven't got your *dress*? You know these bridal boutiques can take like nine months to get the bloody things brought in and altered.'

'She doesn't need a bridal boutique,' Sonia said. 'They're all pomp and frills and jacked-up prices.'

'Pomp and frills is *all* a wedding is, Sonia! Remove that and what do you have?'

'A commitment between two people who love each other, witnessed by a collection of friends and family?' Mia suggested.

'God, Mia, you're no craic. Just promise me you'll try a boutique, okay? I don't want you just . . . heading off to some charity shop or Lost Property box, and slipping into someone else's wedding day, you hear me?'

Mia's thoughts caught on the idea of wearing Kelsey Cunningham's dress. Where was it now, she wondered; up in an attic, forgotten? Burned on a bonfire after the marriage went south, or indeed, lying in a Lost Property box somewhere unexpected?

'Hey, Ballinadrum's got a Lost Property box, doesn't it?'

Ruby nearly choked. 'Mia, *what* did I just say?'

'No, not for the dress – just for . . . I'm doing a research thing.'

'If it's for Cormac, forget about it. He's taking time off, so you should, too.'

'But there *is* a Lost Property box, isn't there?'

'Yeah,' Sonia said. 'Henry's in charge of it – like a well-organised dragon sitting on a hoard of crap.'

There was a crash across the room.

All three women spun to face it.

'This place is falling apart!' Ruby cried, hands to chest. 'Is that another thing to replace?'

The clock had fallen from the wall, and was now lying on the floor – face shattered, wooden surrounds cracked.

Its golden hands were the only things that had been spared.

Mia was the first to reach it. She crouched, and lifted the clock's broken body.

'I think so,' she said.

'You know,' Sonia said. '*That* was spooky.'

Mia agreed.

*

Mia did not like it, but she could not deny that she was getting good at lying. For a worthy cause, *of course*, but lying all the same.

Today, she was lying to Henry – and, more specifically, about why she wanted to rifle through the hotel's Lost Property cupboard.

Henry turned from his computer screen with a dubious expression. 'Marketing purposes?'

'Yeah. Cormac thought there might be some old photograph or maybe an old diary left lying around and it could be a good . . . story for the hotel.'

'*Cormac* did?'

'Yes. He texted me. Very briefly.'

If she feared that Henry would have probed this utterly fictitious conversation further, she needn't have. 'Well, if it's *marketing* he's looking for,' he said, turning back to his computer. 'I actually already have a few ideas – some notes on similar hotels and their strategies and . . .'

'And the Lost Property?' Mia reminded him gently.

It was another few minutes before she could tear Henry away from the newly loaded series of spreadsheets and images displayed on his screen, but tear him away she did, and soon, she was looking at the most untidy, disorganised, and chaotically uncategorised space she had ever come across within Ballinadrum Hotel.

Henry *had* warned her, of course – more than three times, in fact – but she thought he was just being Henry. Instead, what she found – tucked away in a corner of the basement – was a cupboard that looked as though it had only ever been opened long enough to cram some other misplaced item inside.

But Mia had high hopes for such forgotten things.

With a bulletproof sense of determination, she pushed and dragged the boxes along the floor to the lift, one at a time – occasionally drawing the attention of those passing through the lobby. At one point, Ruby appeared and insisted on helping, despite Mia's best efforts to assure her she was fine. She was spared only when one of the waiters emerged from the dining hall, waving his hands.

'Broken?' Ruby repeated. 'The entire table?'

'Right in two!' he said. 'And the whole afternoon tea set in the middle of it!'

As she watched her friend retreat to the dining room, Mia considered going with her, to see this broken table for herself, and deduce whether its demise had supernatural causes. But, really, she already knew.

The ghosts had been unfortunately unsettled as of late, and she could not help but notice their impact on the hotel around them. She had taken more time with them, been especially careful with her words and questions, and yet to little avail. A broken *something* did not come as a surprise to Mia.

Sighing, she shoved the boxes from Lost Property into the lift, and then pushed them along the third floor to the secret passageway. There, she stacked them in piles, and once the collection was complete, moved them with infuriating slowness to the ballroom.

It was more strenuous exercise than Mia had done perhaps *ever*, and the whole process took an hour. The ghosts, at least, seemed pleased by the new arrivals.

'This is *disgusting*,' the Bride announced, waltzing about in a misshapen knitted vest, while the Nanny picked over a tall stack of magazines and the Little Girl twirled a collection of bracelets and necklaces into impossible knots.

Old coats were kicked here and there, purses flung over shoulders, wallets rifled through, books opened and closed and, in some cases, torn. Hairbrushes. Clips. Half-used hand creams and plastic water bottles. A set of pale grinning dentures and a jar of unidentified pills – neither of which Mia wanted to investigate further.

She imagined Donahue here with her, and the stories he would spin. He would probably say something like every single item on display had dropped out of a dream, or another world, or been bargained for by a mysterious stranger, and that he had refused to part with a single piece, lest anything fall into the wrong hands – all while dusting his face with an old make-up brush and brandishing the ugly *Kiss Me I'm Irish* mug.

If Cormac was here, she could imagine a scoff and a roll of the eyes.

How many are left? is all he would say, she thought.

Today, though, Mia was quite interested in this question too, and not just the general emotional wellbeing of her ballroom occupants. As she looked about, she kept a special eye out for two ghosts in particular: the Writer and, of course, the Reverend.

In Mia's compilation of the Writer's short tales, a vague, shimmering thread of continuity – a theme of regret and disappointment – had at last emerged. *Ballroom Imaginings*, she had entitled the collection when she had typed it out and published it on an open submissions board under the name *Rebecca Davies.* It had gotten a few 'hearts' and a comment or two in the first few hours it was live, and then notifications had gone quiet as new submissions pushed it off the first page.

Mia had feared this lack of attention would have rendered the exercise fruitless. However, whether her work found fame didn't seem to have bothered the Writer. It seemed to be enough that it had been released – and thus, so had she.

There was no sign of the Reverend either, not since Mia had posted his letter, and the camera consistently totalled fifteen dots of white. It wasn't bulletproof evidence, but it was as close as Mia ever got with her ghosts.

She made marks by each of their names in her notebook – she had a good feeling that she would not be seeing either of them again.

Just then, one of the Soldiers, Blond Moustache, approached Mia, wearing his usual scowl.

'This,' he said, lifting a pocket-sized tin case and holding it out so that Mia could see, 'shouldn't be here.'

It had been plucked from a pile of other metallic goods – shrapnel, tag-less ball chains, coins – and was not an item she had expected anyone to find issue with.

Mia tried to assure him it was, indeed, supposed to be here, but he wouldn't have it, so she tried something different.

'John Cooney,' she said.

It was not a question nor an accusation, but simply his name – returned through the majesty of the internet from a genealogy website that had, as Granny had foretold, recognised his service number.

Now there was a true possibility it was being spoken aloud for the very first time this century.

The Soldier cocked his head, but his eyes were clear and focused when they moved from Mia and back to the tin box. He opened it as though it held a collection of butterflies, slow and slight, and Mia leaned forward so she might catch a glimpse of what he thought so important.

All at once, he snapped the box shut and drifted across the room.

Typical, she thought. What else would she have expected of Blond Moustache but more difficulty?

Despite this, Mia felt she was finally making progress. The other night, after trawling various local primary schools' webpages searching for information on past staff, she had, to her delight, discovered the Headmaster smiling up from an old staff photograph on the website of the sixth school she had tried: *Barrymore Primary School*. And just yesterday, Mia had learned, by playing a fraught game of Eye-Spy, the Little Girl's name was Anna Loughran – and while her *ghost* was a child, in life she'd grown up, married, and had children of her own.

Mia lifted one of the many stuffed animals that had been squashed into disfigurement from their years in their boxes. 'What do you think *this* one's name is?'

The Little Girl screwed up her nose at the felt monkey. 'He looks nasty.'

'Well, how about this one?' Mia lifted a scruffy bear. 'He's smiling.'

'Only for show.'

'And this one?'

'I don't like dogs.' The Little Girl's eyes flitted upon the box of other stuffed animals. 'I like cats, though. And cats should always be somewhere sunny. He looks *so* sad in that box, doesn't he?'

Mia looked upon the heap of playthings. 'A cat, you say? I don't see any cats.'

'I *know* there's a cat. A teddy-bear cat.'

Mia reached into the box. 'Well, in that case, I'm sure we could find . . . something . . .'

Arm deep in a tunnel of fuzzy bodies, Mia was not expecting her hand to brush anything hard or cold. She jerked backwards, and then, after laughing at her own nervousness, sought out the item once more.

With a little prodding, she finally took hold of it and pulled it into the daylight.

It was a folded frame, no bigger than the size of her hand. Granny had a few scattered about the house, often with a smaller Mia, chubby and cherub-like, as the subject – but unlike those, which Granny regularly dusted, this was tarnished and vaguely yellowed.

Mia worked at the stiff catch to flip it open.

Twin boys looked up at her in dreary black and white, or rather, the same small skinny child was pictured in both halves of the folding frame, neither looking particularly happy to be there at all.

Whoever he was, he had sunken eyes and white tufty hair, and was drowned in a large sports sweatshirt. His ears, by contrast to the rest of his minute features, were comically large, which Mia might have had a giggle about, if he didn't already look painfully aware of them.

He must have been ten or twelve, no more than thirteen, when the picture was taken.

Mia glanced up from the picture to her remaining ghosts. There were no little boys among the dancers, but that was not to say this little boy had not grown into one of the ballroom's occupants. That being said, though, the clothing was too modern for it to be any of the Soldiers, and even though age may have changed his face, none of his features resembled those of the Headmaster, Blue Dungarees, or the Butler.

Yet Mia was sure she had seen this person before. There was some familiarity to those narrowed eyes, the pinched mouth . . .

She almost dropped the frame altogether.

Mia Anne Moran took a second look at this young Cormac Byrnes. She had heard enough in recent days about the child Cormac had been – nervous, quiet – but she still felt ill-prepared for physical evidence that he had not simply emerged, already grey and jaded, from some distant dark portal.

Mia tried to imagine him with Donahue, walking hand in hand throughout the hotel's hallways, but failed.

She thought, instead, of this boy – this Cormac – discovering the strange and unsettling creatures of the ballroom for the first time. She thought of him watching their eyes darken and their mouths blur as the room around him got colder, and of him waking in the night to find that his father was not sleeping next door where he had hoped to find him.

The image took shape too easily, and Mia snapped the frame closed.

'What have you there?'

'Oh, just a . . .' Mia dropped the pictures back into the box of stuffed animals. 'Silly old thing. What about you – what's that?'

The Nanny grinned darkly and held out a handful of old mottled coins. 'I'm buying tonight at the bar. Are you going?'

'Which bar?'

'Ballinadrum's, obviously.'

Mia looked her over. 'You meet many people there?'

'I know a Gerry Finnerty who spends a lot of time around the old place.'

'*You* know a Gerry Finnerty? *I* know Gerry Finnerty.'

'Works the doors? About . . . *this* height, green eyes?'

'Yes!' Mia could hardly keep the excitement from her voice.

'You might even say I know him *biblically*.' The Nanny tipped her head back and laughed, and a blush reddened Mia's cheeks.

'But you know these country boy sorts . . . *ditherers*. Won't tell you yes and won't tell you no – just string you out as long as you like. Although, I can't say I made it easy on them either. Think I must have scared them off a little, you know, but yeah, he was the one to get away, I'm telling you. Quite the bombshell.'

'Bombshell,' Mia repeated, and a smile warmed her face. This was, perhaps, the third or fourth time she had heard the Nanny use this particular phrase and it felt so near to the reason the Nanny was here at all, Mia could hardly bear it.

She grabbed her notebook and began to scribble.

'Think I'll head out to the bar, though, now,' the Nanny went on. 'This place is kind of dead.'

'You think so?' Mia asked, eyes still on her pen. 'I thought it was just getting started.'

'Maybe. But if I go to Ballinadrum, I always get a free drink – on account of knowing the owner.'

Mia stopped writing. 'Donahue – Donahue Byrnes?'

'Of course. We play cards most Friday nights down at the bar, and I'll have you know I've beaten him at blackjack more times than I can count.'

'And was there . . . Did you . . . Who else played cards with you?'

'Oh, just boys from about town. This *enormous* woman, too, with arms like tree trunks and—'

'Any Owens?'

The ghost's gaze lit upon her. 'Who's Owens?'

'Owen Buckley. I heard he was close to Donahue and—'

'Didn't know any Owens. Don't know what you're talking about.'

'Oh.' Mia should have known not to get her hopes too high. 'How about Francis Croft?'

This time the ghost narrowed her eyes. 'Why are you talking so much?'

'I'm sorry—'

'You're always talking – just talking, talking, talking—'

'I didn't mean to pry, I just wanted to—'

The ghost rounded on her suddenly, leering so close it struck Mia how real she looked. There were pores on her skin, and purple bruising under her tired eyes. Spit gathered at the corners of her sharp angular lips.

She waited for Mia to finish.

'To know about *The Field by Our House.*'

The mean smile she wore opened into a look of surprise – like Mia had reached out and slapped her.

The hotel shuddered.

Mia stood, clinging to the key through her shirt. It was over in an instant, but the cold still lingered, and when Mia turned around, she found the Nanny gone, and the Little Girl was no longer digging amongst the teddies and lost things, but standing, hands outstretched.

'Teddy-cat,' she said, and resting in her open palms was just that.

The toy was matted and faded, and its ears were folded flat after years of confinement, but it was still obviously a cat. It had two glassy eyes and a wriggle of a tail, and even one fine nylon whisker, sprouting in the shadow of its tarnished pink nose.

Mia cast a look about the ballroom, searching for the Nanny, waiting for her to reappear. The seconds mounted up, her unease coiling tighter, and then – *there*. The Nanny marched briskly through the centre of the dance floor, splitting some partners and distracting others. She seemed . . . unhappy, but *present*, and that was enough for now.

Mia returned her attention to the Little Girl.

‘He seems like a very nice cat,’ she said. ‘How did you know he was there?’

‘Because he’s *my cat*,’ was the ghost’s answer. ‘He was always my cat – until . . .’

‘Yes?’

‘Until I left him at the hotel. And then, I suppose, he wasn’t my cat anymore.’

‘Oh, I wouldn’t say that,’ Mia said, smiling. ‘You were just separated for a little while, but he was always *your* cat. And now look at you – back together again. He looks happy to be found, doesn’t he?’

The Little Girl seemed pensive. “Yes, he does – but only because he wanted to be found.”

chapter 25
ninety

HILLWOOD HOTEL WAS A small building sandwiched between tidy bricked houses on the main street of a sleepy nowhere town. It was like Ballinadrum that way, although from what Mia had seen of it online, it didn't appear to be as grand as Ballinadrum Hotel. It did not tower, and it did not loom. The doors were all glossy white, and it had given Mia the impression of a fashionable town house where people walked in heels across the sunlit wood floors.

Ballinadrum, by contrast, was more the sort of place those fashionable people escaped to. It was where they pretended to be invisible, lost amongst the old oaks and the unassuming way of the place.

As of late, it had taken on even more of a gothic air, with its increasing late-night noises and brushes of cold in various unexpected places. The electricity had even gone out again, one perfectly still and uninteresting night, across the whole hotel this time, with staff guiding guests about by flickering candlelight, until the problem was corrected – seemingly by itself.

Old buildings, they said, old wiring. Mia did not enlighten them.

Despite these new inconveniences and ghostly goings-on, Mia knew without a doubt which of the two hotels she preferred. But Ballinadrum was no longer an option, and truthfully, as Heather would say, Hillwood Hotel was perfectly lovely.

She did not say it now, however. She had been explicitly banned from today's outing. Her presence persisted in text messages, regardless.

Remember to stop for those brownies you wont regret it!!! xxx

Send pics ok?? xxx

Love you both xxx

As though her phone wasn't busy enough with this stream of messages, both Sonia and Ruby had the evening off and were also texting in the group chat.

Any word on Cormac? @Mia??? I'm two clicks away from a naughty clown costume and need to know if I'm wasting my hard earned coin on a non-existent Halloween party.

Havent heard anything. Think Mias venue hunting today.

OOH exciting – whens the dress fitting though?!?!

'Can you stop that?'

She knew Rosco was frowning without even having to look at him.

'It's your mum,' she said.

'Yeah, and it's annoying. Don't you want to actually *talk* anymore?'

'What do you want to talk about?'

He exhaled noisily. 'Well, that's one way to kill a conversation.'

She tried again. 'Ruby is buying a clown costume.'

'Post-hotel career options really that bad?'

'It's for the Halloween party.'

'What Halloween party?'

'Well, Ballinadrum always . . . I don't really know, really. She wanted me to ask Cormac about it, but obviously, I haven't seen him, and if I'm honest, it sounds like a lot of work when the hotel has other problems.'

For a second, he said nothing, and then: 'No hotel talk either.'

'Okay, well . . . How's your day going?'

'Fine,' he said. 'Until you insisted on stopping here on the way. Why can't we just go straight to Hillwood?'

Mia folded her hands in her lap. She didn't know how to talk to him when he was like this, even with all the practice he had given her recently.

'Why'd you invite yourself over anyway?' he went on. 'We *never* go to see Aunt Olive.'

'Exactly,' Mia said. 'Maybe it would be good to, and seeing as we're already heading to Hillwood . . .'

'You just thought we'd take a twenty-minute detour?'

It was another addition to the long list of things Mia could not tell Rosco about, and it should have been more painful, but it felt distant in comparison to the cool press of the key to her chest, to the thrumming world within her leather journal.

The last time Mia had visited Olive's house, she was eighteen, and all of the Buckleys had been invited to the birthday party of someone none of them were acquainted with. Upon arrival, however, they discovered said person had actually died four years prior, and so the polite gifts and cards were left in the car.

Four years later, Olive, wrapped in a brown shawl, greeted them at the gate. 'I'll make tea.'

Inside, Mia remembered just how cluttered and chaotic the house was. The details had been a wash of colours and angles in her memory, but now each snow globe, crystal paperweight and vase of old dried flowers came into vibrant focus.

Mia was given a cup with a royal blue swirl painted on the side, and Rosco one with green stripes. Olive herself chose the most worn, tea-stained cup in once-been white.

'You never visit, Rosco,' Olive said. 'In fact, I don't know if you've ever visited alone – and even now, Mia's here. Tell me, whose suggestion was it to come?'

Mia bit her tongue and Rosco gave a mechanical laugh.

'That's not fair, Olive. I'm here today, aren't I? And thanks for the tea.'

'Do you know that cup?'

He inspected it briefly. 'No.'

'It was your father's. Got it at a Sunday School prize day forty-seven years ago.'

'Oh. That's . . . nice you kept it so long.'

'Of course. If I'd gone out and bought some brand-new mug, what would I have to say to you about it?'

'That you bought it just the other—'

'*Nothing*,' she corrected. 'And Mia's cup . . . Have you any idea where it's been, Mia? I purchased it on a trip to Santorini twelve years ago. They were selling them at a little stall, and it was half off because of the little splash of green on the bottom.'

Not wishing to upturn her mug of scalding tea, Mia decided to trust the old woman's tale.

'And this one . . .' she said fondly, rubbing her mug like a genie's lamp. 'It's from a set of mugs I was gifted the day after your grandfather Eamonn died. I don't know anyone else who brings a present to a wake, but Valerie from down the road did and it fits so nicely in my hand.'

Rosco cut Mia a nettled look, and she jumped to steer the conversation.

'I actually wanted to visit to ask you about the pictures you showed us last time,' she said. 'I would love to have known a little bit more about your brothers. Especially Owen Buckley?'

The smile that stretched across Olive's face scored deep lines across her cheeks. 'I knew it couldn't have been this one who wanted to see me. Now, what do you want to know?'

'Well, just more about his history, really,' Mia said. 'You said he died, but there wasn't a lot of . . .'

'Wanted the beginning and middle, as well? I sympathise with you, Mia Anne. Most people don't care for those parts. It's only the ending that anyone seems to remember, and you know, those are such brief moments of life, you wonder they have the power to define a person at all. But they do.

'For me, though, I'll remember him best as my favourite brother. You shouldn't have favourites, of course, but I do, and always will, because he was kind when he didn't have to be and patient, even though I was the smallest and couldn't keep up. And you know, he was so energetic as a boy, so well liked, you would never have guessed how his life would pan out.'

'What happened?' Mia asked.

'Well, he killed himself, Mia Anne. Didn't you know that?'

Mia's eyes widened. 'No, I didn't realise . . . I'm—'

'Oh, don't. No need for apologies. I've had enough of them over the years, and well, it doesn't change anything, does it? He was in jail at the time, off in the city.

'Sometimes I sit back and think *why*? Why did he do it, when it was only going to be six weeks, and then he'd be home, and he'd have the rest of his life? But it wasn't about the sentence. It wasn't even about the trial, I'd imagine, but that couldn't have helped. He wasn't well. He hadn't been for years – though when he had worked at the hotel . . . we'd thought he was better then.'

Mia felt a pang of sympathy. 'He liked the hotel?'

'Oh, yes. It was his first "proper" job after being a farm hand, and I think he liked his colleagues. Met Melanie, his wife, there, too, and that Donahue of yours took a real shine to him. We used to tease him that Donahue had replaced our father – he was dead a long time then. Cancer. In the blood.'

Mia had almost begun into more apologies but stopped herself. She simply nodded with a frown she hoped conveyed all the *sorrys* she meant.

'But we shouldn't have teased too much: Donahue was *very* good to him. Had him round for dinner, their children used to play together, and after a few years, maybe more, he got this big promotion. What that entailed, no one's ever told me, but he was making a lot of money and was away from home a lot more. In fact, he could be gone all night on occasion, if there'd been some incident at the hotel he had to attend to. No one at the hotel ever knew what this mysterious incident could be, but perhaps that just meant he was doing his job right. If things go well, no one has to know you did anything at all.'

Mia blinked. The tale she was being told felt so familiar, so akin to her own, she wondered whether Donahue had hired Owen, just as Cormac had hired her – but that was wild, mad.

Wasn't it?

'Of course, that wasn't the case with our Maria. Now *that* was an incident.'

Mia's mind returned to the incident report she had found. 'I think I read about that,' she said. 'Was she Owen's daughter? She needed an ambulance, didn't she – for an asthma attack?'

'Asthma attack, panic attack . . . The girl – yes, she was Owen's – couldn't breathe for the life of her, and whether she made up the ghosts after that, or scared herself enough to bring it on, I'll never know. Regardless, she ranted about these *spirits*, and honestly, I'm not sure she ever recovered, even when she grew into a young woman.'

The hairs on Mia's arm stood at attention. 'Where is she now?'

'Oh, hard to say. Last I heard she'd gone over to Scotland or something with some man, though if there was a wedding, we weren't invited. It wasn't the same after Owen, really – lost touch over the years.'

'And the painting was stolen *after* her . . . asthma attack?'

'Oh, yes. They do say terrible things come in threes, you know. First, Maria, then the painting.' Her eyes glimmered. 'Then, we lost Owen entirely.'

Rosco shifted in his seat. 'What painting is this, then?' he asked, sounding vaguely annoyed.

'*The Field by Our House*,' Mia said quickly. 'Remember – I told you about it the other night?'

He frowned as he asked Olive, 'Do you have it, then?'

'It's been missing since nineteen sixty-nine,' Olive said flatly. She turned her gaze back to Mia. 'Owen never mentioned the painting to anyone at home, and they didn't even know it was worth anything. All a bit strange, really, but he was on hard times, I suppose, house repayments, car needing fixed . . . A little extra cash wouldn't have been a bad thing, but then again, is it for anyone?

'We never really did figure out why he did it – just that whatever the jury heard that day was enough to convince all twelve of them he was guilty.'

Olive's gaze was taut and appraising. 'I would have thought,' she said, 'that Cormac Byrnes would have told you all about *The Field by Our House*. He was just a boy when it happened, but he'll remember. Everyone remembers.'

'Oh, he . . . he isn't at the hotel at the moment,' Mia said. 'But I think he'll be back soon.'

'Well, when he is, make sure you ask *him* about the painting, and Owen and . . . that other one . . . that . . .'

'Francis?'

'Francis Croft,' Olive said with a smile. '*Frankie.* They were quite the collection before that awful autumn. I remember hearing about him, too. He left town, right after the whole incident. I'd say it would have been hard to work in that hotel after what went down between the three of them, but before all of that, before the painting . . . my, there would have been enough dinners with the Byrnes' family for Cormac to remember something of my Owen.'

'I'll make sure to ask him,' Mia said.

'And remember to tell me what he says, too, won't you? I'm always looking for little pieces of him.'

'I think, Olive,' Rosco said, 'it might be time for us to go.'

'Nonsense. You've hardly drunk your tea. Don't you know it's rude to leave before the third cup?'

'We're actually going to visit a venue today.' He was already on his feet, dragging Mia onto hers as well. 'Been meaning to do it for ages, and with the wedding so soon . . .'

Mia went to argue, but Rosco was pulling her towards the door. She offered Olive an apologetic smile, but the old woman just held a tight polite expression, which, in its rigidity, didn't seem polite at all.

Not that Rosco cared, Mia thought bitterly, as he more or less pushed her into the car. He was so . . . *so* . . .

'Do you have to do that?' she snapped, as he drove and flicked through radio channels simultaneously.

'I'm just finding something to listen to.'

'Well, maybe you could start with your great aunt.'

That was new, Mia thought, and dangerous, and Rosco must have thought it, too, because he looked at her with more shock than anger for the initial seconds.

Then, his anger sparked into life. He began to speed up.

Mia watched the little dial creep into the fifties, and then sixties. Each bump in the road felt like a mile-deep pothole, and when they came to the little humpback bridge, they practically took flight. He was at seventy by the time she said, 'Stop.'

'You're always worrying,' he told her. 'Always worrying about the hotel, or Cormac, or something else. It's always something *else* with you, isn't it?'

'I know,' she said, because it had worked before, and she didn't like this foreign, frightening place. She didn't like how each winding turn threw her into the car door, or how she could feel every jolt through her spine. 'I know I've been spaced out, so just – just *stop*.'

Eighty. They were at eighty, and this was a country road, not a place to be doing anything more than half this really, but he just kept going, his brow low, his eyes burning.

'Please,' she cried out, voice suddenly hysterical. 'Please slow down. I can't – I don't—'

He didn't respond and he didn't hit the brakes, but somewhere between her clawing the seats and reaching for the door handle, Mia noticed she wasn't being thrown about so much, and the fields beside her weren't frantic lines of yellow and gold.

Her gaze flicked to the speed dial. Sixty-five. Fifty. They sailed along and she felt relief fill her eyes with tears but there was something horrible in being safe now, something that made her feel the panic she had felt seconds before was a gross overreaction – was gross, full stop.

She glanced at him, and he was smiling.

'You should've seen your face,' he said. 'You were terrified.'

Mia said nothing. She tried to breathe without him hearing the way it caught.

'Hey, lighten up. I was just messing around.'

'I didn't like it,' she said after a moment.

'Yeah,' he said, straightening his shoulders. 'There's lots of things you do that I don't like, too.'

chapter 26
a more personal matter

WHEN ROSCO DROPPED HER OFF at Granny's later that evening, she did not let him kiss her goodbye. He made a *tsk* noise when she got out of the car.

Granny Brea was curled up on the sofa, Muriel a ball of white fur on her knee and Handsome Boy leaning against her shoulder.

An old movie was playing, a video of Granny's. Mia had tried time and time again to convert her to digital downloads, but Granny seemingly preferred the rewinding, shuddering, and clicking of her old VHS player.

Mia kicked off her shoes at the door and went to join her.

'You're home early,' Granny said. 'Did you like Hillwood?'

'Yep. We're booked in.'

'Oh, that's wonderful, Mia. Was it as nice as the pictures?'

'Yeah. Very clean.'

'And the food? How was that?'

'Have to go to the tasting yet.'

The man who had led their tour through the hotel's gleaming hallways and spacious wedding suite had explained, cheerfully, that they could arrange a tasting at their earliest convenience, if they would like to wait until then to put down their deposit. Rosco had been adamant that wasn't necessary, and Mia hadn't argued.

There was nothing to argue about.

Mia's eyes tracked the characters on the screen. She had seen this one a dozen or more times: a pretty girl writing to her lover gone abroad, while a heavily accented vampire plotted against them both. No matter how many times Granny had seen it, she made sure to watch it every October, and Mia often accompanied her.

Now, she settled into the sofa and let the music wash over her.

After a few minutes, she asked, 'Do you remember Donahue's friends from the old days?'

'How old are we talking?'

'I don't know,' Mia said. 'Fifties. Sixties.'

'I think you know as well as I do that that man had too many friends to count.'

'Well, what about . . . Frankie?'

Granny Brea smiled. 'Vaguely. Him and that other one – that Buckley – had stories follow them about until . . . Oh, well, until it all fell apart.'

'What kind of stories?'

'Just . . .' She was distracted by an intense kissing scene, and slowly re-joined the conversation. 'Silly things. Nights at the hotel that went on too late, and racing to the beach in a car that shouldn't have been on the road. I have the notion something happened with a particularly grumpy bullock, but exactly who was chased out of the field, I can't quite remember. These were grown men, of course, but how grown they were was debatable.'

'And the painting?'

'Ah, yes, the painting, and Owen left us, then Francis, too.'

'Where did Francis go?'

'The next town or something. He probably wanted a fresh start after all of that.' At last, Granny looked at Mia. 'It's not a very nice story, though, Mia Anne. What's your interest in it all of a sudden?'

'Just curious.' She tucked her feet underneath her. 'I'm tired.'

'Me too,' Granny said. 'But then again, I'm always tired. You want me to catch you up on the movie, love?'

Mia knew she should go upstairs, to her files and notes, to have another look online for *Anna Loughran*, or consider where the Soldier might have stashed that ever elusive tin he'd been so interested in . . . but the night had been long and unpleasant, and the sofa was so comfortable, Granny's company so uncomplicated.

The vampire leered through a window to a sleeping figure dressed in blue taffeta, and Mia let her head fall against Granny's shoulder.

'Please.'

*

Granny Brea was first admitted to hospital when Mia was seventeen years old. It was an angina attack, the doctors had told her, and she would need to stay overnight for observations. It was *reasonably common* amongst people of Granny Brea's age, though, and with *proper treatment* and *healthy lifestyle choices*, it could be *easily managed.*

Angina, however, was not a cold or a cough, and one didn't just leave it behind in the spring.

Mia had cried all the way home. Rosco had tried to console her, but it proved impossible.

He had driven up to Granny Brea's empty house, Mia trying to choke back tears, and then pulled off again, taking her hand in his and squeezing tight.

'We have a spare room,' he'd said, and those five words had felt like a lifeline.

At the Buckleys house that night, the fire had been lit, the kettle flicked on as soon as Mia walked in the door, and Heather had found her a pair of fleecy pyjamas she'd bought new and never worn. Mia had watched a steady stream of sitcoms, the evening news, and watched, too, as the family had shifted and risen and drifted off to bed.

She hadn't made use of the spare room that night, but had sat up for hours talking to Rosco, who had held her tight until at last, he had fallen asleep, and his hand had gone slack.

In the morning, he had not asked how she was feeling but if she wanted breakfast, whether she needed to borrow a toothbrush – normal things. She had liked that, that there could be many Mias: the one still at the hospital, sitting in a grey waiting room, and the one who had a cup of her choosing at the Buckleys' house and no other concerns except whether she wanted jam or marmalade on her toast.

The day after Mia visited Great Aunt Olive, she threw herself into *normal.* She got up, made breakfast, and put on her usual sensible, patent shoes. She kissed Granny Brea's cheek and asked if she had taken her heart medication.

She got into Rosco's car and, with some frigidity, let him kiss her cheek. He played with the radio. She watched the speedometer.

'You doing okay?' Rosco asked, as they drove up Ballinadrum Hotel's driveway.

'Yeah,' she told him.

'Yesterday was . . .'

Awful. Unfair. Unkind.

'Stupid,' he finished. 'It was a daft thing to fight about.'

'It was,' she said.

'But at least we got the venue sorted, huh? Not long now. Hey, you know, I was going to call by The Burning Lamp on my lunch break. You want me to get you something?'

'No, it's okay.'

'Come on,' he said, and nipped her knee lightly. 'Tell me what you want.'

Mia took a breath. 'You know what I like.'

And then he smiled at her, like all was forgiven – like the Mia who sat in his car was the same one who had done so all summer. And Mia tried to pretend that was true, too, so when he parked outside the hotel, she, once again, allowed him to kiss her cheek, and waved goodbye to him from the top of the steps.

'Mia! Come here!'

By the front desk, Sonia and Ruby waved her over.

With barely concealed reluctance, Mia made her way across the lobby, but was interrupted mid-journey. Sonia's daughter Lily appeared to be playing a game of hopscotch on some imaginary pattern she had found in the terrazzo.

'I can do ten hops on both feet,' she told Mia proudly.

'Is that so?'

'See – ten on this side, ten on this one—'

'Lily, leave Mia alone.'

'I was *showing her* my *hopping*.'

'She can watch it from over here. Mia, come on.' Sonia waved her closer, more insistently this time, and Lily, nose screwed up and eyes livid, hopped off with new force.

'I can do twenty now!' she called. 'I bet you can't do twenty!'

'Sorry about her,' Sonia said. 'Neil just dropped her off with a pack of Skittles, so you can imagine how my evening is going to go.'

'We'll be praying,' Ruby said.

Sonia rolled her eyes, and stooped behind the desk. When she reappeared, it was with a stack of books.

'Delivery for Mia Anne Moran.'

'Me?' Mia tensed, mind immediately going to Cormac.

Sonia thumped the pile on the desk. Mia read the title of the top volume. It read *A History of Modern Marketing*, and when she tilted her head to read the spines of the others, she found them to be in a similar category: *Your Brand Needs You*, *Traditional VS Digital: Where Do We Go From Here?*, *A Beginner's Guide to Going Global.*

'I didn't know you were into all this business stuff,' Ruby said.

'I'm not.'

'Henry,' Sonia said, 'thought you were. He told me to give them to you.'

Clarity dawned on Mia then, and she scrabbled for the same explanation about Cormac she had given before.

'Mummy, see what I'm doing – it's two at a time!' Lily called from across the room.

'I see you!' Sonia called back, though her eyes only left Mia for the briefest of seconds. 'So, what, you're some sort of marketing person for the hotel now?'

'But I thought this was just temporary,' Ruby said. 'Aren't you coming back to the kitchen?'

'I am,' Mia said. 'I think.'

'Oh, for goodness' sake – I thought he was *borrowing* you. I'm down three waiters, a cook, and you're being shipped off to a new department permanently? How am I supposed to run a restaurant with next to no staff?'

'Mummy, *look*—'

'I *am* looking—'

'It's not like that,' Mia tried to argue.

'Then, what is it like?' Sonia asked. 'What do you *do* for him?'

'*Mummy*—'

'I *saw* you, Lily, I—'

At that moment there was a crash from across the room. All three dropped the conversation and whirled about to see what had happened.

Lily began to cry.

Mia could see white shards scattered across the lavender floor, and her gaze travelled to the row of decorative plates, printed hydrangeas of all shades – from bruised-blue to tenderest pink – that hung on the wall. Plates that were no longer there, but instead lying in pieces – and Lily, on hands and knees, amongst them.

'They just fell,' Mia could hear someone say – an older woman, a guest by the looks of things. 'She didn't touch them.'

Sonia hauled Lily off the floor into her arms to cradle her like a newborn, while the girl howled, pink-faced and terrified.

At this angle, Mia could see the red painting Lily's hands.

'It's okay – it's only a little cut,' Sonia was saying. 'It's just a few little—'

Ruby rushed along beside her. 'There's the first aid kit, just in the back. I'll grab it and—'

Mia should have gone with them, she knew. She should have been on Sonia's left side, just as Ruby was on her right, and she should have told stories to make Lily laugh while Ruby handled the disinfectant, and together they should have fixed this. That's what would have happened on any normal occasion, but Mia knew – so well it hurt – this was not normal.

She stayed in the lobby long enough to see other members of staff arrive to brush up the blood-smeared china, and then she rushed to the third floor.

'Owen Buckley!' she called. 'Owen Buckley, I know you're here.'

The ballroom was utterly silent. The ghosts parted around her like she was magnetised, continuing with their conversations, carrying on with their dancing, as Mia marched through the middle of them.

She called again, but the Rogue did not answer.

At the door to the back room, she wavered. This was the room she had to be careful not to think about late at night, for fear it would linger in her dreams.

'Owen,' she said again, hands rigid by her side. 'Owen Buckley.'

There was still no response, no movement – nothing.

'My cat,' said a small voice. 'He likes to be in the sun.'

Mia turned to see the Little Girl, holding the stuffed cat they had found together the other day. Its glassy eyes stared into nothingness while the ghost petted its matted tail.

All the other ghosts carried on as though nothing had changed. Nothing had, Mia supposed, for them.

'He hates to be in the dark,' the Little Girl went on. 'He's frightened of the dark.'

Mia looked at the spirit – her blonde hair, her large blue eyes – and part of her crumpled. She got down on one knee to be at eye level and said, 'Of course he is. Who likes to be in the dark? We can find him a lovely place to sit, can't we? Somewhere warm, and sunny, and bright.'

'But not too hot,' the ghost insisted.

'Not too hot,' Mia agreed. 'And he'll be happy there, and no one will hurt him, and he'll never have to be in the dark ever again.'

The ghost grinned, and then, all at once, frowned. She turned around, as though someone had called her name, and as she did so, faded out of view. The little ginger cat fell to the floor soundlessly.

Mia picked it up and turned it over in her hand. She could find somewhere bright and warm for it, somewhere beyond the hotel and all its shadows.

Now, though, she had to open the door. For Lily's sake. For all their sakes.

Mia straightened, then stopped dead.

Across the ballroom, someone was standing in the doorway.

She half-thought he was a vision, but she blinked twice, and he was still there, dressed in a greyish green suit and his usual spectacles.

Cormac Byrnes.

'You,' Mia said without a second thought. She dropped the cat. 'You're back.'

'Last night,' he said, looking appraisingly at the ballroom. She crossed the room towards him. 'Flight was a little bumpy, but what can you expect in a place with such appalling weather. You know, I'd half forgotten that London was actually relatively bright compared with here.'

She stopped ten steps from him, hardly believing what she was hearing.

'When . . . how . . .'

'It helps when you communicate in full sentences, Mia Anne.'

Redder now, she asked, 'What are you doing here?'

The ghosts were unbothered by his presence, but Mia felt her special space trespassed.

'I believe as Ballinadrum Hotel's *owner*, I have a right to be *here*. What are *you* doing here?'

'My job.' She pulled a packet of custard creams out as though that was suitable proof.

'Ah, excellent. I had half-feared you would have taken off after your run-in with our rogue. How has he been behaving?'

Mia was bereft of an explanation.

Cormac snorted. 'Hm. Figures. Well, I'm sure I'll wrangle him up.'

'*You*? *You're* going to . . . go after a ghost?'

He slipped his hands into his pockets. 'Yes. I feel this is a more *personal* matter than I had originally believed, and so, here I am.'

'What about our deal?' she asked.

'Oh, it still stands. I don't mean *these* creatures.' He took a step further into the room and gestured widely to the rest of the ballroom. 'I only mean to get rid of our rogue. I've been doing some thinking, you know, about why he might be here, and have decided it's only fitting I should be the one to send him on his way.'

Mia frowned. 'You . . . you know how to get rid of him? How? I've been looking through the files and I—'

'Yes, that's very studious of you, Mia Anne, and I'm sure it's worked with your other spirits, but trust me on this one: I'll handle it. After all, no one knows him better.'

'You . . . you know him?' She felt a sinking embarrassment come over her: the mystery that had transfixed her over the last ten days had seemingly already been solved by someone who wasn't even in the country. 'Did you . . . know all along?'

'I had a feeling. It just took me some time to work out the *why*.'

'The painting?'

'The what? No, no painting. It's *me.* He needs to tell me something, and as much as I would like to leave him here for all of time, I'd really rather get this place sold on – *ghost-less*. And honestly, I'm quite interested in what he has to say.'

He did a sweeping circle, calling out, 'You hear that? *I'm not scared of you anymore*. You think you can hide here among all these lost souls, but I *know you*. I'll *find you*.'

It was always cold in the ballroom, but suddenly, it was colder than it should be. This chill came with malice. It was unwelcome and unkind.

It had only felt like this once before.

'I don't understand,' Mia said. 'Weren't you small when Owen was here?'

'Owen?' the hotelier repeated. 'What on earth are you on about?'

And then, she saw him: the Rogue.

He materialised like a shadow, a long slip of darkness, and then his uniform came into focus, his fist tight around something Mia could not see. He did not advance, however, but merely watched – curious, it seemed, as to what Cormac might do next.

'Mr Byrnes,' she whispered. 'Maybe you shouldn't—'

He tipped back his head and laughed at her. 'Don't tell me you're afraid of *offending* these characters now, are you, Mia Anne? I thought you would have grown braver over these weeks.'

'I'm not *scared*, I'm—'

'Please do tell your crouching, then. It's doing you an awful injustice.'

She shook her head. 'Mr Byrnes, he's here.'

Cormac Byrnes had always been a grey man, but now he was ghostly white. It was in this moment that Mia could see it most clearly – those ears he grew into, those fluffy tufts he cut short. The boys in the frames, grown into this.

He jerked around to follow Mia's gaze, and then stumbled backwards before righting himself once more.

The Rogue did not move, and Mia took note of his features this time: the near-black, slicked-back hair, the pale skin. He seemed to be in his late thirties, or perhaps forties. She could not yet glimpse what he was gripping in his hand, though.

Cormac cleared his throat. 'Well, Father, it's been a while.'

Mia's head snapped around to look at him.

'Donahue Eagan Byrnes,' Cormac went on. 'The light of Ballinadrum Hotel come to a grisly end, and then a more pitiful afterlife. Didn't you think it best to leave it after all these years, or are you still of the opinion there is nothing more important? Or perhaps, you have finally seen the error of your ways? I can only imagine that death has lent some clarity to your priorities. So, what is it – what have you come to tell me?'

Mia could see how the Rogue flickered – how his mouth thinned with indignation, his eyes darkening with every ill-timed word.

Cormac was angering it. He was ruining everything.

'Somehow,' he continued, 'I don't think anything you could tell me now will be any different to that last letter, but I will express, *once again*, that a few nice words cannot and will not brush over all the damage you did, Father.'

The ghost stepped forward, and its eyes were so black, its expression so unknowable, if Mia didn't do something, she knew something awful would happen.

Before she could talk herself out of it, Mia marched past Cormac Byrnes to the centre of the ballroom. She stared across the divide to the Rogue.

'Owen,' she called. 'Owen Buckley.'

All was cold and silent. The Rogue was not called back to himself, but he did cock his head as though curious about this strange young woman and what she had to say.

'What are you doing?' Cormac hissed from behind her.

Mia tried to ignore him, but he pulled on her sleeve.

'Let *go*,' she told him. 'I'm helping.'

'This is my business. This is *my father*.'

Mia could have slapped him then and there. 'You have no idea what you're talking about!'

'And you do?'

'*Yes*. Yes, I do – because I read the files. I wrote the journal. I come here every day and I *know* this has to do with *The Field by Our House*, and Donahue Byrnes, and Francis Croft, and *yes*, Owen Buckley, but it has *nothing* to do with whatever it is you're prattling on about.'

She turned back to the Rogue. She stepped closer.

'What's in your hand?' she asked it. 'What are you holding?'

The Rogue shifted slightly.

'I know you, Owen Buckley,' she said. 'And I would bet good money to say that . . . that you're holding a key in that hand. I've got one, too.' She pulled the key from beneath her shirt and held it out on its chain. 'I'd bet it's the same key. I bet you and I aren't so different either.'

Then, the Rogue smiled. It was not a gentle thing. It was a jagged wound, and Mia did not know whether to be comforted by it or take her leave and run.

The ghost moved first, though.

Slowly but surely, and smiling all the while, he closed the space between them.

She remembered vividly how she had been this close to him before, when he had stood on those stairs in the back hallway, the world all black but for her phone light. Today, he met her in daylight, and she felt no braver.

He opened his hand, which held a perfect match for the key Mia wore about her neck.

She looked from the key to his face, but all at once, he was gone, and Mia felt her relief like vertigo.

She turned to look at Cormac Byrnes, but he, too, had vanished.

chapter 27
adequate warning

Lily had needed two stitches in her left hand. The right had been solved entirely by the contents of the hotel's first aid kit.

Judging by the photographs Sonia had sent Mia that evening – after a long six-hour sit in A&E at the hospital forty minutes away – Lily's mental state hadn't taken much hurt, either. Her smiling face had been decorated with an assortment of children's plasters, all puppy dogs and unicorns, and she showed the camera a thumbs up.

'Ruby's work,' Sonia said of the plasters in her text. 'Think we owe the hotel about six boxes.'

It had been a relief to Mia to know Lily was okay, but it niggled at her still that she had not been there. She could have helped Ruby with the plasters. She could have held Sonia's hand, or offered to go for food while they sat in the waiting room. Instead, Mia had been where she always was. The ballroom.

It was – surprise, surprise – where she was today, as well.

Despite all the activity these last few days, the ghosts were oddly cheerful. They played with the Lost Property items, danced in circles, and laughed with one another over jokes that made no sense whatsoever.

And the Rogue . . . mercifully, his only appearance came in the form of a brief white dot in Mia's camera screen, before it vanished once again, to whatever dark recess it normally hid in.

Mia even got to leave the ballroom for twenty minutes to see Granny, who was having a cup of tea in the dining room with a few of the choir girls. They wanted all of the gossip on *the accident* the day before, as though it was a celebrity news piece, and when Mia described the events in as ordinary terms as she could, they questioned her further.

'I heard they fell off themselves—'

'Did you see her touch them, *really*?'

'All those ghost stories are really getting to you, Marigold—'

Mia quietly excused herself to *get back to Cormac*.

It was in this brief and relative peace that she had finally decided to trawl through the Lost Property items again. She inspected the clothing with renewed interest – names stitched into jackets, stains spilled down satin shirts – and looked into each stuffed animal's eyes, daring them to confess their owner's names.

She then came across something she had not noticed before: a red scarf, bundled up and tied. It seemed such a curious thing that Mia didn't know how she had missed it the last time she had looked, but as she unfurled the length of red fabric, she realised that it *hadn't* been here last time.

Inside lay the tin – the tin Blond Moustache had not wanted her to touch, and had clearly since tried to hide.

She looked up at the ballroom and searched him out. He was by the door with his comrades, looking as unhappy as ever.

Mia took her chance and flipped the lid on the tin.

A loose collection of coins gleamed back her. *No*, she realised – not coins. *Medals.* Printed with heads and lions and attached to striped lengths of fabric, apparently untouched by time or its ill-effects.

She looked back to the soldiers, still wearing their uniforms for a war that had so long ended, and realised, with some surprise, a new body had joined her ballroom.

She wasn't sure how long he had been standing there, but when Cormac Byrnes cleared his throat for her attention, he appeared to have been waiting some time.

'What have you there?' he asked, as though this were a perfectly reasonable greeting.

'A tin,' she told him flatly.

'Is it a . . . special tin?'

'I hope so.'

With some reluctance, she crossed the floor to meet him.

'With war medals inside. I think. Might have something to do with the Soldiers . . . You know – buried on Irish soil, never made home. Like the stories?'

'You think these are what could be tying them here?'

Mia shrugged. 'I need to find out. Maybe. I mean, I have the service number for one of them, so I know that he definitely died here, and that he was originally from Eastbourne, and he was only thirty-seven when he died, and was married—'

'You found all of that out? By yourself?'

She frowned and bit back the urge to say, *do you see anyone else standing here?* Instead, she said, 'Yes, with a little help from the genealogy archives online . . . and those files you left me.'

He nodded slowly. Today, he was wearing a blue sweater underneath his usual grey suit, a sure sign that winter's chill was making its way across the country – and Mia's time was running out.

'How many then?' he asked. 'Are left, that is?'

'Sixteen, counting the Rogue,' she said. 'Fifteen, if not. I've recorded the Singer a few times, but she keeps getting distracted mid-song, and the Little Girl's cat has been moved to my room at home, but seeing as she's still here . . .' Mia gestured to the twirling blonde child at the centre of the ballroom.

'And you're doing that because . . . ?'

'Well, the Singer wants to be heard – by a thousand people, supposedly, or at least, that's the most consistent thing she's told me in all these weeks. And the Little Girl's toy cat was stuffed in a box for who knows how many years, and she goes on and on about how she wants it to sit in the sun, so that's what I did – what I've been doing.'

'Odd,' Cormac said, 'that those things should be important to them, now when they're dead and gone. Cats and songs.'

'Not really,' Mia told him. 'I've found that . . . well, these people feel just as much alive as we do, and we care about all sorts of silly things. I'm sure you've noticed how Henry likes to organise his keys downstairs, and that's hardly a matter of life and death.'

'I suppose you're right,' Cormac said, and it struck Mia as being one of the first times he had ever told her as much. 'You do well to remember all of their names.'

'Well, they're hardly names. They're just . . . nicknames. Identifiers. It would be kinder if I did call them by their real names, but I can't ever be sure of them. They're so . . . fussy with information. I mean, I can't even be sure the Little Girl is here because of that cat at all, especially as it hasn't worked so far . . .'

She tailed off and he frowned.

'What are you doing here?' she asked, doing well to avoid adding *really* to her question.

Cormac looked ill-prepared for such a query.

'I'm . . . Well, I . . .' He folded his hands in front of him. 'I'm the owner of this property. I can go where I please.'

Mia suppressed a sigh. 'Alright,' she said. 'I must admit, it's rather boring work to watch, but if that's what you're here for . . . I do hope . . . Well, I assume you're not back to speak to . . .'

'No, no,' he said quickly. 'That was a . . . foolish endeavour on my part. I had only thought . . .'

'Yes?'

'I had so deeply believed it was him.'

Mia looked away. 'I would tell you I'm sorry it wasn't, but I don't feel I am.'

'You told me, I know, but it wasn't until I saw him . . . Why, it looked nothing like him. I tried to tell myself that . . . well, he was a young man once. Perhaps he had been that thin, his hair that dark, but when he came close . . . close to you, Mia Anne, I didn't see one trace of my father in him.'

She looked at him, studying the stiff way he held himself, the wariness in his gaze.

'Before he died,' Cormac said, 'my father sent me a letter. It asked me to come back here, and return to the work I had long rejected. I didn't reply because I had made myself clear – had done so, for years. You can understand why I might have thought he would have reason to stay here.'

'For you,' she said.

His mouth contorted into something like a smile. 'Foolish, I know. But, despite how it sounds, I did not come here to offer you some pathetic little story. I actually wanted to ask you—'

Just then, the Nanny drifted between them, and caught Cormac by the elbow.

'Won't you dance with me, stranger?' she asked.

Cormac stumbled after her, before ripping his arm back and righting himself. The ghost seemed tickled by his reluctance.

'You must know how to dance,' she went on, plucking at his jacket lapels. 'Don't you like music?'

'*Music* – I'll tell you about *music*.' The Singer appeared at his other elbow.

'Beverly,' Mia called. The ghost stood to attention. 'Weren't there a few free drinks going at the bar? And, Syvita, they're missing a singer for the lounge tonight. Maybe speak to the manager?'

As Mia knew they would, both spirits were transformed with excitement. They dashed off in different directions, Syvita already warming up her voice, and Beverly calling to some fictious barman that she would have *the usual* – before becoming distracted by the tray of stale cupcakes Mia had left on a folding stepladder.

Cormac looked at Mia as though he might thank her.

'Do they still do that?' he said instead.

'What?'

'The . . . crowding. Pulling.'

Mia thought briefly. 'Not around me.'

He nodded, looking absent.

'I'm sorry if they upset you,' Mia went on. 'I know they can be frightening, Mr Byrnes but, for the most part, I think they're just confused.'

'They know me.'

This surprised Mia. 'They don't know anybody. Not really. They don't know my name—'

'No, they do. Those ones – I don't know how, or from when, but—'

What Mia had anticipated would be a minor discomfort seemed to have unravelled Cormac. He watched the ghosts with an age-old distrust, and she saw him draw his limbs closer to his centre.

'You don't have to be here,' she said more quietly. 'I know you don't like—'

'I'm perfectly fine.' The firm set of his lip told Mia he would never tell her anything but. 'But I'm not here for the enjoyment of it. I wanted to talk to you – about *The Field*—'

Mia held up her hands, alarmed. 'Don't.'

Cormac's unease sprung to panic. 'What? Are they—'

'No, it's fine. It's just . . . don't talk about it.'

'The . . . ?' He outlined a rectangular frame in the air with his fingers.

Mia gave the ballroom a long look. 'They don't like to talk about it. I've only done it a few times myself but every time I do . . . they disappear, or begin to wander. I'm sure you'll agree it's best if they do neither.' She crossed her arms. 'But if you do know about *that*, I would like to hear what you have to say.'

'My office, then.'

'Yes, but after dark.' She smiled. 'I have some work here still to do, and I'm not sure if you remember, but a deal to be met, too.'

'And you . . . You really aren't afraid of them? Still?'

She thought. 'I wouldn't say that. Not exactly.'

'And yet . . .'

'I have a job to do,' she said, and her smile was tight and grim.

*

That evening, Mia knocked on Cormac Byrnes' door and showed herself inside.

All was as it had been the last time she had visited, save for a second chair – stolen, it seemed, from the dining room.

The man himself was on his phone, but as Mia entered, he clicked the screen to black and slipped it into his pocket.

'So,' he said, all business. '*The Field by Our House.* That's a name I didn't think I'd be hearing too much of this millennium. Anything in particular that caught your eye about it?'

Mia took the dining-room chair. 'It's just been adding up.'

'Hm. And what exactly have you been adding?'

Mia told him as much as she could recall, in an imperfect order, with lots of jumping back and forth, much to her embarrassment. Her notebook, it seemed, was as cluttered as her own thoughts.

'Olive . . .' the old man said. 'I can't say I recall her.'

'No, she didn't think you would remember *her*, but her brother – Owen. Do you?'

Cormac nodded. 'He was a friend of my father's. And like you, he helped with the spirits.'

Mia had wondered as much.

'I was too young, and my mother wanted nothing to do with the ballroom. Francis and Owen, though—'

'Francis *and* Owen? Both of them?'

'Yes, they were his helpers, so to speak. It's not that he *needed* the help, but . . . Well, they lessened the load, while they were here. You know yourself how time-consuming the ghosts can be, Mia, so you can see why that was of interest to a man with a wife who often complained of how little she saw him, and a young son . . .'

He shook his head and turned the conversation.

'They were . . . older than me, Francis and Owen – by twenty years or more – and eager to prove themselves. Francis Croft was a rather earnest young man, dedicated to a fault to this hotel and its ghosts. Owen Buckley was a different sort. Quiet, unassuming. He was hard to read for his silence, or so I thought when he ate with us. Still though, it was obvious how much he loved my father, in an unordinary sort of way.'

'He didn't have a father,' Mia said softly. 'Olive told me that.'

'Well, that might explain it.' Cormac gave a short sigh. 'Regardless, though, it came to a crashing end, after the painting was stolen.'

'My grandmother told me they weren't the same that autumn, and then Owen . . .'

'Took his own life. Yes, I recall the funeral. Large turnout. My father spoke.' Cormac shook his head. 'Francis had already left town, though.'

'But why did he take the picture?' Mia asked. 'If he loved your father and the hotel.'

'It's a mystery to this day, but I do recall they had a blistering argument the day before it was reported missing.'

'About what?'

'About me.' Cormac took a long breath. 'My father used to tell me I was his heir and how, one day, I would be the one to care for the hotel, and its ghosts. I had been . . . frightened of the ghosts, in truth, since I was small, but I wanted to be brave – for him, you see. I wanted to make him proud.

'But that was the bother, wasn't it? One night, not long before the painting went missing, I was playing with Owen's daughter, Maria. She was eight years old and didn't come to the hotel all that often, but when she did, my father would ask me to entertain her – get her dessert in the dining room, show her where the board games were kept in the lounge.

'I was ten at the time, and thought myself quite grown up. I knew all the secret passages about the hotel, and the staff knew me by name. She seemed to think I was something of a celebrity, and I let her. I enjoyed it. But that night, she wasn't impressed with trifles or board games. She was bored, she said, and I could see her interest in me waning, so I offered to show her something interesting. Something *amazing*. As you may have guessed, I took her to the ballroom.'

'She didn't like it?' Mia asked.

'Oh no. She thought it quite fantastical. The ghosts, however . . . Well, they seemed fine at first, uninterested as they had always been with me, but then . . . They must have been overexcited because she was different – new. They were suddenly all around us, pulling at our clothing, Maria's hair. They wanted to ask us questions, have us dance, but they were . . . They were so cold, and close.'

Mia saw Cormac's hands clench.

'I was scared,' he explained. 'I didn't know what to do. I had only been there with my father, and I felt *safe* with him. And then Maria had . . . I didn't know she had asthma. She was suddenly gasping for breath, and the ghosts were still picking over her. I'm ashamed to say that I . . . I ran away. For my father.

'He was up in our suite, and when I got there – I'll never forget how he looked at me. He was . . . so angry, so utterly furious with me, he actually pushed me away in his haste to get to the ballroom. I'm not sure he even noticed, but my mother did. It was she who scooped me up, and washed my face. I didn't even realise I'd been crying until she wiped my tears with her handkerchief.

'Maria was fine after a night or two in the hospital, though according to her mother, she could hardly sleep for the fright she had suffered. No one believed her, of course, about the ghosts. But – the rest of it, well . . . When my father came back, he didn't speak to me. When I went to him, asking about Maria, he told me to go to my room.

'The next day, when he finally looked at me, he told me I was too young to visit the ballroom. He wanted my key back, and for me to promise never to go to the west wing. I didn't argue, and I pleaded with him not to go back either. He refused, and told me the ghosts needed him.'

Mia was unsure of how to picture the interaction. Donahue . . . angry? Donahue unkind and unforgiving? She listened with a face of neutrality.

'It felt like a lifetime before he spoke to me again, though it was probably no more than a few days – perhaps just a week – and after . . . that . . . he changed utterly. Suddenly, he was offering me piggybacks around the lobby, and pointing out which birds had come to peck over the crumbs one of the cooks had thrown onto the steps. He was good at making up that way, but I never forgot that when it came to it, he chose the ghosts. He chose them time and time again. Even when I turned fourteen or fifteen, and he asked if I'd like my key back so he could finally teach me to care for the ghosts properly, I wouldn't do it. I couldn't.'

Cormac looked at Mia then, as though checking for derision or disbelief in her eyes. She offered only confusion.

'The argument my father and his friends had, of course, was about Maria and that day I took her to the ballroom. It came less than a week after the incident, and they met in our apartments. I pretended to be asleep, as did my mother, but we were both wide awake, listening. How could we not? They had never fought like this before, and the things being said . . . *Enough. Dangerous. They should know.* There was even something said about *giving adequate warning.*

'My father was . . . upset about it. He said terrible things, but that was his temper. He didn't mean it. He never did mean the terrible things he said, but it didn't matter. Owen left that night in a hurry, but Francis stayed with my father, the two talking into the night.'

'So, that night . . . the argument . . .' Mia said. 'That's when Owen took the painting?'

'I can only assume it was a message to my father – a burnt bridge, an act of treachery – rather than for money. I'm not sure if my father would have reported the crime, but Francis, loyal as ever, did. Once the police were involved, of course, my father couldn't put the brakes on it, though he tried.'

'He did?'

Cormac rose from his chair and opened a drawer in the tall cabinet. He withdrew a small stack of newspapers and set them before Mia.

They were dated from nineteen sixty-nine and the headline screamed:

PAINTING THEFT SHAKES BALLINADRUM HOTEL

'You kept these?' Mia asked, placing a delicate finger upon the front page.

'God, no,' Cormac said. 'My father did. I found them recently. If you look at page six, you'll find that my father claimed Owen was a good employee and he hoped he'd be found innocent by the jury.'

'But he wasn't.'

'Well, it was Buckley's own fault for taking it.' Cormac shook his head. 'What a waste.'

'But then . . . what is he still doing here?'

'That's what I wanted to ask you, Mia Anne.'

She thought for a moment. 'I don't know,' she said at last. 'Not yet. This . . . what you've told me . . . it's made everything look so different. What do you think?'

'Haven't a clue. He got away with the painting and then took his life. Seemingly, he was the coordinator of his own fate.'

Mia thought back to Olive's conversation, to the man whose sadness persisted without cause or end.

'I wouldn't say that exactly,' she said. 'And the painting wasn't found.'

'No,' Cormac agreed.

Mia let the silence yawn between them.

'You've given me a lot to think about,' she said finally. 'Thank you.'

Cormac shook his head brusquely. 'No matter. And take those with you if you're going.'

Mia had not been, but she nodded and slid the old papers into her satchel as carefully as she could. She stood and headed for the door.

'Was the weather really better?' she asked before leaving.

Cormac frowned at her, but it lacked its usual glacial edge. 'No,' he said.

chapter 28
silk and taffeta

THE HOTEL WELCOMED CORMAC back like a cold winter wind. The staff buttoned their uniforms more tightly and, where there had been a breath out, the team now collectively took a sharp breath in.

Only Ruby seemed vaguely pleased, which shocked Mia until she learned it had less to do with Cormac and more to do with Mia's proximity to him.

'*Clown costume*,' she reminded her. 'Still in my basket – *waiting*.'

This proximity was more than anyone could have anticipated. Cormac and Mia's old pattern had been to see one another just once or twice a day – namely at Mia's arrival and departure – but now, Cormac made a habit of visiting her in the ballroom, too.

For the last three days, he had hung around the entryway, asking odd questions such as *How do you know to do that?* and *Will you write that bit down?*

It surprised Mia that she did not mind his company terribly.

On a practical note, it was simply good sense to have a second body to run errands outside of the ballroom. She had already sent Cormac to the post office with a padded envelope addressed to a small war museum based in Sussex. When she had emailed their curation department, they had been all too keen to receive a few genuine war medals, and while Cormac had grumbled about it – he was not an entirely changed man – the task was complete, and the three soldiers now seemingly . . . gone.

More than that, though, Mia thought she might actually *like* having someone witness this thing she did all day, every day. It was silly work, of course – offering biscuits to the dead and asking them how their mothers were could be nothing else – but it was nice, Mia thought, to have someone there. To be at least somewhat impressed by her new skills.

That said, in the days following Cormac's return, those skills were certainly put to the test. Gone were her cheerful dancers, and in their place . . .

'I heard a rumour,' the Gossip announced on this particular Tuesday afternoon, 'that something terrible is going to happen to you.'

Mia looked for the joke in her words, but didn't find it.

'What sort of something?' she asked.

'You'll know it when you see it,' the Gossip went on. 'Nothing good can come of this place. No, nothing good at all.'

Mia tried to keep her expression bright – she was all too conscious of the grey hotelier watching her from afar – and tried to divert the ghost, instead.

'And where did you hear this rumour – from anyone in particular?'

The Gossip, an ordinarily calm and orderly ghost – as much as any ghost could be – sniffed twice as though suddenly overcome with emotion, then disappeared.

Mia, surprised, stared into the space where she'd been. It was, by far, the shortest conversation she had ever had with the Gossip – and the darkest – and she watched as the ghost reappeared, mid-stride, across the room.

She looked to Cormac.

'She's normally chattier than this,' Mia said. 'She could talk for hours, and—' She paused as she took in the ballroom again. The Gossip had faded from view.

'She's over there,' Cormac said with a nod of the head, and indeed, when Mia looked, she could see the Gossip, standing on the edge of the dance floor, watching the others – and not talking.

She didn't want to tell Cormac what she was thinking – *I don't know what's wrong with them* – but needed to tell him something.

'I ought to say,' Mia said, 'the numbers were wrong yesterday.'

'Excuse me?'

'The ghosts. I told you eleven, but there's actually still twelve, plus the Rogue. I missed one.'

'Missed one? How do you miss one?'

'They move a lot,' she said. She did not say *they move a lot* more *now*. In fact, they had been flitting in and out of view so much more frequently that Mia had to photograph the ballroom three or four times before she could be satisfied with her count – and even then, might get it wrong.

'I really did think the Little Girl had vanished,' she continued, 'but she turned up . . .'

'Yes?'

The answer to this was that she had turned up in the dining room, after closing time, refusing to answer any questions about where her mummy and daddy were. Ruby had been rather alarmed by the entire exchange, though Mia had done her best to smooth the situation over – with promises of cake for the ghost, and tales of fictional parents staying on the second floor for Ruby.

'She turned up,' Mia repeated, more firmly. 'So, she's still here. But the Soldiers haven't been seen – not since you sent their medals off for me – and I haven't counted them in my photos either, so they seem to be gone.'

'Seem,' Cormac repeated without warmth.

'But I think I know what was wrong with the Singer now. You see, the other day I uploaded her song online, and I had hoped that would have done it, but it clearly hasn't.'

She gestured to the red-headed ghost near the piano.

'The thing is, though, the song didn't get very many hits, and I'm almost certain that's what she's really after. It's only part of a song, though. That can't help.'

'Does it matter?'

'Of course, it matters,' Mia huffed. 'I still intend on having you sell this hotel as a full piece, you know.'

'No, the song. I mean . . . Can't you just title it something eye-catching like . . . *ghost song captured live on tape*? Or, you know, some rubbish clickbait headline like that.'

'It's not clickbait if it's true,' Mia countered, but the idea was good, and she tucked it away for later. She drew herself a little straighter for her next words. 'You know, you don't have to be here.'

Cormac frowned. 'I know that.'

'And . . . well, I wondered—'

'What?'

'The ghosts haven't been themselves. I'm not sure if it's you, or me, or the . . .' *Rogue.* 'But they're different.'

Fortunately, the Rogue hadn't actually made an appearance since Cormac's ill-conceived confrontation, and the hotel hadn't suffered any of his misdeeds either.

That being said, it was a disquieting sort of absence – a watchful, waiting one. It made Mia think of shrill screams and bloodied china, and she kept a careful eye on that back door.

'Different how?' Cormac asked.

'Like . . . how it just was with the Gossip. They're quiet when they aren't normally, and agitated where they're usually calm. I half-thought maybe it was to do with the Soldiers, at first. You know, in losing the original spirits – the ones who actually died here – the others might feel . . . off kilter. Not themselves.'

'I suppose there's some logic to that.'

'But then, when I thought about it, they were a little . . . odd before that, too.'

'Since the day I showed up,' Cormac surmised. 'And you want me to go?'

'It's not about what I *want*—'

'What if you need help?'

It reminded her of the first day, when he had left her for a three-hour-long stretch without concern. She shrugged.

'I don't like them,' he countered.

'You never have.'

'And if you say they're worse—'

'Possibly *because* you're here—'

'And if that's not it?'

Mia looked at him, unsure how to respond.

'Mia Anne, if they're not behaving as they should, then . . . Then, surely, that's all the more reason for me to be nearby. I mean, how can it be *better* for me to be further away if you're noticing odd patterns, particularly now you're aware of what they are capable of? What if – what if they do something and no one is here to help you?'

His tone told her there wasn't room for argument in this, and in truth, Mia Anne didn't want to argue. (She *did* want to note that *he* had always known what the ghosts were capable of, but she didn't think that was particularly conducive to their improved working relationship.)

'Do you think that old ghost hunting website would want the Singer's recording, then?' she asked instead. 'Or do you have some other supernatural publication in mind?'

*

When Mia left that evening, she was smiling into her phone.

'What's that there, then?' Gerry asked, holding the door for her.

'Oh – a text.'

'From the *fiancé*?'

She nodded. Gerry didn't need to know that *GhostHuntHub.com* had just requested exclusivity on her ghostly song recording. 'Who else?'

'You hang on to that now, Miss Mia. I have the suit all ready for February.'

Out on the steps, October had truly nestled in for the year. Night had come early, there was a chill in the air, and oak leaves skittered about their feet in a party of mauves and indigos. The hotel's chimney smoke settled over the grounds and through the trees as well, thickening the evening's fog and spicing the air.

She turned back to the warm glow of the hotel.

'Were you ever married, Gerry?'

His eyebrows jumped with surprise. 'Why, no, I wasn't. I was *close*, but . . . couldn't pin me down, Miss Mia. Bachelor at heart, you see.'

She nodded. 'I only ask because, well, maybe it's a long shot, but I knew a Beverly a long time ago, and she talked about a Gerry. She said he was a *bombshell*, and I always wondered whether her Gerry was you.'

'Beverly,' he echoed. 'You knew Beverly?'

'Oh, not very well. I think we met at a party of the Buckleys or something – forever ago. I was thinking about weddings, and I remembered suddenly she had said once . . . she wanted to ask this Gerry to marry her. She didn't want to seem un-lady-like, though.'

To this, Gerry burst out with a laugh. '*That* Beverly was no more a lady than I was.'

'So, you *did* know her!'

'A long time ago,' Gerry said with a wan smile. 'A very, very long time ago.'

'That's small towns, I guess,' Mia said. 'Can't bury any secret around here.'

With that, she walked out to the dark car park, feeling she might like to dance on the spot, or photograph the doorman's wonderful, wistful expression, or perhaps rush back past him, to the ballroom, to tell the Nanny what she had done.

If she had done anything right, however, Mia thought, there would be no Nanny there to tell it to.

A car horn sounded. Mia leapt, almost dropping her phone.

Ruby's high cackle poured into the night, and Mia could see she was parked on the corner, engine idling. Sonia was in the backseat, grinning.

Approaching, Mia asked, 'Are there . . . plans I should be aware of?'

'Oh, there are plans,' Ruby said. 'But you definitely should *not* be aware of them. Hop in.'

Mia felt a ripple of unease, and her thoughts kicked into high speed.

'Are they at least . . .' she asked, slipping into the passenger seat, 'nice plans?'

Ruby revved the engine. 'The best.'

*

Mia's bedroom was a wash of white silk and taffeta and a dozen other fabrics she couldn't name. Bridal gowns seemed to hang from every edge and lip of furniture: the wardrobe, the chair, the curtain railings, the end of Mia's bed – and between them stood Granny Brea and Heather Buckley.

'Surprise!'

Granny handed Mia a cold, slick bottle of champagne, and Heather kissed her cheek.

Mia, half-dazed with the relief that she had not been whisked away to an intervention, asked, 'What is this?'

'We knew you wouldn't go yourself,' Ruby said.

'And the wedding is four months away . . .' Sonia continued.

'So, we brought the bridal shop to you!'

Mia's gaze drifted from one perfect shimmering dress to the next. 'Where did you . . . ?'

'High street's best,' Ruby explained. 'Much to my credit card's horror – so you can't keep them all, got it?'

'And you *have* to try them on tonight,' Sonia said. 'I had to work serious magic on my mother to get her to look after Lily last minute.'

'Go on, Mia,' Granny said, reaching a hand over to touch the top of the champagne bottle. 'Enough chatter and let's get that thing popped!'

It was very un-movie like, Mia thought, with the tricky cork coming out in her hand and a plume of bubbles escaping afterwards. They grabbed loo roll and mopped it up, and served what was left into glasses, clinking them delicately.

'To Mrs Buckley!' Sonia said, raising her glass, and then giving Heather an apologetic look. 'Or maybe *another* Mrs Buckley!'

'New and improved,' Heather said, squeezing Mia's shoulder.

'It's pretty,' Mia said of the first dress.

It was off-white and satin, a slippery nod to the nineteen twenties, which nipped in at Mia's small waist.

'Pretty?' Sonia repeated. 'Pretty isn't *wow*.'

'It isn't *bury me in this*,' Ruby added.

Mia looked herself up and down in the mirror. 'Does it have to be . . . *bury me*?'

'It should be a little closer than *pretty*,' Heather said. 'Let's try another.'

Rather quickly, Mia realised that a key problem with this endeavour was that *all* of the dresses were *pretty*. And *pretty*, she thought miserably, was the *lovely* of wedding dresses.

'I had no idea you were so into photography,' Heather said from across the room. She was looking over the photo wall with great interest, while Mia was released from a rejected dress with a corset bodice.

'Oh, that?' she said with a little difficulty. 'I wouldn't call it photography. I just . . . like pictures, you know?'

'But they're really lovely, Mia. *Different.* You've never thought of doing this as a career? I don't mean to be rude but with talent like this, you're wasted as a waitress.'

'Mia's not a waitress, actually,' Ruby said. 'She's Cormac's assistant.'

Mia felt her cheeks pink.

'Assistant?' Heather said. 'Rosco never mentioned it.'

'It's relatively new,' Mia explained hurriedly. 'Nothing major.'

'Nothing major? You're at the hotel *all the time*,' Sonia said with a laugh.

'And then up half the night, looking through files for the man,' Granny added on. 'I've never seen you work as hard in all my days, and trust me, I would have liked to have seen a little more ambition when you were at your GCSEs.'

'Well, you really do have a good eye,' Heather said. 'And I'm not saying I *could* pull strings for family, but the newspaper could do with some young blood if you're looking for a leg up.'

'Thank you,' was all Mia could think to say. Her gaze flitted from the photograph wall, with the hotel in all its angles and Donahue, to the dress now pooling around her knees.

'Imagine trying to get that one off in the honeymoon suite,' Ruby puffed. 'It's a *no* from me.'

Mia darted a look at Heather, who merely giggled, and then Granny, who busied herself with straightening out another dress.

'Have you a favourite yet?' she asked.

'The one with lace around the bodice,' Mia said with forced confidence. 'It's comfortable.'

'What about that slippery little one in dove white?' Ruby asked. 'Maybe we could try it again?'

'Yes, I think we're almost finished with all the dresses, except – oh, you haven't tried this one, Mia.'

Unlike the others, this one had a bulky brown bag, the zip of which was rather dull, and a little stiff, too. It didn't carry the synthetic scent of new things, either, but a familiar smell that Mia recognised at once.

She looked to Heather, who beamed back at her.

'It's *mine*,' she said, her voice as tight and small as Mia had ever heard it. 'Your friends said you were having a little bother finding one, and well, I don't have any daughters of my own, so I thought . . . Well, it's an option, isn't it?'

'How long have you held on to this?' Ruby asked, slipping the dress from its bag so the full length of the gown could flutter to the floor.

'Thirty years, if you'd believe it – so if it's not for you, Mia, you just say. It can sit in the attic a little longer, I promise you.'

The women dressed Mia, pulling the lace sleeves over her arms, and fastening the buttons along her spine. They fluffed the pleated skirt around her bare feet and adjusted the scooped neck so that it lay flat against her chest.

'Now, that's a good fit actually,' Sonia said. 'Maybe take it up an inch or two—'

'And let the shoulders out a pinch—'

'Oh, wait, let me just—'

Heather pulled a long, shimmery thing from the old dress bag, attached the veil delicately to Mia's short hair, and stood back.

The room quietened. Mia watched her reflection.

It was a classic style, one that made her think of old movies and doe-eyed women. It cinched in at the waist to give her a more womanly shape than she actually had, and dipped around the neckline to accentuate the pale peaks of her collarbones. The long sleeves made her think of fairy tales where swans were turned into young women – or perhaps it was the other way around.

'Well?' Granny asked now at her shoulder.

Mia held her breath. The rest of the room seemed to have followed suit.

'It's perfect, Heather,' she said, a little shakily.

'See,' Ruby told her. 'See, *that's* how you're supposed to react with *the one*!'

The women cheered and *aw*'d. Granny came around so she might *get a better look* at her *little girl* and Heather began fussing about the hem saying, 'Yes, definitely two inches, see this – two.'

'My credit card is going to be so happy,' Ruby said, feigning a tear, and Sonia gave her a shove.

Mia laughed, though the knots in her stomach threatened to turn it to tears.

'Oh, send Rosco a picture!' Ruby cried, going to grab Mia's satchel by the door. 'Just a corner or something!'

'I'll get it,' Mia said, a little sharply. Ruby was too elated to notice, and Mia withdrew her phone. Then, she buckled the satchel and swept it under her bed, away from inquisitive eyes and fingers.

'Now, hold out your hand . . .'

Ruby snapped the edge of the intricate white details by Mia's wrist, clicked a few buttons and then handed it back to its owner.

'Sent!'

'I guess you're going to have a lot of returns to sort out,' Mia said apologetically, looking around the room of garments.

'Oh, like we care. I've had a ball. In fact, if *you're* not wearing them . . .' Ruby held up a dress to her chest and shimmied behind it.

Mia's phone pinged, and the women gathered about her to see the response:

Can't wait for the full view xxx

They cooed appreciatively.

'Is he always like that?' Heather asked. 'He's always such a grump with me, I can't tell if he's secretly a romantic or not.'

Mia thought about Rosco twirling her about in the little rented semi they would call their own in February. She thought of the boy in beat-up Converse, too afraid to talk to her in person, and the way he had kissed her when she had told him *yes*, she would marry him, just last year.

She thought of the nights she had fallen asleep in his bed and awoken to his dark eyelashes, long and feathery against his cheeks, and nights she had watched him laughing with Ethan and the others from her barstool.

She thought of the way he had looked at her in The Burning Lamp and the way he had held her afterwards. She thought of the days he had brought her home and the nights he had changed his mind.

She thought of his passenger seat and the accelerator.

'He takes notions,' she said, forcing a smile.

chapter 29
the receipt

'MY FATHER WAS A POOR ACCOUNTANT,' Cormac told Mia when she arrived at the hotel that morning. He had met her in the lobby and bid her to accompany him to his office for some *mysterious thing* he had come across – which turned out to be a pile of papers and numbers Mia wasn't sure she was qualified to unravel.

'Is that so?' she said, eyeing the cluttered desk.

'Woeful would be a better descriptive,' Cormac went on. 'I mean, where is the boundary between generosity and folly? I'm a cold-hearted man so perhaps I'm not really at liberty to decide. You're young and not quite as jaded as myself. What do you think of three hundred pounds for a lounge singer in nineteen sixty-nine?'

'Well, I'd have to do the exchange and—'

'It's about five grand today.'

'Oh,' Mia said, lips pulled to one side. 'Maybe they were a really great singer? Who is it made out to anyway?'

Cormac passed the slip of paper to Mia. The name it bore was *Syvita Angelica Green*.

'Syvita!' Mia gasped. 'That's my Singer!'

'Oh, so that's helpful, is it?'

'Well, it might have been, but I'm quite sure she's taken her leave. I took your advice and sent her song to *GhostHuntHub*.

com, and they published it the other day. It's already got a thousand views. In fact . . .' Mia pulled her phone out and brought up the website. 'Yes, there, two thousand views as of today! I couldn't see her yesterday at all. I'm pretty sure that'll have done it.'

'Pretty sure?'

'Yes, well . . . You know how they've been. It's like they're *trying* to hide from me. I didn't get a single decent conversation out of any of them yesterday, actually. I even had details about the Little Girl's wedding, and she didn't want to hear a thing.'

'The Little Girl's *wedding*?'

'Yes, she looks young, but didn't die until she was seventy-six. They don't always take their most recent appearance, remember.' She looked up at him. 'You told me that.'

He cut her an unappreciative glance, and she carried on.

'Anyway, she told me one day that she was married, so I've been looking through marriage registrations online, and what turns up but our ghost: Anna Loughran, married in nineteen-fifty-five to Simon Loughran, in County Armagh. But when I mentioned this to her . . . Well, I thought she'd have been keener to talk, but she got fussy instead.'

'Are you sure it's the right Anna Loughran?'

'Well, it better be. It cost me five pounds ninety to access it.' Mia slipped her notebook from her satchel. 'You wouldn't mind if I . . . copied that receipt out, would you? I like to keep everything together.'

Cormac shrugged. 'Sure. But don't crouch like that. Take this.' He rose from his chair. 'You'll break your knees doing that, and I've heard you need them later in life.'

With some caution, Mia got to her feet and eased herself into Cormac's warm chair.

'There's more where that came from,' he continued once Mia was seated, gesturing to a pile he had set aside. 'Have a look at the dates.'

Mia fanned the handwritten slips in front of her. They were in black ballpoint ink and dated September nineteen sixty-nine.

'The year the painting went missing,' Mia said.

'The *month* it went missing,' Cormac corrected.

She frowned. 'That's strange. Why was Donahue paying so many different people at that time?'

'Well, I don't know. That's why I called it *mysterious*.'

Mia copied the receipts out quietly and when finished, tapped the one made out to *Barrymore Primary School.*

'I know that school,' she said. 'The Headmaster upstairs used to work there.'

'Do you think he could shed some light on all of this?'

Mia stared at her list, the back of her mind itching with some inexplicable discomfort – the same as when her ghosts started talking about things she knew were important but couldn't place.

'Is it strange,' she asked slowly, 'that they all seem . . . linked in some way or another to this painting?'

Cormac frowned. 'Strange how?'

'Strange like . . . Well, I mean, they don't even like us *mentioning* the painting and then all of these payments . . .'

'It *was* quite the scandal of the time. Maybe it's a sensitive topic for them.'

'But is all of this . . . *too* coincidental?'

'What are you saying? That they're all connected?'

Mia's mind whirred for an answer, before she finally settled with, 'I don't know. I don't see *how*.'

'Well, if it helps,' Cormac said, tapping the school receipt, 'you can take that with you. I'll be here, sorting through . . . *this*.

Honestly, you would think I had enough work of my own, never mind the accounts of the dead, too.'

Mia returned his seat to him and went to leave. Something stopped her, however.

'Mr Byrnes?'

'Yes?'

'Do you remember Ballinadrum Hotel's Halloween party?'

Cormac gave her a wearied look. 'How could I forget? The one night a year when anarchy reigned through these halls. Well, more than usual. Why?'

'Oh, it's just . . . You know what? Never mind.'

'Mia Anne, what is it?'

Mia didn't quite know where to look. 'Well, it's just . . . It's silly, but my friend has been asking about this *Halloween party* thing for a while, and nobody really knows if it's happening—'

'I'm quite sure it's not.'

'Yes, and that's . . . Well . . . From what I've heard from people . . . It seems they would quite like it to . . . go ahead.'

Cormac frowned. 'You want to throw a Halloween party?'

'Not me personally.' She gestured to the air about her. 'The hotel.'

'You know the hotel doesn't have feelings either.'

'The *staff*. You know what I mean.'

He rolled his eyes. 'Well, it makes little difference to me. Ideally, I'll already be gone – if you do your job that is. And if not . . . you don't mind dancing on a building site, do you?'

'That's not very nice,' Mia said, but he was laughing.

'Trust me, Mia Anne. Your precious Ballinadrum Hotel is safe until Halloween at the very least. I may consider myself a decent businessman but I'm not that good.'

'So that's a . . . yes?'

'The closest you'll get to it anyway.'

She burst into a smile. 'Thanks, Cormac!'

Before he might question this use of *Cormac* or even change his mind about the party, she rushed off to her ballroom of ghosts, hoping they were feeling chatty.

As it turned out, they were not.

The ghosts were more interested in confusing Mia instead, flitting in and out of sight near enough with every other step. The Bride, for example, would almost fade to nothing, with just the ends of her lace veil visible, before suddenly bursting into full colour and twirling about the dance floor.

Mia didn't even try to count them by eye. She pressed herself against the wall and clicked the shutter of her camera.

Looking down, she could see twelve spots – two more than she'd hoped. She frowned at them, unsure of *who* was even present anymore. The Bride was there, as was Blue Dungarees, and the Headmaster, the Clown dancing all by himself. The Soldiers didn't appear, or at least, hadn't yet.

Feeling deflated, she snapped another picture, but the result was worse. Thirteen lights now floated in the photograph.

She took another, and another, and counted them one by one with her finger against the screen.

Thirteen.

'You know, if you keep your nose in that thing all day, you'll miss out on the whole party,' a familiar voice purred.

Mia wheeled on the Singer, almost dropping her camera entirely. 'You're . . .'

'Syvita Green,' the ghost said. 'Everybody knows that.'

Mia's heart sank; she'd been sure that loading the Singer's song onto *GhostHuntHub.com* had done the trick. Before she could dwell on her failure, though, another voice cut through the air.

'Watch me! Watch what I can do!'

Mia's gaze drifted back to the Little Girl, who appeared to be addressing her, because as soon as Mia's eyes lit on her, she threw herself into a graceless cartwheel. Upon righting herself, the Little Girl tossed her arms up like a gold medallist.

Standing beside her was, to Mia's disappointment, the Nanny – apparently, her conversation with Gerry had not been enough to shift her, after all.

Mia braved a smile.

'That's very impressive,' Mia told the Little Girl, who was still waiting for some sort of congratulations on her gymnastics. 'How long have you been practising that?'

'I could always do it. It's my *innate talent*.'

'You've been at it all morning,' the Nanny corrected. 'You shouldn't lie, Anna.'

The Little Girl stopped immediately. '*You* lied.'

The Nanny raised a hand and slapped it across the Little Girl's face.

It came so quickly, so unexpectedly, that Mia did not register what had happened until it was over, and the Little Girl had taken a stumbling step backwards, holding her cheek.

It couldn't have hurt, not really. There was no skin-to-skin contact, no blood to rush to the Little Girl's face, but Mia still dashed forward to take the young ghost's hand in hers.

'Are you okay?'

The Little Girl did not look up. 'I'm not a liar.'

'I know, it's okay. We all tell fibs sometimes, but I know you're not—'

The ghost's gaze drifted upwards, and Mia could see her blurred pupils and creased brow. 'I'm not a liar. You can't prove it. You can't prove I lied.'

Mia held tight to her hand, refusing to be scared. 'I know that. You're not a liar, Anna, of course, you're not. Your cartwheel was—'

But it wasn't about the cartwheel. Mia could see that by the blackness of the Little Girl's eyes.

'You know, Anna,' Mia went on, 'this party is a little dull, I think. It could do with some extra sweeties. I should order cake. What do you think? Or maybe . . . maybe lemonade? Or how about a plate of chips, or biscuits, or . . .'

'Biscuits,' said the Nanny. Mia glowered at the ghost, who wore a vague, unconcerned expression. 'Those chocolate ones – you know, with the creamy layer in the middle. I love those.'

Except when I last offered them, you told me they tasted like dog food, Mia thought.

With her eyes still on the Little Girl, she said, 'Anna. Anna Loughran.'

Slowly, the Little Girl's face brightened. Her eyes were blue once more, and her mouth upturned in a smile.

'Biscuits,' said the ghost. 'What kind do you have?'

Mia breathed a sigh, and finally let go of the Little Girl's hands. Her own fingers felt numb with the cold, and she rubbed them together before reaching into her satchel for a packet of ginger nuts.

'Your favourite,' Mia told her.

'Cookies!' the Little Girl cried, receiving one of the rust-coloured biscuits happily – before reaching for another, and another. When she dashed off, her fists were crammed full.

Mia heaved another sigh, just as the Nanny disappeared entirely.

There was something wrong with them, Mia knew. She just couldn't figure out what.

Cormac's receipt, however, was at least one clue she still had in her arsenal.

Mia slipped it from her pocket and sought out the Headmaster. It took some wandering about the ballroom, offering biscuits to various other ghosts and bidding them to stay a little longer – *just one more dance* – but he finally came into view and took one of the Ginger Nuts.

'Wonderful appetisers at this function,' he said. 'Very good, indeed.'

'Oh, we only serve the best at Ballinadrum Hotel,' Mia said, smiling. 'Especially with our good friends in attendance. You know, we were happy to help with that donation to your school.'

'Donation?' he said, frowning. 'I don't . . . There was no donation.'

'Oh, there should have been, so if you didn't receive it, I could—'

Irritation cast a shadow across his wrinkled face. 'Yes, well, it was a long time ago and trust me, that money was put to good use. The school stayed open, didn't it? It was worth it, wasn't it?'

He began to blur a little.

'Of course,' Mia said, relenting. 'You're perfectly right. Could I possibly offer you another . . . uh . . .'

'Shrimp cocktail?'

'Oh, yes, shrimp cocktail.'

But he didn't take a biscuit, just gave her a stiff nod, and wandered off.

She looked down at the little slip of paper, hanging on to it like her last lifeline. She could ask him another time, she told herself – when he wasn't threatening to break loose of himself and the ballroom's confinements.

And then she noticed something curious.

When Cormac gave her the receipt, she'd assumed it had been written by Donahue Byrnes. However, looking at it now, she could see it was not his handwriting at all.

A scream sliced through the ballroom.

Mia's heart lurched. Her first thought was that the Little Girl had come to blows with the Nanny again, but when she turned, the former was stamping about in the centre of the room, quite gleefully. Her foot came down again and again on the mess of biscuit crumbs, and Mia frowned. It had definitely been a child screaming. Screaming in pain.

Then Mia ran, Lily vivid in her mind. She didn't have to think about where she was going, because she knew – she needed to get to the lobby, to Sonia, to wherever it was Lily could be playing. Her thoughts swung from kitchen knives to tall bookcases, and her feet flew all the faster for it.

Breathless, she thundered down the last of the stairs, into the lobby, and almost onto the toes of some guest who was just checking out.

Sonia looked . . . unbothered.

'Where's Lily?' Mia asked with uncharacteristic sharpness.

With a wrinkle of a frown, Sonia said, 'Excuse me?'

'Lily – where is she?'

'What do you mean, where is she? Not here.'

'The grounds, then – or the dining room, or—'

'What? Mia, she's with her dad. She's not here.'

'But I thought—'

'I'm so sorry,' Sonia said to the guest, who seemed irritated by the interruption, and gave Mia an aggrieved look. 'If you could just sign here, and then . . .'

Mia stared from the man to Sonia and then the rest of the lobby. The few people present seemed unfazed, and a scream like that should have prompted *some* concern.

There was only one person Mia could think to ask: Cormac.

She found him pacing his office, on the phone. He quickly finished the call when he saw the look on her face.

'What's happened?'

'A scream. Did you hear a scream?'

As with Sonia, he had not, and was puzzled by the suggestion.

'But . . .' Mia frowned, confused, 'it sounded *real*.'

'I didn't hear anything,' he told her again.

Mia stopped. She thought.

'I need to get back.'

'Mia, what's wrong?'

'It's nothing, it's—'

'You look worried.'

Mia left Cormac's office with the same haste with which she had arrived – chasing the hotel's steps around and around until she arrived on the third floor – and Cormac, despite his age, followed her nearly step for step.

'It's probably nothing,' she tried to explain, but it didn't *feel* like nothing – and Cormac knew that too. 'I just want to check the receipt . . .'

Back in the ballroom, she looked at the dancers. They were . . . calm. Happy. The Bride posed and blushed. The Butler bowed here and there. The Little Girl was spinning in circles, and the Singer was seated at the piano, surveying the dance floor as though receiving a standing ovation. To see this particular scene, no one would think anything was wrong.

No one but Mia.

The ghosts did not acknowledge her, even when she crossed through their dancing steps and in between their conversations, and not when she stopped at the very centre of the room.

The marble floor was peppered with white.

'What is it?' Cormac asked, drawing alongside her.

Mia stooped to pick a small piece of confetti from the dust. 'The receipt you gave me,' she told him.

chapter 30
this person whom she loved

CORMAC ASSURED HER IT wasn't her fault, but Mia still felt responsible for having been tricked by the ghosts.

They had never tampered with her belongings before – at least, not like this – but there was no other explanation. There was no one else there and, in truth, she could just imagine them doing it: the Little Girl stamping all over it, the Bride shredding it. The Butler slicing it in two like unwanted post and the Gossip turning it to tiny pieces in her fingers.

Later that same day, in Cormac's office, Mia inspected another receipt – the one marked Syvita Green, in fact – and came to the same conclusion as before: it was *not* Donahue's handwriting.

Who it *did* belong to, however, was still a mystery – even to Cormac.

'I can look through other files and notes, if you think it would help,' he said, and she told him, without hesitation, *yes*.

Because if there was one thing Mia was now surer of than anything, it was that the remaining ghosts weren't hanging around for radio listeners or a stuffed toy.

They were here because of Owen Buckley.

But why?

Being so close to the answer and yet having no idea how to reach it was maddening. There was *something* – something to do with the painting, and Donahue, and that list of payments Cormac had showed her. Something the ghosts didn't *want* her to know.

It was with this in mind that Mia threw herself all the more fanatically into her research, concentrating specifically on Owen Buckley – his birthday, his teachers in the old Ballinadrum primary school, and how he had played on the local football team. His job before the hotel, and his wife and child, Maria.

None of it told her what her ghosts were trying to hide from her.

Every moment she did not spend in the ballroom, Mia spent in her journal and her thoughts, despite knowing full well that there were other, better things to think about – namely, her wedding, growing ever nearer, and the list of additional hair and beauty appointments she ought to be making. But time was so short, and becoming more so every single day and hour. She didn't want to fail – not when she was this close.

Tonight, she was up late again – her bed splayed with the newspapers Cormac had given her. Her fingers were already blotted by the old ink, and she'd committed the headlines to memory, but still, she thought, she may have missed something – something small and uninteresting at first glance.

First glances were so misleading, after all.

It was on page four, the picture of bodies emerging from the court room, where Mia found something that tugged on her memory.

Suddenly, the doorbell chimed. She sat bolt upright.

She glanced at the clock, just to be sure that it was in fact *too late* for anyone to be calling, and slipped out of bed.

Out in the hall, Granny Brea, too, was out in her pyjamas, her robe pulled tight to her chest.

'Who could that be?' she asked.

'I'll check,' Mia told her, passing by her to the stairs. 'You stay here.'

'And let my granddaughter open the door to who knows—'

'I'll not open the door, Granny. I'll look through the window.'

This, it seemed, was enough to satisfy the elderly woman, and she stayed put while Mia went to investigate.

Downstairs, a shadow moved behind the sheer lace curtain by the front door, seemingly rocking from foot to foot – waiting.

Mia leaned forward, fingers outstretched and pulled back the lace, just a hair.

The body moved. It faced her.

Mia felt a *whoosh* of air leave her. When she had steadied herself enough, she unlocked the door quickly and opened it just wide enough to peek her head out.

'*What are you doing here*?'

Rosco Buckley swayed in Granny Brea's porch light.

'*At last!*' This was not Rosco, but Ethan, who Mia could now see at the other side of the fence. Mia gripped the door tighter.

'Hey, Mia,' Rosco said. 'I wanted to see what you were doing.'

His voice was low and while he did not slur, Mia knew this careful pronunciation to be Rosco's own personal giveaway. That was, of course, if the stink of alcohol had not already done it for him.

'So, what are you doing?' he asked.

'Sleeping,' she told him flatly. 'It's two in the morning.'

'You weren't answering my texts.'

'I just told you I was—'

'Not all night. You weren't sleeping all night.'

'Well, I'm *busy.* It's not like I've been texting everybody else. You should see the number of messages I have from Ruby about this stupid Halloween party and—'

'But I'm not everybody else, am I?'

Mia looked at him, at a loss for words. 'I'm sorry,' she said at last. 'I'm sorry I didn't reply, but it's really late, and . . . well, you're drunk, Ros. You scared Granny.'

He looked down, as though only now realising what a fool's errand this was. 'Sorry, I just . . . I thought I'd come see you.'

'You'll see me in the morning.'

He took a step back. The porch light caught his lashes and made kindling of them. It struck Mia now just how unlike the Rogue Rosco looked. True, both were dark-haired, like all the Buckley men, but their faces were different. Their noses. Had the darkness inside Owen cast out his Buckley-ness?

'I miss you, Mia. I never see you anymore. You're always . . . somewhere else. In your head.'

'Rosco, I . . .'

'And I *love* you. I want to get married tomorrow and move into the House, and I want you to come out with us on a Friday, because you're . . . You're so pretty, Mia.'

'Ros, don't. I . . . Ros, Ethan's in Granny's bushes.'

Rosco swivelled, losing his balance a little but recovering adeptly. Ethan was, indeed, warring with Granny's front hedge, seemingly having stumbled into it and now facing the difficulty of detaching himself without any solid handholds out of it.

'For fuck's sake,' Rosco said under his breath, before turning back to Mia.

'Tomorrow,' he said.

'Tomorrow,' she repeated.

'And you won't be mad? Tell Granny I'm sorry, okay? I didn't mean to . . . Well, it's a bit of a dick thing to do now you've said that. I wasn't . . . It was Ethan's idea.'

'I figured.'

'I just missed you.'

'And I missed you too.'

'I love you, Mia. I don't want to lose you.'

She leaned on the door, and it swung open, just an inch. It was all Rosco needed. He lunged forward and his arms encased her, his face in her neck.

'Ros, you're . . . hurting me.'

He didn't let go, not immediately. If anything, he held tighter, as though worried such a protest was a sign she was about to wriggle from his grasp, and when he finally drew back, he took her face in his hands.

His fingers smelt like soap and coins and liquor, but she let him hold her. She let him see her tired eyes and her wary expression.

'Tomorrow,' he said again, and he kissed her.

It felt so simple, to be kissed by this person she loved, that for a moment, she was not present. She was reading a newspaper in her bedroom, and she was with her ghosts, unboxing their conversations.

It was only when he was out on the pavement, waving at her, and hauling his stupid friend from the hedge, that Mia realised she had not been a participant in the kiss at all, and how sad that was, not just for Rosco, but for her.

And she realised what had snagged on her mind in that newspaper photograph.

chapter 31
perfect typed ink

It was quarter to seven when Mia decided that she had waited long enough for Rosco Buckley.

It was a wet morning and rain fell like sparks through the orange lamplight glow.

'Are you sure he's not coming?' Granny asked at the door.

Mia, already on the street, popped up her umbrella. 'If he is, I can't afford to wait.'

She hurried on to the hotel with a crackling candy-like anticipation and more energy than her few hours of sleep should have produced. Not even the dark morning shadows and the puddles seeping into her shoes could dampen her mood.

When she reached the oak-lined avenue of Ballinadrum Hotel – the brown and orange leaves shaded purple by the early morning – she broke into a run. The windows of the hotel were dim and glowing like candles, and the dark roof blended into the heavily hung sky so that it seemed ever taller and more looming.

It was a beautiful thing, she thought.

Gerry had not yet started his shift, so she grabbed the door herself, eager to rid herself of her coat and wet shoes.

A flash of grey passed her shoulder.

Her first thought was it was one of her ghosts, escaping the hotel at long last for mischief in the wider world, but with her hand clutched to her chest, she looked down to find the thing that had hurtled by her was made of more substantial stuff.

A roof tile, smashed to pieces on the wet cobbles.

Inches from her head.

She looked up, rain spitting upon her cheeks and eyelashes. There was nothing but deep, dark cloud and pale flecks of rain.

'It wasn't an accident.'

Cormac Byrnes wasn't in his office when Mia arrived, but in his bedroom, asleep, and so Mia called him on the phone. He appeared in a matter of minutes, looking unusually rumpled in a grey woollen jumper and corduroy trousers instead of his typical suit.

Now seated opposite Mia on one of the lounge's armchairs, he was still a little grumpy. 'What do you mean it wasn't an accident? The building is ancient.'

They were alone, save for the flickering flames in the fireplace and the tick of the clock on the wall, but Mia still felt watched.

'Old, yes, but the roof was checked last summer, and there hasn't been a single bad storm since then. It *shouldn't* have fallen.'

'Yes, well, strange things happen in old buildings. They're liabilities at the end of the day.'

'*Those ghosts*,' Mia said under her breath, 'are the liability.'

'Ah, we're on the same page about them. You think they have something to do with it?'

'I think *one* of them did. In fact, I think he's been involved in a few strange things going on around here, and I'm pretty sure it's because we're catching up with him. He knows we've got him.'

'But we haven't.'

'I disagree. Last night, I was looking through the newspapers you lent me, and I'm surer than ever the ghosts have something to do with *The Field by Our House*. I hadn't seen it before, but I wasn't looking closely enough and—'

'Get to the point, Mia Anne.'

'The Bride,' she said. 'The Bride was in the photograph at the court case.'

Cormac, who had been rubbing his brow, sat back. 'She was?'

'*Yes*. And when you look at the notes I've gathered on the ghosts, they've all worked or been baptised or married in the same thirty-year span. That means there's every likelihood they were alive at the *same time*.'

'Is that important?'

'On its own, maybe not. But think about it: we have *thirteen* ghosts, and if you take away Owen Buckley, that leaves . . .'

'Twelve,' he said.

'And in a court case, there are twelve—'

'You don't really think . . .'

'*Jurors* – there are twelve *jurors*. This is *the* jury that put Owen Buckley away in nineteen-sixty-nine.'

'Are you sure? I mean, are you going on solid evidence or a hunch here?'

Mia's shoulders sank. 'Well . . . I don't have anything *solid*, but it all adds up.'

'Does it? Do you know *why* they're here, or just that they're connected to the case?'

Mia opened her mouth and closed it again. 'I suppose not,' she said at last. 'Do you at least think it's . . . a good hunch?'

Cormac leaned forward. 'How am I to know? I thought you were the one leading this investigation?'

'Yes, I suppose I—'

'And stop saying you *suppose*. Look, let me give you some advice: if you're going to wake an old man before sunrise, you best have a good reason to do so, and if you've got a good reason, you damned better be prepared to convince him of the same. Got it?'

She nodded.

'Mia Anne, your work with these creatures has been . . . satisfactory. You should learn to take some pride in it, because you know well enough that no one else will do it for you.'

'Satisfactory, huh?' she said, smiling despite herself. 'Well, in that case . . . I *do* have a good reason. And I'm . . . I'm going to convince you, too.'

'I welcome the challenge,' he said, and just about smiled back.

*

The rain was unending, and when Mia Anne Moran and Cormac Byrnes left the hotel later that morning underneath the small cover of Mia's umbrella, they agreed one of them should really have brought a car.

'I can't drive,' Mia told him sheepishly. 'I never learned.'

'You never . . . *Why*?'

'I wasn't good at it. My fiancé said it's not for everyone.'

'I have to disagree. How do you function in a place like this without a car? There's only one bus every hour and I can't imagine we're any closer to a train station than twenty minutes. What, do you walk everywhere?'

'My fiancé drives.'

'Ah, well, I suppose that's to be expected if he discouraged you from finding your own means of transportation. Did he deliver you to these dark doors this morning?'

'No. He . . . was late.'

'So, you *did* walk.'

'It's not that far.'

He rolled his eyes. 'And this *fiancé* of yours – does he know what you're doing at the hotel?'

Mia hesitated. 'He thinks I'm your assistant.'

'That's more or less the truth.'

Less, Mia thought.

'I don't like lying to him,' she said. 'But he . . . he didn't believe me when I told him I'd seen things in the hotel before, and I . . .'

'Didn't want to convince him?'

'Well, I could hardly bring him to the hotel and *show him*. And what if I did? He'd probably not want me working here even more. It's just . . . easier to keep them separate.'

'So, to keep the boy *and* the hotel, you must court them individually and make sure neither finds out about the other.'

Mia bristled. 'Well, what would be your suggestion?'

'Oh, I'm not suggesting anything. In fact, if I give you any romantic advice, don't use it.'

'Not so successful in love?'

He cut her with a sideways look. 'I'm sorry, I didn't realise we were swapping stories at a sleepover.'

'I only thought if we were discussing fiancés and driving skills . . .'

'Well, we're not.'

Cormac took hold of the umbrella so that he might position it better over Mia's head and they completed their journey in silence, save for his occasional curses at the wind and rain and cars splashing by.

*

Ballinadrum Library was a creaky old building of grey bricks and windows. Inside, Mia could have counted the patrons on one hand.

The librarian on duty stood crouched over her desk, studying a large textbook with apparent enthusiasm.

As the two approached, she greeted them with a hundred-watt smile.

'*Mia*,' she said in a breathy whisper, 'I haven't seen you in *forever*.'

Mia's eyes widened. 'Miss Barry?'

'*Mrs Davison*, now, actually. Didn't you hear?'

'You're not at the primary school anymore?'

'Nope. Been here for about six months, actually.' Mrs Davison readjusted her ponytail, and then, swishing it about, asked, 'And who's *this?* An uncle, grandfather?'

'Her employer,' Cormac said flatly.

'*Employer?* I thought you were still working at that old hotel? You have to tell me, sweetheart, what on earth did you—'

'Miss Moran's place of work has not changed.'

Mrs Davison blinked a few times, then gave a giddy laugh, which prompted the few readers present to shoot her deadly glances.

'Cormac Byrnes! *Of course.* I've heard *so* much about you! My auntie remembers you when you were still in your teens – said you had a head of blonde hair back then.' She gave a breathy cackle. 'Seems things have changed somewhat. Where have you been hiding out?'

'I've been working. Look, what we need—'

'And thirty years in London, I hear. You really have lost the accent.'

'Yes, I'm aware. What I need from you is—'

'You thinking of staying? That would be so wonderful for the hotel; it really should stay in the family. That's what everybody's been saying.'

Before Cormac could reach across the counter to strangle the librarian, Mia cut in.

'I'm sorry, Miss Bar – I mean, Mrs Davison. We're in a bit of a rush. We need to see the public records – specifically, court cases in nineteen sixty-nine.'

'September nineteen sixty-nine,' Cormac clarified. 'Something like Buckley versus—'

Mrs Davison gave a little gasp, eyes sparkling. 'Buckley versus Byrnes? The painting theft, right? What was the name of that thing . . . *House Field* or something, right?'

'I don't think that's any of your—'

'Yes, that one,' Mia said. 'Do you have it?'

'Well, I haven't looked in the old records in a while, but I'm sure the biggest criminal case in Ballinadrum's history will be back there somewhere. What on *earth* are you looking at that for?'

Cormac spluttered with indignation, but Mia just smiled.

'Research,' she said. 'Marketing stuff. We're trying to . . . you know, think about how to bring out the historical side of

Ballinadrum Hotel. Not a lot of places have these kinds of stories to tell.'

'I've been saying that for *years*. Like, the ghosts. *There's* a story. When did the hauntings start? Must have been in your daddy's heyday, hm, Cormac?'

'We're in a rush,' Cormac reminded her.

'Yes, sorry about that,' Mia added.

'Oh, of course! There's me, gabbing again. I'll go have a look for it, sure. You two take a little seat and I'll be back, quick as a—'

'Quick will do,' Cormac growled.

Mrs Davison gave a laugh as though it was the funniest joke in the whole world, before disappearing through a door behind her.

Cormac cocked an eyebrow at Mia. 'Stories to tell, hm? Seems you've been doing a little more thinking about the hotel than I had thought.'

'It's hard not to think about the future of the place you spend every waking second.'

'Well, it's a lovely idea, but I hardly think ghost stories make for a particularly relaxing or family-friendly atmosphere.'

'That's not strictly true,' Mia said. 'Granny used to take me to this Halloween festival down south and we'd pick pumpkins, get toffee apples, and they did all these scary story readings. It's really about how you frame it. You know, I was actually talking to a couple who booked a stay at Ballinadrum *because* of the ghosts.'

'Halfwits,' Cormac said.

'And Henry gave me this textbook about marketing from his university days, and it says what you're selling isn't always the product itself, but rather the *feeling* of the product. What if we sold something . . . fun, and magical?'

Something like Donahue Byrnes.

'You want to sell the hotel as a ghost story?'

'I'm just saying there might be something more important to the hotel than . . . copper and tiles and what you can get for scrap.'

'Yes, and you certainly think so. I must admit I've been curious about your fascination with the place. Did my father really make that much of an impact on you?'

'He made things seem . . . brighter,' Mia said. 'I know that's not *your* memory of him, but for me . . . he was a wonderful man, and I . . .' She looked to the door through which Mrs Davison had disappeared. 'I'm a little nervous about all of this if I'm honest. I'm worried about what I'll find.'

'So am I.'

Mia looked up at him. His face was unusually soft, though he did not meet her gaze.

'You are?' she asked.

'I like to be right,' he said slowly. 'I like it very much, and I . . . Well, I was wrong about the Rogue, Mia Anne. You knew it before I did, and I just kept barrelling on like there was no other version of the truth but the one I knew. My father, the villain, come to haunt me. And yet, that wasn't it at all.'

He finally looked at her.

'I'm nervous that I spent over forty years believing something that wasn't true, and I'm . . . I'm also a little nervous in case it was. I remember him as the man who chose his ghosts over his son, but perhaps it was a more tangled story than I allowed it to be. Perhaps I . . . *was* wrong, and still am all these years later, and I hate to think I simply squandered every chance I had to reconnect with him.

'Yet despite it all, and how . . . curt I've been, about my father and your experience of him, I would quite like it if you were right about this, too.'

Cormac dropped his gaze, while Mia's held on. He looked both older and younger in the sallow library light, a drop of rain idly hanging on to his left eyebrow.

'Do your best to know your parents while you have them, Mia Anne,' he said. 'It really is a journey we tend to neglect.'

Mia's eyes finally fell away. 'Oh . . . Well, my parents are actually dead – but I know what you mean.'

Cormac frowned, gathered his thoughts, and said, 'You must think me the rudest arse to ever cross your path, Mia Anne. I am so sorry—'

'It's okay. I was three.' She shrugged as though to say *it happens* except, when it came to all her classmates and nearly everyone in town, Mia knew it *did not*. 'I don't remember much about it.'

'May I ask how—'

'Car accident. There's this bendy road out on the other side of town, and they've put up slow signs there, but—'

'No,' Cormac said gently. 'Sorry, I didn't mean that; I was going to say . . . How do you . . . *feel*?'

She looked at him, a question tightening her brow.

'About the hotel,' he went on. 'And . . . what you do. I didn't realise when I asked you to . . . Well, I didn't know—'

'I love the hotel,' she said. 'That hasn't changed.'

He nodded, slowly, and Mia wasn't sure what he was thinking, but it didn't look like pity.

'They got married at Ballinadrum, you know,' Mia said.

'Oh?'

'Yeah. Granny said it was a really wet day, absolutely pouring, but it was November, so they had planned for that possibility. Most of the photos are all inside the hotel – in the lobby, by the fireplace. There's one where they're in the bar with champagne glasses, and it's all done up with flowers and everything. It's beautiful.

'But my favourite photo is this one that Granny keeps in one of the albums. She doesn't think it has *photo-frame potential* because . . . well, it's quite blurry. See, they're running to the doors of the hotel in the rain, and you can hardly see their faces because of the umbrella and all these little white flecks, but you know that they're laughing, and it's . . . It's my favourite, even if it's not perfect.'

He looked at her, a question in his eyes.

Mrs Davison suddenly appeared through the door wearing a dimpled smile. '*Found it.*'

Cormac reached out. 'Thank—'

'It's *so* interesting. In fact, I had a little flick through, and I *really* think—'

'I said *thank you.*'

Cormac pulled the record from her hands, and though Mrs Davison's smile faded a little, it didn't quite slip from her face.

'Well, you'll let me know if you need anything, won't you? *Anything* at all.'

Cormac did not grace her with an answer, but stepped quickly in the direction of a cluster of desks in the far corner of the library – as far away from Mrs Davison as possible. Mia followed, offering an apologetic smile over her shoulder.

She pulled up a chair opposite Cormac, who was already flicking through the report, his blue eyes small and shrewd.

Mia's, by contrast, were as wide as dinner plates.

'Well?' she asked.

Cormac glanced up at her, down at the report, and back again. 'In truth,' he said slowly, 'I don't know what I'm looking for.'

Mia rolled her eyes with an impatient sigh, whipping the report around so it faced her instead.

'You don't have to be so rude about it,' he told her.

'Is that advice you live by?' she asked, and he glowered at her.

Mia returned to the report, handling it like a newborn – pages lifted with measured slowness, gaze moving with care. Much of it appeared to be legal jargon, but she knew the names in between.

Ballinadrum Hotel
Donahue Byrnes
September 1969
The Field by Our House, 1912
Owen Buckley

Only three witnesses seemed to have been called: a waitress named Sheila who had been on duty that night and spoken to Owen in passing; Owen's wife, who insisted he was only at the hotel because he had been called in last minute by his manager, Francis Croft; and Francis Croft himself.

His wife had sworn up and down to his innocence, the waitress had testified to him being a *lovely fella*, and Francis Croft had described him as *lingering* in the lounge where the painting had gone missing.

'Look here,' Mia hissed, pointing out a list of names. 'It's our ghosts.'

Cormac leaned over the table, his brow furrowed and eyes sharp.

'I don't have all of their first *and* last names, but . . .' She ran a finger along the page. 'Kelsey Cunningham: the Bride. Syvita Angelica Green: the Singer. Anna Loughran: the Little Girl. Arnold McVee: the Headmaster.'

Mia reeled off the rest of her ghosts, each one faster than the next. 'The Butler. The Florist. The Butcher. The Lady. The Nanny. The Clown. Blue Dungarees. The Gossip.'

In a flurry, she reached into her satchel. She laid her notebook out flat on the table, comparing the two lists.

The ghosts of Ballinadrum were in perfect typed ink – and had been so this entire time. She just hadn't known where to look.

'I was right. I was right.' Mia's voice grew higher and softer, until her words sounded like one insistent breath. 'It's why we can't get rid of them. It's what they've been keeping secret. *This* is why they're here, Cormac.'

'What is?'

'The case, the robbery, the—'

'Yes, but they *caught a criminal*. How would that be cause for hanging around the hotel for fifty years after?'

'But the painting,' Mia said. 'It was never found. You said it yourself.'

'Because it was obviously sold on. What of it?'

'But what if it wasn't sold? What if it's . . .'

'Still there?'

'What if *that's* why Owen is hanging around? And the others are hanging around because . . . Well, because they know it, too.'

The hotelier did not appear wholly convinced. 'It just doesn't feel . . . neat.'

'Neat?'

'Like when two jigsaw pieces just fall together.'

Mia studied the names. 'It's the closest thing we've got. Maybe if we went back to the hotel . . . Maybe he *was* guarding something after all.'

'The painting,' Cormac repeated. 'You really think so?'

'There's only one way to find out.'

chapter 32
owen buckley

SOMETHING WAS WRONG. Mia knew it from the moment they rounded the gates of Ballinadrum Hotel: the noise, the cars. The ambulance.

The pair picked up the pace, and as they arrived at the steps of the hotel, they joined a small crowd. Lorna McGowan was on the phone, her red boots luminous, while Ruby was talking animatedly to one of the waiters, and Henry paced back and forth.

More alarming still was Rosco's red car.

'Oh no,' Mia said.

Rosco, soaked through in a T-shirt and jeans, closed the space between Mia and himself in a heartbeat.

Without thinking, she asked, 'Why are you here?'

Rosco's already dim expression darkened. 'Why am I here? Are you serious?'

He seemed to wait for an answer, but Mia didn't have one. She flushed.

'I'm *here* because a couple of guys in work said they saw an ambulance come up here, and you didn't answer your phone. I was worried.' His tone faltered, and Mia found her own steely resolve give way, too.

'I'm sorry,' she said. 'I didn't—'

'Yeah, I *know*.'

The coarseness surprised her. 'Is . . . Is everything alright?'

'No, it's not. Gerry's hurt. A roof tile fell on him.'

Mia felt the ground under her tilt, just an inch. 'What? Just now?'

'I don't know – I got here ten minutes ago. *You* should know, though. *You're* meant to be here. Where were you?'

Mia hesitated, unsure of how to begin.

Cormac tried for her. 'She was—'

'I didn't ask you.'

'*Rosco*,' Mia hissed.

'Well, I didn't. I asked *you*.'

'I was at the library, doing research. My phone was—'

'Off.'

'On silent.'

'Same difference. And before that?'

'I went to work early.'

'So why didn't you text?'

Mia glanced between Rosco and Cormac meaningfully, but Rosco didn't seem to care about the company. He waited. 'You were late,' she said quietly.

'By ten minutes. You couldn't wait?'

Cormac cleared his throat. 'Mia Anne, perhaps we could . . . pick this task up again tomorrow? It looks like I'll be dealing with this issue here the rest of the today. Go home. Get some rest.'

Before Mia could argue with him that she didn't *want* to rest, she wanted to find *The Field by Our House*, he had tipped his head and was making his way towards the scene in front of the hotel.

'He's so stuck up,' Rosco said, leading the way to his car. 'With that fake accent. Everybody knows he's from Ballinadrum anyway.'

'He's been away a while.'

'Yeah, well, he should have stayed away. Things were easier before he got here.'

Mia looked back at the crowd – to Sonia who had finally noticed her and held up a hand of greeting and concern, and the old shining doors that were now without their warden.

For once, she agreed with Rosco.

*

'Poor *Gerry*,' Granny Brea said, blowing steam off the surface of her teacup. 'Hit him on the shoulder you said, Rosco?'

Rosco had his hand on Handsome Boy's head, ruffling his ears. 'So I heard. The place is a death trap, Brea.'

'Well, he's a tough old cookie,' Granny said. 'Hopefully the worst we'll have to deal with is the milking he'll do afterwards. You should have heard him the year he sprained his ankle on the ice. I never thought I'd hear the end of it.'

'Still,' Rosco said, covering Mia's hand with his own, 'I don't know if you should be working in a place like that anymore. Not when it's being sold anyway.'

Mia resisted the urge to pull her hand away. 'Just because it's for sale, doesn't mean it's *closing*.'

Rosco scoffed. 'As if anyone will keep it open. Besides, Mum was saying the other day about getting you on the paper. Photographer. *That* would be a smart move.'

'You are very talented, Mia,' Granny said. 'And with all the time you've been spending at the hotel, I haven't seen you working over your pictures much these days.'

'See,' Rosco said, 'you're overworked. You can't put any time into your passions.'

'That's not true.'

'Well, what do you do besides work?'

Mia thought of Ginger Nuts and newspapers from another lifetime. She thought of a box of Lost Property treasures and music no one in the world had ever heard besides herself, Cormac, and Donahue.

'Just give it a think,' Rosco said. 'You'd see it our way if you took a step back from it.' He rose from his seat. 'I better get back to the garage, though. Thanks for the tea, Brea.'

'No problem at all, Rosco, sweetheart. And remember – come back tomorrow and we'll all go visit Gerry in the hospital. Get him some nice grapes on the way, hm?'

Granny Brea walked him to the door, thanking him, again, for dropping Mia home. 'That sounded positive,' she said, returning to the room.

'What?'

'The paper. Heather must have really meant it when she said you were talented if she's still talking about it. This could be good for you.'

'Can't *I* decide what's good?'

It came out sharper than Mia had meant.

'I'm only saying,' Granny said, tone disapproving. 'No need to snap at me – or Rosco, for that matter. You hardly said a word to him all afternoon.'

'What did you want me to say? "Thanks, Rosco, for asking me to quit a job I love"?'

'He's only looking out for you, Mia. He probably doesn't understand how much it means to you, so if you just *tell* him you'd rather stay at the hotel—'

'I literally just did. You heard me.'

'Well, tell him again.'

'I don't want to have to repeat myself.'

'Then where does that leave you, hm?'

Mia frowned and let the quiet stretch on. 'I don't know,' she said at last.

Granny watched her, a knot working at her brow. 'You know, Mia Anne, if you're not careful, you could lose that boy.'

*

Mia woke in a worse mood than the one she had worn to bed.

She had lain awake the night before, turning to her phone for distraction, and her friends for support. It didn't come as she had hoped, though: Ruby and Sonia were as excited about Heather's job suggestion as Granny, it seemed.

Do photographers get to go to cool press events? Begsy plus one!

Begsy other plus one! That would be so great!

Sorry, not taking it. Ballinadrum FOREVER.

Honey, I dont even know if Ballinadrum Hotel is Ballinadrum forever.

After that, Mia had put her phone away. She didn't know how to correct them – how to tell them about the time and effort she had put into saving the place, or the magic it had in its very bones.

No one understood.

No one but Cormac.

She dressed quickly, grabbed her satchel, and hurried to the hotel. Cormac was waiting for her by the lift.

'Got your text,' he said. 'Are you ready?'

She nodded.

'You seem . . . upset,' he said inside the lift. 'Are you sure you want to do this?'

'Yes, so don't try to talk me out of it.'

They rode in silence, until the doors opened, and they stepped onto the third floor.

'Is this to do with that young man yesterday?'

'I'd rather not talk about it.'

'I only wanted to say . . . Well, I don't think you should let him talk to you like that.'

'Mr Byrnes, *you* talk to me like that.'

Cormac made a *tsk* sound. 'Need I remind you that you're not marrying me? I'm speaking from experience when I say people don't actually change as you think they will when you marry. As someone who's been through a divorce—'

'Mr Byrnes, I don't want a lecture right now.' Mia stopped in the small passageway, the cold from the ballroom drifting about her ankles. 'I want to . . . fix this whole mess. And I don't want to think about what happened yesterday. Is that okay?'

Cormac nodded. 'Okay.'

The ghosts were unhappy when they arrived. Mia could feel it.

The Lady was weeping, and Syvita Green was whispering to herself. The Little Girl stood atop the piano, flinging music sheets into the air, while the Butler made some attempt to catch them. His movements were sluggish though, and he stumbled about in the shower of the paper.

Mia raised her camera to the scene.

'How many?' Cormac asked.

'Twelve, I think.' She tried again. 'Still twelve. He's not here.'

Cormac's gaze turned to the back door. 'Then let's keep going.'

The Little Girl stopped playing the piano and trailed alongside Mia instead.

'Do you want to see me cartwheel?' she asked.

'Of course,' Mia said, eyes still looking ahead. 'Go ahead.'

'You have to watch.'

'Yes, I will—'

'No, watch me. *Watch me.*'

She grabbed at Mia's hand, and it felt like Mia had plunged it into ice water. She pulled back, hissing.

'Watch me,' the Little Girl continued. 'Watchme watchmewatchme—'

'Anna Loughran,' she said to the ghost, whose lips were still moving though not making a sound. Her eyes were darker than before, and Mia didn't like it. 'Anna Loughran, I can see you. I'm watching.'

She felt a tug on her arm, and expected more cold, but none came. It was Cormac, forcing her on.

'Wait—' Mia began, but as she moved, she realised why Cormac had grabbed her.

The ghosts – all of them – were suddenly here. Suddenly watching, in a way Mia had only ever seen them do the once, on the first day she had stepped into the ballroom.

It was as if they didn't know her – except they *didn't*, she reminded herself. They never had. It was only that now . . . Now it seemed they did not *like* her.

They knew, Mia thought.

Cormac and Mia increased their pace across the room, and Mia wanted to say *don't* – she didn't want to go to that back room. Not ever, but especially now, with her ghosts all quiet and all staring.

Waiting.

But for what?

Cormac opened the door before Mia could argue, and she stumbled into the dark after him. Shadow enveloped them until he lit a path before them with his phone – which gave Mia an uneasy feeling they had given away their position. It was foolish, though, she knew, because what she was frightened of didn't need a light to know she was there.

The room at the top of the stairs contained the same mess and line of lockers as before. It might have been comforting to find some bird's nest or a family of mice, but there was nothing living to be found. It was utterly dead and unused – dull, really, if it hadn't been for the way the shadows from their phones' torches spilled across each object, giving claws and teeth to things that had neither.

'Start looking,' Cormac said under his breath.

'You go left,' was Mia's whispered reply.

There was nothing new to be found with a superficial search, so Mia forced herself onto hands and knees to look beneath the lockers.

When Cormac gave a small gasp, Mia rushed to his side. 'What?'

'Up there,' he said softly, as though there was anyone else to hear them. Perhaps there was.

'The painting?'

'No . . . a book, I think.'

'Can you reach it?'

'I'm . . . trying.'

'Let me give you a boost.'

Cormac scoffed. '*You?* Give *me* a boost?'

'Well, I'm—'

'Smaller. Undoubtedly lighter.'

'But I'm younger. And you've a bad back.'

He offered her only a glare as an answer, bending forward and lacing his fingers together as a suitable step for her.

She obliged. He huffed under her weight, but otherwise did not complain, and Mia swept her phone across the top of the locker space.

It was dusty and dirty and, as per Cormac's supposition, hid a squat little book.

'Well?' Cormac said, his voice noticeably strained.

Mia tucked her phone into the pocket of her skirt and, holding Cormac's shoulder just a little tighter, reached out into the darkness. Her fingertips brushed leather and she took hold of it.

Hopping down from Cormac's hands, she held the book out in front of them.

Cormac staggered upright, panting a little. 'Is that . . . ?'

'No,' Mia said. 'Mine is in my bag.'

'It looks just the same.'

'My Granny said that Donahue gave it to her as a gift. Maybe . . . Maybe he had lots of them.'

'Well, open it. What are you waiting for?'

Mia held her breath as she turned to the first page, the second, then the third. She flicked through the whole book.

'Nothing.'

'Nothing?'

Cormac took the book from her. 'There can't be nothing. There's got to be—'

A small, feather-like thing fell from the pages and Cormac stooped to grab it.

A sharp bang shattered the silence.

'What was that?' Cormac asked.

'I don't know—'

'Was it the door?'

Mia rushed to investigate, and quickly confirmed said door was, indeed, closed. Moreover, when she tried the knob, it wouldn't give.

'It's locked,' she said, voice rising.

'It must lock automatically. I'll just . . .' Cormac withdrew his key, but when he went to turn it, it made a sickening *click, click click.*

'Isn't it working?'

'It's just old, it's . . .' Cormac's turning grew more insistent, his voice frayed. 'Goddamn it, Mia Anne, it's just an old door. It's an old building. Stop panicking.'

'I'm—'

'I just said *stop.* Don't you listen to anything?'

He kicked. The door shuddered.

Mia then tried her own key, to the same useless clicking.

'Look,' she said, 'I'll just call Ruby or Sonia. It'll be . . .'

She turned to look at Cormac and her words dried up.

Over his shoulder, she saw the Rogue.

His hair was pushed back just the same, and he wore the same smart suit from years gone by, but this was not how Mia knew him. No, rather, it was his eyes – his unflinching stare.

Cormac spun. The light of his phone did not pass through the figure before them, but cut his face into ugly angles and shadows, allowing Mia to see just how dark his eyes truly were, how warped his smile.

Whatever it was he saw, whatever he had heard, Owen Buckley appeared to find it funny.

Mia did the only thing she knew. She spoke his name.

'Owen,' she said, voice thin as a wire. 'Owen Buckley.'

The man before her tilted his head. And his mouth curled upwards.

He took a step towards them, and Cormac pushed back against the door.

'Owen Buckley,' she said again, louder. 'Owen Buckley, I know you.'

He did not slow. His mouth hung slack, his eyes predatory.

'Owen Buckley. I know you.' Mia was shouting now, only vaguely aware of the tears springing to her eyes. 'I know what happened, and I know what you did. We don't want to bother you. We just want to leave.'

Cormac began kicking the door. He pounded and it banged, but it did not give and the man in front of them took another step.

'Owen Buckley, I know your family. *Olive* – I know your sister. And I know your friends – Donahue Byrnes, and Francis Croft and—'

All at once, the lights above came on.

Cormac was shouting too now, and Mia's eyes darted between the lights and the ghost in front of them and the floor she had already run out of.

The bulb grew brighter and brighter, until Mia could not bear to look at it – and then it exploded.

The lights went out and they were plunged into perfect darkness.

Until they weren't.

A flicker of flames dripped down from the light above, onto the boxes, the folded curtains, the frayed carpet. They only smouldered at first, little sparks, little flashes of light, but they soon flared to life and became great licks of yellow and orange.

And the Rogue was gone.

Mia coughed. Cormac swore.

He threw himself against the door again, and this time, miraculously, it opened. The hotelier stumbled out into the dust and debris on the other side, and, coughing, turned back to Mia.

'Quickly,' he said, and held out a hand.

She took it without a word.

chapter 33
silly little girl

MIA STOOD IN THE FRAGILE DARK, looking up at her beautiful hotel. Ruby held on to one elbow, and Sonia the other.

'It'll be alright,' Ruby said. 'She's a tough old girl.'

'And it's mostly just the west wing, right? We don't even use the west wing.'

Mia didn't answer either of them. She didn't know how to, nor how to cry, nor do anything but stand and stare, shivering in the smoke-laced air.

The fire engines had already arrived, and a short while after, police cars pulled alongside them.

Guests stood in the car park, wrapped in their hastily grabbed coats, and conversing in low, concerned tones.

Cormac, with Henry in tow, had been called away for questioning a little while ago, though before then, he had stood with Mia, and allowed her to tuck her hand into the crook of his elbow.

'Do you think they saw?' she had whispered to him.

'I don't know,' was his faint reply.

The firefighters had gone through the windows of the west wing's corridor. It was the easiest access point to the origin of the fire, they said, raising their ladders to the old hotel's walls and laying siege to it – and windows could be replaced. Windows weren't lives.

But somehow, it felt a bit like a life to Mia. She did not know how long those windows had been there, protecting the corridor and the adjacent ballroom from light and wind and rain.

According to the firefighters, the damage was limited, and they were all very lucky – particularly because Mia had been outside and noticed the fire. Otherwise, who knew how far it might have travelled, and what more damage it might have wreaked, before anyone had realised? As it was, only the carpet, floorboards, and insulation in between had been truly damaged, and while the ceiling wasn't in great shape, it was still intact.

It was hard to feel lucky, though, Mia thought, and harder still to feel anything but frightened, staring up at her hotel, thinking of her ghosts.

Thinking of Owen Buckley.

Suddenly somebody gripped her from behind.

'My girl,' Granny said. 'My Mia, are you alright?'

'Granny,' Mia said, vaguely dazed. 'I'm . . . I'm fine. But the – the hotel, Granny.'

'I know, my love. I know.'

Mia was about to ask how Granny had arrived when the answer came onto the scene and stood nearby, his face marred with a scowl.

'Rosco,' she said, and he just about looked up. It felt all too similar to that last day, when Gerry had ridden off in an ambulance, that Mia almost tried a joke: *we really must stop meeting like this*. But she knew Rosco well enough to know how that would go. The time for jokes had long since passed.

'He was so worried,' Granny answered for him. 'He saw it on the internet – the smoke. Someone posted a photo and when he couldn't get you on the phone, he came straight to our house.'

'And then we came here,' Rosco answered. His voice was hoarse, and he, too, looked the hotel over, though not with a gentle gaze. Rather, his glare told Mia he wished the fire had taken more than just insulation.

'We should go,' he said at last. 'You'll freeze out here.'

Granny agreed before Mia could offer any counterargument. She would have preferred to stay with Ruby and Sonia, but wasn't about to make a fuss – not here, in front of everybody when things were already this bleak.

'Okay,' she said softly.

Her friends hugged and kissed her goodbye, and when she left, she saw them loop arms around one another – gazing upwards still, like the hotel was a simmering sunset, too beautiful not to watch.

On the way back to the car, Rosco took Mia's hand. He held it loose, and she didn't know what to think, and then – then, there was Cormac, standing with two policemen, looking distant and ashen.

Suddenly, Rosco dropped Mia's hand and marched up to Cormac – so quickly, she didn't even have a moment to give chase.

'If you were as smart as you think you are,' she heard Rosco say in a low, angry tone, 'you'd get rid of this place before it really does kill someone.'

Mia found her feet then, rushing forward to intervene in some undetermined way, but Rosco had already turned away. He looked as cold and unlike himself as he ever had as he took her hand once more, urging her towards his car.

Mia took one look back at Cormac. She wanted him to know that Rosco was wrong about the hotel, and that what they were doing was important – and she wasn't finished. Not yet.

*

Mia woke and did not immediately recall the night before. For a half-second, she only knew that her room was soft grey, and it was morning.

Then, the memory came back to her. She balled her sheets in her fists.

It shouldn't have happened.

Owen Buckley should have stopped. He should have calmed at the sound of his name, or at least recognised someone was speaking to him. He had only smiled. He had come closer, gone further. How far must he have lost himself?

It was hard to remember anything clearly but those eyes and the flames and the running.

Mia pulled on a knitted jumper and a pair of jeans, smoothing out her stubborn bed head with her fingers, but her movements were all habit. Her mind was on Owen Buckley and whatever mysterious thing it was that had fallen from the empty journal.

It must have been important, she thought. They must have got too close.

She searched out her satchel. Perhaps she had missed some key part in her research.

The satchel was, peculiarly, on its side by her dresser with some of its contents tipped out: lip balm, a purse, headphones, a couple of pens. No notebook.

A ribbon of unease unfurled within Mia, and she thrust her hand inside, finding only further useless items. She tossed them onto the floor and then turned the whole bag upside down.

Another pen, a scattering of receipts, and a half-opened blister pack of ibuprofen, but still no notebook amongst them.

Mia surged into the hallway, and thundered down the stairs where the warm, buttery scent of breakfast found her.

'Granny, have you seen my notebook, I—'

Granny Brea sat at the dining table, upon which was a tray of bacon and stack of buttered toast. She was pouring tea for Rosco, sitting opposite.

'I thought you left,' she said unthinkingly.

Granny barked a laugh. 'And good morning to you, too.'

Rosco looked darkly across the room.

'Sorry,' she said. 'But I . . . I lost my notebook and I—'

'You should eat,' Rosco interrupted. 'You didn't have much dinner last night.'

'Yes, Mia,' Granny said. 'Have some breakfast. And say a proper hello to Rosco. He's been so worried, he was back first thing this morning.'

Rosco pulled out a seat beside him. 'Sit down.'

Granny poured another cup of tea, offering it to Mia. Mia, unsure of how else to respond, took it, and the chair beside Rosco.

'I . . . I can't find my notebook,' she said.

'Your notebook? Which one?' Granny asked.

'The one you gave me. It's brown, leather. Donahue gave it to you.'

'Oh, *that* one. Haven't come across it, sorry, sweetheart. Do you think you left it at the hotel?'

'No, it was in my satchel.'

'We'll have a good look for it then, after breakfast. Can it wait that long?'

Granny rose from the table, giving her granddaughter a quick squeeze on the shoulder.

Mia's eyes snapped back to Rosco.

'When did you leave last night?'

'After you fell asleep.'

They surveyed each other, and Mia felt a chill like a wind blowing through a valley. There was something so foreign about him in that moment, something alien and untouchable.

She had never quite recognised how grown up he had become.

'You took it,' she said.

His expression didn't change, but his silence was all Mia needed to hear.

'How could you?'

With his jaw set, he said, 'You forced me to.'

'I've never been able to make you do anything.'

He rolled his eyes and shifted to retrieve something from his pocket. Her notebook.

She reached out to grab it, and he snatched it back.

'Give it to me,' she said quietly.

'How long have you been writing this?'

'I said give it to me.'

He flipped through it carelessly. '*How long?* Because the stuff in here is *insane*. Ghosts and butlers and dead soldiers. This *Field by Our House* painting.'

She sat there, hating the heat in her face.

'Look, I know you took Donahue's death hard, but this isn't any way to deal with those things. The hotel isn't haunted. It's not special. What you're writing in here . . . is it a story? Is it made up? *What is this?*'

'Don't.'

'I mean, it's crazy, Mia—'

'*Don't*—'

'I don't think I want a wife who—'

'You don't want a wife who does what, Rosco – believes in ghosts? Who's a waitress? Who does things you don't always approve of?' Mia felt tears push behind her eyes. 'Because if that's the case, it doesn't sound like you want *me* as your wife.'

He levelled her with a serious look. 'Now, you're being ridiculous.'

'No,' Mia said. 'I'm being serious, and I'm – I'm *annoyed*, Rosco. I'm annoyed that you took that, and I'm annoyed you keep telling me to leave the hotel, and—'

'Alright – I think you've made your point, Mia.'

'And you – *you shouldn't speak to me like that*.'

He narrowed his eyes. 'Like what?'

'Like I'm crazy. Like – like you know better, even when you don't.' She took a breath. 'I don't want a husband who speaks down to me, just as much as you don't want a wife who believes in ghosts.'

She looked at him, and some part of her was still sixteen, she thought – still quivering under his gaze, still believing he was too handsome to even look at her. For a moment, she thought maybe he felt that, too: all the time between them coming to this moment, all the love between them spinning out of control like a car off the road.

He held her gaze until his straight mouth curved upwards, and he asked, 'Is that so?'

'It is.'

'So, what are you saying here?' he asked, still with that smile – that awful, infuriating smile. 'You want to break up?

Because, you know, Mia, you haven't been easy to deal with recently, and I've been more than patient—'

'I'm *saying* that I . . . that I don't know. I don't know if we're right for each other. You just said it. *You* said it first – you don't want a wife who—'

'I didn't mean it like that.'

'But that is the way it is.'

At last, the smile faded. 'That's the way it is?'

'Yes.'

'We're breaking up?'

Mia paused a moment. 'I think we are.'

Something akin to hurt crossed Rosco's face – before it was replaced with derision. He shook his head, and laughed. 'You've totally lost it, Mia. You are a one hundred per cent, grade A *mental case*. And all because of this hotel—'

'Not just because of the hotel. Because – because of *this*—'

She leaned forward again, and this time, managed to take the journal from him. In an instant, she was on her feet, and heading for the front door, breathing hard.

It was a bright morning, the clouds thin and wispy overhead, and Mia was running before she even knew where to.

But there was only one place to run.

*

The hotel was quiet like a still night, each step she took like the crunch of untouched snow.

She could still hear the pipes at work, the breathing of the floorboards, but the murmur of voices, in the dining room and bar, and the lobby, was gone.

It was strange to see it utterly deserted, for the only light to reach the terrazzo floor to be that which streamed through the windows. Part of her expected to see someone behind the desk, or to hear the *ding* of the lift, but of course, nothing stirred, and the blue hydrangeas looked on in silence.

She reached Cormac's office, and knocked twice, trying not to take much notice of the ring on her left hand.

There was a shuffling behind the door – he was probably searching for insurance documents and other important things – and Mia didn't wait, but opened it herself.

What she did not expect to find was a stranger staring back at her.

'I'm so sorry, this is a . . . staff member,' Cormac was saying. 'You know how these types of businesses are, I'm sure.'

He was tidying papers at the desk, forcing them clumsily into a file, so they bent and split. He did not meet her gaze, but rather continued to talk to the man beside him.

This man was tall and dark, with a thick beard and leather jacket. Surprised by Mia's entrance as he looked, he did not appear angry, but bemused – as if her presence was laughable.

There was nothing funny, however, about the twist in her gut when she remembered where she recognised him from.

'Mr Gurning? Why . . . Why are you here?'

'Mia, that is none of your business,' Cormac hissed.

Mr Gurning's gaze shifted to Cormac, wearing that same amused smile. 'Didn't you say the hotel was closed today, Mr Byrnes?'

'I did,' Cormac said stiffly. 'It is.'

'It seems as though you have a few cracks in your defences, then.' Mr Gurning chuckled, the only sound in a too quiet room. 'I'll call you in the morning once everything has been processed. A pleasure doing business, Mr Byrnes.'

Cormac nodded with pursed lips and once the door was securely shut behind Mr Gurning, he asked, 'What do you want?'

'He bought the hotel,' Mia said. 'Or did he just . . . buy the bits?'

Cormac began to tidy his desk, though it was practically empty. 'I'm not going to explain my actions to a—'

'We had a deal!'

'We had a . . . pinkie promise, a silly child's game of a thing, Mia Anne, and you know that as well as I do. What was I supposed to say when someone came knocking, actually wanting to *buy* the place?'

'*No*,' she said. 'You were supposed to say *no*.'

'Well, I didn't.'

At last, he looked at her, and his eyes were as stony and unforgiving as the day she had met him.

'You were only able to sell it because of me,' she told him. It was meant to sound hard and spiteful, but it just sounded miserable. Lost. 'You were too scared to do it alone.'

'And for that, I thank you. It was a great help.'

The full meaning of those words cut through her then, cold and mean as a knife. *She* had done this. *She* had been the one to help Cormac with his ghost problems, the one to get rid of them and keep them under control. She had been his sole secret keeper, the only one stupid enough to walk amongst the dead and call it purpose.

She had ruined everything.

'Donahue loved this hotel,' she said. 'I hope you realise what you've done.'

'I'm well aware of it, Mia Anne,' he replied. 'I've cut my losses and made some profit. I would say that I'm sorry for all of this, but really, this is probably the best thing that could have happened to you, too.'

She felt his words like the slap they were.

For one single heartbeat, he met her eyes again. Then, he looked away.

'You really should be getting home now. The hotel is closed.'

She was breathless, dizzy – too shocked to cry and too embarrassed to argue. She turned for the door, but stopped just briefly, hand on the doorknob.

In a low, brittle voice, she asked, 'What was inside that journal?'

Cormac paused, and then said, 'I don't know what you're talking about.'

Outside, it had started to rain. The sky filled with dark, heavy clouds and puddles shivered on the pavement.

Mia took out her phone, considered calling someone, then thought better of it. She slipped it back into her pocket, and that's when she saw the glint of red paint, the arm hanging crookedly from the car window.

Rosco got out, holding the car door in front of him like a shield.

She waited for him to tell her how dramatic she was, how foolish. She waited for the cruel edge in his voice. *What was she doing running away from him like a child? Did she think the ghosts would be waiting for her? Wasn't she too old to believe in Donahue's stories?*

'Do you want a lift?' he asked instead.

She felt a tear slip over her eyelashes.

'Oh, Mia,' he said, so soft and gentle that she felt at once that she must still be seventeen and staying over at his house in a pair of his mother's pyjamas. 'Come here.'

She half-fell into him, her nose crushed against his chest. He folded his arms around her and told her everything was going to be okay.

chapter 34
sorry

MIA THREW OUT HER JOURNAL the next day.

Rosco watched her do so, and although he had not asked her to do it, she knew it made him happy by the way he drew her into his arms afterwards.

'I love you,' he whispered.

It was her first day off in weeks and she was spending it at the Buckleys' house, curled up on their sofa with the fire murmuring over the coals. Rosco had thought it best for her to be away from her bedroom and her photograph wall with all its memories in plain sight.

Still, Ballinadrum Hotel could not be escaped.

'Awful about the hotel,' Joseph Buckley said in passing. 'All those jobs.'

Mia nodded listlessly, and let the conversation skate by.

She ignored the notifications buzzing through on her phone, too. She knew they were from Sonia and Ruby, and she didn't want to talk to them.

'What about this one?'

Mia looked down at the job advert Rosco had slid under her nose, for a housekeeping manager in an upmarket hotel.

'You could do that,' he said.

'I'm not a manager.'

'But you should apply. You have a lot of experience.'

'As a waitress.'

'In a hotel.'

She looked up at him, his insistence grating against her own. They both knew whose would win.

'Sure,' she said.

At some point in the afternoon, Heather Buckley returned with a banging door and excitable shout of *hello*. She burst into the living room, still wearing her coat and checked scarf.

'We have budget!' she announced with elation. 'Can you believe it?'

'Budget,' Rosco repeated. 'For Mia?'

'For Mia! Well, for a *photographer*, but I'll be running the interviews myself and I know who my favourite candidate is already. When are you free to come in, Mia?'

Mia had said so little all day that when it came to such a direct question, she fumbled. 'What?'

'She's shocked,' Heather said with a laugh. 'I want you to come in for an *interview* for the position as our new photographer. It'll just be a little chat, and we can go through the sort of things you'll be doing day to day, and *oh*, maybe we should look at a new camera for you. Rossy was saying you just have that little digital thing.'

That *little digital thing* was lying at the bottom of Mia's wardrobe, every image in its memory deleted.

'That's . . . great,' Mia said. Her face was slow to catch up with the sentiment, and Heather's own enthusiasm dulled.

'Perhaps this isn't the right time,' she said.

'No, of course it is,' Rosco insisted. He squeezed Mia's shoulder. 'You're just surprised, aren't you?'

Mia found herself nodding. 'I didn't . . . expect it to be that fast.'

Heather found her smile again. 'Well, of course. I am the editor, you know. I can work *magic* overnight – if you're ready for it, of course.'

'She is,' Rosco said. 'Aren't you, Mia?'

If she'd been standing in front of him, she wouldn't have known where to look, but sitting like this, curled under his arm, she let her head nod.

'Look, I'll go pop the kettle on and then we can have a chat, okay? I'm not here to railroad you, but . . .' Heather beamed. 'I just think it would be *wonderful.*' She stripped off her winter coat and took to the hallway again.

Rosco didn't loosen his grip on Mia's shoulder. 'That's great, isn't it? You don't have to worry about any of these stupid hotel jobs anymore – you can throw out the whole applications list!'

Mia did not meet his gaze, but picked apart the carpet with her eyes.

'You *are* excited about this, right?'

'Yeah,' she said softly. 'Of course I am.'

'Well, you don't look it.'

'I'm just . . . I'm surprised. Like you said.'

'Good.' Rosco drew close to her so that she felt his breath on her cheek. 'You know,' he said slowly. 'You never said sorry.'

A coldness found her. 'For what?'

'For when you went running off to the hotel yesterday – you said we weren't right for each other, Mia. And you know, it wasn't just that. It was *all* the times you did things like that – ran off and didn't say where you were, the late nights, early mornings. All the secrets and quiet car journeys. You upset me, Mia. And you didn't say sorry.'

His fingers trailed along her shoulder.

'We can move on once you say it,' he said. 'You'll get this job at the paper, and we can get married, and everything will be normal again. All you need to do is stop making things up and say sorry.'

Finally, Mia looked at him. Everything was starry, like a head rush or fainting fit. If she could have photographed the moment, it would all be a blur—all overexposed colour and jagged sound waves and Rosco's eyes like two burn marks in the centre.

'Sorry,' she heard herself saying. 'I'm sorry.'

That night, Mia regarded her photo wall. The yellow lamplight illuminated it with the cheap tones of an all-night garage, and she approached them, slowly, almost unwillingly.

So many memories had been pinned up against that pale-blue paint, so much time and effort put into preserving moments that had already passed.

She would take new photographs, she thought, of their semi in town and parties with friends, of the paper's offices and the report-worthy scenes she was sent to. She'd take new pictures of Ruby and Sonia and Granny. She'd find new places to eat cheesecake and drink tea.

Mia reached forward, silver glinting on her ring finger, and plucked a photograph from the wall.

It was a fuzzy picture of the hotel lobby at Christmas, all reds and greens and speckled with gold. What was the point in keeping it now? It was over, and even if it wasn't, what business did she have trying to capture time when all it ever did was flow through her fingers?

Slowly, her hand moved to another photo, and she let it fall to the floor without even examining its contents, and then she ripped off another, and another, with increasing haste.

Soon, there were more pictures on the floor than on the wall, and before she knew it, Mia's fingers touched the last photograph.

Donahue smiled up at her. His blue eyes twinkled more in memory than in ink, but there was the smile that had always hinted at some fantastic secret, which she had never known in full – and had never expected to run so deep or so dark.

She held Donahue's photo a breath longer, then took it down with the rest.

chapter 35
halloween

HALLOWEEN NIGHT WAITED for no one. It arrived just as planned, without halting or slowing even a second, though Mia had long given up asking that it might.

Pumpkins glimmered outside neighbours' doors and the cackle of teenagers rang through the night. There was a delicious anticipation of something unknown and unspeakable, and it felt as though the very evening air, cold and spiced with woodsmoke, was holding its breath.

The Buckley house was warm. Strings of spider webs were draped across the back of sofas, and scented candles, named things like *Sweater Weather* and *You're My Boo*, sizzled and sputtered. Heather had donned a felt witch's hat, and Joseph, in a leather jacket, had greased back his hair. The twins wore torn and bloodied shirts, and a black-and-white monster movie flickered on the television.

'It's great,' Rosco was saying. 'It's got six different lens settings, and she's still getting used to it, but I think it'll give some really amazing pictures.'

'Suppose you'll be learning on the job,' Joseph said. 'Best way to do it, in my opinion.'

'But weren't any *hotels* hiring?'

Mia could hardly look at Olive. She had hoped the old woman wouldn't have appeared tonight, but of course, it was

Halloween – the only holiday of the year she could *actually* be expected to observe.

'She's trying something new, Olive,' Rosco said. 'It's a good thing.'

'I suppose that makes sense. I only assumed you might have mourned Ballinadrum a little longer before moving on to the next job.'

'*Olive*,' Joseph laughed. 'It's a building, not a person. And how else is Mia supposed to be paying bills if she's wearing widows' weeds over the fate of a *business*?'

Olive's interest moved from her nephew to Mia.

'I've brought a few albums with me,' she said. 'If you'd like to have a look.'

'Oh, it's okay,' Mia told her. 'I wouldn't like you to have to get up.'

'I don't have to at all.' Olive rocked forward to the large leather handbag at her feet. 'They're right here.'

'Oh, well, I, uh—'

'Mia's finally got bored of it, too,' Matthew stage-whispered to Grant. The two of them tittered to themselves, picking more biscuits from the spread of foods on the coffee table.

'No, I haven't,' Mia said quickly.

'Yeah, and I'm sure you'll say you actually *want* to be here next,' Grant said.

'I do, actually.'

'You don't want to be at the hotel? Big party, you know. Isn't that where your granny is tonight?'

'Yeah, but—' Mia began, just as Rosco cut in with, 'It's just the bar.'

The twins had an impish glint in their eyes. 'But it's the last night the hotel will be open. Didn't you want to see it one more time?'

'Well, it might have been nice, but like I said, we're here and—'

'So, you *did* want to go?'

'No, that's not—'

'Mia's left the hotel,' Rosco told them, his voice tight. 'So, stop dragging it up and find someone else to bother. What are you supposed to be anyway, chavs on a night out?'

Joseph whistled a chiding sound, and Heather sucked her teeth.

'Behave, boys,' she told all three of them, and then, to Olive, 'We'd love to see your photographs, Olive.'

'Is this book just full of dead people?' Grant said, playing for laughs from his twin.

'It's Halloween,' Aunt Olive said in a cool tone. 'Is it not well suited to the occasion? We're closer to the dead now than on any other night of the year, what with these lines between our worlds blurring and thinning. Or were you under the impression that Samhain was all about . . .' She gestured blithely to the room of plastic decorations and silly costumes. 'This,' she said flatly.

The twins didn't answer, but swapped unimpressed glances.

Olive slowly withdrew a thick, black photo album, her eyes just as dark as she fixed them on Mia.

'Come here,' she said. 'Come and see it more closely.'

Mia hesitated, as did Rosco, who still had her hand tightly closed within his. Then, she rose, and crossed the room to perch gingerly at Olive's side.

'I remember you asking about Owen,' she said, quietly enough that the television almost drowned her out. 'And I thought it was a shame you got rushed away so quickly.'

Mia met her beetle-like eyes. They were searching, she felt, for some sense of likeness, a hint they were more a matched set than the others.

Olive pointed at the photograph in front of her.

'Do you know who these young men are?'

The picture was of an old kitchen, four men seated about it – three of which were obvious Buckleys for their dark hair and tanned complexions.

'Buckleys?' Mia said with a small smile.

Olive cackled. 'Buckley breeding is potent, alright. But . . . do you know them?'

'Trevor,' Mia said, pointing to Rosco's grandfather. His picture appeared around the Buckley house often enough for Mia to recognise him, though she had never met him. 'Mm. You told me last time, but I . . .'

'That's alright. Samuel, here in the blue, and Dennis. You didn't see the fourth last time.' She pointed to the man on the end, the only one with hair lighter than chestnut. 'That's Owen.'

Mia felt the room around her still, or rather all of the sounds of bickering and television clustered into the distant, cottony noises of air travel. Even Rosco's dark gaze, the loudest thing in Mia's world, was just part of the roar.

'*This* is Owen?'

'Mhm.'

Owen Buckley was thin and angular, with the same short, sharp nose Rosco had. His brown, downturned eyes looked directly into the camera, and in this particular image, he was dressed in a pale turtleneck and blue jeans, holding a cup of tea to his chin.

Was it right that the Rogue ghost in the hotel didn't look like Owen Buckley *at all*? Ghosts didn't always take the shape of their most recent likeness, but . . .

'What age was he there?' Mia asked Olive quietly.

'Twenty, twenty-five perhaps? Quite handsome, hm?' She sighed. 'Poor lad. The mind can be a difficult place for some people.'

Mia had been scared, panicked. Her torch had distorted his features, surely. Because it made sense, didn't it? Hiding his crimes even in death was a suitable explanation – it fitted, it worked. She and Cormac had already agreed.

But.

She could not help the *but*, and thought back to her ghosts, to the room of dead people talking in circles, circles, circles.

If it wasn't Owen, who was it? If he wasn't haunting the hotel to hide his crime, who was?

I'm not a liar, the Little Girl had said. *You can't prove I lied.*

And then she understood. Mia gasped.

'Mia?' Rosco was at her side in an instant. 'What's wrong?'

'I'm so sorry,' she said, or perhaps whispered, or just breathed. 'I have to go.'

She knew there was a commotion behind her, a chorus of voices asking where she was going and if she was alright, but there was a thumping in her head that raged over it all. It pulled her forward, pushed everything else out, and Mia had left the living room before she even quite knew what she was doing herself.

Rosco was close behind. 'Where are you going?'

She was slinging her scarf about her neck, throwing her satchel over her head. 'To the hotel. I have to tell Cormac—'

'You've got to be kidding me.'

'I'll only be—'

'No, Mia. You'll not *be* anything. You're not going anywhere. You're going to go back into the living room and have a cup of tea.'

'But I don't want to.'

She hardly knew the words had escaped her mouth, they were so far away and foreign to her. She only knew that his face twisted angrily and his eyes were on her.

'What do you mean you don't *want* to?'

'I mean . . .' She took a breath, and another, but neither seemed to help. 'I mean what I said. I don't . . . I don't want to.'

'And what *do* you want to do?'

He asked it like she should be embarrassed, like a teacher asking a misbehaving pupil what they had done wrong. He asked it like she wouldn't tell the truth.

'To go to the hotel,' she said, and grabbed the door handle just as he moved in front of it.

'You're being dramatic again, and ridiculous—'

'Says the person *blocking the door.*'

'Because I'm trying *to help you.* It's gone, Mia. The hotel is gone. I mean, what are you even running *to*? Cormac doesn't care about you. *I* was the one who followed you. *I* was the one waiting outside for you. *Me*, Mia. I'm the only one who's there for you. And I . . . Mia, fuck, *I love you so much.* What are you doing?'

He was right, she thought, the truth of it all burning cruelly in her mind. She was twenty-two, pinning her whole future on a hotel she didn't even know would be standing at the end of the year, and when she was thirty-two, unmarried and alone in Granny's empty house, while her friends had moved on with their lives, and Cormac couldn't remember her name, would this night have been worth it? Would any of it have been worthwhile?

She thought of Heather's wedding dress. She thought of that semi in town. She thought of all the photographs she had boxed up and the notebook she had left in the wastepaper bin.

She thought of Donahue, dancing on the tables at a Christmas party.

'I didn't mean it,' she said. 'When I told you I was sorry – I wasn't. I wish . . . I wish I could be, but . . . I'm just not.'

She flung open the door.

Rosco chased her down the driveway.

'You've never appreciated me. This relationship never meant a damn thing to you, Mia; I had to put in all the work, and for what—'

Mia kept on walking.

'You walk there in the dark, you'll get knocked down and it'll be all your fault, and if you do come back, I won't be waiting for you this time. You . . . You leave, Mia, and that's it.'

She paused at the post box at the end of the drive.

'We're over,' he called. 'You take another step, and we're done.'

Mia Anne Moran looked back, just once. She could see the triumph in his face – the almost-smile that told her he thought he had won, yet again.

She turned into the night.

chapter 36
the last piece

BALLINADRUM HOTEL THUMPED WITH MUSIC. Mia could hear the pulse of the bass as she crossed through the gates, and it got louder as she approached.

There was no Gerry on duty, of course, but a cluster of people talking and laughing beneath a hazy cloud of their own smoke. Mia dodged through them and into the lobby.

It was a stark contrast to the last time she had been here, and busier than she had anticipated. In previous years there had been fifty or sixty people maximum, but tonight there was hardly room to breathe. Nylon capes rubbed against nylon wings, and plastic masks were pushed back onto foreheads. Children in garish face paint rushed about the lobby, their plastic pitchforks and brooms swinging through the air, while a group of partygoers in minimalistic animal ears perched on the front desk.

A green-skinned gargoyle grabbed Mia's shoulder.

'You came!' it exclaimed.

'Uhh—'

'It's me! Hugh!'

'*Oh*. Of course! I, uh, like the green.'

'Thanks. Ruby did it.'

'Where is she?'

'At the bar! I'm running to the bathroom, but hey – it's good to see you. I heard you were leaving and then Ruby said you weren't going to come and, well, that seemed like a shame.'

'Oh, thanks, Hugh, I . . . Uh – you haven't seen Cormac, have you?'

'Hm . . . I think he was here earlier on, but haven't noticed him recently.' He patted her on the shoulder. 'Really good seeing you, Mia.'

He strode off to the bathrooms, the edges of his face paint just visible around his ears as he turned, and Mia headed for the lift.

Nothing stirred and all was black.

Mia stepped out of the lift and into the darkness, fumbling for her phone's white torchlight. The third floor was eerie, but this was her hotel.

She tamped her fear down just enough to make the journey from the lift to the ballroom possible, and all at once, she was there – pushing the unlocked door open and peering down into the lonely passageway.

Overhead, the lights were already on, and a breeze blew over her – along with a voice. It was low and gravelly, and made her think of greying temples, pressed white cuffs and the blue of a winter's morning.

She rushed towards it, her chest suddenly so full she might have sobbed right there for how she had missed this walk, this passage to another world.

The ballroom was a terrible beauty to behold.

The doors to the corridor were blown open, and glass glittered on the floor. The windows themselves were all shining edges, crystalline and perfect even in their brokenness.

The wind outside breathed cold and chimney smoke through to this once airless place, and moonlight touched it with magic.

Cormac Byrnes stood at its centre, a cluster of spectres surrounding him.

'Stay back,' he was saying. 'Get away.'

But the ghosts, Mia could see, were confused. Their home had been cracked, their hive punched through.

'Syvita Green,' she called to them. 'Kelsey Cunningham.'

At once, the ghosts turned their attention on her, and Cormac did the same. There was a satisfying surprise to his face, Mia thought, though the same could not be said of the rest.

The ghosts did not look happy. Their eyes and mouths all tugged at the corners.

'You're not supposed to be here,' Cormac said, rushing from the ghosts to Mia.

Mia had a hundred and one things she wanted to say, triumphant and bold and sure, but the ghosts spoke first.

'We're not liars,' the Little Girl sang out. 'I'm not, we're not.'

'He told us,' said Blue Dungarees.

'He never left,' said the Gossip.

'What did you do to them?' Mia whispered to Cormac.

'Nothing,' he snapped. 'I came up here *because* they were like this. I've been trying to calm them down but . . .'

'You can't prove it!' the Little Girl shrieked, and her eyes were just a shade too dark.

'They know,' Mia said.

'Know what?'

'Why I'm here.' She grabbed Cormac's elbow, urging him away from the ghosts. 'Cormac, the painting, the Rogue – it's not Buckley.'

He frowned. 'I know.'

'You . . . *know*? But you never . . . You closed the hotel.'

'I know what I did.'

'But *why*?'

'I didn't mean to,' the Little Girl wailed, stumbling towards them. 'I didn't know what would happen.'

Mia stepped in front of Cormac.

'Anna,' she said in a commanding tone. 'Anna Loughran.'

Immediately, the Little Girl's face brightened – but only for a second. In the next instant it was somehow more shadowed than ever, and her fists curled up to her eyes, which sprung with tears.

'You can't prove it. *You can't prove it.*'

Her cry tore through the building like an electric shock, the bricks shuddering and glass tinkling.

'Anna, I understand. It's okay. Anna Loughran, you—'

Her mouth opened wide, and a shriek poured into the air. And then, Anna Loughran disappeared through the floor.

Mia dived after her, but her palms slapped against impenetrable terrazzo. Still on her knees, she looked up at the ghosts, all a mixture of shame and longing and fear.

And each of their eyes held that little spot of black.

Mia scrabbled to her feet. 'We have to go.'

'Go where? After her? We don't even—'

'We just have to *go*.'

'He's still here,' the Singer sang after them, as Mia and Cormac plunged back towards the third floor. 'He's still here.'

'Explain yourself,' Cormac huffed as they reached the lift.

Mia pressed the button furiously. '*Me?* I have nothing to explain. You, on the other hand—'

'*I* don't need to explain anything—'

'How about why you sold me out? Or better yet, what you found in that journal?'

The hotel shuddered. The lights overhead flickered.

'I don't see how it's of any relevance to you, Mia Anne.'

'Relevance? After all I've done for you these last weeks, you really think this has no *relevance to me*? I came here tonight *for you*.'

Another shudder went through the building. The lift still had not arrived.

'This isn't working,' Cormac said. 'The stairs.'

Mia chased after him.

'Tell me,' she said. 'Tell me what was in that journal. I need to know.'

'Mia, can you just—'

'I already know it was Francis Croft, Cormac.'

She stopped on the stairs and so did he.

'He framed Owen Buckley and bribed the jury. The receipts – they weren't in Donahue's handwriting but *his*. And the ghosts . . . Well, you heard them. They accepted the bribes and that's why they're here. Isn't it?'

'Croft died,' Cormac said slowly, 'in September last year.'

'How long have you known? How long did you let me think it was—'

'It was . . . It was that last day – the day of the fire. I hadn't seen the ghost so close before, hadn't made the connection, it was so long ago that I had seen him. But after that, when he was right there in the room with us . . . I recognised him. I looked through the files again, and checked the handwriting against those receipts we found and . . . well, that confirmed it.'

'Then, why didn't you *tell* me?'

'Because it didn't matter. The hotel was—'

'It did matter! It mattered to *me*.'

'Well, it doesn't anymore, does it? So go home—'

'Home? I *left* a perfectly good home tonight to be here. Because this is where I *want* to be – where I feel smart, and useful, and capable. Why can't you understand that? Why are you pushing me like this? We had a deal and I'm just—'

'The deal is *off*. I told you that.'

'Well, I still want to fix this.'

'Mia—'

'No, you can't just invite me into all of this and then slam the door in my face one day without warning.'

'You've *had* warning. Were the flames not enough?'

'So, that's what this is? You think it's too dangerous? That was *one* time—'

'And it could happen again. I know now I should never have made that deal with you, Mia Anne. It was too much to ask. Too reckless, and selfish. I never wanted to be like—'

'Like what? Like *him*?'

'Mia,' he said warningly.

'Because I think maybe you should be *more* like him, Cormac – more like Donahue,' she went on. 'I know he wasn't perfect, but he would understand *this* – why it's important. He wouldn't have sold it off to the highest bidder, especially after making me a promise. He would have stuck to his word. He would have—'

'He would have put this building first, regardless of the consequences and however many people got hurt in the process.'

Cormac was angry, but Mia was too.

'So that's what it is,' she said. 'After all this time, you still hate him.'

'No, after all this time *you* still don't *know him.*'

'And you do?'

Something in the way he flinched surprised her.

'Do you?' she asked.

He was slow to answer. 'Mia Anne, I . . . I don't want you to know what's in that journal because I already know it will matter to you, and that you won't like it. And despite what you may think of me . . . I don't want that for you.'

'But that's not your decision to make.'

'It was the one I thought best.'

'Well, it wasn't. It was selfish and mean and—'

'Nothing worse than what you already thought about me.'

She stared at him, unwavering, and the creases about his eyes folded, the anger going out of him. With a heavy sigh, he thrust his hand into his pocket, and withdrew what looked to be a small, frail feather. He placed it into her hand, and when she looked down at her open palm, a pressed hydrangea bloom lay crookedly against her skin.

A purple hydrangea.

There was another rattle, another shudder. Mia tried to pretend it wasn't colder than ever.

'Let's go,' Cormac said. 'I don't like it here.'

He rushed ahead of her, and Mia followed.

'I don't understand,' she said, her fist around the little flower. 'What does this mean? Why was this left in the journal?'

His trademark. His signature.

'You know as well as I do,' Cormac replied.

'But what does Donahue have to do with any of this?'

'You put this much together, and yet falter at the last piece?'

'The Rogue . . . It didn't want us to go into the back room, to the journal, with this inside, and the hydrangea . . .' She gasped, faltering on the stairs. 'It was there because Donahue left it there. Because it points to where the painting is hidden. It means that Donahue and Francis – they were working together.'

'I told you that you wouldn't like it.'

Mia didn't know how she felt. There was the insistent howl of her nerves telling her to keep moving, to keep running from the Rogue that undoubtedly lurked in the shadows all around them, and then some ill-conceived thrill, singing out with elation that they were this close to their mystery's end.

'That can't be it,' she choked out. 'There has to be another reason.'

'No? Then what is your explanation?'

She didn't have one. 'But you can't really think—'

'That the night my father argued with Owen Buckley it was because Owen wanted to out the hotel and its ghosts? That my father disagreed and so did Francis? Yes, I *can* think that. And I also think they needed something to discredit him – make him disappear – and all it took was one painting and a lie. They got away with it, Mia Anne. Until now. Until—'

'Me,' she said, barely a whisper, and then sped down the last of the steps to round on him.

'But the painting,' she said. 'If Francis took the painting – if *Donahue* – it means it's still here. The painting is still here.'

'I knew you would do this.'

'What?'

'Make excuses for him. Try to fix all of his mistakes. He doesn't—'

'Deserve it? I don't care. *I* deserve it, don't you think?' Mia took a steadying breath. 'So, where is it? You know, don't you?'

'I have my suspicions.'

A scream cut through the hallway. Mia had heard it before but that didn't make it any less jarring. Lily and the lobby and her red hands flashed in Mia's memory, before she squashed it down, breathing hard.

'Maria?' Cormac's eyes darted about the hallway, searching. 'I heard—'

'No,' Mia said. 'You didn't.'

The lights on the lower floor flickered on, while Mia and Cormac's floor remained in darkness. Then, there were footsteps – the hotel groaning, a rhythmic tapping. It sounded as though someone was walking just one floor below, and—

'Cormac, it's not real,' Mia said.

He shook his head. 'There *is*—'

'*No*. This isn't anything. They're scaring you, Cormac. You're letting them *scare you* and there is *no one there*. We need to leave. Come on—'

'But that *crying*—'

'Cormac, I need you to take me to wherever *The Field* is. Now.'

The lights suddenly came on overhead, and Mia flinched at the new shadows all around them.

Then there was another sound – a soft *ding*. Mia turned to see the lift's golden doors slide open.

She could feel the cold from where they stood.

'We need to take the stairs,' she whispered.

Cormac was pale. 'Yes. The stairs. We'll take the stairs.'

'We'll go to *The Field by Our House*,' she said. 'So, tell me where it is.'

'You know it as well as I do, Mia Anne.'

For a beat, she just looked at him, frustration and fear heated to a melting point. And then, all at once, she did know.

She looked down at the hydrangea bloom, crumpled in her hand.

chapter 37
the field by our house

THEY KEPT STEP WITH ONE ANOTHER, and though they were now on the stairs, the guest corridor left behind, they could hear knocking and banging. The sounds were in the walls, along the stairs, and paired with crying – soft, at first, but then sobs gave way to wails of despair, and among it, snatches of words:

I didn't mean to—

It wasn't supposed to happen—

I'm not a liar—

Mia forced herself to keep her eyes on the path of light as the voices grew ever louder, more insistent.

When they reached the ground floor, it was as if some portal had transported them from a shadowed old building, laced with misery, to – a party.

Mia watched as costumed figures drifted here and there, drinks in hand and smiles on faces. They danced to music that had never stopped, under lights that had never cut out.

It unnerved Mia to see these people – her friends, her colleagues – carrying on as though nothing was wrong. But perhaps, nothing *was* wrong, down here. None of *these* people had been poking around a rogue ghost's business, after all.

But Mia had. Cormac had.

They hurried across the lobby floor, edging through groups of partygoers. It was all still so cold, despite the close bodies, and Mia carried with her a piercing sense of unease. Had the chandelier really quivered, its glass shards tinkling together with menace, or had she imagined it? Had the music jumped, for the briefest seconds before blaring again, or was it just her nerves?

'Quickly,' she said to Cormac. 'He's following.'

Outside, it was chilly and dark. Clouds had skated across the moon, and it shone through just barely, like a pale face through a lace veil. Apparently, it was too cold for smokers, and Cormac and Mia were alone.

Or so she hoped.

'He won't be able to follow us out there,' Cormac said. 'He's tied to the hotel like the rest of them.'

Mia nodded, chasing the steps, eager to be free of the building's eyes in favour of the trees.

The hydrangeas lay out there. As still and silent as ever.

Cormac followed her, seeming just as keen to flee the hotel, but both came to a sudden stop when the lights went out.

Now there *were* screams. And panic.

'Granny—' Mia gasped, and rushed back up the steps. As she did so, the lights, miraculously, flickered on once more.

She heard the shouts of confusion and worry from the party die away. She heard the music restart, and laughter return.

Was it real? Mia asked herself, and when she looked at Cormac, he wore the same wary expression.

She fixed her feet to the steps. 'You go,' she instructed. 'You go and bring it back here. I can keep watch and make sure . . .'

She didn't know what she would do exactly if the Rogue did decide to cut the lights again – or anything worse for that matter – but she knew more than any of the partygoers inside. That was, of course, if it was real at all.

Cormac shook his head. 'You can't stay here.'

'There isn't any other way.'

He put a hand to her shoulder and pushed. 'You go. I'll take care of the hotel. He can't follow you, so you'll be safe, and . . . Well, you knew my father better than I did. You'll find it.'

'Knew your—' She could have cried. 'Cormac, this whole thing has only proven I didn't know him at all. I don't—'

'Mia Anne, *you knew him better than I*,' he repeated firmly. 'Now *go*.'

This time, Mia did not argue. There wasn't enough time to debate Donahue Byrnes. There wasn't enough time in all her life, she imagined, and right now, she had to find the place where fairies made mischief and books went unread.

The undergrowth before her shivered with a light breeze and things alive – familiar as an old friend but made unknowable by the dark.

The hydrangeas were not the buxom blooms of springtime. They were brown and crisp, and she pushed her way through their brittle branches, her phone light blazing a path before her.

Ferns brushed against her legs. Nettles bit at her ankles.

At the heart of the hydrangea bushes, Mia found her old playfellow: the little wooden library.

It had weathered so many cold nights and all-day rain showers even in her lifetime that Mia wondered it still stood upright. Moss crawled over its flat roof, and leaves were caught in the spider web strung across one side of it. The purple paint was peeling, and the metallic lock rusty.

She hadn't been able to open it last time, but she hadn't been prepared then.

Tonight, she took the key from about her neck and unlocked the library.

An absurd faith. A good friend of mine.

There was a painful crunch as she opened the aged wood, and there in the gloom, like ribs pulled apart to reveal a heart in a dead man's chest, lay a collection of mouldy books.

Mia pushed the latter to one side so she might see to the back. There was nothing there, though, and she wondered if the painting might be *between* the books.

No, it was not, and, panicked at the thought of having got it wrong, she now took to pulling them out, one by one: *Frankenstein*, *Hamlet*, a couple of pastel-coloured romances and a tattered spy drama with fat red lettering.

It was *King Lear*, however, that weighed less than Mia had expected. The cover sagged and, as she held it out in front of her, fell away entirely.

Mia saw then that it did not hold pages at all, but instead, a brown paper package, and inside—

She held *The Field by Our House* in her hands.

It was small, she thought. Smaller than she had ever imagined. Smaller than its tremendous price tag, and smaller than the aftershock of its disappearance. Yellow-green grass swayed in the painter's breeze and a white cottage was dabbed into the distance.

It was held in a simple brass frame, and when turned over, there was a slip of paper tucked into one of its edges. Mia recognised Donahue's loopy *y*s and *g*s, and larger than necessary capitals but couldn't understand its meaning.

There was a rustle behind her. She jumped.

A figure emerged from the hydrangeas.

With a hand to her chest, she breathed, 'It's *you*. You scared me.'

Cormac strode from between the trees, hands in his pockets, face unreadable.

Mia's heart skipped. 'Is everything okay? Is it the hotel?'

He did not answer but closed the space between them. When he was standing toe-to-toe with her, he looked down at the painting in her hands.

'It's *The Field by Our House*,' Mia whispered. 'It's been here all this time – just like you said. We found it.'

Cormac reached out. It was dark but Mia could have sworn there was a tremor to his hands as they took hold of it.

Then, all at once, he ripped the painting from Mia's fingers, with such force she breathed a quick *Ow*.

She looked at him, confusion at her brow and a question on her lips.

Then, she saw his eyes.

Instead of ice blue, there was a charcoal smudge to his irises, and a hunger to them she had never seen on Cormac Byrnes.

She knew then. It was Francis Croft.

But he shouldn't have been here – especially not wearing Cormac like a macabre Halloween costume. Hadn't he always said they couldn't leave the hotel? They had never done so before, and never given reason for Mia to believe they might, but—

It didn't matter.

Francis Croft was here, and he had *The Field by Our House*.

When he looked at her now, Mia could see the ghost all the more – the blurred expression, the anger.

He pushed her – with all the physicality of a human man – and she stumbled backwards, knocking against the little library. The edges caught her back and pain flared through her, but she kept her eyes on the ghost.

He looked back. Then, to the painting, and to Mia again.

'It stays here,' the ghost hissed with Cormac's mouth. 'It stays hidden.'

It raised the painting so that it obscured Cormac's face and then, all at once, Francis Croft brought *The Field by Our House* down onto the earth. Mia heard the crack of the frame, just as the ghost drove Cormac's smart shoe down on top of it, puncturing the canvas.

Mia cried out as if it were her own body – and perhaps, she thought, it was. Perhaps there was something inside her irreversibly linked to this small yet significant artwork, a link she had forged in time, energy, love and effort. Something that stopped her from giving up – even when she thought she had, taking down all of her photographs, and throwing away her notebook, and even now, alone in the shadows with a dead man.

'Stop it!' she shouted, taking a step forward. 'Get away from it!'

And maybe the ghost felt it, too – that scaring her away hadn't worked before, and would not work now – because something shifted in Cormac's unpleasantly distant expression.

Where she had taken a step closer, he did the same. Mia, seeing this, took her own step back, but the ghost did not change his path.

She backed away, and then – took off running.

Flying through the undergrowth, Mia's feet hardly touched the ground, but she still felt impossibly slow. The rustle of leaves and the crunch of twigs were so close behind, and she knew Cormac was following, and that he was taller than her, his legs longer. He might have been older, but right now, he was deathless, and fast.

She cut through the brambles onto the hotel's tarmac drive, her feet slapping hard against it.

Maybe it was just the grounds the ghost was fixed to, she thought, or maybe it was a particular distance from the hotel. Maybe if she just got *far enough*—

He appeared from the trees.

While Mia felt winded from the effort, he looked utterly unbothered, and she knew she could not outrun him. Not for much longer.

But she could make it to the end of the road.

Her chest tightened with the effort of breaking into a run again, and her breath came in fast gasps.

Weeks ago, in a previous lifetime, on the night she had first seen Jim McGowan, and his blurred, unfamiliar expression, she had fled from the hotel just like this, so scared she could hardly think. She hadn't stopped until she reached the soft, safe porchlight at Granny's house and then – and then . . .

And then, she had gone back, she remembered. She had danced in a lonely ballroom of spirits and heard Jim McGowan laugh anew and he had *changed*. Everything had changed after that, in fact – Mia included.

She had stayed to pour empty champagne bottles for a wedding party that had long since passed, and learned to play the most basic piano tunes so her charges might dance a little longer into the night.

She had posted long-lost love letters. She had uncovered secret gifts.

She spoke to ghosts and, more importantly, she listened.

Mia found her feet slowing. The slap of shoes on the pavement came to nothing, and maybe it was stupid, maybe she would regret it forever, but in that moment, she stopped, right there in the middle of the road.

She turned to face the ghost.

Cormac Byrnes, just eight or ten feet away, looked back at her. Except, of course, it was not Cormac Byrnes, but the ghost within him, and while Mia knew that Cormac Byrnes may long be a mystery to her, the same could not be said of her ghosts.

Because she *knew* her ghosts – knew they were not evil spirits or demons or anything to be exorcised from Ballinadrum Hotel, but simply *lost.* They wanted and needed and reached across death itself to undo years-old regrets, and they needed Mia to *help them.*

And despite everything she felt about him, she knew that Francis Croft was just another ghost – just another of her ballroom guests.

She met his gaze and called his name.

'Francis Croft,' she said. 'Francis Croft, I know your name, and I know what you're doing here tonight.'

He stepped towards her. She did not move.

'I know that you took *The Field by Our House*, Francis Croft. I know you framed Owen Buckley for the theft and that when it went to trial, you made sure he was found guilty by paying off the jury. I know the picture has been out here all these years, and your secret has been safe until now. Until me.'

He was closer now – close enough she could see the specific shade of black in his eyes. The way the corner of his lips lifted in an unsettling half-smile.

'Francis Croft,' she said again, and her voice was stronger than she felt. 'I want to help you.'

Francis Croft stopped. It was so sudden that Mia jerked backwards, ready to run once again, but then, he held up his hands. He looked at them as though he had never seen them before, and then he looked at Mia.

His eyes were bright and concerned. They were *blue*.

'Cormac?' she asked.

'*Mia*,' he said. 'Mia, I don't . . . Are you—'

'I'm fine. I'm okay.'

'I'm so sorry,' he said in a tight voice. 'I don't understand how . . . I had no control. He had me. It was so cold and . . . Are you hurt, Mia Anne?'

Mia shook her head. 'No, I'm fine—'

'No,' he said. 'You're not. We need to go. We should—'

'Cormac,' she said. 'He's still here.'

'What?'

Mia looked past Cormac, and the hotelier followed her gaze.

Francis Croft stood in what appeared to be mortal flesh. He wore his hotel uniform and his hair greased back, holding his fist tight around an all-too-familiar key.

It was then Mia noticed his eyes. Instead of hollowed-out points, they were searching, and pale – almost grey, by this light, but perhaps a soft green, or blue like Donahue's.

'Francis Croft,' she said in a whisper.

'Don't come any closer!' Cormac shouted, stepping between the two. 'Stay where you are, Francis Croft.'

Slowly, Mia came to stand beside Cormac, and then, to Cormac's horror, past him.

'Let me help,' she said to the ghost.

Francis Croft watched her with a curious expression, and then turned. He flickered in and out of vision like an old film reel, and Mia followed his soundless steps.

Cormac rushed to her side, taking her elbow. 'What are you—'

'Trust me,' she said. 'I know what I'm doing.' She managed a grim little smile and added, 'I mean, what do you pay me for?'

Cormac looked between Mia and the ghost, who, seemingly hearing their conversation, had stopped again. His gaze surveyed them both, until Mia took another step forward – this time, with Cormac's arm through hers.

'Let me help,' she said again, and together, Cormac and Mia followed the ghost into the undergrowth.

He took them to the library. There, he stopped, and turned back to them.

Mia's gaze moved from the ghost to the ground, and then slowly, haltingly, she crouched to touch the broken painting, still lying among the autumn leaves and tree roots. She only took her eyes off Francis Croft for the briefest of heartbeats, and he watched her all the while.

Cormac sucked in a breath. 'The painting.'

He took his phone from his pocket and stabbed in some number, but Mia shook her head.

'No,' she said. 'Not if we want Francis to leave this place. That's his final wish, his unfinished business. He doesn't want anyone to know, and the painting – it's the last thing to tie him, and Donahue, to the crime.'

'So, what do we with it?'

She looked down at the painting. 'We burn it.'

Cormac blinked at her, disbelieving, and then, both of them turned their gazes upon Francis Croft.

He watched them still, gripping the key in his hand harder, and then – Francis Croft gave one definite nod of the head.

'Burn it,' Cormac said. 'After all this time . . .'

He took the painting from Mia's hands, shoulders heaving with a sigh. He turned to the ghost, and closed the space between them until they were but a handshake apart.

'I know you,' Cormac said.

The ghost cocked his head. 'I know you, too.'

'Mia Anne,' Cormac said, not looking back. 'Come with me.'

Together, Cormac and Mia left the hydrangeas and the trees, stepped onto the black avenue and into the yellow light of the hotel.

When Mia looked to see if Francis Croft had followed them, he had already gone.

chapter 38
mistruth

The field by our house burned slowly, Cormac's lighter catching its centre with a spark of blue before it melted into yellow flame.

Mia felt her chest loosen at the sight.

Out on the edge of the hotel's grounds, they had found a rocky patch to put the painting to rest, away from flammable ferns and ringlets of ivy, as well as the eyes of hotel partygoers. There was plenty of cover, from the night and the trees, but Mia still jumped at every broken twig, every sigh of the wind.

She and Cormac watched until it was finished.

'Was it awful?' Mia asked.

Light flickered upon Cormac's shadowed face. He knew what she meant. 'I don't think I'd recommend you try it,' he said. 'If that's what you're asking.'

'I'm asking if you're okay.'

After a moment, he said, 'I am. It wasn't . . . painful. Just cold. It was something like a dream, or rather a nightmare, where your feet move too slowly, or you try to talk, and your teeth fall out.' He looked at her. 'In truth, I didn't know they could do that.'

'I didn't even think they could leave the hotel,' Mia said, and thought again of Aunt Olive's words from earlier in the evening. 'But they say the spirits are closer to us on nights like Halloween – that the divide between us thins, or something like that.'

'You should write that down. In your little book. And I know I've said it a dozen times or more now, but . . . I truly am sorry, Mia Anne, for hurting you.'

'It wasn't you, though, Mr Byrnes.'

'Yes, but if you hadn't . . . If you hadn't worked it out . . .' His voice was tight. 'You were . . . wonderful – braver than I could have ever been myself.'

Mia pressed her lips thin and then said, 'You say that, but . . . you stayed behind at the hotel when the ghost came after us – so I could get away. You stood between Francis and me when you thought he was trying to hurt us. So, for what it's worth—'

'Don't,' he said.

'You don't know what I was going to say.'

'I know it was some compliment I don't deserve.'

'*I* think you're brave,' Mia went on. 'And it doesn't matter what you or anybody else thinks.'

He gave her a narrow sidelong look, and she knew even if he appreciated it, he would never say it out loud. She had something more important to ask him anyway.

'The slip,' she said. 'Attached to the painting . . .'

'Yes?'

'It was an invoice, addressed to Francis.'

'Yes.'

'In Donahue's handwriting.'

'Indeed.'

They lapsed into more silence, and Mia listened to the night: the distant thumps of the party, the cool breeze through the bushes. A fire crackling at her feet.

'Why?' she said at last.

'Why what?'

'Why was it there? Why was it addressed to him? I know you know.'

He took a long breath. 'It was an invoice for ten thousand and forty-three pounds. That was the total for those receipts we found. The bribes. Why my father would have asked Croft to pay it, concealed within a book about betrayal and an old, proud fool, is not entirely unclear, but . . .'

'Does that mean . . . ? Are you saying that Donahue was innocent? It was all Francis Croft? That Donahue had never asked him to pay the bribes, and the invoice was his way of showing that?'

'No. My father played a part. He hid that painting out here and never told anyone what he or Croft had done – even when Buckley stood trial.'

'But he defended Owen at the trial! And—'

'Perhaps my father did not intend for things to go as far as they did. Perhaps he had nothing to do with the bribery of the jury. However, there is no man or woman here to tell the true course of events, if there ever was a true course.'

There were twelve ghosts, of course, Mia thought – though, they were twelve *unreliable, unhelpful* ghosts.

'No true course? There must be, there has to be *one way*—'

'Say my father told Croft something vague and Croft did something stupid under the impression it was what he had been ordered to do. If my father was to tell the story, he would claim innocence, that it was a foolhardy deed gone too far. If Croft were to tell the same story, he would have his defence, too.

'If my father laid these things out in such a way that he wasn't implicated in the plot, but Francis was, then the pieces he left behind would have done their job, because you sit here and you believe in him and his goodness.'

Mia felt the suck of the tide again, those cold, dark waters.

'But what do you *think* happened?' she asked.

'Well,' Cormac said, 'I think that the three men argued that night. I think that Buckley wanted to have the hotel shut down after his daughter was hurt by the very ghosts they were trying to hide. I think my father and Croft wanted to protect the hotel, and wanted to discredit Buckley, and decided on this painting theft as the way to do it.

'I think my father only wanted to discredit the man, not imprison him, but Croft fixed the court case with a series of bribes to punish Buckley severely for his betrayal of the ghosts – and the hotel.

'I don't think either of them expected Buckley to end his own life, and that when my father found out about the bribes, he asked Croft to leave. I think the invoice was a bitter farewell and an acknowledgement he knew what Francis had done behind his back.'

'And the journal – it was a sign to Francis?'

'I think so. I imagine it was left to point Francis to the painting's hiding place. Perhaps so he would take it with him when he left the hotel. Maybe after he had cleared the back-room's locker of the rest of his belongings.'

'Do you really think so?'

Cormac gave a small shrug. 'The invoice is clearly meant for him, so it stands to reason that the journal was directed at him, too. The only thing I don't know is why Francis never took it – why he left it behind when my father, seemingly, wanted him to have it.'

'Was it too risky?' Mia asked. 'Or . . . maybe he meant to punish your father, by making him keep it instead, not knowing about the invoice attached? Maybe there was a misunderstanding – he didn't know he was meant to take it. Or maybe . . .' She paused. 'Maybe Donahue didn't mean for him to take it, and the journal doesn't mean anything at all. Maybe he wanted it so that if anyone ever found the painting, they would see the invoice and blame Francis, and not him.'

Cormac looked down at Mia.

'Is that what you think?' he asked gently.

Mia felt close to tears and her mouth fought for an answer that didn't come.

'I don't know,' she said. 'I . . . I love him, and I don't know why. I don't know if he was good or bad, but I love him anyway.'

'That's okay. You should love him. He loved you.'

'But I don't *know* that.'

'You felt it,' Cormac told her. 'And that's as close to a truth as you will get this evening.'

'Do you think we did the wrong thing?' she asked after a moment.

'I'm not sure. I think telling the truth is, *technically*, the right thing, but . . . Croft was dangerous.'

'And if we hadn't destroyed it, then he would have stayed forever. He would have—'

'You don't have to explain it to me, Mia Anne. Some people *may* argue that keeping *twelve* ghosts is hardly the better of our options, but *some people* aren't privy to this whole affair, so I'd say you're in the clear. Now, with those twelve ghosts, do you think . . .'

Mia shook her head. 'I don't know. They stayed because they'd been bribed, and I don't know how to get rid of them if the painting is gone. They might . . . always be here.'

'Then the hotel may always be haunted.'

'It *was* the wrong thing, wasn't it?'

Cormac gave her a weak smile. 'Did I ever tell you why my father enjoyed the hydrangeas so much?'

Mia shook her head.

'The bushes planted out here,' he said, 'as I'm sure you've seen, grow in blues and pinks and purples, and yet they're the same variety. My father liked they could be anything, and that when they were planted, it was a mystery to him which might spring up from the ground.'

Cormac held Mia's gaze.

'There is no *blue* hydrangea to be planted, you see, nor a pink, nor purple. Their colour depends entirely on the soil in which they grow. One plant in an acidic ground will bloom blue. In alkaline, pink. Some combination of the two will grow purple flowers or those little mottled ones, which can't make up their mind. You might even change a pink flower to blue or purple if you add a little tea or coffee to the soil around it. He showed me that when I was small.'

Soft firelight danced in the glass of his spectacles.

'Do you understand, Mia Anne?'

'Yes,' she said.

'Good.'

'What will you do now?' she asked a minute later. 'Do you have a flight in the morning?'

'Oh, I'm not leaving. Not yet. I have a few business matters to take care of first.'

'Oh,' Mia said dully. 'Deeds and that?'

'Not quite.' Cormac put his hands in his pockets and turned away from the embers. 'I still have to make a sale before we can get to that business.'

Mia frowned, hardly daring to hope. 'You mean . . . Mr Gurning . . . He didn't want it?'

'Oh, he wanted it. Very much. But he wanted it for bits, and . . . Well, when we spoke again, I had to tell him I had already given a guarantee the hotel would remain standing and therefore, unless it was sold in entirety, it could not be sold at all.' Cormac did not look at her, but the old building itself, glowing in the night. 'It awaits a new buyer, still.'

Mia wanted to throw her arms about him, but thought better of it.

'And what will you do?' Cormac asked.

'I have a job waiting for me at the paper.'

'Is that right?'

'Photographer,' Mia said, and the old man laughed.

'Did you inform them of your rare experience photographing the supernatural?'

'I didn't, actually. Perhaps I should.'

'I'm sure you will do very well for yourself, Mia Anne. You did very well here, despite the odds – and despite me. My father would be very proud of all you have achieved.'

She looked down at her hands, where her ring glinted dimly.

'I would stay, though,' she said, 'if you need someone to keep your . . . guests in order, while you look for a new buyer.'

'Mia Anne,' he said. 'I don't want you to throw away your potential on an old place with nothing to offer you. Not when you have new opportunities.'

'But what do those opportunities matter, if they don't make me happy?'

Cormac did not speak, but turned his gaze upon the ashes.

'I want to stay here,' she said. 'And be part of this story.'

'You already are,' he told her.

'Then I want more chapters, more pages.' She took a breath. 'If there is work for me, of course. I could, after all, go and find another haunted hotel that might appreciate my unique skills.'

He smiled at last. 'Competition, hm? That's one way to wrangle better pay. I suppose there's a conversation to be had about that, but for now, let's say you keep your job – if that is what you truly wish?'

'It is,' she said.

'Then who am I to stand in your way? God knows I've tried and failed.'

She beamed. 'Thank you, Mr Byrnes.'

He clasped his hands behind his back and with a tip of the head, gestured for her to walk with him, up the grassy hill to the hotel.

'I've been thinking,' he said, 'about what you said about the ghosts and the story here and . . . I think we should tell people the truth.'

Her eyebrows shot up. 'About the ghosts?'

'Indeed.'

'No one would believe you.'

'And that's okay. Truth becomes mistruth becomes legend.' He rolled his eyes, some ghostly smile passing over his face. 'I'm sure it's just as my father would have wished it.'

*

In the morning, Mia brought Granny a cup of tea. The old woman was half-dozing, propped up against the headboard.

Mia asked about the night before – about the girls, and whether she tried one of Alex's winning cocktails. And then, when it was clear that Mia had more to say, Granny fixed her with one of those long, patient looks, and it all came out.

Mia explained her own version of the night before or, at least, some sanitised version in which she fought with Rosco and went to the hotel to be with her friends.

'I'm not marrying him,' Mia told her. 'I don't want to, and we're better apart.'

'All couples have arguments,' Granny tried to reason. 'It's how you work through them that matters.'

'I don't want to work through it.'

'We'll see.'

'No,' Mia said firmly. 'We'll not see, because I've made up my mind. This is me telling you, before I have to tell everybody else.'

Granny stared at her across the stretch of duvet, teacup tilted in her lap.

'I thought you loved him,' Granny said softly.

'I thought so too,' Mia said. 'But I'm not sure I knew what love was. I don't think I really do now.'

There was grief on Granny's face, some deep-wrinkled concern, but at last, she reached out a hand and Mia answered by closing the distance. Granny squeezed once.

'You have to make these choices for yourself.'

Then, as she typically did in times of crisis, Granny suggested another cup of tea, and some buttered toast, too, but Mia could not stay for breakfast. She had to see Rosco, she said. She had to explain.

Mia did not begin her day at the Buckley house, though. Instead, she went to the hotel.

It was crisply quiet – an anticipatory lull before the hotel might reopen with an orchestra of activity.

Cormac was on the phone when she arrived – arguing, it seemed, with some repair man about the windows – and hung up when he caught sight of her.

'Do you think,' he asked, 'Henry would come back if I called him?'

'I think nearly everyone would.'

Then, he was on the phone again, to someone else about the broken windows, and the carpet upstairs, too. A few doors needed tweaking, and a clock replaced. They needed the damage from the fire properly assessed and dealt with before they might reopen, and then, who would order the food, how long did it take to announce these things?

Mia drifted back to the ballroom before Cormac could interrogate her on the practicalities of the hotel further. She harboured a silent yet palpable joy at the idea of being able to call Ruby and Sonia later, and tell them that Ballinadrum Hotel was not dead at all, but shuddering with buds of new life.

She would also have to tell them about Rosco, of course, and she hoped they did not respond as Granny had. She hoped they would buy a cake, offer her a spoon and an ear, and give her the space to explain, as best she could, how he preferred strawberry jam, and she was going to have blackberry, no matter what anyone had to say about it.

But that would wait. Because her ghosts needed her first.

As expected, twelve of them remained, both by her eyes *and* her camera's count.

'May I offer you a cup of tea?' Mia asked them as they gathered about her – eager, it seemed, for someone to listen to them.

'I can sing, you know,' the Singer professed.

'Watch my cartwheel,' the Little Girl cried out.

The Lady sniffed the air as she always had done, and the Florist squeezed the china cup in his hands like he could still feel the warmth of steaming tea. The Gossip insisted that *things were about to change around here*, and Mia told her she was right.

The others drank down cups of anything they imagined and whatever they liked best, and the piano played its tinkling song.

All quiet and all settled, Mia took the journal from her satchel, flicking through pages of her own handwriting, dedicated to ghosts both here and gone, and pressed down on a brand-new page.

'What have you there?' the Bride asked, reading over her shoulder. 'The future of . . . '

'*The future of Ballinadrum Hotel.* I have a few ideas for what I would like this place to look like . . . for what I think people should know about it – like how it's haunted.'

'By ghosts?' the Bride asked.

'That's what people say.'

'And are they dangerous?'

'Sometimes, but not really. Not if you know how to help them. And if you stayed here, for instance, you might hear the loveliest piano melodies in the middle of the night, or try out foods and wines that have been approved from beyond the grave.

'You could learn about the history of the building, and all the different uses it has had over the years, from a wedding venue to a country escape, and the *Byrnes family* – how important they were in changing this whole place from a simple inn to the hotel it is today – and – and *Donahue Byrnes*, most of all. I have lots of photographs of him, you know. That could be nice.'

She thought a moment.

'I don't have any photographs of Cormac Byrnes – *yet* – but he should get a mention, too, on the website or some article somewhere. Just to say that he . . . Well, he helped save the building when it was at its worst. He changed it for the better, too. He's as part of its story as anyone.'

The ghost nodded, thoughtful.

'What do you think?' Mia asked eventually.

'Well, I do quite like it here already,' the Bride whispered.

With a smile, Mia replied, 'Yes. So do I.'

acknowledgements

This book was written in the wildest hopes that it would one day be published, and I am exceedingly grateful that all the planets and stars and powers beyond my understanding aligned just so to make that happen.

Stars and planets besides, though, I must stress that no novel is truly written alone, and as such, I would like to extend my gratitude to the great many individuals who helped me to complete this one.

Thank you, firstly, to my wonderful agent Thérèse Coen, whose unexpected email describing her interest in the world of Mia, Cormac, and this haunted hotel made me sob into my laptop on a grey Thursday morning. Her advice and encouragement in both editing and publishing this work has been kind, wise, and utterly invaluable. She was, and is, a dream to work with.

Thank you, as well, to my sage editor Sam Humphreys, who saw all the light and wonder in this story of hauntings and ghostly happenings, and helped me to see it, too. She has bettered this novel in ways I had scarcely imagined, and it would not be as it is printed here if not for her careful and joyful guidance.

I was also very lucky to have had a collection of wonderful people read and help shape this book in its earliest utterances. Thank you to Michelle Hackett (Shell, Shoos, wondrous best friend), Joshua Hackett (proof-reader extraordinaire), James Lyttle (yes, I changed the ending), Amy Watson (who, indeed, *got me the notebook*), Sam McCready (who asks the most thoughtful questions), and Mark Fulton (my one-man Rosco fan club).

Thank you, as well, to my mother, Deborah Fulton, who has always said that I would succeed despite her, but should know that I am only where I am and who I am now because of her love and friendship. I am also extremely grateful to my father, Richard Fulton, who has supported me in everything I have ever done, and foresaw all of my successes long before I was even close to reaching them.

Though they cannot read, I would also like to say to Mr Cash that he was no help whatsoever and I love him very much, and to my sweet baby Kipper that he was another beloved distraction. I hope he never changes.

And of course, in closing, I must say thank you to my husband Blair McLoughlin, to whom this book is dedicated and without whom it would likely still be hidden in my laptop. For his very good advice and endless belief in my dreams – no matter how outlandish – he has all of my thanks and all of my love, forever and always.